FANTASTIC FOUR PRESENTS
FRANKLIN RICHARDS
SON OF A GENIUS

LAB
BRAT

FANTASTIC FOUR PRESENTS:
FRANKLIN RICHARDS
SON OF A GENIUS

LAB BRAT

Story: Chris Eliopoulos & Marc Sumerak
Script: Marc Sumerak
Art & Letters: Chris Eliopoulos
Colors: Gurihiru, Lovern Kindzierski & Brad Anderson
Assistant Editor: Nathan Cosby
Editors: MacKenzie Cadenhead & Mark Paniccia

Masked Marvel
Writer: Karl Kesel
Art: David Hahn
Colors: Pete Pantazis
Letters: VC's Rus Wooton & Cory Petit
Editor: Nicole Boose

Digest Re-Lettering: Dave Sharpe

Collection Editor: Jennifer Grünwald
Assistant Editor: Michael Short
Associate Editor: Mark D. Beazley
Senior Editor, Special Projects: Jeff Youngquist
Vice President of Sales: David Gabriel
Book Designer: Dayle Chesler
Senior Vice President of Creative: Tom Marvelli

Editor in Chief: Joe Quesada
Publisher: Dan Buckley

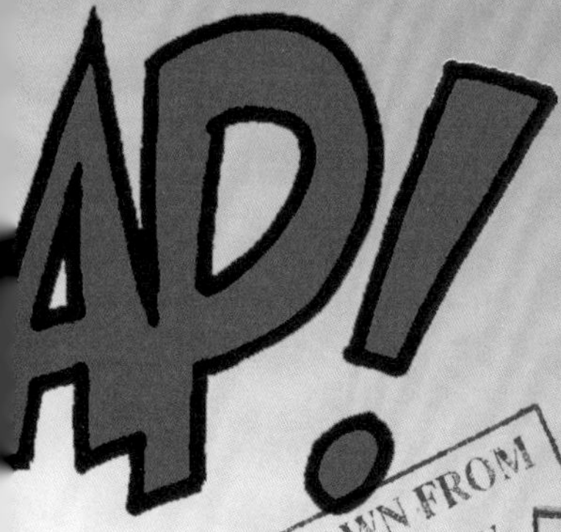
AP!

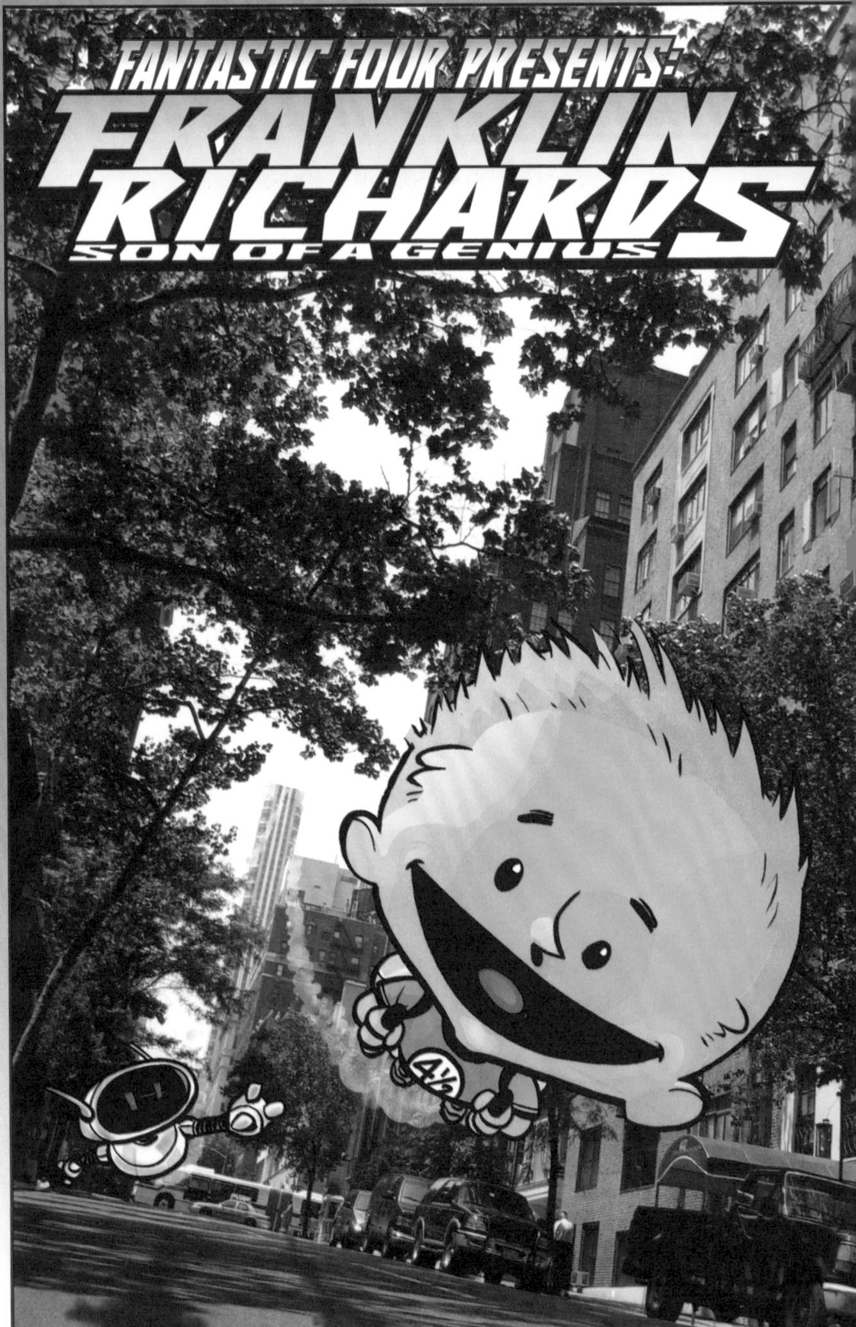

FANTASTIC FOUR PRESENTS:
FRANKLIN RICHARDS
SON OF A GENIUS
4½

FRANKLIN RICHARDS SON OF A GENIUS IN: MICROSCOPIC!

BY CHRIS ELIOPOULOS & MARC SUMERAK

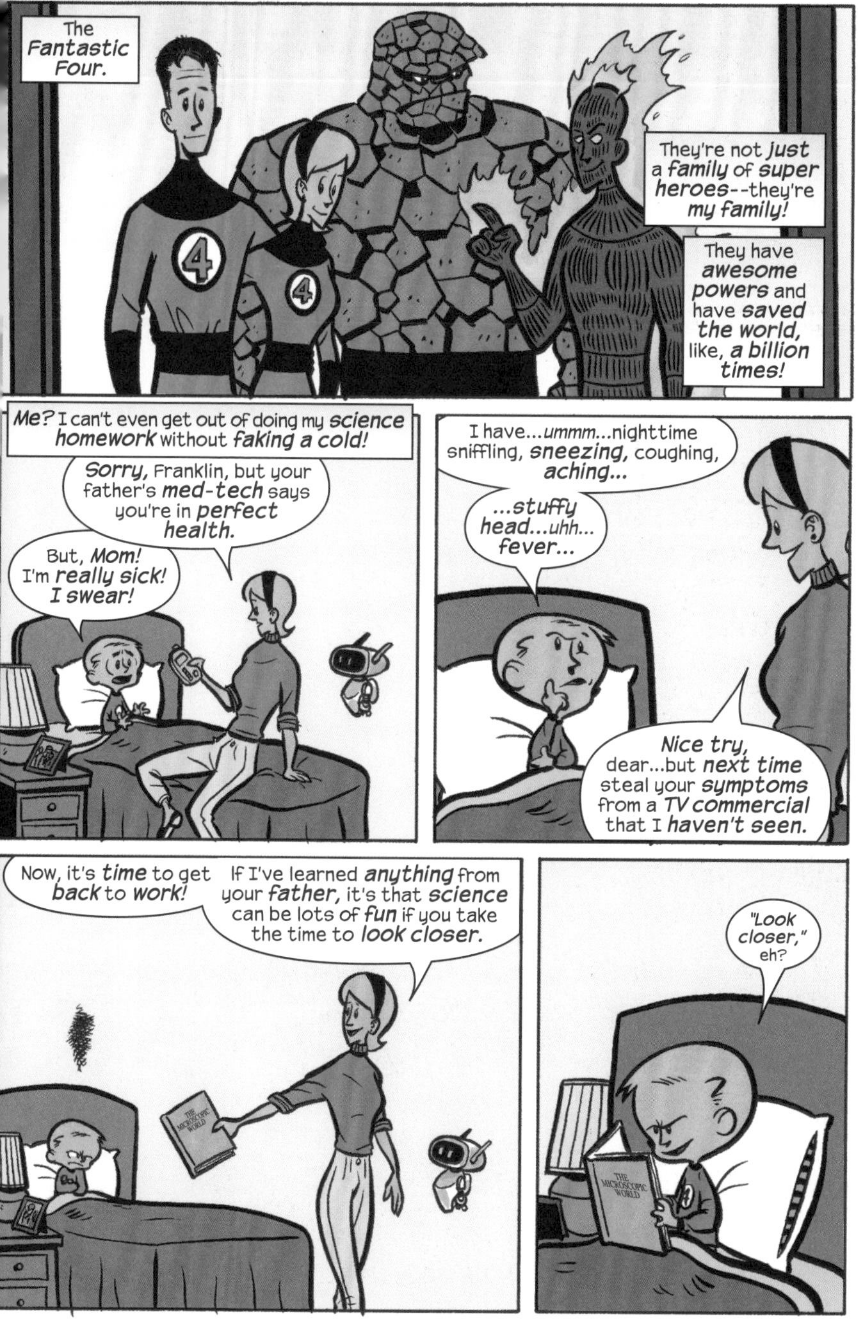
The Fantastic Four.
They're not just a family of super heroes--they're my family!
They have awesome powers and have saved the world, like, a billion times!
Me? I can't even get out of doing my science homework without faking a cold!
Sorry, Franklin, but your father's med-tech says you're in perfect health.
But, Mom! I'm really sick! I swear!
I have...ummm...nighttime sniffling, sneezing, coughing, aching...
...stuffy head...uhh... fever...
Nice try, dear...but next time steal your symptoms from a TV commercial that I haven't seen.
Now, it's time to get back to work!
If I've learned anything from your father, it's that science can be lots of fun if you take the time to look closer.
THE MICROSCOPIC WORLD
"Look closer," eh?
THE MICROSCOPIC WORLD

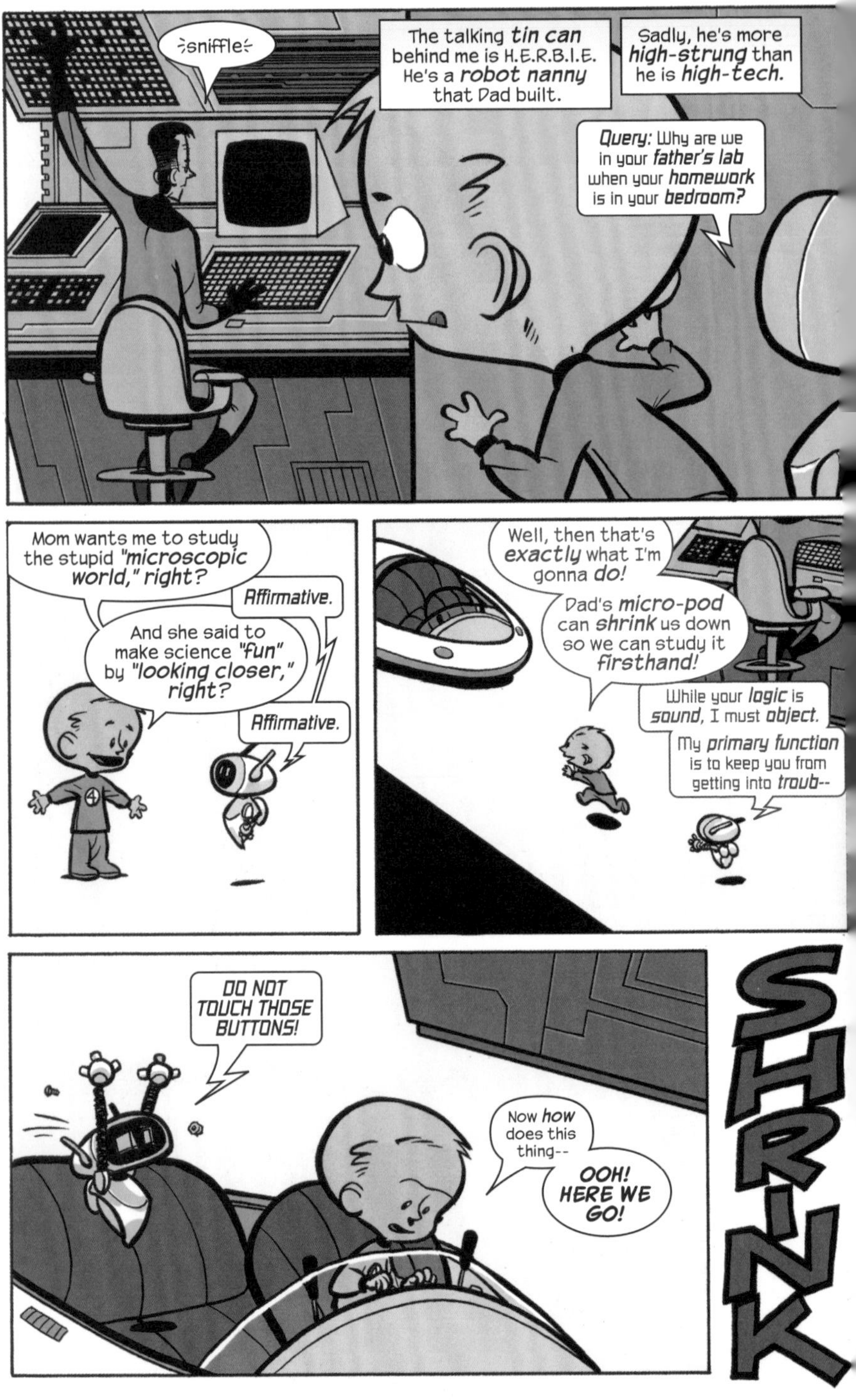

sniffle
The talking tin can behind me is H.E.R.B.I.E. He's a robot nanny that Dad built.
Sadly, he's more high-strung than he is high-tech.
Query: Why are we in your father's lab when your homework is in your bedroom?
Mom wants me to study the stupid "microscopic world," right?
Affirmative.
And she said to make science "fun" by "looking closer," right?
Affirmative.
Well, then that's exactly what I'm gonna do!
Dad's micro-pod can shrink us down so we can study it firsthand!
While your logic is sound, I must object.
My primary function is to keep you from getting into troub--
DO NOT TOUCH THOSE BUTTONS!
Now how does this thing--
OOH! HERE WE GO!
SHRINK

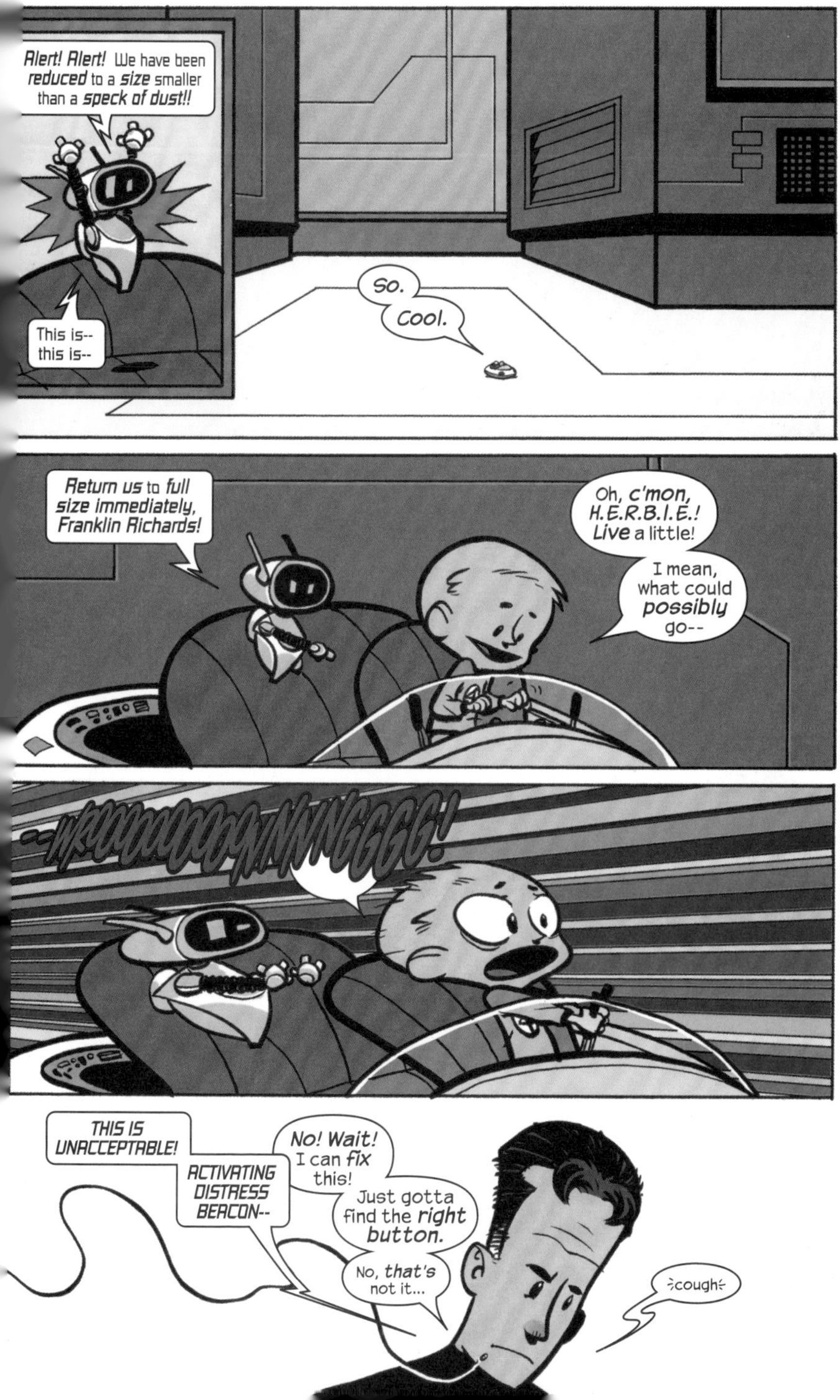

Alert! Alert! We have been reduced to a size smaller than a speck of dust!!
This is-- this is--
So.
Cool.
Return us to full size immediately, Franklin Richards!
Oh, c'mon, H.E.R.B.I.E.! Live a little!
I mean, what could possibly go--
--WRRRRRRRRRGNNNNGGGG!
THIS IS UNACCEPTABLE!
ACTIVATING DISTRESS BEACON--
No! Wait! I can fix this!
Just gotta find the right button.
No, that's not it...
cough

ALERT! ALERT!
Chill out, H.E.R.B.I.E. Before you know it we'll be--
--GOING RIGHT UP YOUR FATHER'S NOSE!!!
GAAAHH!
Hmm. That wasn't so bad.
Not so bad? When your father finds out about this, he will dismantle me!
No, he won't! 'Cause he'll never even know we did this.
We are in his nose! How can he not--
YAAH!
Some kinda giant germ!!
HELP ME, H.E.R.B.I.E.!
ACTIVATING SECURITY PROTOCOL 1870.
PROTECT FRANKLIN RICHARDS AT ANY COST.
You are safe now, Franklin.
All danger is being eliminated.
Oh, yeah?
What about THAT?!

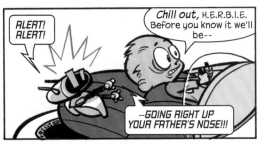

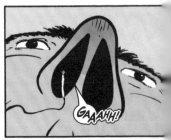

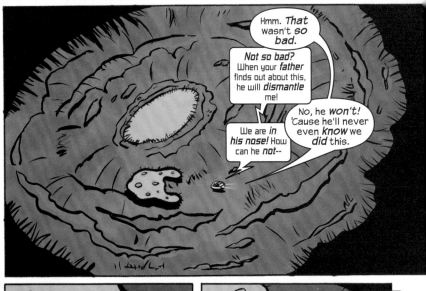

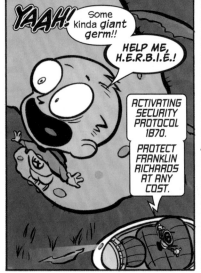

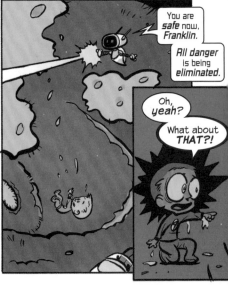

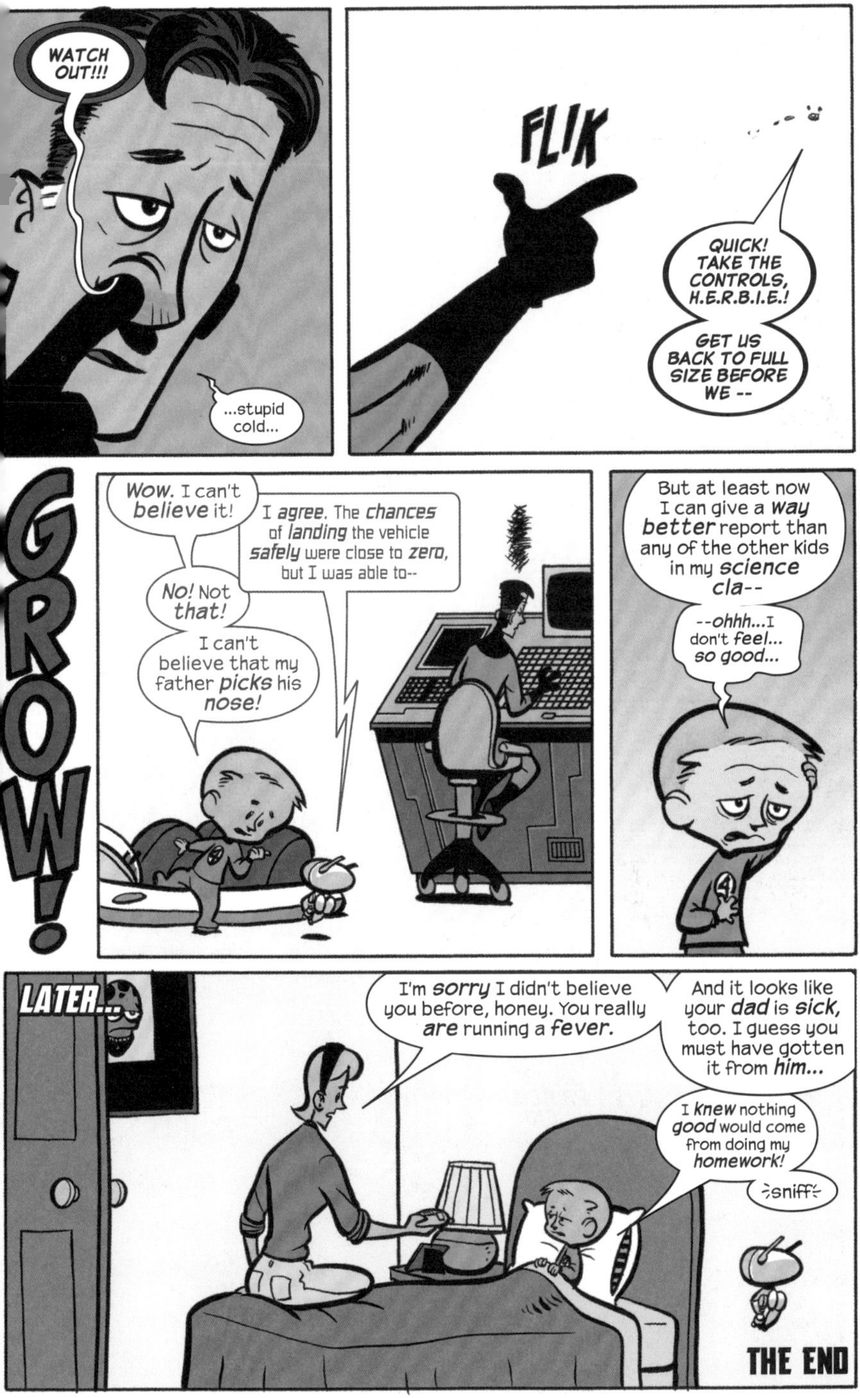
WATCH OUT!!!
...stupid cold...
FLIK
QUICK! TAKE THE CONTROLS, H.E.R.B.I.E.!
GET US BACK TO FULL SIZE BEFORE WE --
GROW!
Wow. I can't believe it!
I agree. The chances of landing the vehicle safely were close to zero, but I was able to--
No! Not that!
I can't believe that my father picks his nose!
But at least now I can give a way better report than any of the other kids in my science cla--
--ohhh...I don't feel... so good...
LATER...
I'm sorry I didn't believe you before, honey. You really are running a fever.
And it looks like your dad is sick, too. I guess you must have gotten it from him...
I knew nothing good would come from doing my homework!
sniff
THE END

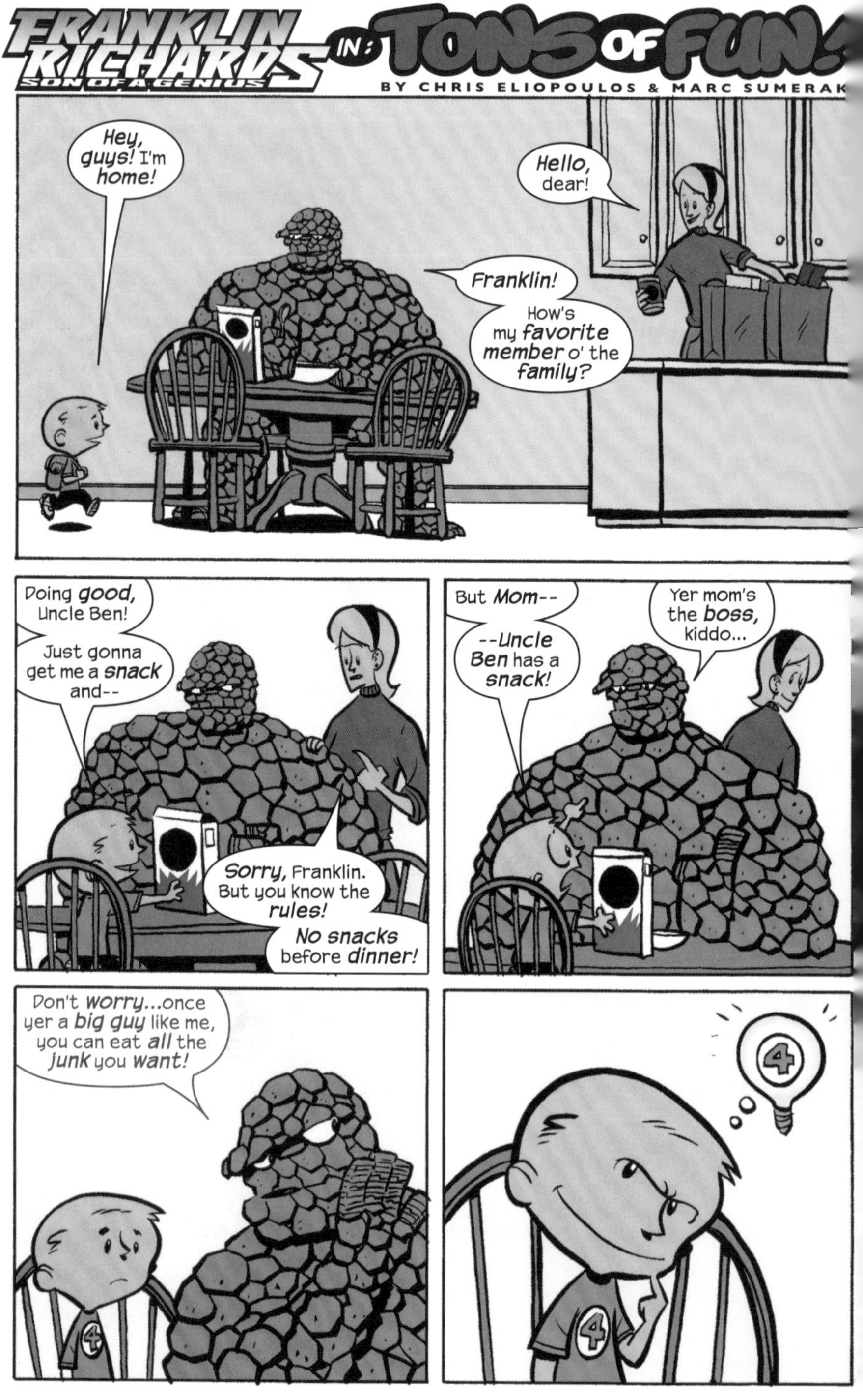
FRANKLIN RICHARDS SON OF A GENIUS IN: TONS OF FUN!
BY CHRIS ELIOPOULOS & MARC SUMERAK
Hey, guys! I'm home!
Hello, dear!
Franklin!
How's my favorite member o' the family?
Doing good, Uncle Ben!
Just gonna get me a snack and--
Sorry, Franklin. But you know the rules!
No snacks before dinner!
But Mom--
--Uncle Ben has a snack!
Yer mom's the boss, kiddo...
Don't worry...once yer a big guy like me, you can eat all the junk you want!

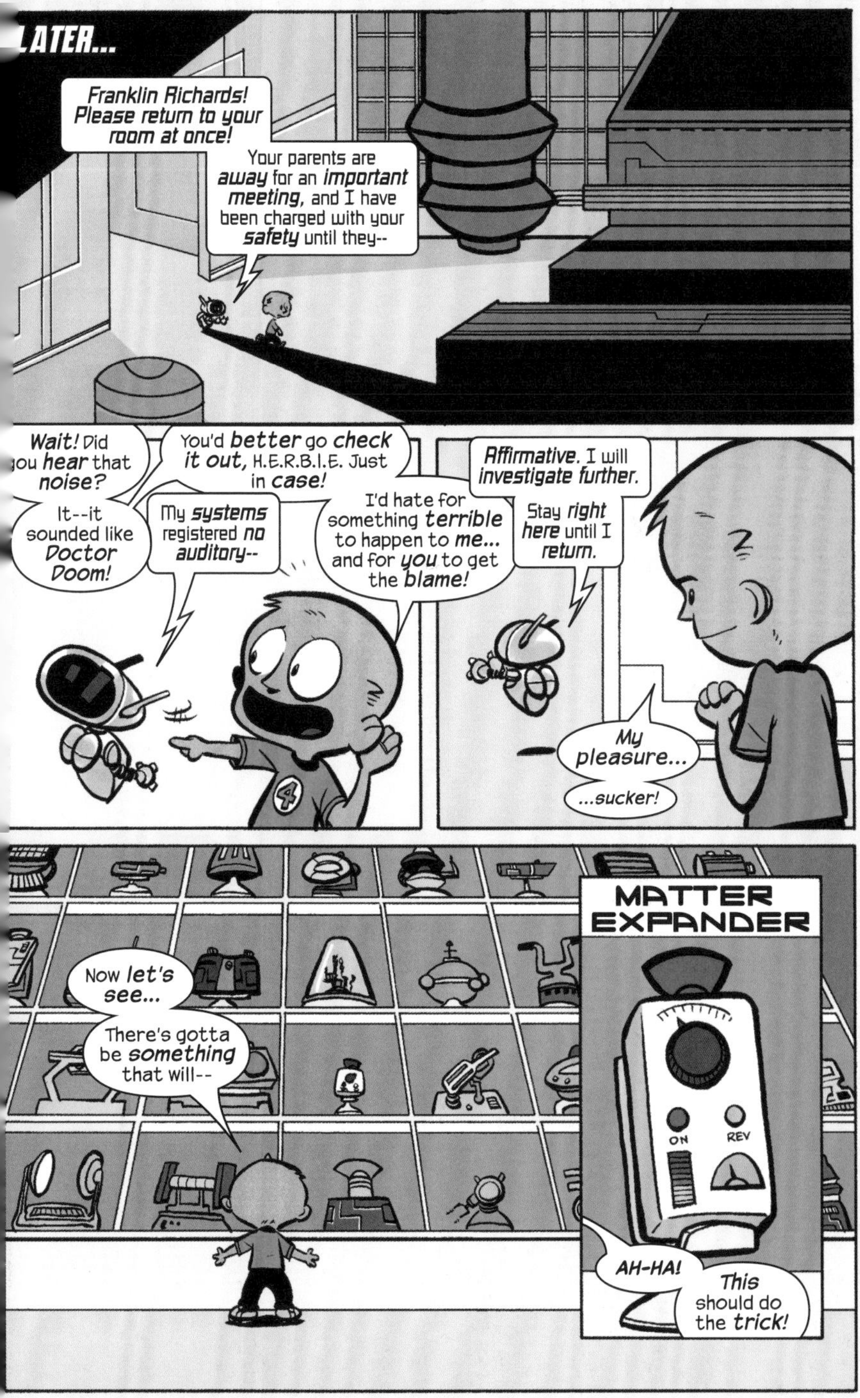
LATER...
Franklin Richards! Please return to your room at once!
Your parents are away for an important meeting, and I have been charged with your safety until they--
Wait! Did you hear that noise?
It--it sounded like Doctor Doom!
You'd better go check it out, H.E.R.B.I.E. Just in case!
My systems registered no auditory--
I'd hate for something terrible to happen to me... and for you to get the blame!
Affirmative. I will investigate further.
Stay right here until I return.
My pleasure...
...sucker!
Now let's see...
There's gotta be something that will--
MATTER EXPANDER
ON
REV
AH-HA!
This should do the trick!

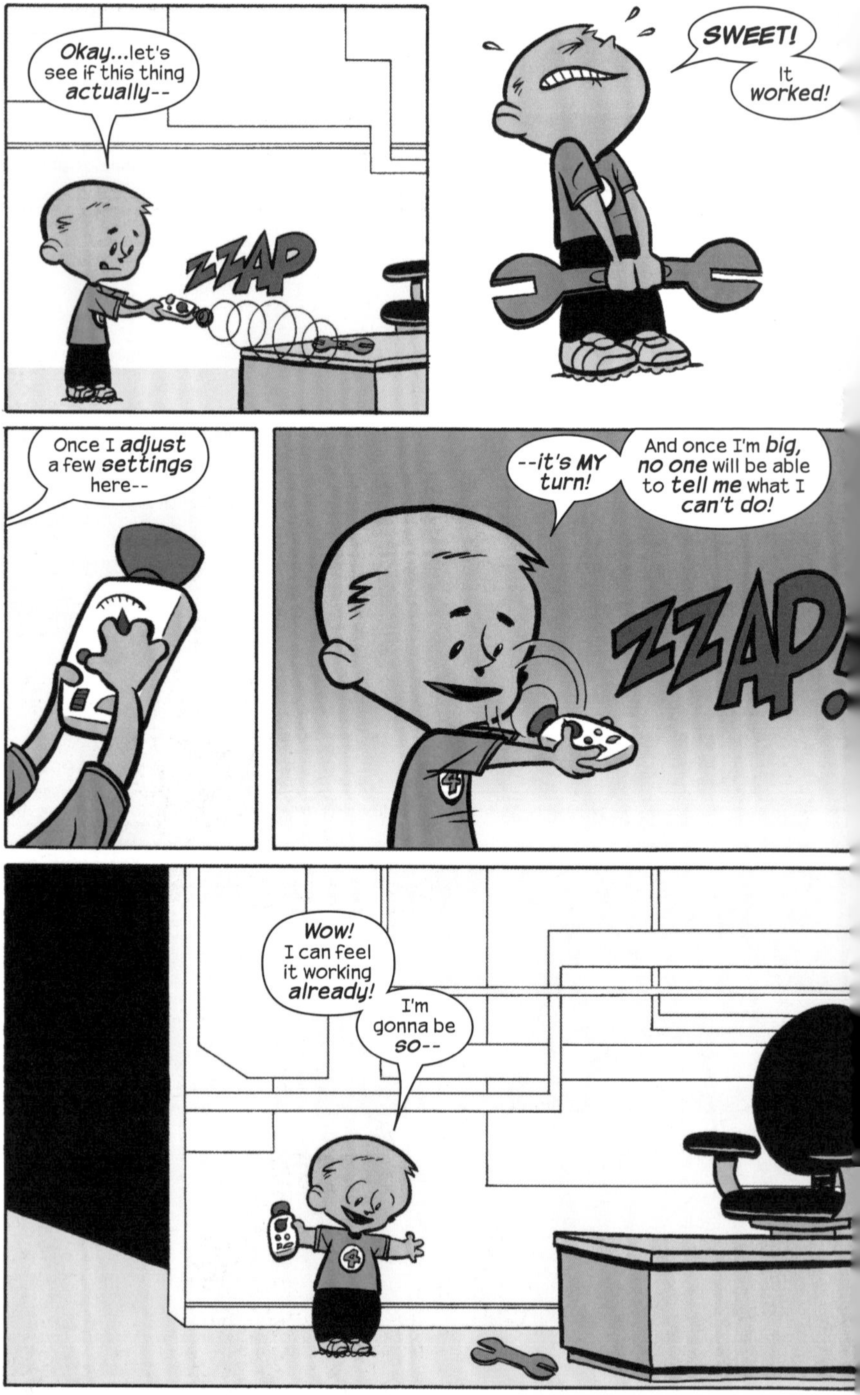

Okay...let's see if this thing actually--
ZZAP
SWEET!
It worked!
Once I adjust a few settings here--
--it's MY turn!
And once I'm big, no one will be able to tell me what I can't do!
ZZAP
Wow! I can feel it working already!
I'm gonna be so--

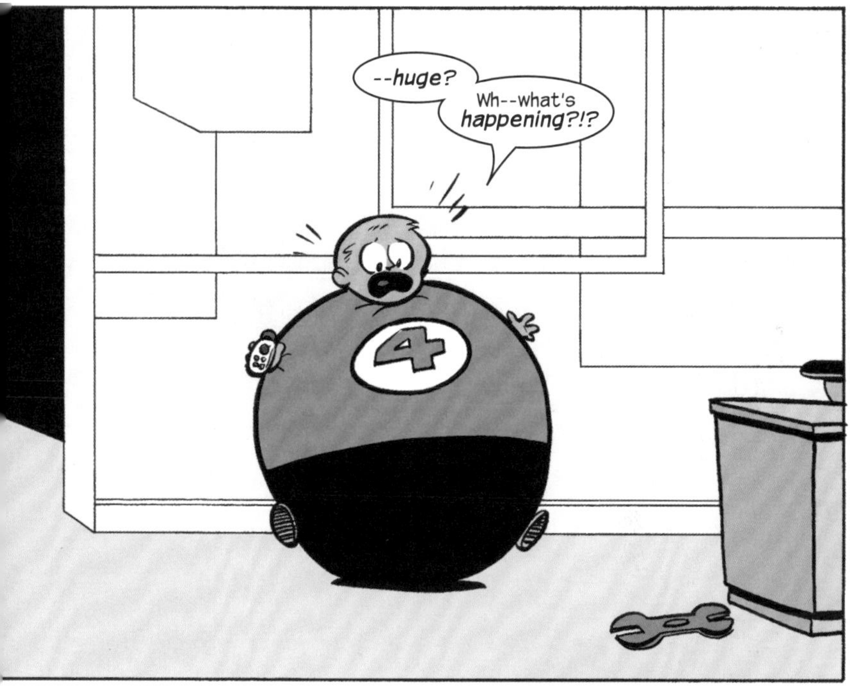
--huge?
Wh--what's happening?!?

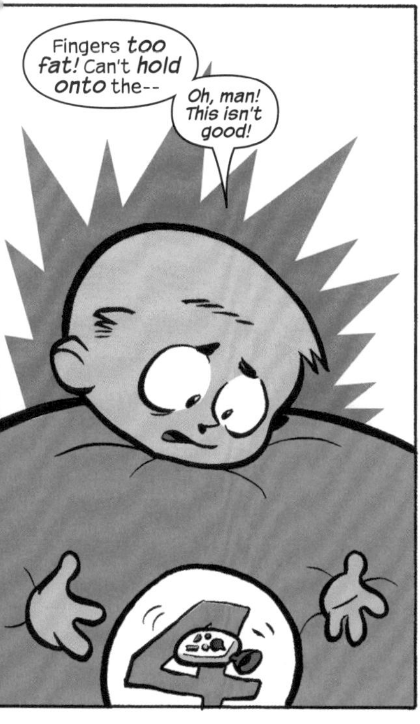
Fingers too fat! Can't hold onto the--
Oh, man! This isn't good!

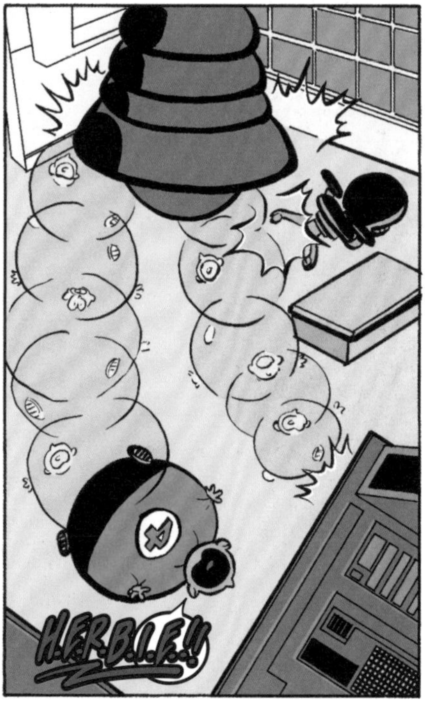
H.E.R.B.I.E.!!

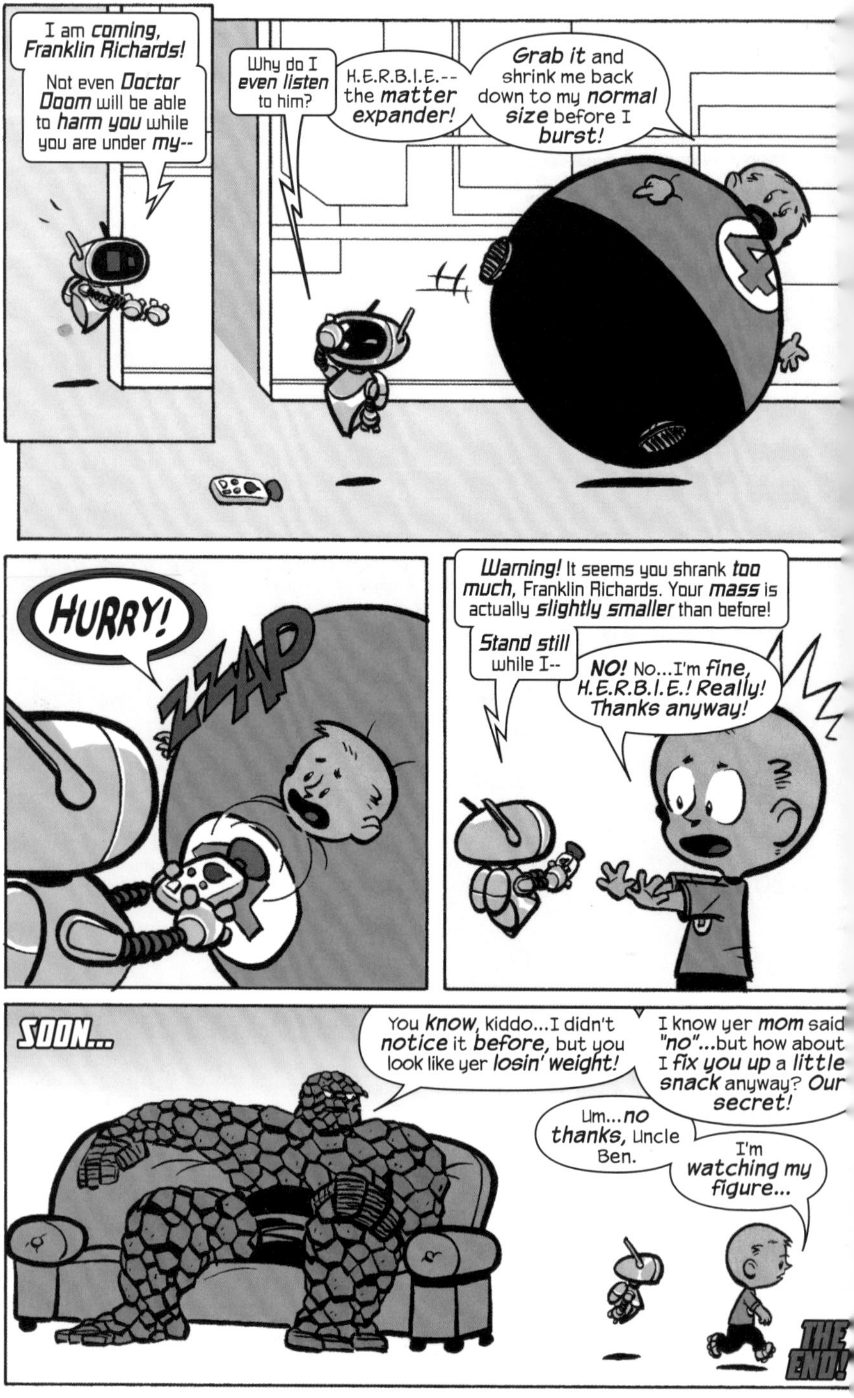
I am coming, Franklin Richards!
Not even Doctor Doom will be able to harm you while you are under my--
Why do I even listen to him?
H.E.R.B.I.E.-- the matter expander!
Grab it and shrink me back down to my normal size before I burst!
HURRY!
ZZAP
Warning! It seems you shrank too much, Franklin Richards. Your mass is actually slightly smaller than before!
Stand still while I--
NO! No...I'm fine, H.E.R.B.I.E.! Really! Thanks anyway!
SOON...
You know, kiddo...I didn't notice it before, but you look like yer losin' weight!
I know yer mom said "no"...but how about I fix you up a little snack anyway? Our secret!
Um...no thanks, Uncle Ben.
I'm watching my figure...
THE END!

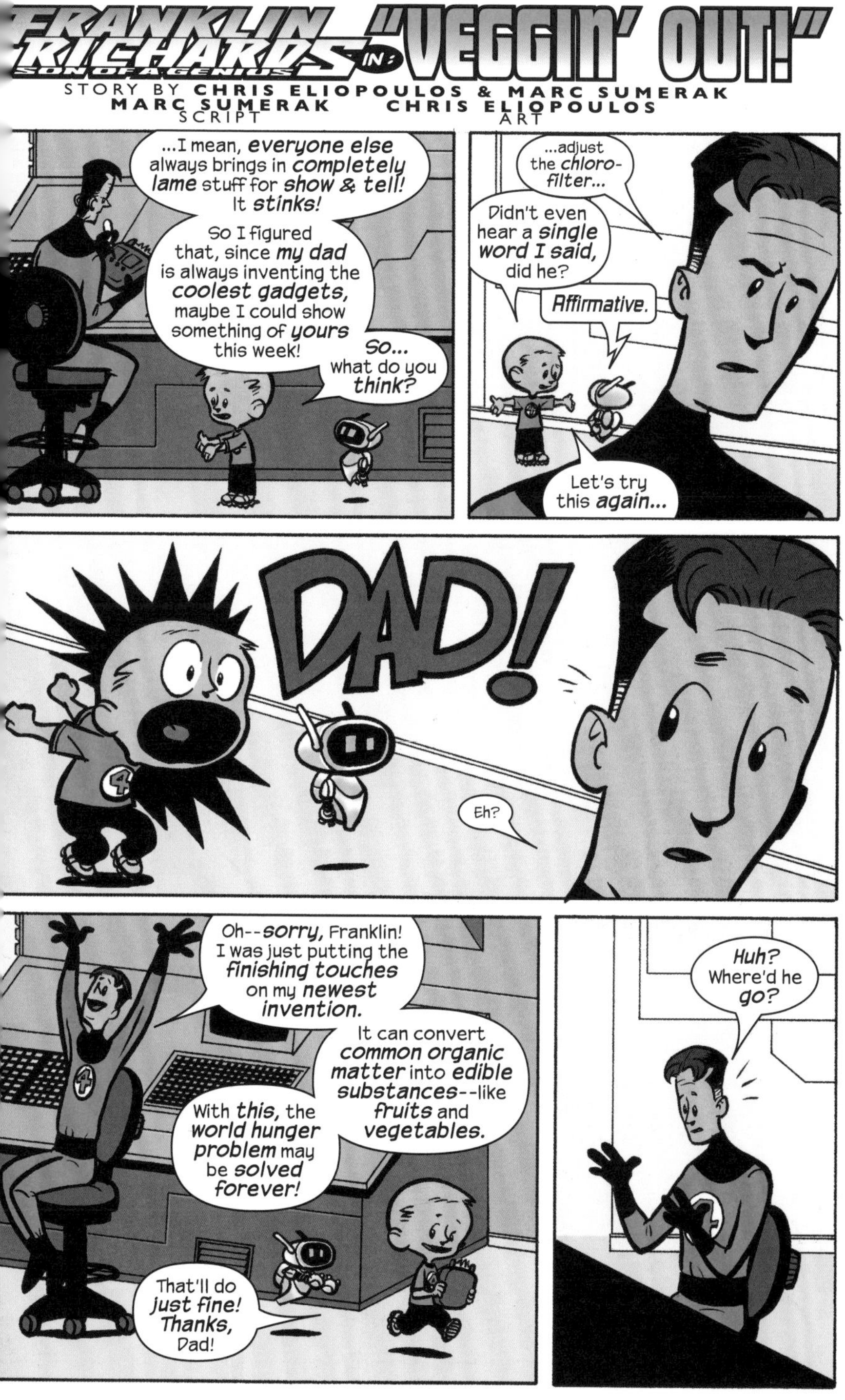
FRANKLIN RICHARDS SON OF A GENIUS IN: "VEGGIN' OUT!"
STORY BY CHRIS ELIOPOULOS & MARC SUMERAK
MARC SUMERAK SCRIPT
CHRIS ELIOPOULOS ART
...I mean, everyone else always brings in completely lame stuff for show & tell! It stinks!
So I figured that, since my dad is always inventing the coolest gadgets, maybe I could show something of yours this week!
So... what do you think?
...adjust the chloro-filter...
Didn't even hear a single word I said, did he?
Affirmative.
Let's try this again...
DAD!
Eh?
Oh--sorry, Franklin! I was just putting the finishing touches on my newest invention.
It can convert common organic matter into edible substances--like fruits and vegetables.
With this, the world hunger problem may be solved forever!
That'll do just fine! Thanks, Dad!
Huh? Where'd he go?

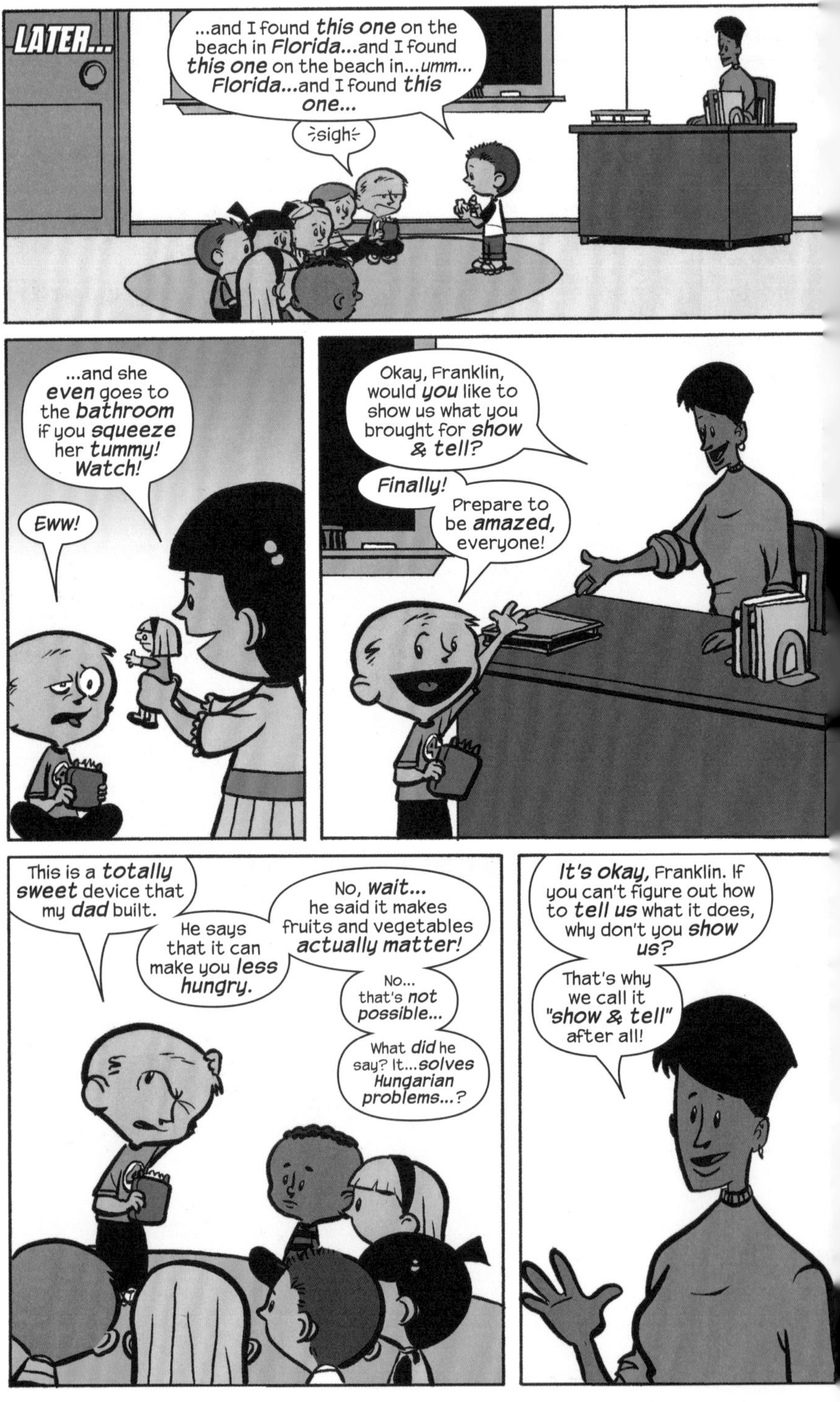
LATER...
...and I found this one on the beach in Florida...and I found this one on the beach in...umm... Florida...and I found this one...
sigh
...and she even goes to the bathroom if you squeeze her tummy! Watch!
Eww!
Okay, Franklin, would you like to show us what you brought for show & tell?
Finally!
Prepare to be amazed, everyone!
This is a totally sweet device that my dad built.
He says that it can make you less hungry.
No, wait... he said it makes fruits and vegetables actually matter!
No... that's not possible...
What did he say? It...solves Hungarian problems...?
It's okay, Franklin. If you can't figure out how to tell us what it does, why don't you show us?
That's why we call it "show & tell" after all!

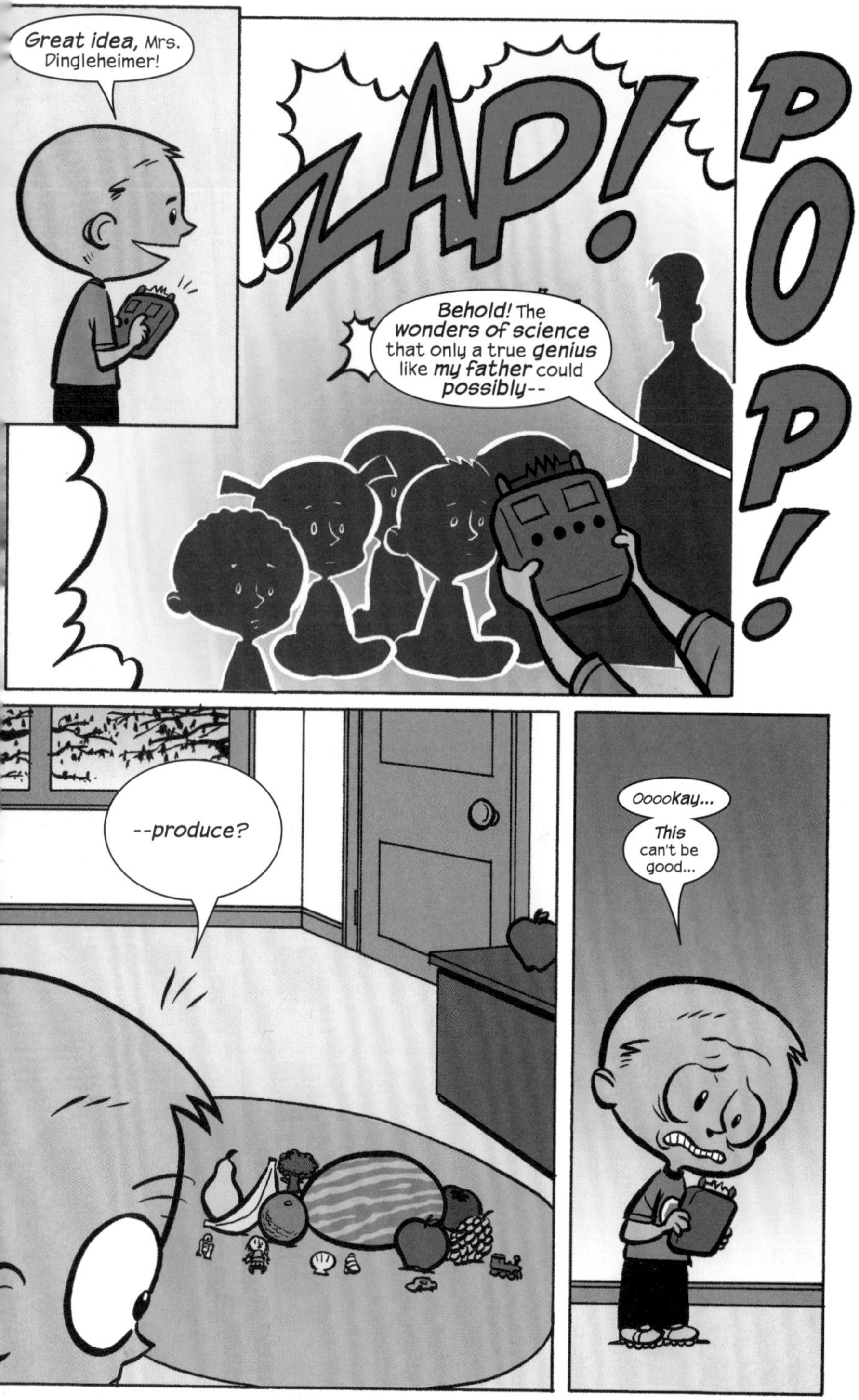

Great idea, Mrs. Dingleheimer!
ZAP!
POP!
Behold! The wonders of science that only a true genius like my father could possibly--
--produce?
Ooookay...
This can't be good...

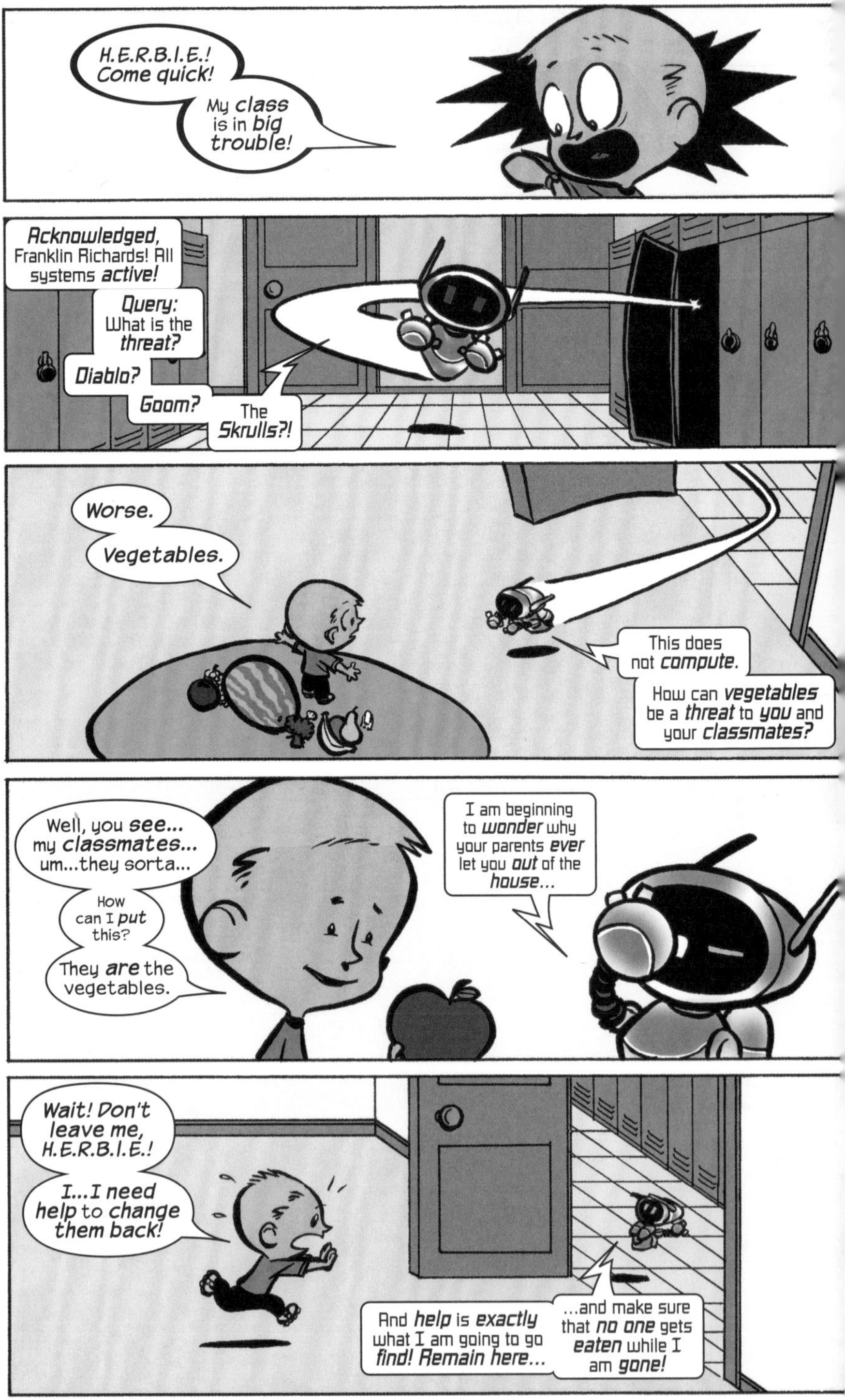

H.E.R.B.I.E.! Come quick!
My class is in big trouble!
Acknowledged, Franklin Richards! All systems active!
Query: What is the threat?
Diablo?
Doom?
The Skrulls?!
Worse.
Vegetables.
This does not compute.
How can vegetables be a threat to you and your classmates?
Well, you see... my classmates... um...they sorta...
How can I put this?
They are the vegetables.
I am beginning to wonder why your parents ever let you out of the house...
Wait! Don't leave me, H.E.R.B.I.E.!
I...I need help to change them back!
And help is exactly what I am going to go find! Remain here...
...and make sure that no one gets eaten while I am gone!

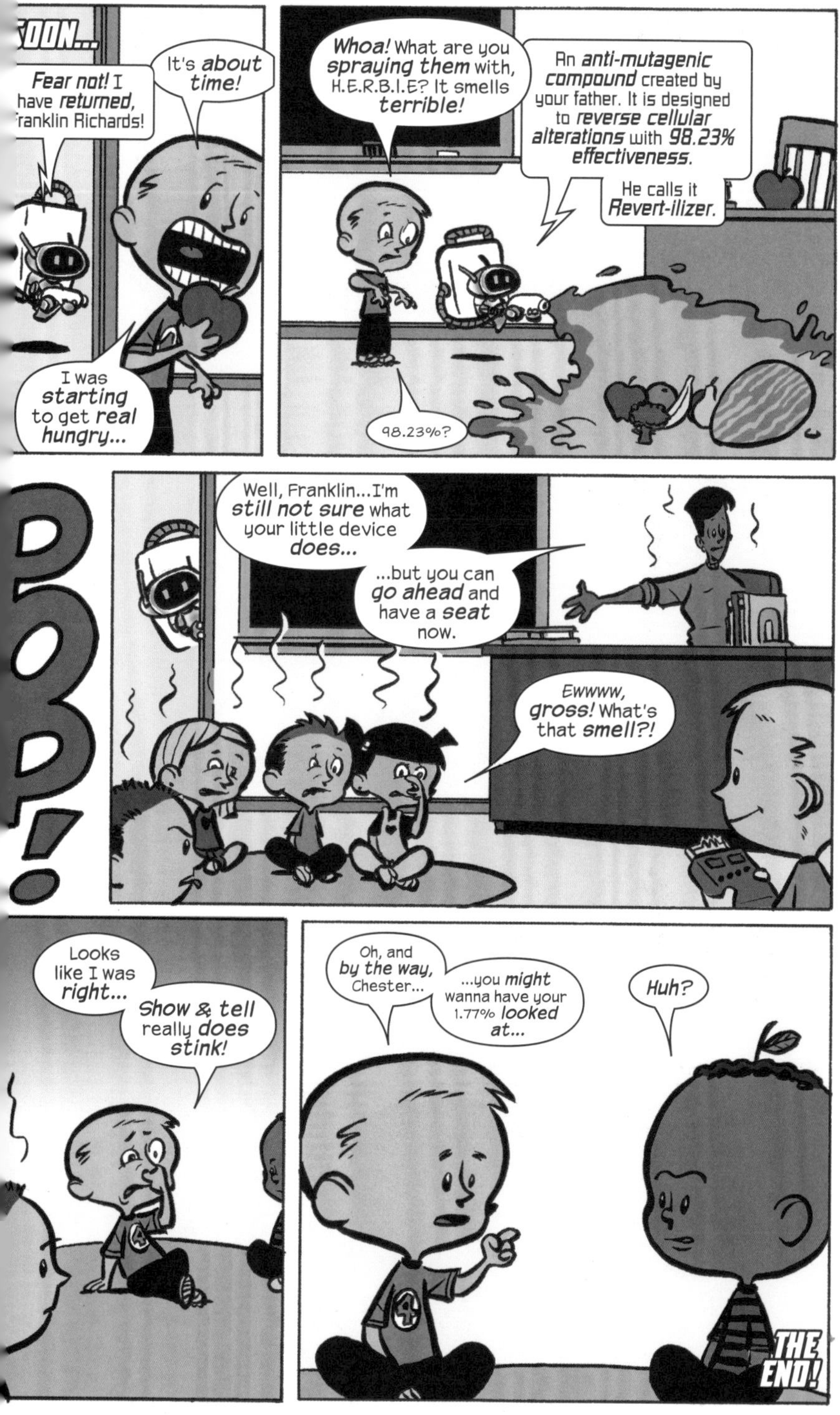
Fear not! I have returned, Franklin Richards!
It's about time!
I was starting to get real hungry...
Whoa! What are you spraying them with, H.E.R.B.I.E? It smells terrible!
An anti-mutagenic compound created by your father. It is designed to reverse cellular alterations with 98.23% effectiveness.
He calls it Revert-ilizer.
98.23%?
POOF!
Well, Franklin...I'm still not sure what your little device does...
...but you can go ahead and have a seat now.
Ewwww, gross! What's that smell?!
Looks like I was right...
Show & tell really does stink!
Oh, and by the way, Chester...
...you might wanna have your 1.77% looked at...
Huh?
THE END!

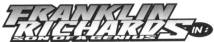

FRANKLIN RICHARDS SON OF A GENIUS IN: WEATHER OR NOT

STORY BY CHRIS ELIOPOULOS & MARC SUMERA
MARC SUMERAK SCRIPT
CHRIS ELIOPOULOS ART

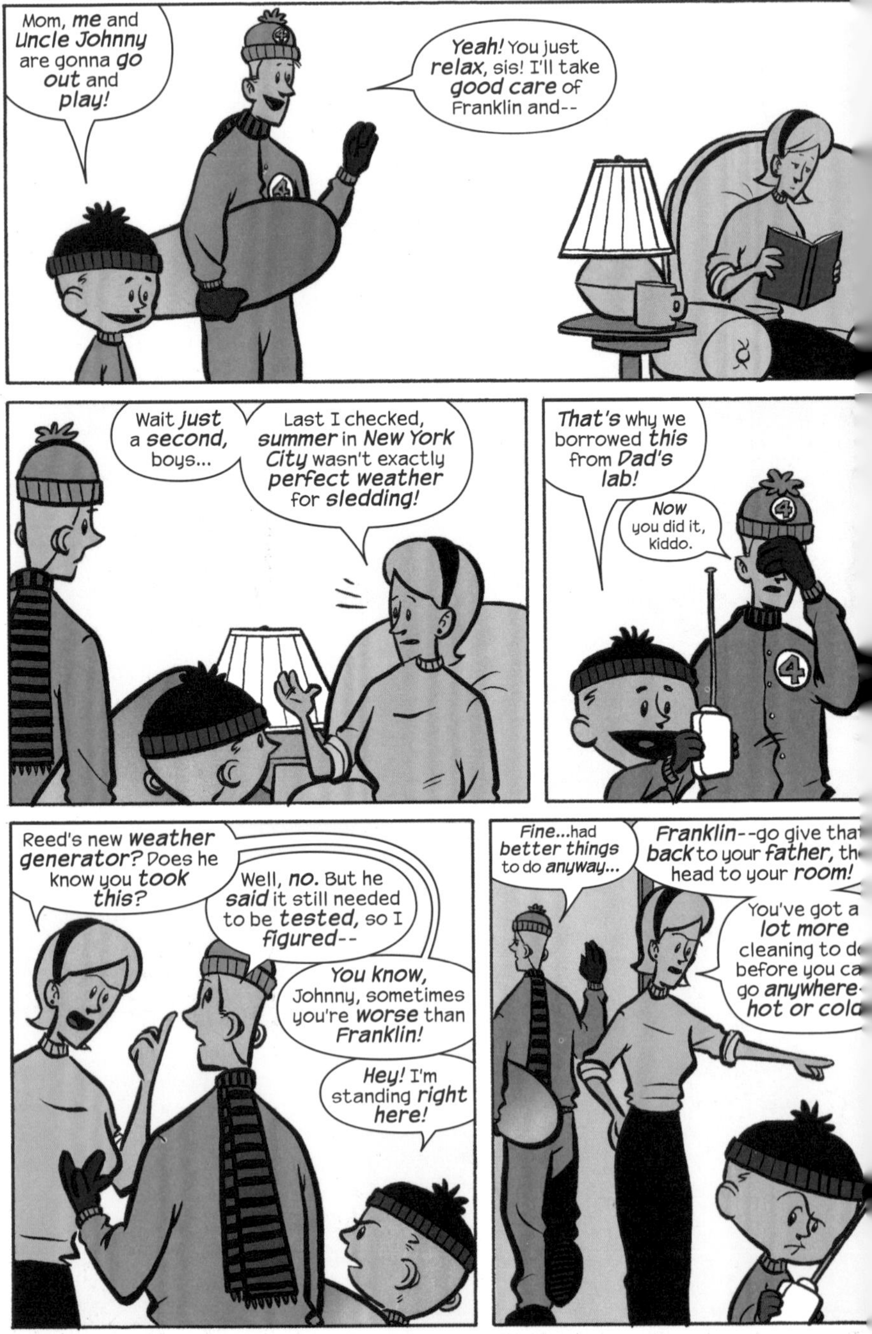
Mom, me and Uncle Johnny are gonna go out and play!
Yeah! You just relax, sis! I'll take good care of Franklin and--
Wait just a second, boys...
Last I checked, summer in New York City wasn't exactly perfect weather for sledding!
That's why we borrowed this from Dad's lab!
Now you did it, kiddo.
Reed's new weather generator? Does he know you took this?
Well, no. But he said it still needed to be tested, so I figured--
You know, Johnny, sometimes you're worse than Franklin!
Hey! I'm standing right here!
Fine...had better things to do anyway...
Franklin--go give tha back to your father, th head to your room!
You've got a lot more cleaning to d before you ca go anywhere hot or cold

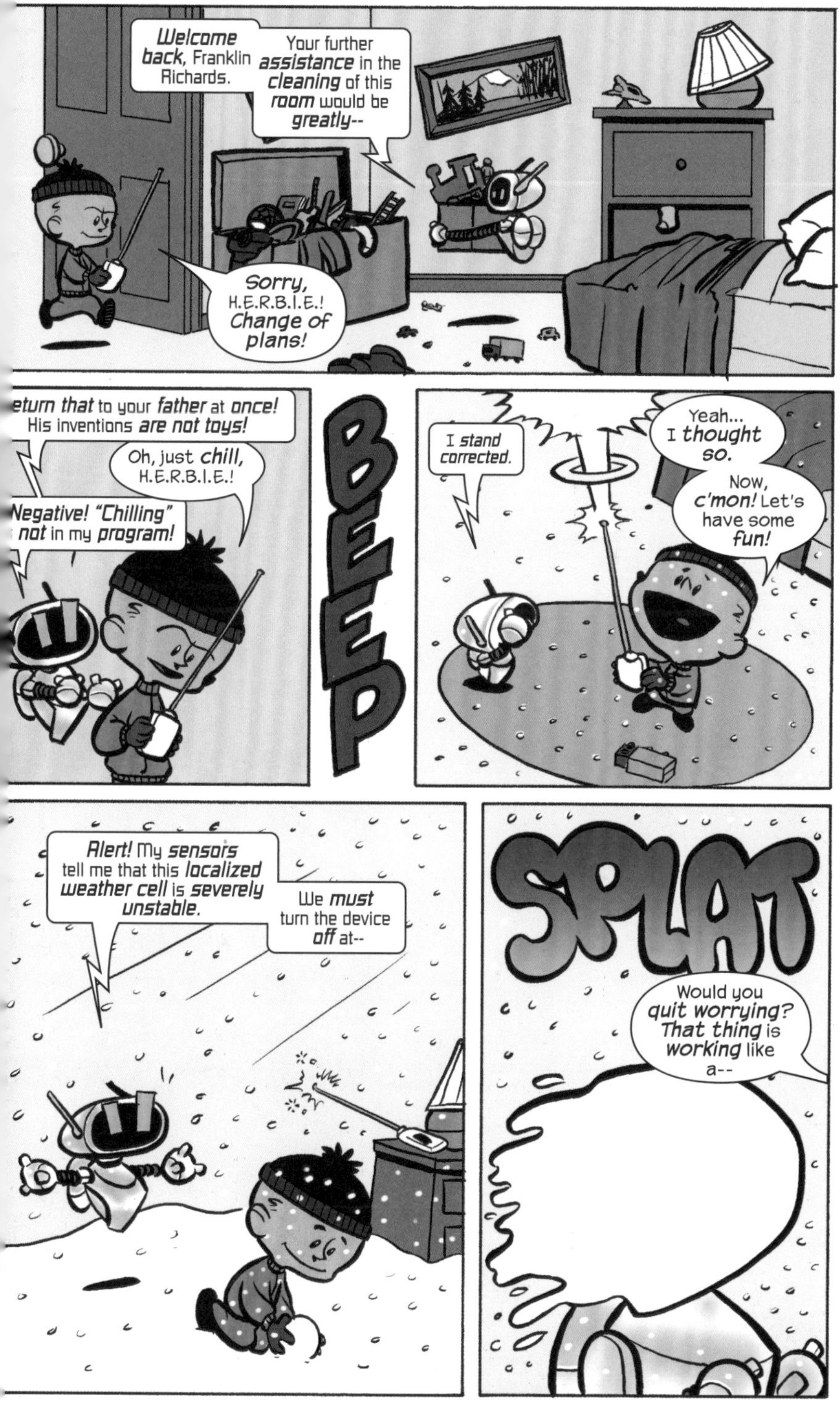

Welcome back, Franklin Richards.
Your further assistance in the cleaning of this room would be greatly--
Sorry, H.E.R.B.I.E.! Change of plans!
eturn that to your father at once! His inventions are not toys!
Oh, just chill, H.E.R.B.I.E.!
Negative! "Chilling" not in my program!
BEEP
I stand corrected.
Yeah... I thought so.
Now, c'mon! Let's have some fun!
Alert! My sensors tell me that this localized weather cell is severely unstable.
We must turn the device off at--
SPLAT
Would you quit worrying? That thing is working like a--

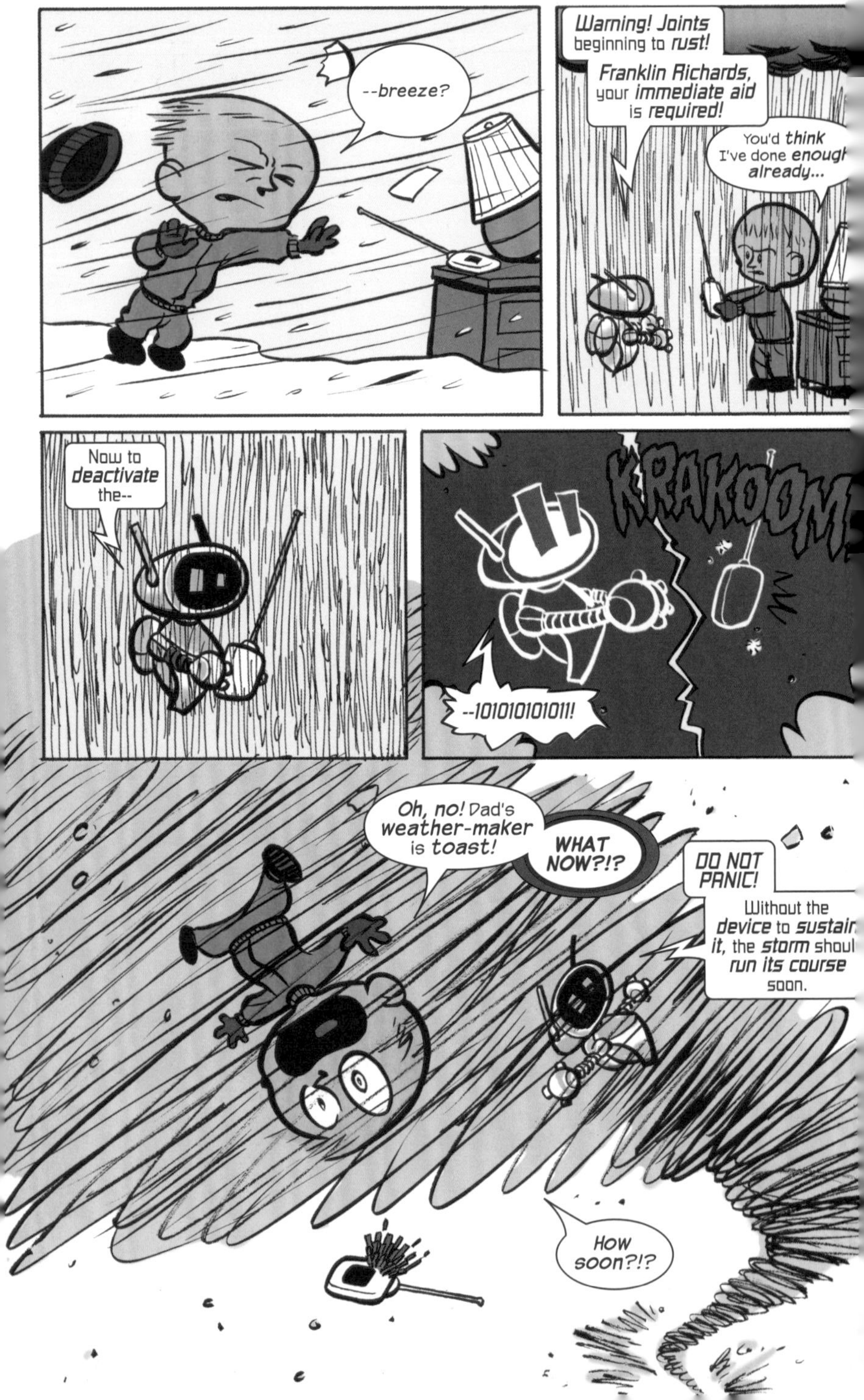
--breeze?
Warning! Joints beginning to rust!
Franklin Richards, your immediate aid is required!
You'd think I've done enough already...
Now to deactivate the--
KRAKOOM
--101010101011!
Oh, no! Dad's weather-maker is toast!
WHAT NOW?!?
DO NOT PANIC!
Without the device to sustain it, the storm should run its course soon.
How soon?!?

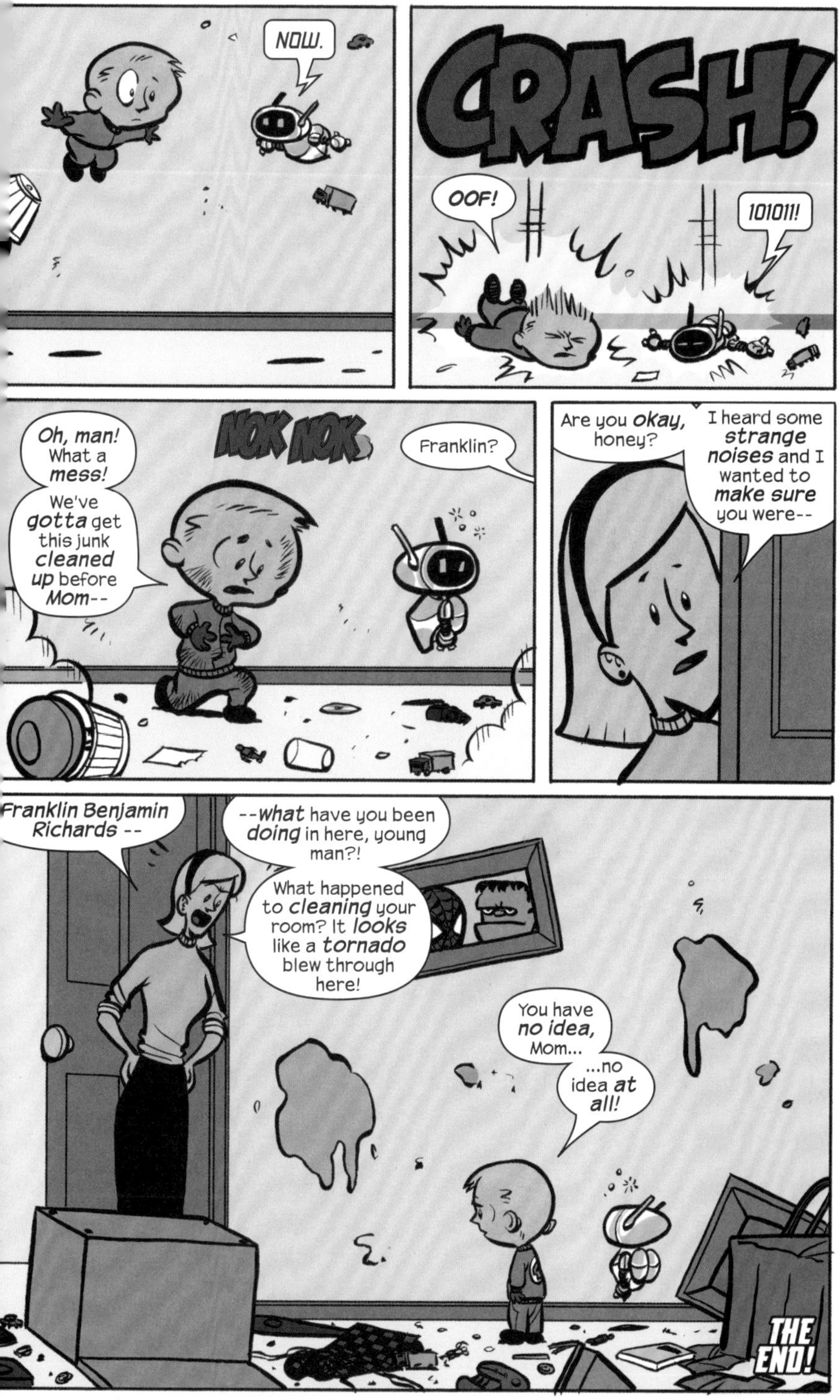
NOW.
CRASH!
OOF!
101011!
Oh, man! What a mess!
We've gotta get this junk cleaned up before Mom--
NOK NOK
Franklin?
Are you okay, honey?
I heard some strange noises and I wanted to make sure you were--
Franklin Benjamin Richards --
--what have you been doing in here, young man?!
What happened to cleaning your room? It looks like a tornado blew through here!
You have no idea, Mom...
...no idea at all!
THE END!

FRANKLIN RICHARDS SON OF A GENIUS IN: "SEND IN THE CLONES"

STORY BY CHRIS ELIOPOULOS & MARC SUMERAK
MARC SUMERAK SCRIPT
CHRIS ELIOPOULO ART

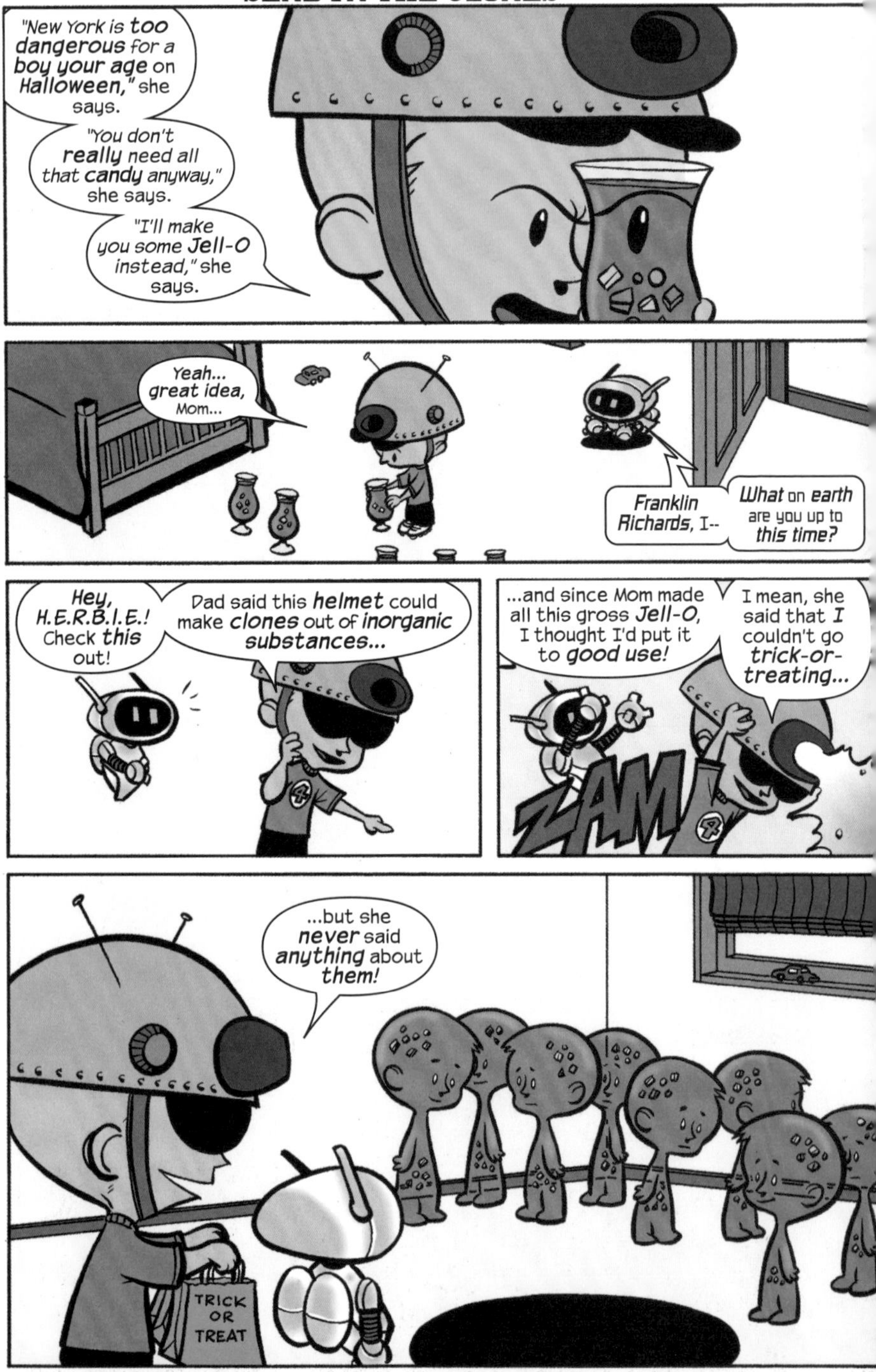
"New York is too dangerous for a boy your age on Halloween," she says.
"You don't really need all that candy anyway," she says.
"I'll make you some Jell-O instead," she says.
Yeah... great idea, Mom...
Franklin Richards, I--
What on earth are you up to this time?
Hey, H.E.R.B.I.E.! Check this out!
Dad said this helmet could make clones out of inorganic substances...
...and since Mom made all this gross Jell-O, I thought I'd put it to good use!
I mean, she said that I couldn't go trick-or-treating...
ZAM
...but she never said anything about them!
TRICK OR TREAT

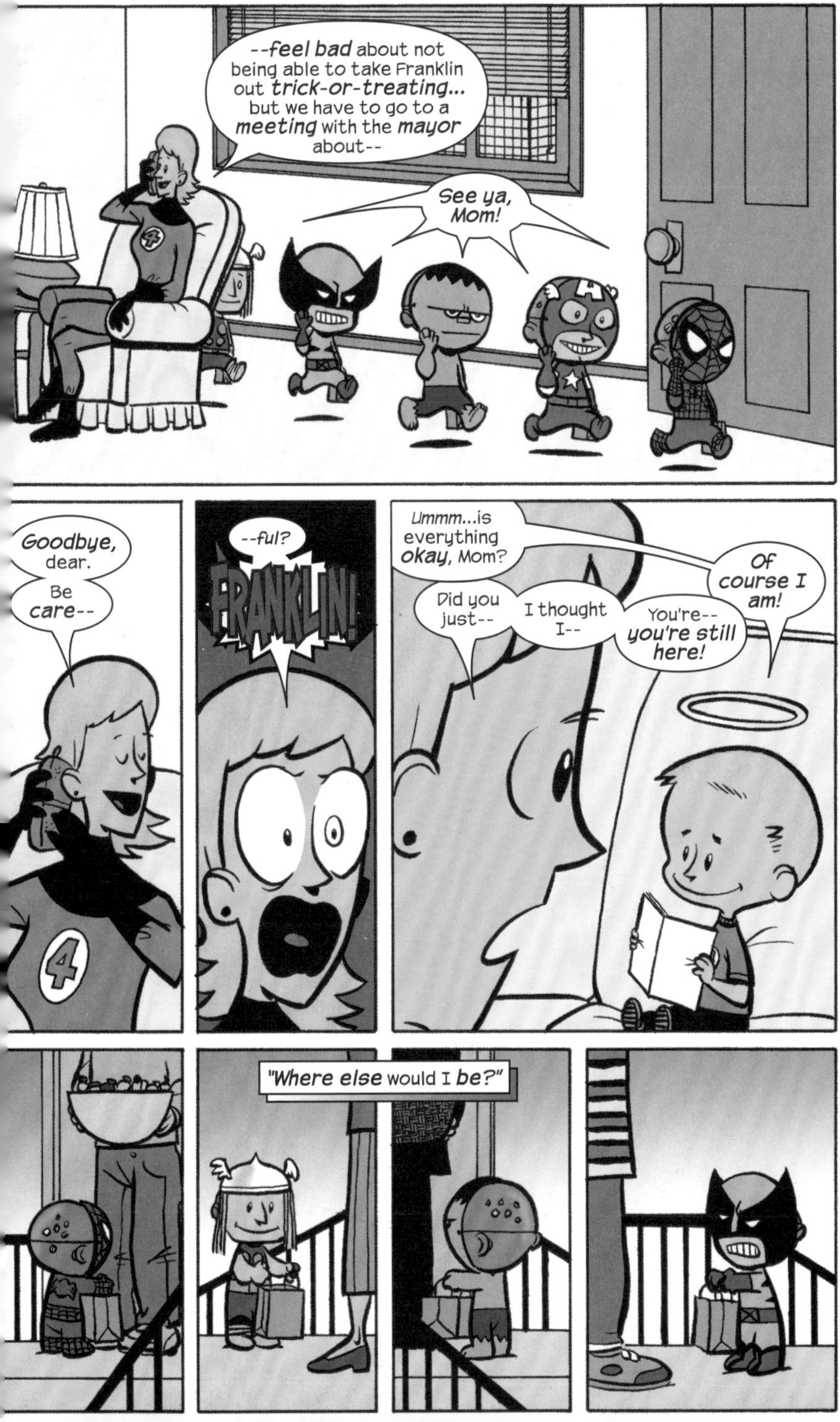
--feel bad about not being able to take Franklin out trick-or-treating... but we have to go to a meeting with the mayor about--
See ya, Mom!
Goodbye, dear.
Be care--
--ful?
FRANKLIN!
Ummm...is everything okay, Mom?
Of course I am!
Did you just--
I thought I--
You're-- you're still here!
"Where else would I be?"

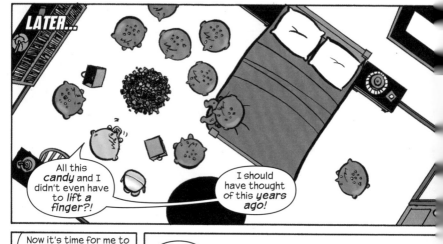

LATER...

All this *candy* and I didn't even have to *lift a finger*?!

I should have thought of this *years ago!*

Now it's time for me to *devour the evidence* before Mom and Dad *get back* from--

--HEY!

What are you *doing*?! Stop it!

Yeah, right, dude!

We *earned* it, we *eat* it!

MMMmmMM!

But those *treats* are for *me*!

They *are "you,"* remember?

Or at least *gelatinous facsimiles* thereof...

Since they were *cloned* from *you,* they naturally *behave* like you too.

Put that candy *down,* you *wobbly weirdos!*

Bad clones! Bad!

Man, why won't they *listen to me?*

I *often* ask myself the *same thing...*

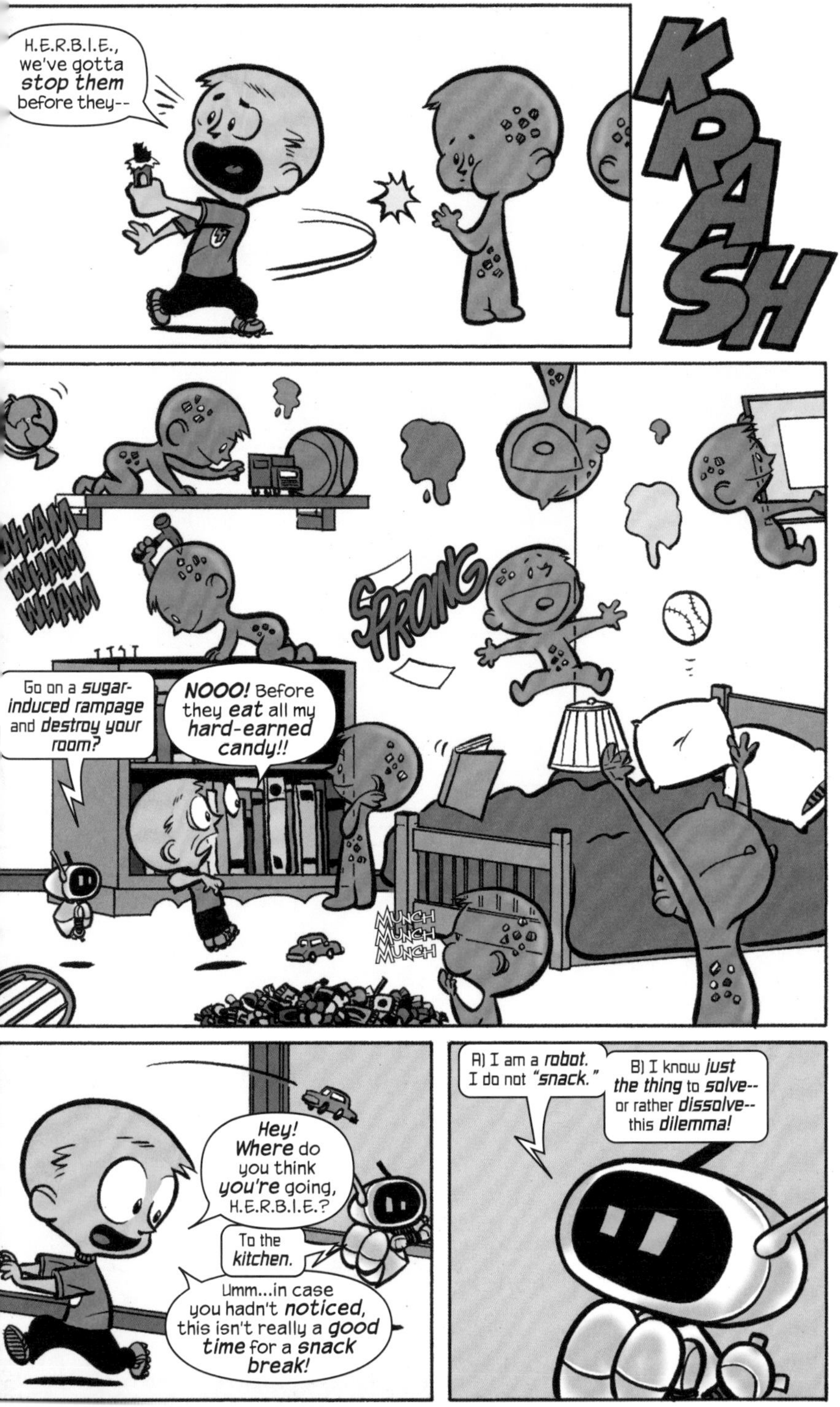
H.E.R.B.I.E., we've gotta stop them before they--
KRASH
WHAM WHAM WHAM
SPROING
Go on a sugar-induced rampage and destroy your room?
NOOO! Before they eat all my hard-earned candy!!
MUNCH MUNCH MUNCH
Hey! Where do you think you're going, H.E.R.B.I.E.?
To the kitchen.
Umm...in case you hadn't noticed, this isn't really a good time for a snack break!
A) I am a robot. I do not "snack."
B) I know just the thing to solve--or rather dissolve--this dilemma!

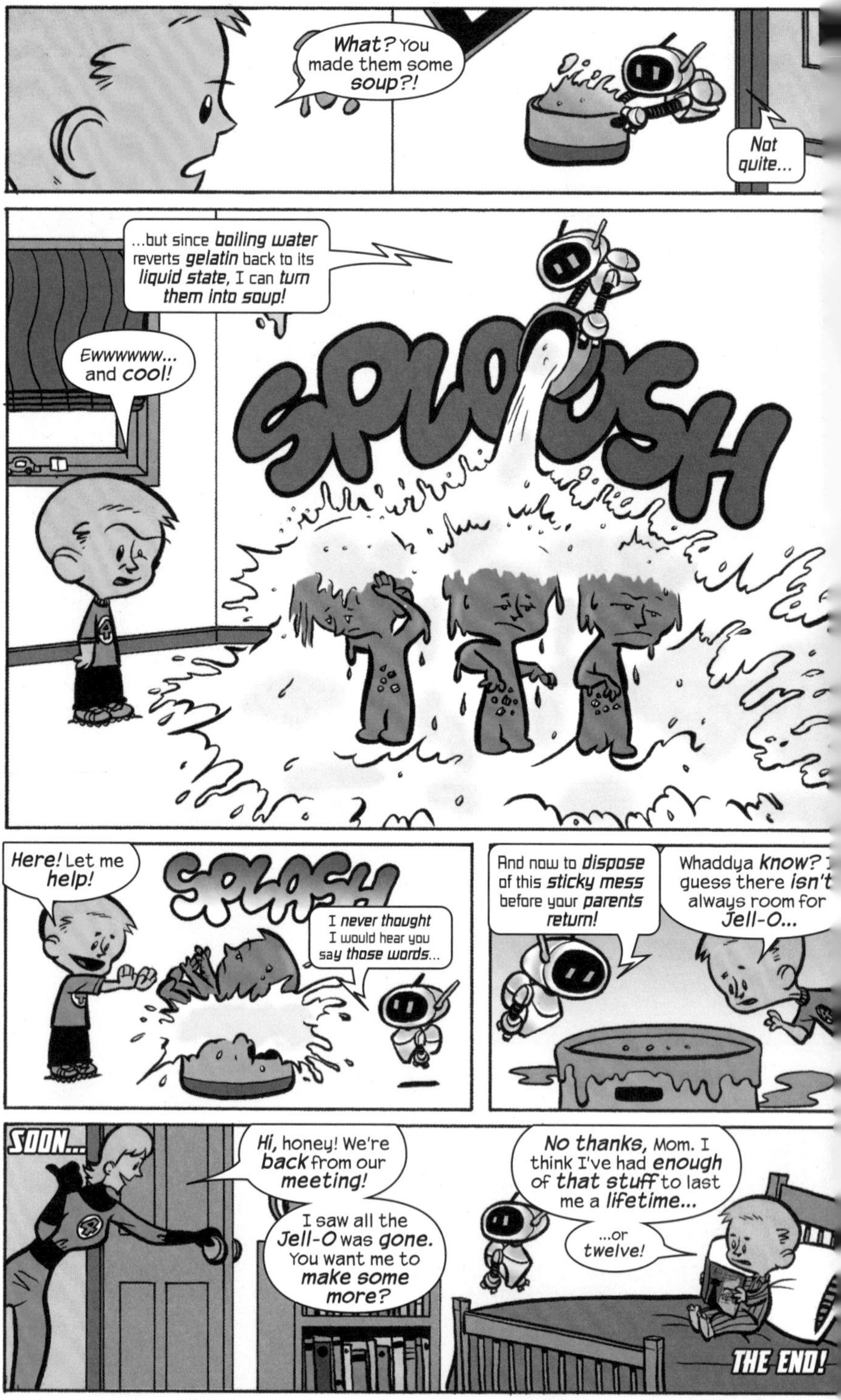

What? You made them some soup?!
Not quite...
...but since boiling water reverts gelatin back to its liquid state, I can turn them into soup!
Ewwwwww... and cool!
SPLOOSH
Here! Let me help!
SPLASH
I never thought I would hear you say those words...
And now to dispose of this sticky mess before your parents return!
Whaddya know? I guess there isn't always room for Jell-O...
SOON...
Hi, honey! We're back from our meeting!
I saw all the Jell-O was gone. You want me to make some more?
No thanks, Mom. I think I've had enough of that stuff to last me a lifetime...
...or twelve!
THE END!

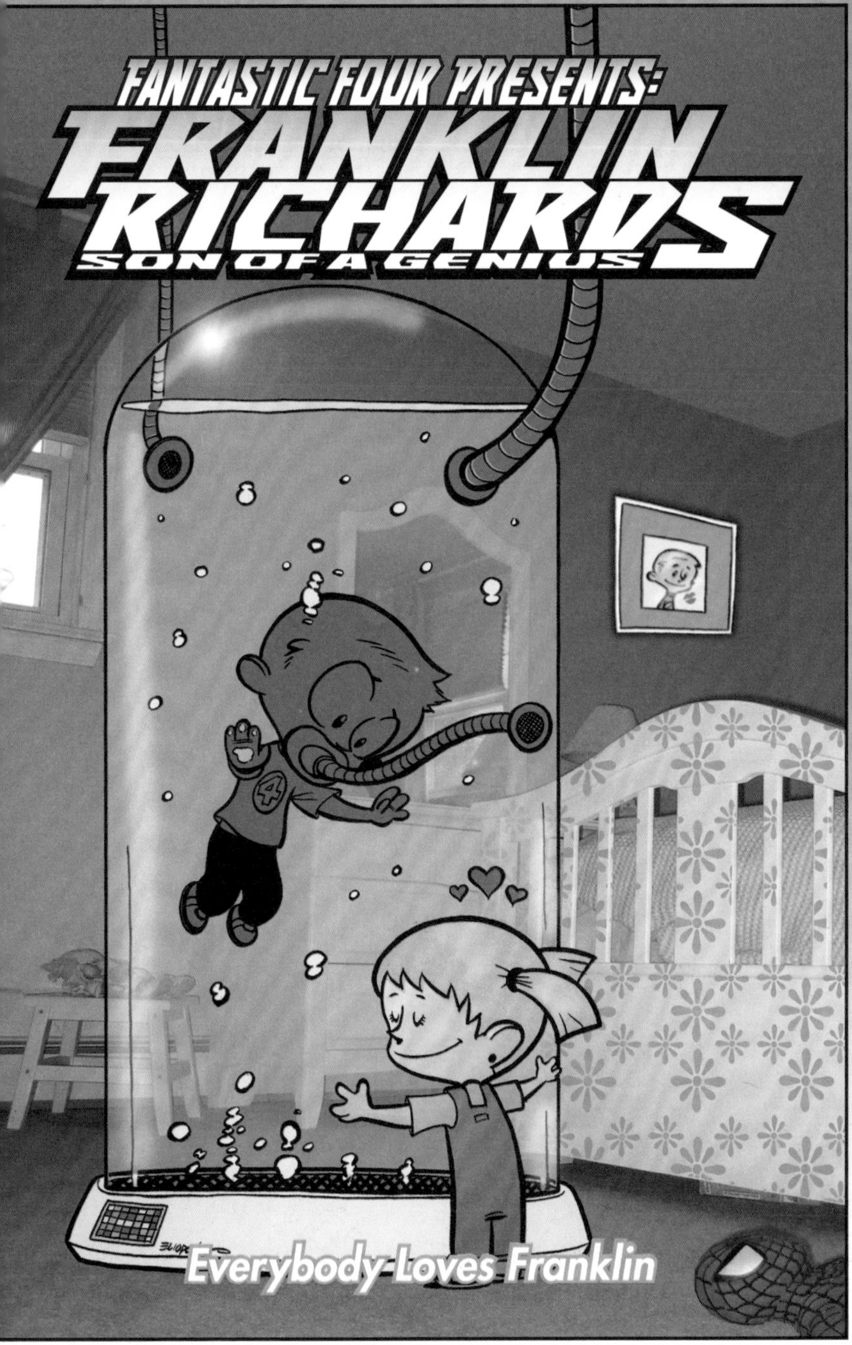
FANTASTIC FOUR PRESENTS:
FRANKLIN RICHARDS
SON OF A GENIUS
Everybody Loves Franklin

FRANKLIN RICHARDS SON OF A GENIUS IN: Christmas Time War

BY CHRIS ELIOPOULOS & MARC SUMERAK

GURIHIRU COLORS · NATHAN COSBY ASSISTANT EDITOR · TOM VALENTE PRODUCTION
MARK PANICCIA CONSULTING EDITOR · MACKENZIE CADENHEAD EDITOR

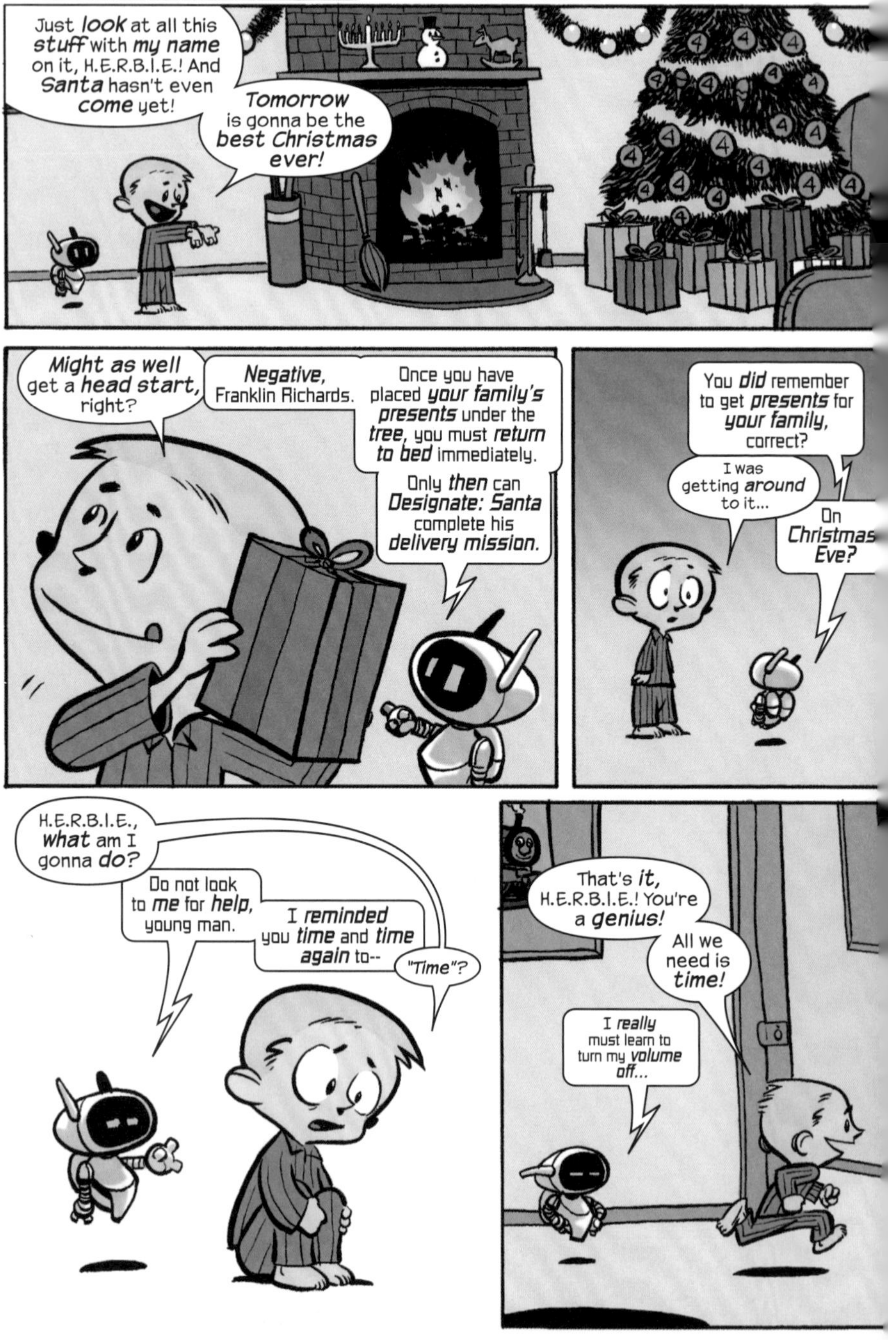

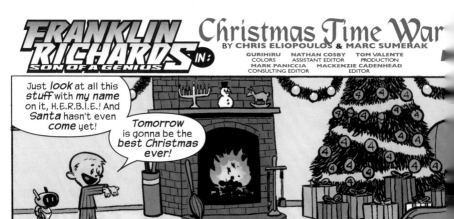

Just look at all this stuff with my name on it, H.E.R.B.I.E.! And Santa hasn't even come yet!
Tomorrow is gonna be the best Christmas ever!
Might as well get a head start, right?
Negative, Franklin Richards.
Once you have placed your family's presents under the tree, you must return to bed immediately.
Only then can Designate: Santa complete his delivery mission.
You did remember to get presents for your family, correct?
I was getting around to it...
On Christmas Eve?
H.E.R.B.I.E., what am I gonna do?
Do not look to me for help, young man.
I reminded you time and time again to--
"Time"?
That's it, H.E.R.B.I.E.! You're a genius!
All we need is time!
I really must learn to turn my volume off...

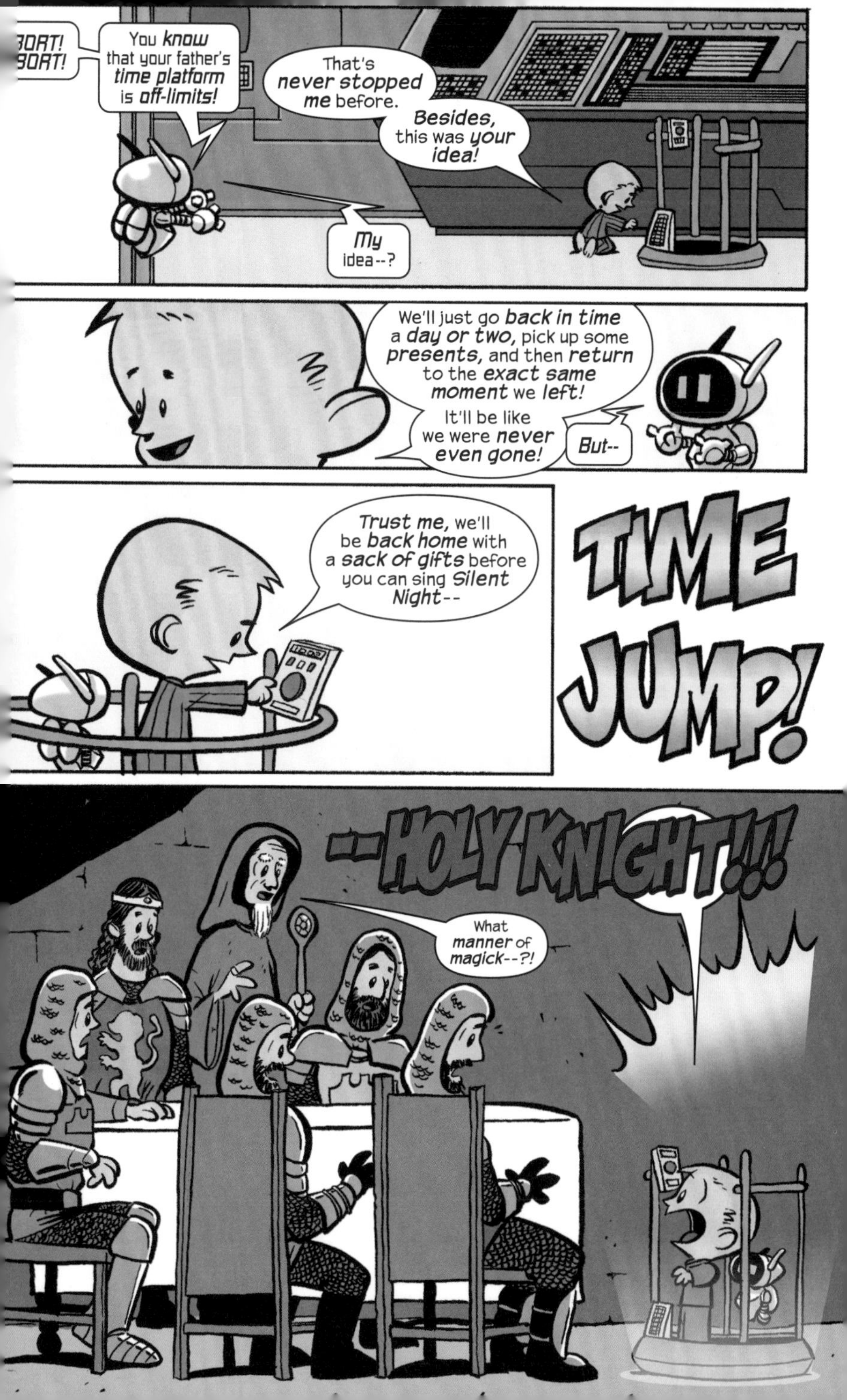
You know that your father's time platform is off-limits!
That's never stopped me before.
Besides, this was your idea!
My idea--?
We'll just go back in time a day or two, pick up some presents, and then return to the exact same moment we left!
It'll be like we were never even gone!
But--
Trust me, we'll be back home with a sack of gifts before you can sing Silent Night--
TIME JUMP!
--HOLY KNIGHT!!!
What manner of magick--?!

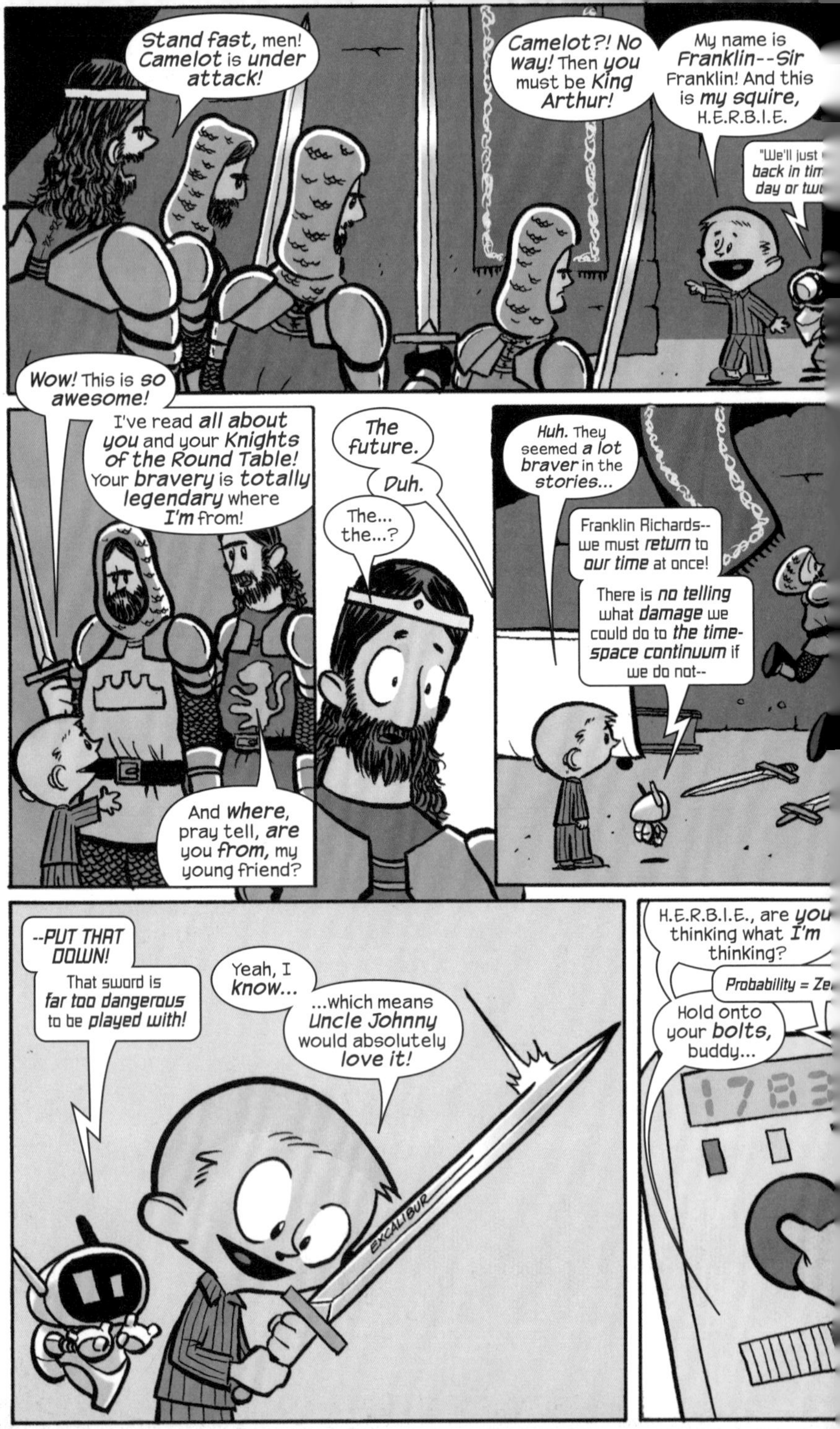

Stand fast, men! Camelot is under attack!
Camelot?! No way! Then you must be King Arthur!
My name is Franklin--Sir Franklin! And this is my squire, H.E.R.B.I.E.
Wow! This is so awesome!
I've read all about you and your Knights of the Round Table! Your bravery is totally legendary where I'm from!
And where, pray tell, are you from, my young friend?
The... the...?
The future.
Duh.
Huh. They seemed a lot braver in the stories...
Franklin Richards-- we must return to our time at once!
There is no telling what damage we could do to the time-space continuum if we do not--
--PUT THAT DOWN!
That sword is far too dangerous to be played with!
Yeah, I know...
...which means Uncle Johnny would absolutely love it!
EXCALIBUR
H.E.R.B.I.E., are you thinking what I'm thinking?
Hold onto your bolts, buddy...

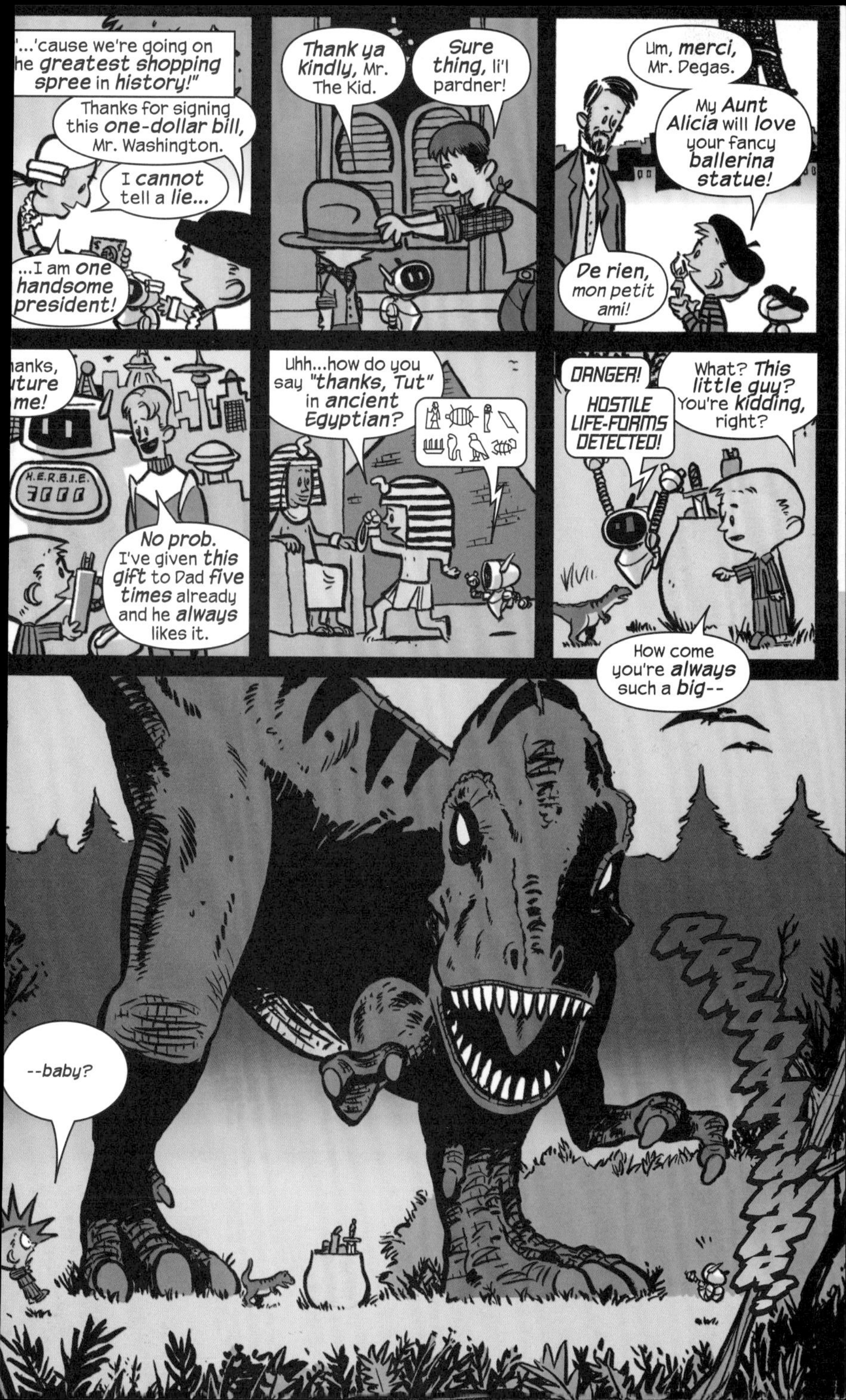
"...'cause we're going on the greatest shopping spree in history!"
Thanks for signing this one-dollar bill, Mr. Washington.
I cannot tell a lie...
...I am one handsome president!
Thank ya kindly, Mr. The Kid.
Sure thing, li'l pardner!
Um, merci, Mr. Degas.
My Aunt Alicia will love your fancy ballerina statue!
De rien, mon petit ami!
hanks, uture me!
H.E.R.B.I.E. 3000
No prob. I've given this gift to Dad five times already and he always likes it.
Uhh...how do you say "thanks, Tut" in ancient Egyptian?
DANGER!
HOSTILE LIFE-FORMS DETECTED!
What? This little guy? You're kidding, right?
How come you're always such a big--
--baby?

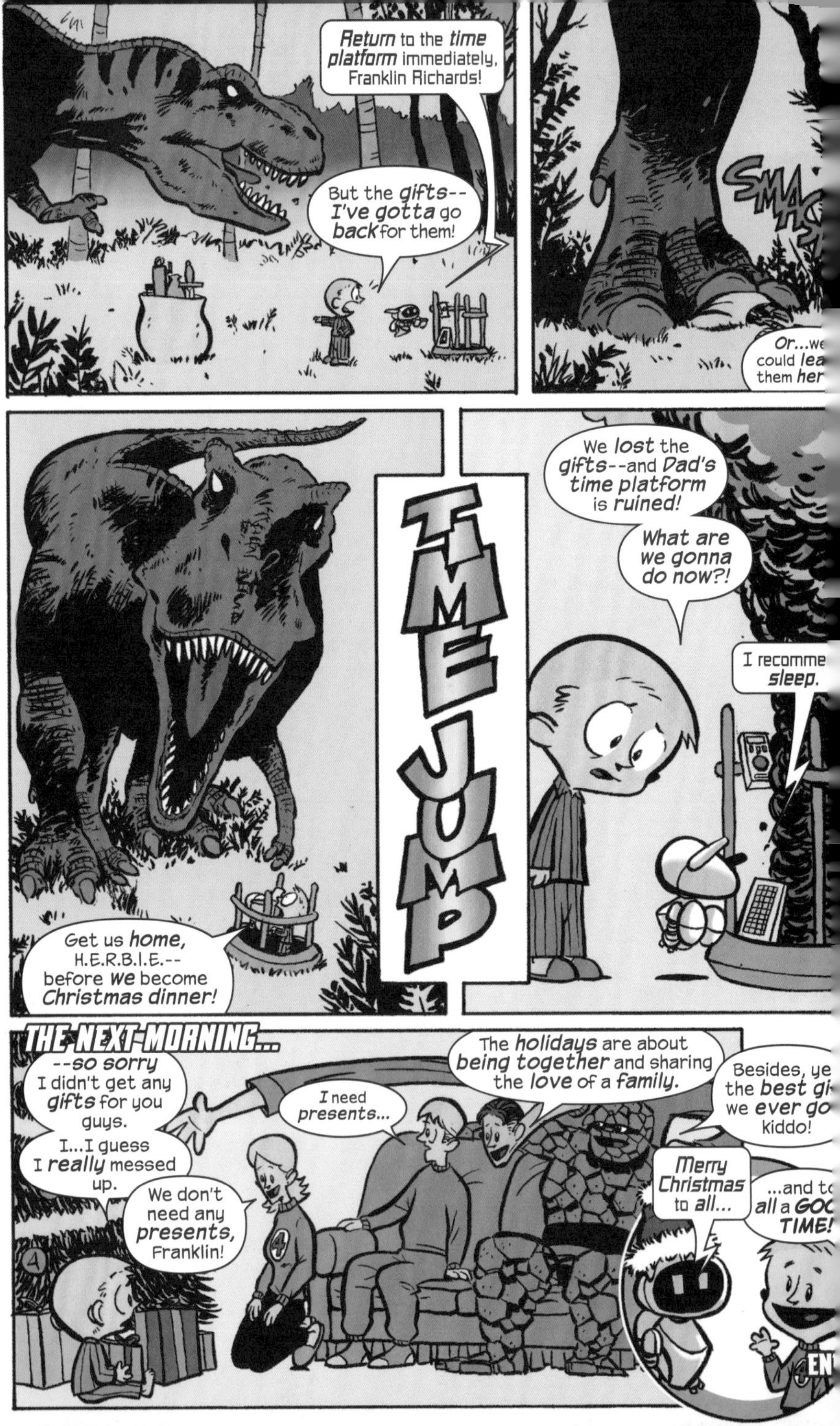

Return to the time platform immediately, Franklin Richards!
But the gifts-- I've gotta go back for them!
SMAS
Or...we could lea them her
Get us home, H.E.R.B.I.E.-- before we become Christmas dinner!
TIME JUMP
We lost the gifts--and Dad's time platform is ruined!
What are we gonna do now?!
I recomme sleep.
THE NEXT MORNING...
--so sorry I didn't get any gifts for you guys.
I...I guess I really messed up.
We don't need any presents, Franklin!
I need presents...
The holidays are about being together and sharing the love of a family.
Besides, ye the best gi we ever go kiddo!
Merry Christmas to all...
...and to all a GOO TIME!
EN

FRANKLIN RICHARDS: SON OF A GENIUS IN: MY DINNER WITH DOOM(BOTS)!

BY CHRIS ELIOPOULOS & MARC SUMERAK

GURIHIRU COLORS
SPECIAL THANKS FOR BUBBLE BOMBS **JEREMY & JUSTIN ELIOPOULOS**
TOM VALENTE PRODUCTION
NATHAN COSBY ASSISTANT EDITOR
MARK PANICCIA CONSULTING EDITOR
MACKENZIE CADENHEAD EDITOR

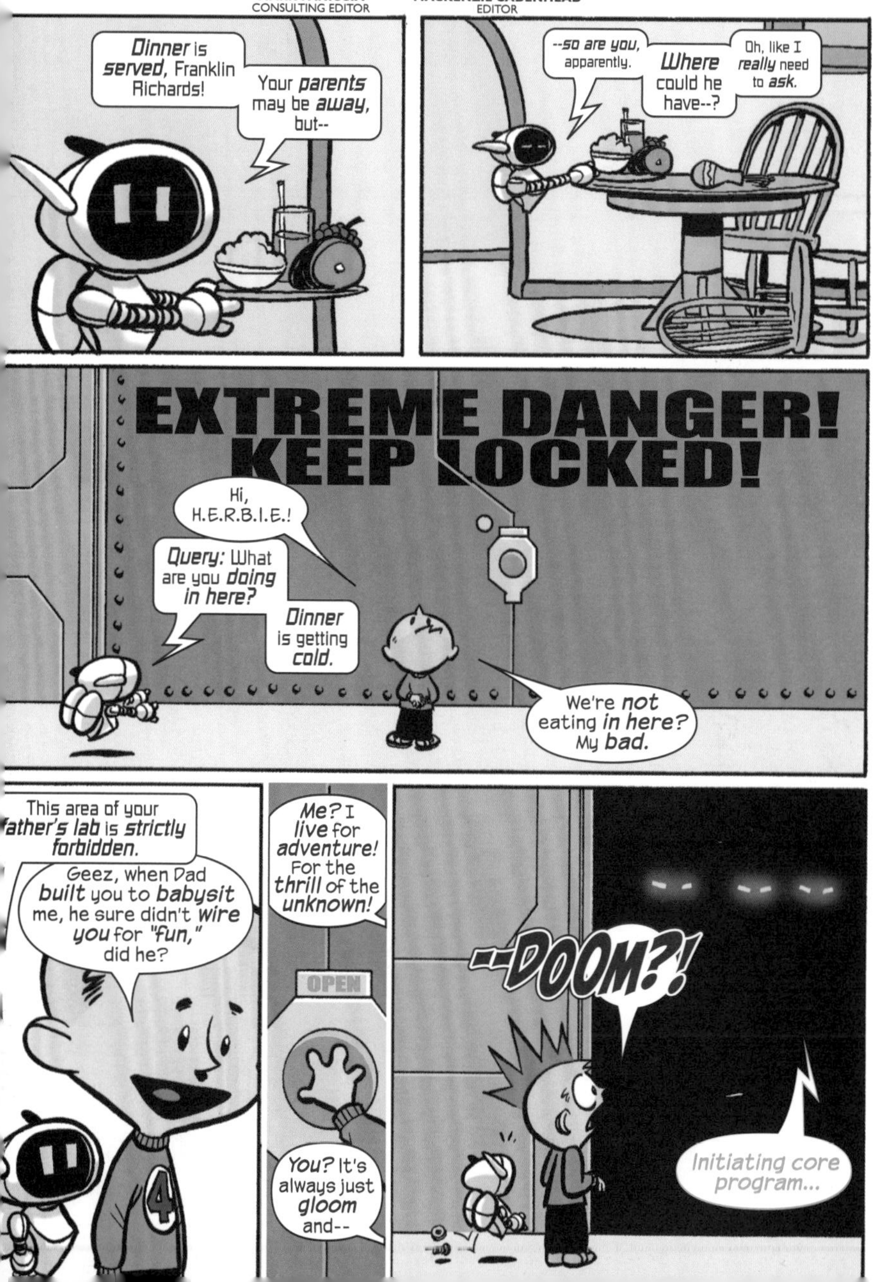
Dinner is served, Franklin Richards!
Your parents may be away, but--
--so are you, apparently.
Where could he have--?
Oh, like I really need to ask.
EXTREME DANGER! KEEP LOCKED!
Hi, H.E.R.B.I.E.!
Query: What are you doing in here?
Dinner is getting cold.
We're not eating in here? My bad.
This area of your father's lab is strictly forbidden.
Geez, when Dad built you to babysit me, he sure didn't wire you for "fun," did he?
Me? I live for adventure! For the thrill of the unknown!
OPEN
You? It's always just gloom and--
--DOOM?!
Initiating core program...

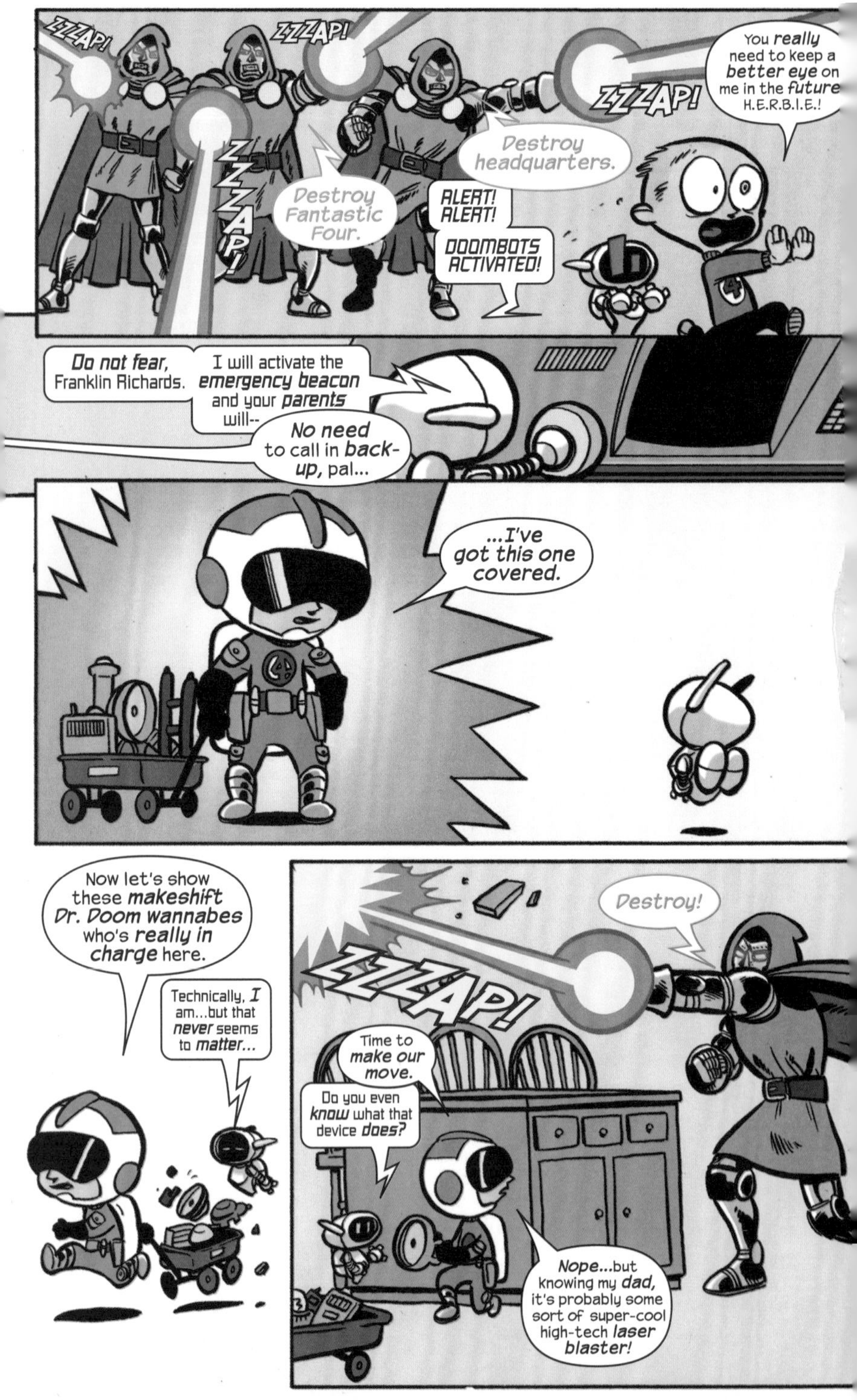
ZZZAP!
ZZZAP!
ZZZAP!
You really need to keep a better eye on me in the future H.E.R.B.I.E.!
ZZZAP!
Destroy headquarters.
Destroy Fantastic Four.
ALERT! ALERT!
DOOMBOTS ACTIVATED!
Do not fear, Franklin Richards.
I will activate the emergency beacon and your parents will--
No need to call in back-up, pal...
...I've got this one covered.
Now let's show these makeshift Dr. Doom wannabes who's really in charge here.
Technically, I am...but that never seems to matter...
Destroy!
ZZZAP!
Time to make our move.
Do you even know what that device does?
Nope...but knowing my dad, it's probably some sort of super-cool high-tech laser blaster!

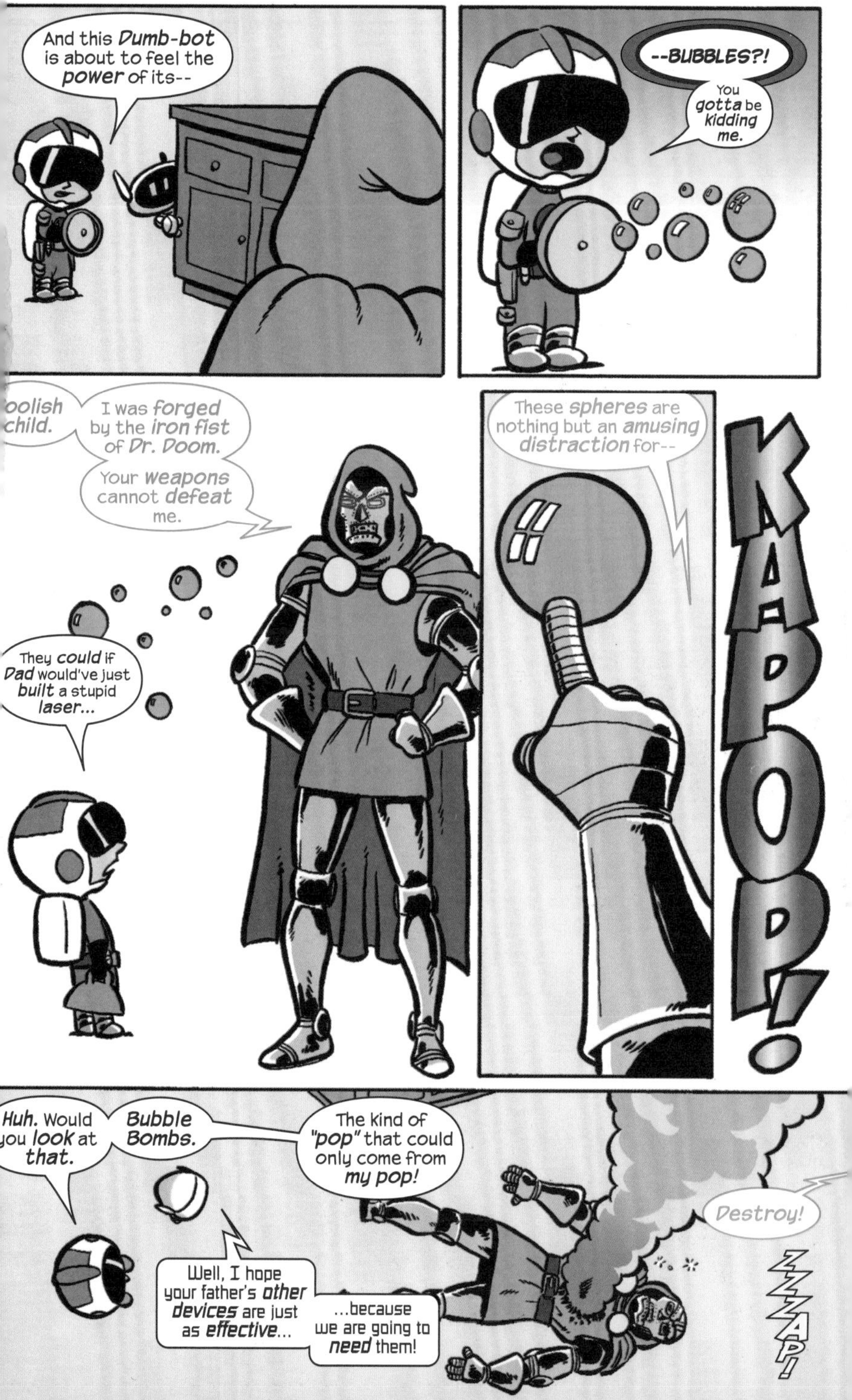
And this Dumb-bot is about to feel the power of its--
--BUBBLES?!
You gotta be kidding me.
oolish child.
I was forged by the iron fist of Dr. Doom.
Your weapons cannot defeat me.
They could if Dad would've just built a stupid laser...
These spheres are nothing but an amusing distraction for--
KAPOP!
Huh. Would you look at that.
Bubble Bombs.
The kind of "pop" that could only come from my pop!
Destroy!
Well, I hope your father's other devices are just as effective...
...because we are going to need them!
ZZZAP!

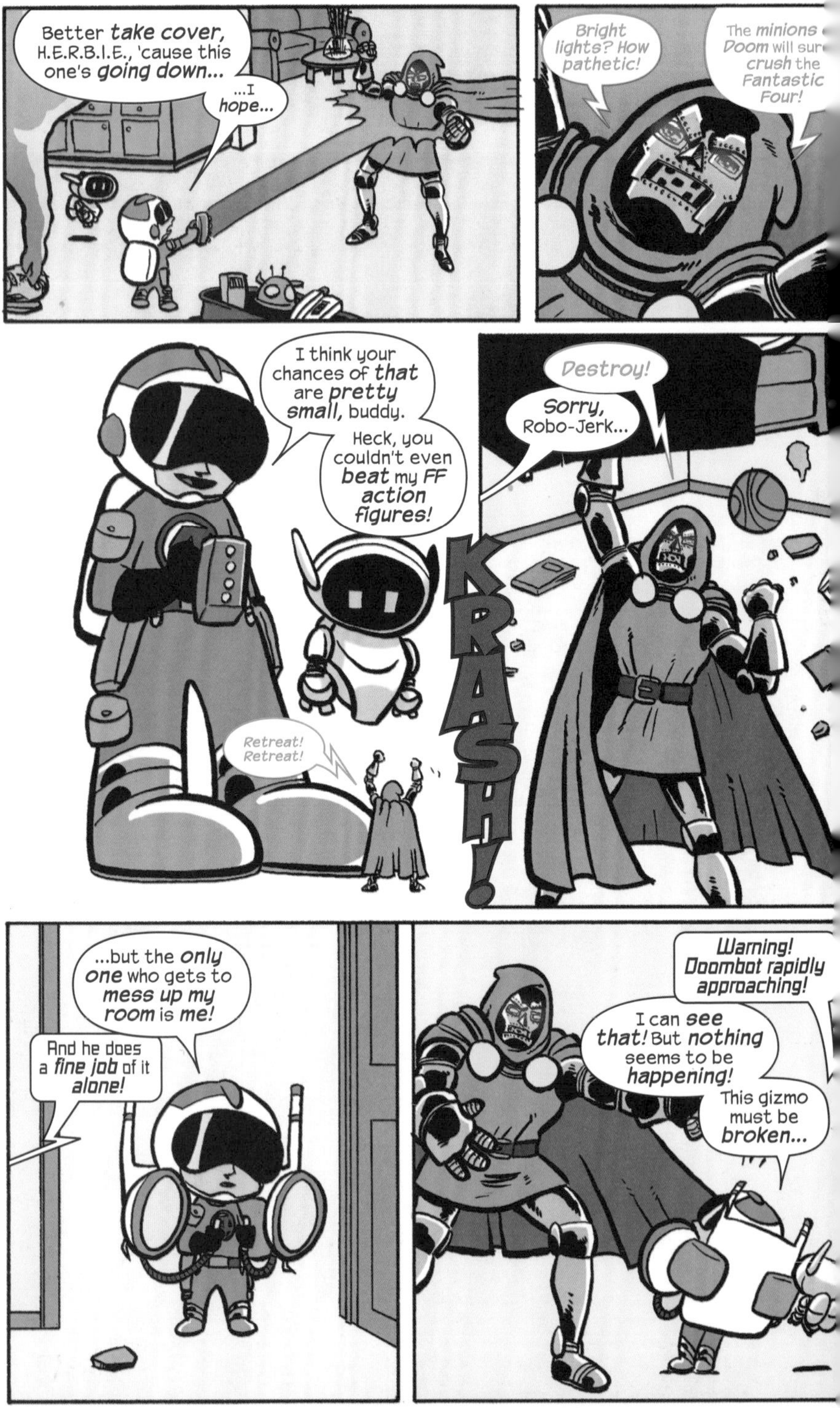

Better take cover, H.E.R.B.I.E., 'cause this one's going down...
...I hope...
Bright lights? How pathetic!
The minions of Doom will surely crush the Fantastic Four!
I think your chances of that are pretty small, buddy.
Heck, you couldn't even beat my FF action figures!
Retreat! Retreat!
KRASH!
Destroy!
Sorry, Robo-Jerk...
...but the only one who gets to mess up my room is me!
And he does a fine job of it alone!
Warning! Doombot rapidly approaching!
I can see that! But nothing seems to be happening!
This gizmo must be broken...

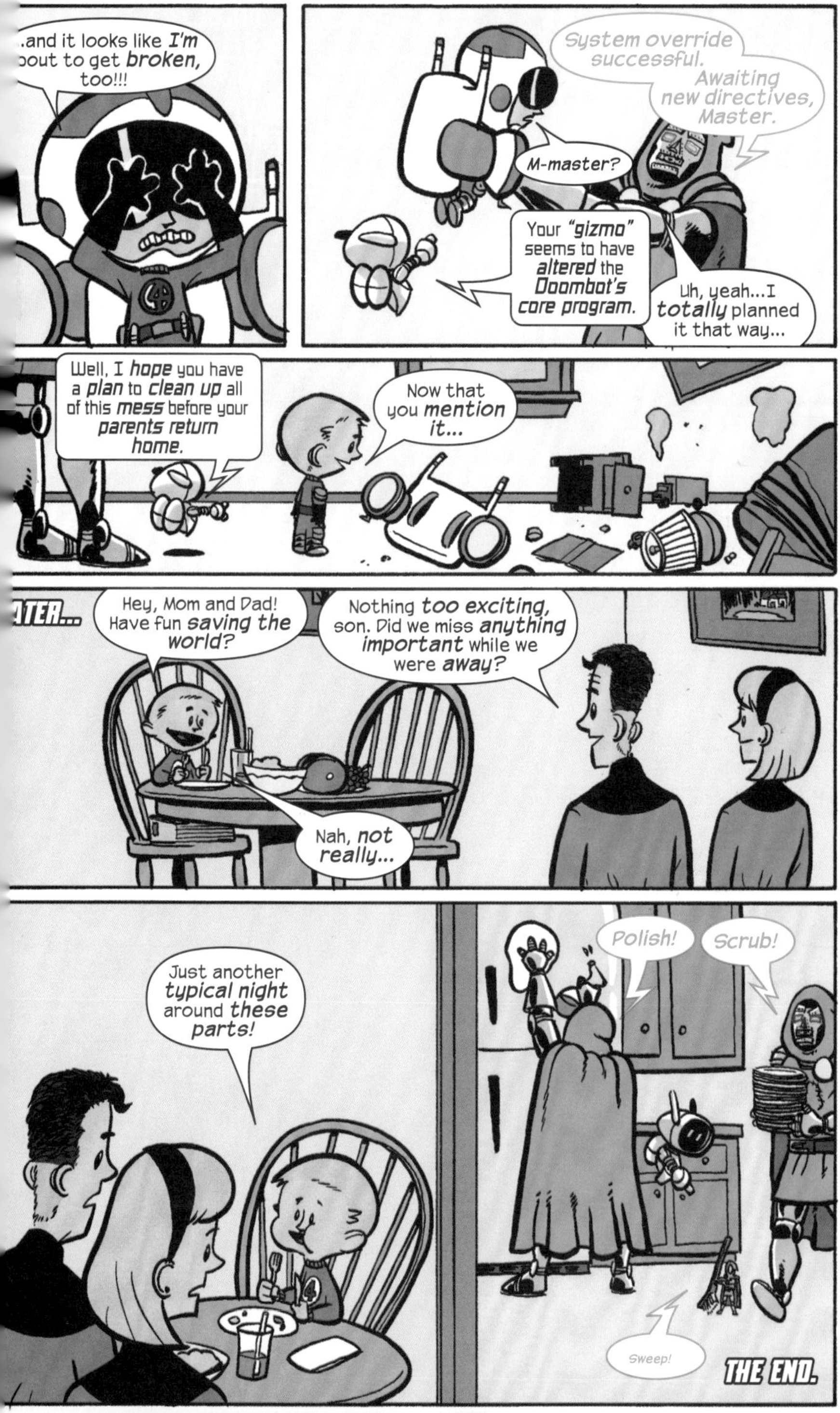

...and it looks like I'm about to get broken, too!!!
System override successful.
Awaiting new directives, Master.
M-master?
Your "gizmo" seems to have altered the Doombot's core program.
Uh, yeah...I totally planned it that way...
Well, I hope you have a plan to clean up all of this mess before your parents return home.
Now that you mention it...
LATER...
Hey, Mom and Dad! Have fun saving the world?
Nothing too exciting, son. Did we miss anything important while we were away?
Nah, not really...
Just another typical night around these parts!
Polish!
Scrub!
Sweep!
THE END.

FRANKLIN RICHARDS SON OF A GENIUS IN: "Frankie, My Dear..."

BY CHRIS ELIOPOULOS & MARC SUMERA

GURIHIRU COLORS · JAMES TAVERAS PRODUCTION · NATHAN COSBY ASSISTANT EDITOR · MARK PANICCIA CONSULTING EDITOR · MACKENZIE CADENHE EDITOR

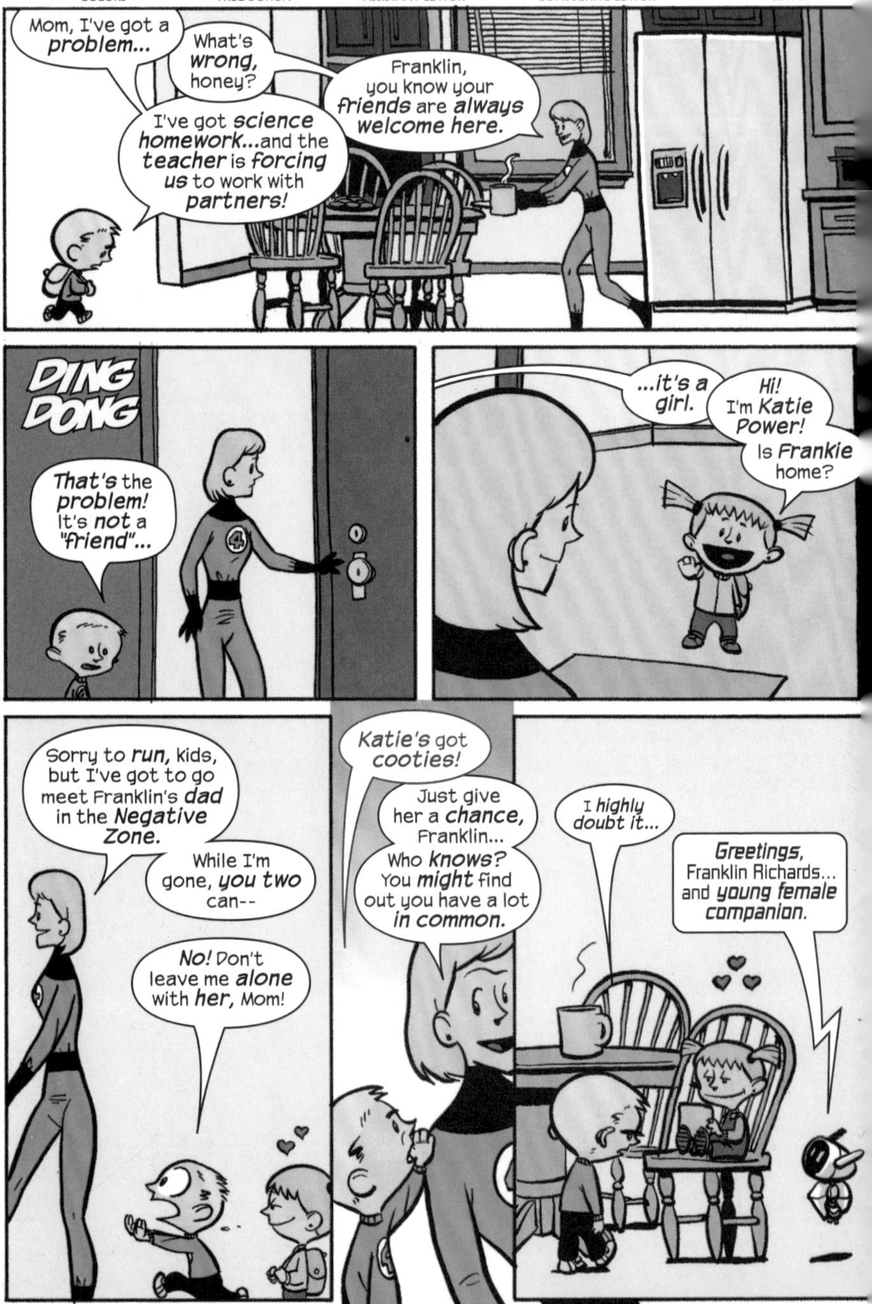

Mom, I've got a problem...
What's wrong, honey?
I've got science homework...and the teacher is forcing us to work with partners!
Franklin, you know your friends are always welcome here.
DING DONG
That's the problem! It's not a "friend"...
...it's a girl.
Hi! I'm Katie Power!
Is Frankie home?
Sorry to run, kids, but I've got to go meet Franklin's dad in the Negative Zone.
While I'm gone, you two can--
No! Don't leave me alone with her, Mom!
Katie's got cooties!
Just give her a chance, Franklin...
Who knows? You might find out you have a lot in common.
I highly doubt it...
Greetings, Franklin Richards... and young female companion.

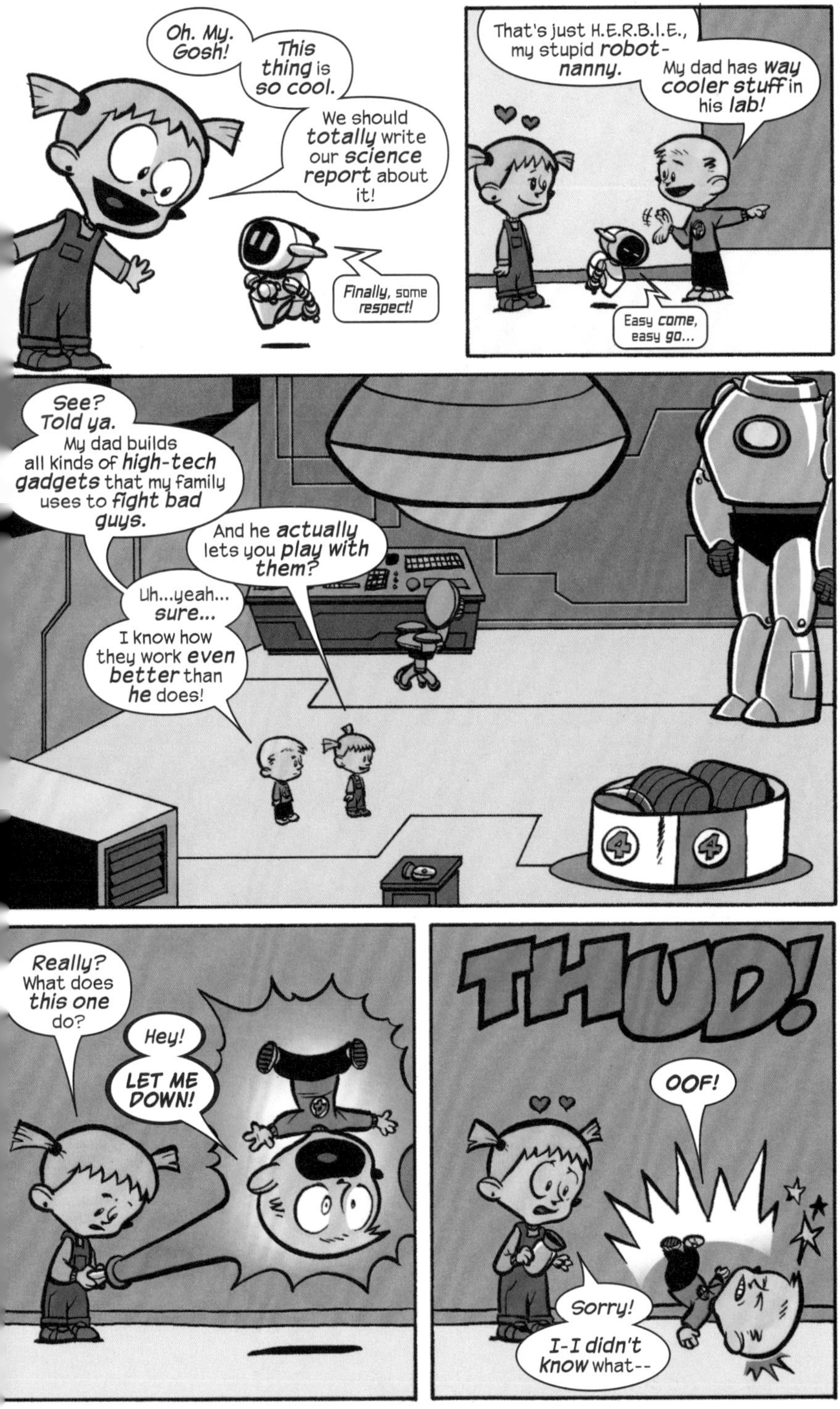

Oh. My. Gosh!
This thing is so cool.
We should totally write our science report about it!
Finally, some respect!
That's just H.E.R.B.I.E., my stupid robot-nanny.
My dad has way cooler stuff in his lab!
Easy come, easy go...
See? Told ya.
My dad builds all kinds of high-tech gadgets that my family uses to fight bad guys.
And he actually lets you play with them?
Uh...yeah... sure...
I know how they work even better than he does!
Really? What does this one do?
Hey!
LET ME DOWN!
THUD!
OOF!
Sorry!
I-I didn't know what--

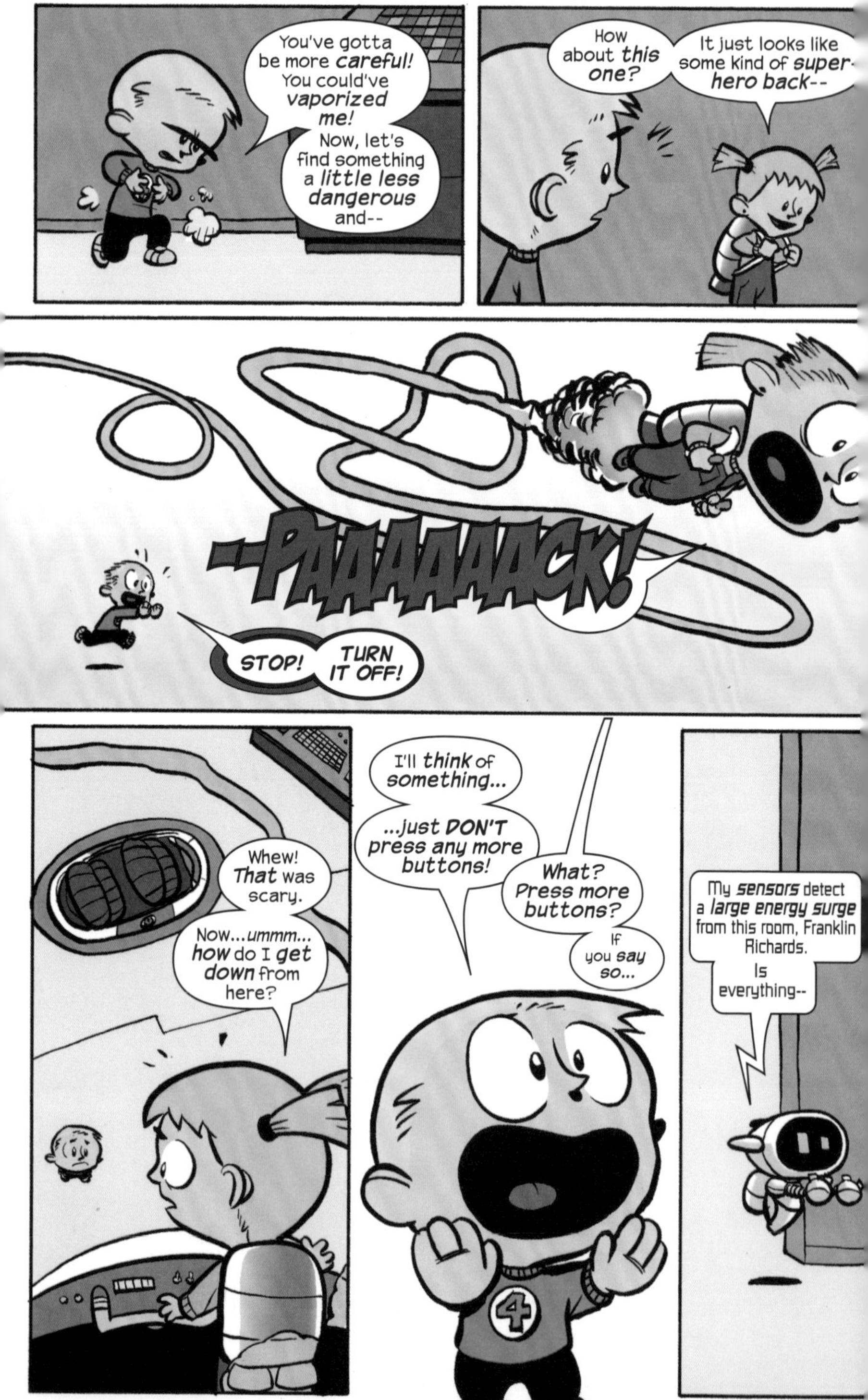

You've gotta be more careful! You could've vaporized me!
Now, let's find something a little less dangerous and--
How about this one?
It just looks like some kind of super-hero back--
--PAAAAAACK!
STOP!
TURN IT OFF!
Whew! That was scary.
Now...ummm... how do I get down from here?
I'll think of something...
...just DON'T press any more buttons!
What? Press more buttons?
If you say so...
My sensors detect a large energy surge from this room, Franklin Richards.
Is everything--

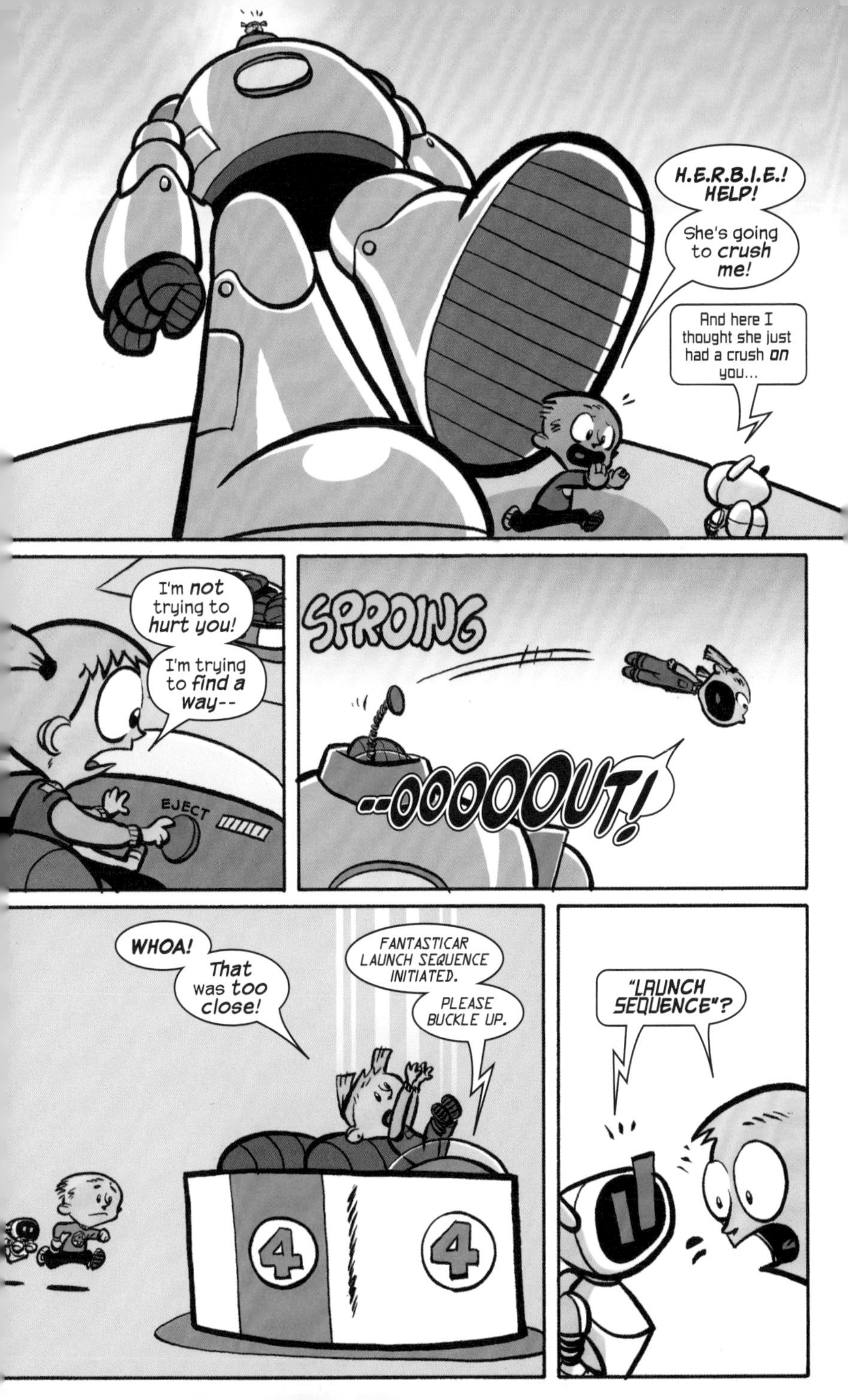
H.E.R.B.I.E.! HELP!
She's going to crush me!
And here I thought she just had a crush on you...
I'm not trying to hurt you!
I'm trying to find a way--
EJECT
SPROING
--OOOOOOUT!
WHOA!
That was too close!
FANTASTICAR LAUNCH SEQUENCE INITIATED.
PLEASE BUCKLE UP.
"LAUNCH SEQUENCE"?

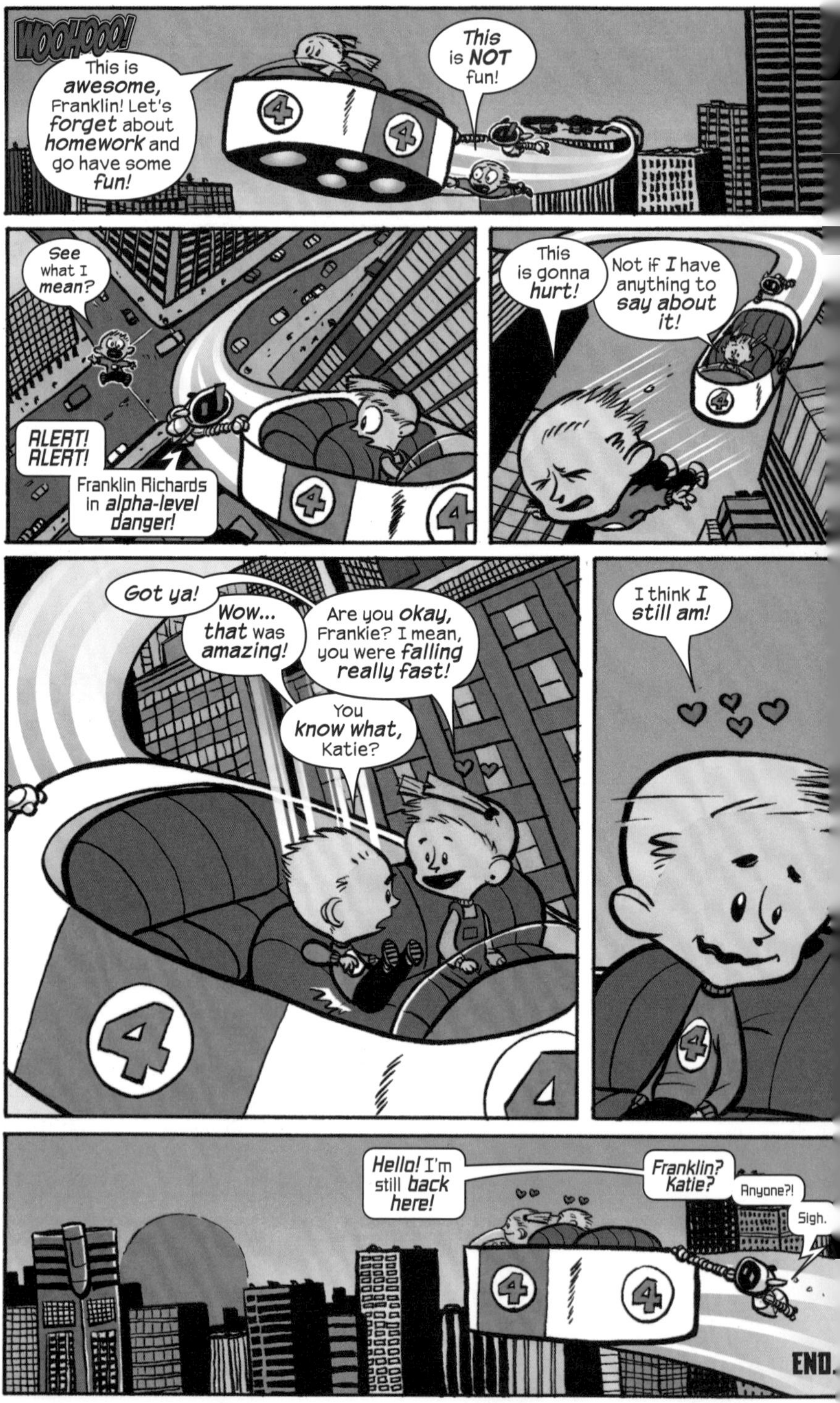
WOOHOOO!
This is awesome, Franklin! Let's forget about homework and go have some fun!
This is NOT fun!
See what I mean?
ALERT! ALERT!
Franklin Richards in alpha-level danger!
This is gonna hurt!
Not if I have anything to say about it!
Got ya!
Wow... that was amazing!
Are you okay, Frankie? I mean, you were falling really fast!
You know what, Katie?
I think I still am!
Hello! I'm still back here!
Franklin? Katie?
Anyone?!
Sigh.
END.

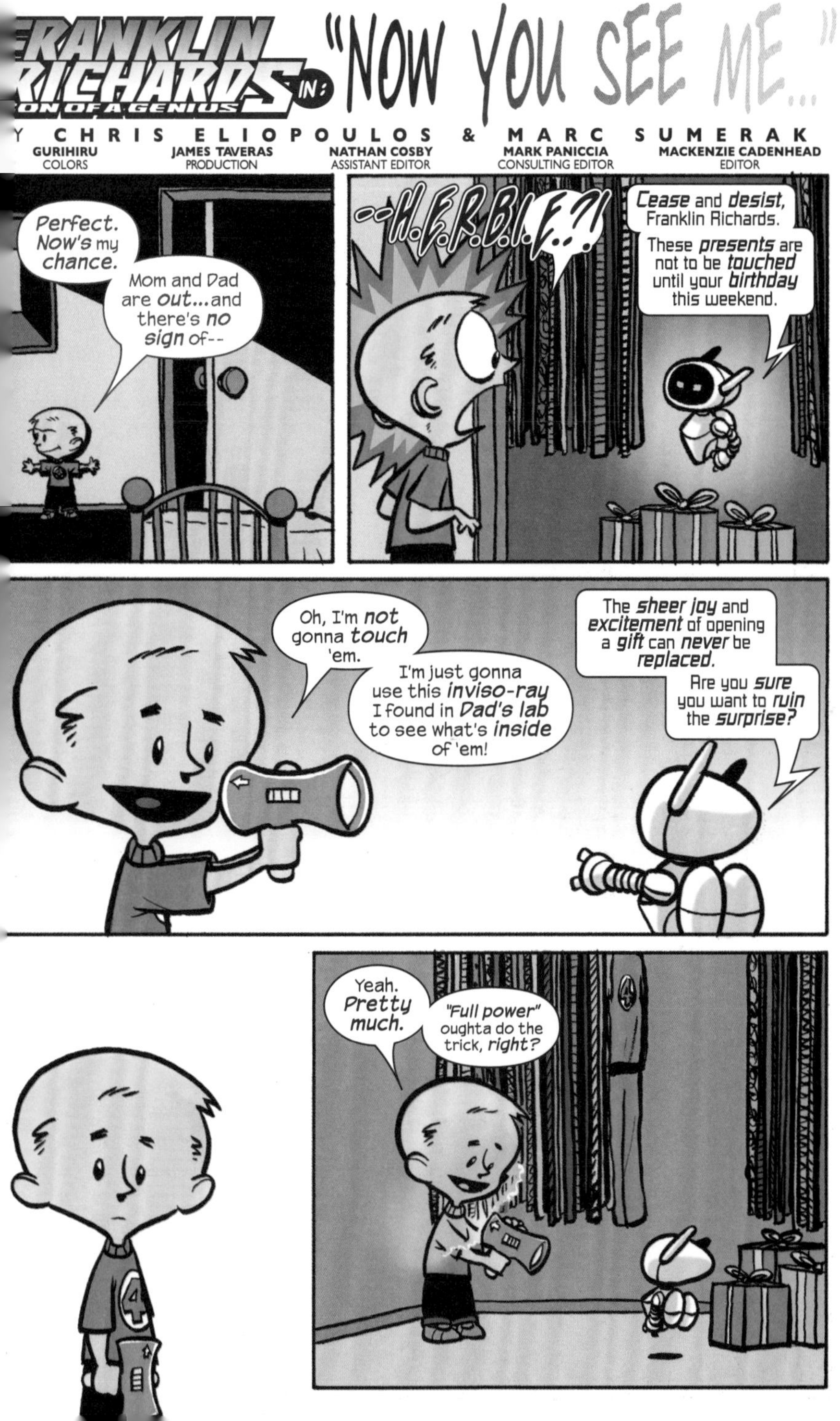

FRANKLIN RICHARDS SON OF A GENIUS IN: "NOW YOU SEE ME..."
BY CHRIS ELIOPOULOS & MARC SUMERAK
GURIHIRU COLORS
JAMES TAVERAS PRODUCTION
NATHAN COSBY ASSISTANT EDITOR
MARK PANICCIA CONSULTING EDITOR
MACKENZIE CADENHEAD EDITOR
Perfect. Now's my chance.
Mom and Dad are out...and there's no sign of--
--H.E.R.B.I.E.?!
Cease and desist, Franklin Richards.
These presents are not to be touched until your birthday this weekend.
Oh, I'm not gonna touch 'em.
I'm just gonna use this inviso-ray I found in Dad's lab to see what's inside of 'em!
The sheer joy and excitement of opening a gift can never be replaced.
Are you sure you want to ruin the surprise?
Yeah. Pretty much.
"Full power" oughta do the trick, right?

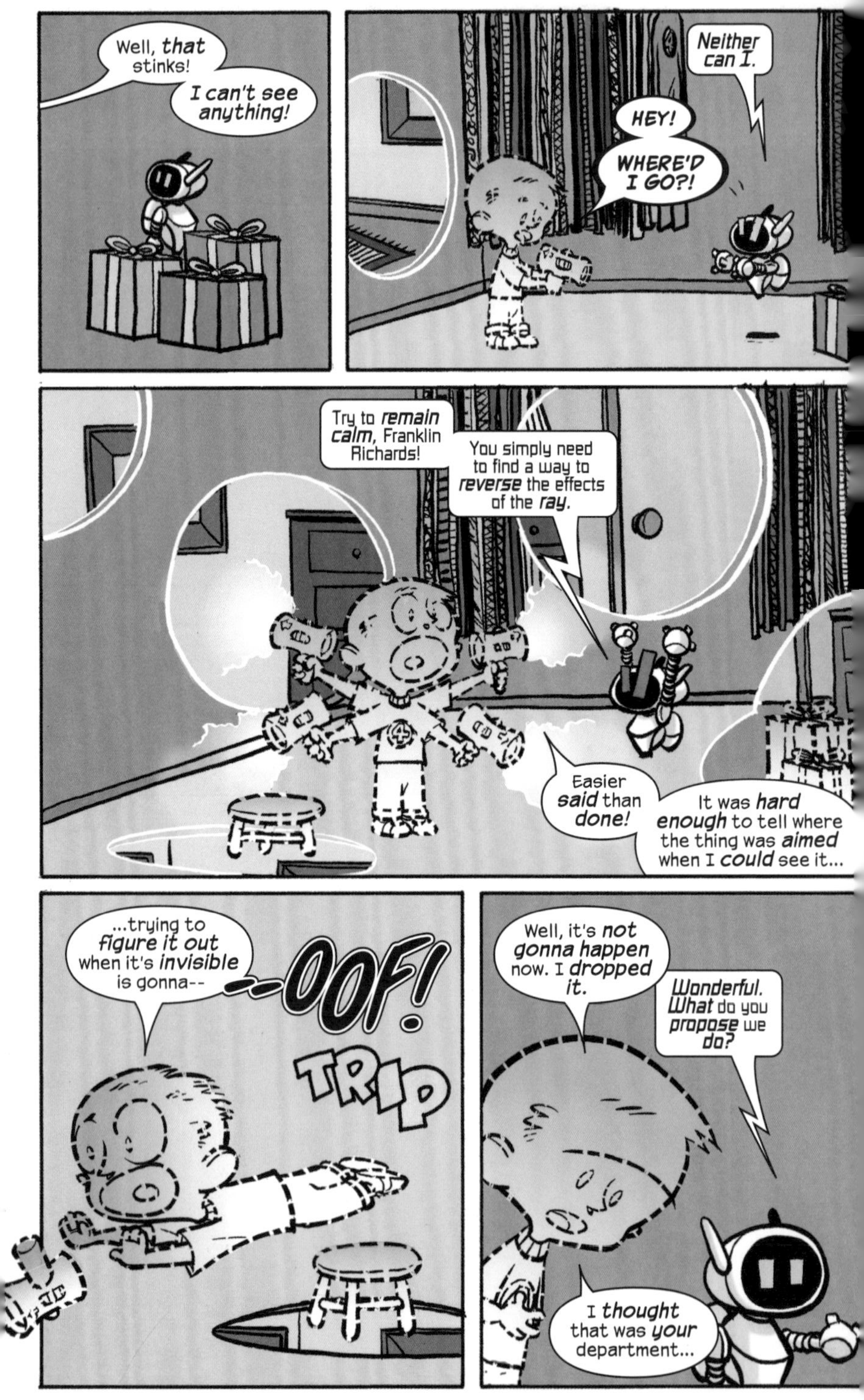
Well, *that* stinks!
I can't see anything!
Neither can I.
HEY!
WHERE'D I GO?!
Try to *remain calm*, Franklin Richards!
You simply need to find a way to *reverse* the effects of the *ray*.
Easier *said* than *done!*
It was *hard enough* to tell where the thing was *aimed* when I *could* see it...
...trying to *figure it out* when it's *invisible* is gonna--
--OOF!
TRIP
Well, it's *not gonna happen* now. I *dropped it.*
Wonderful. What do you *propose* we *do?*
I *thought* that was *your* department...

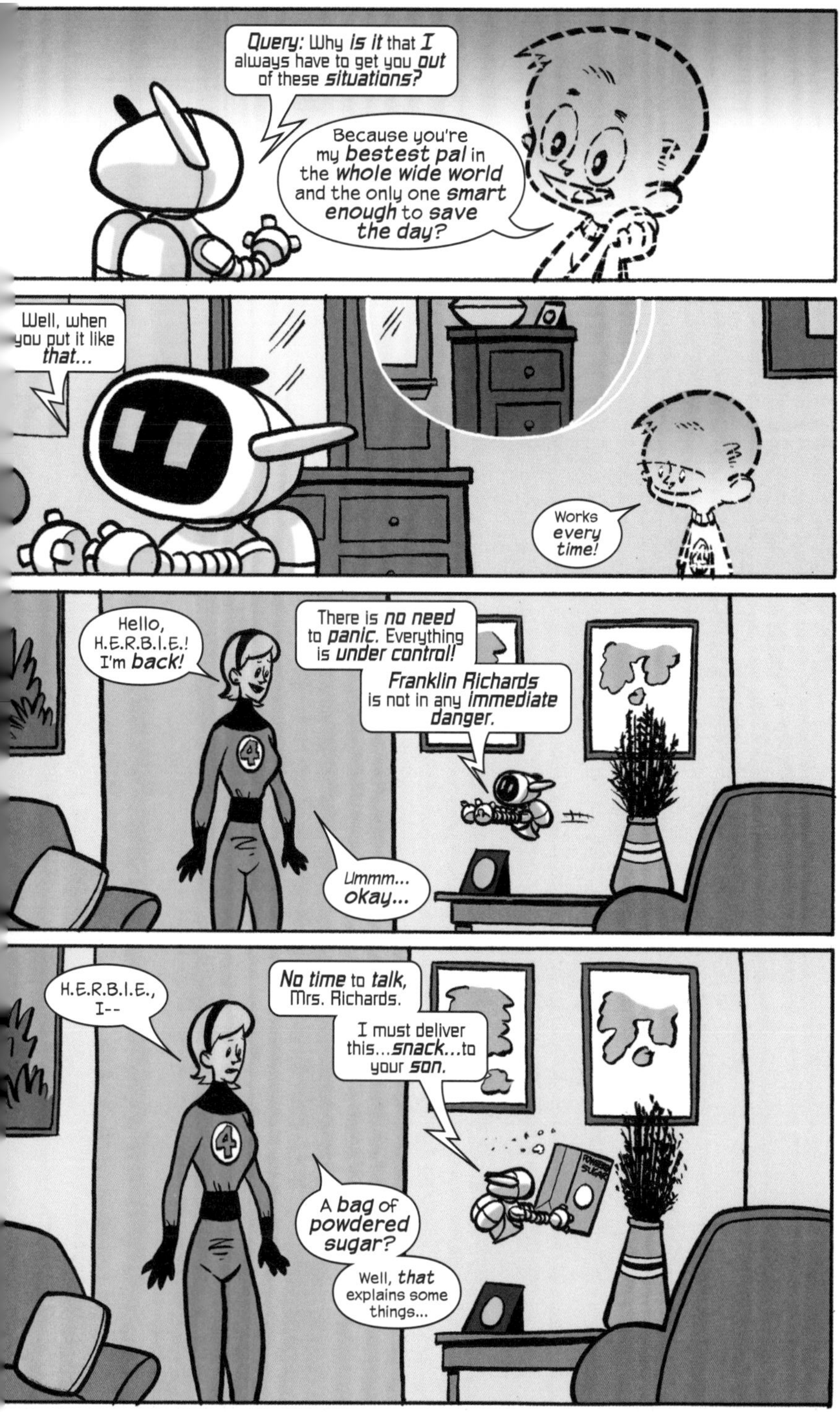
Query: Why is it that I always have to get you out of these situations?
Because you're my bestest pal in the whole wide world and the only one smart enough to save the day?
Well, when you put it like that...
Works every time!
Hello, H.E.R.B.I.E.! I'm back!
There is no need to panic. Everything is under control!
Franklin Richards is not in any immediate danger.
Ummm... okay...
H.E.R.B.I.E., I--
No time to talk, Mrs. Richards.
I must deliver this...snack...to your son.
A bag of powdered sugar?
Well, that explains some things...

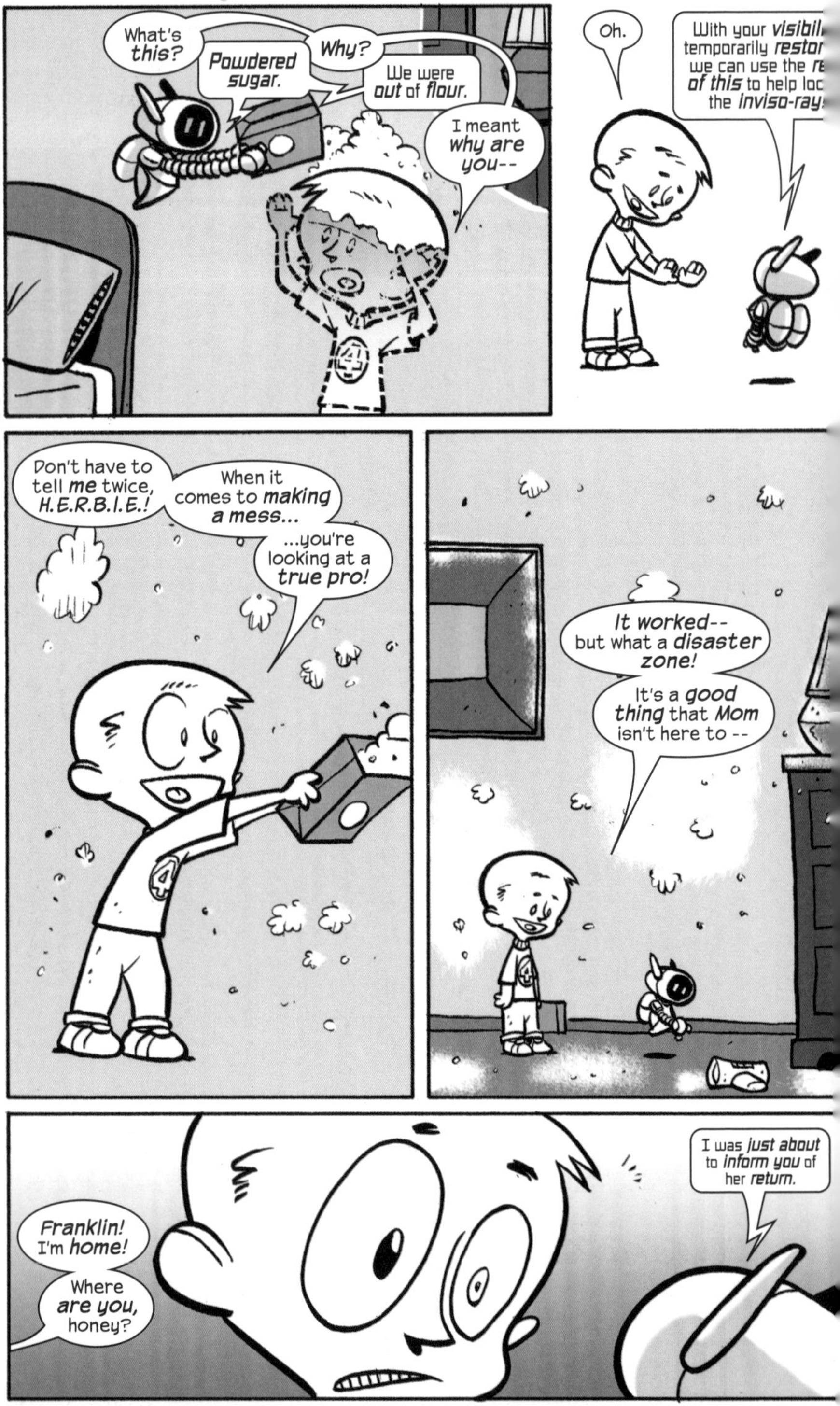

What's this?
Powdered sugar.
Why?
We were out of flour.
I meant why are you--
Oh.
With your visibil
temporarily restor
we can use the re
of this to help loc
the inviso-ray
Don't have to tell me twice, H.E.R.B.I.E.!
When it comes to making a mess...
...you're looking at a true pro!
It worked-- but what a disaster zone!
It's a good thing that Mom isn't here to --
Franklin! I'm home!
Where are you, honey?
I was just about to inform you of her return.

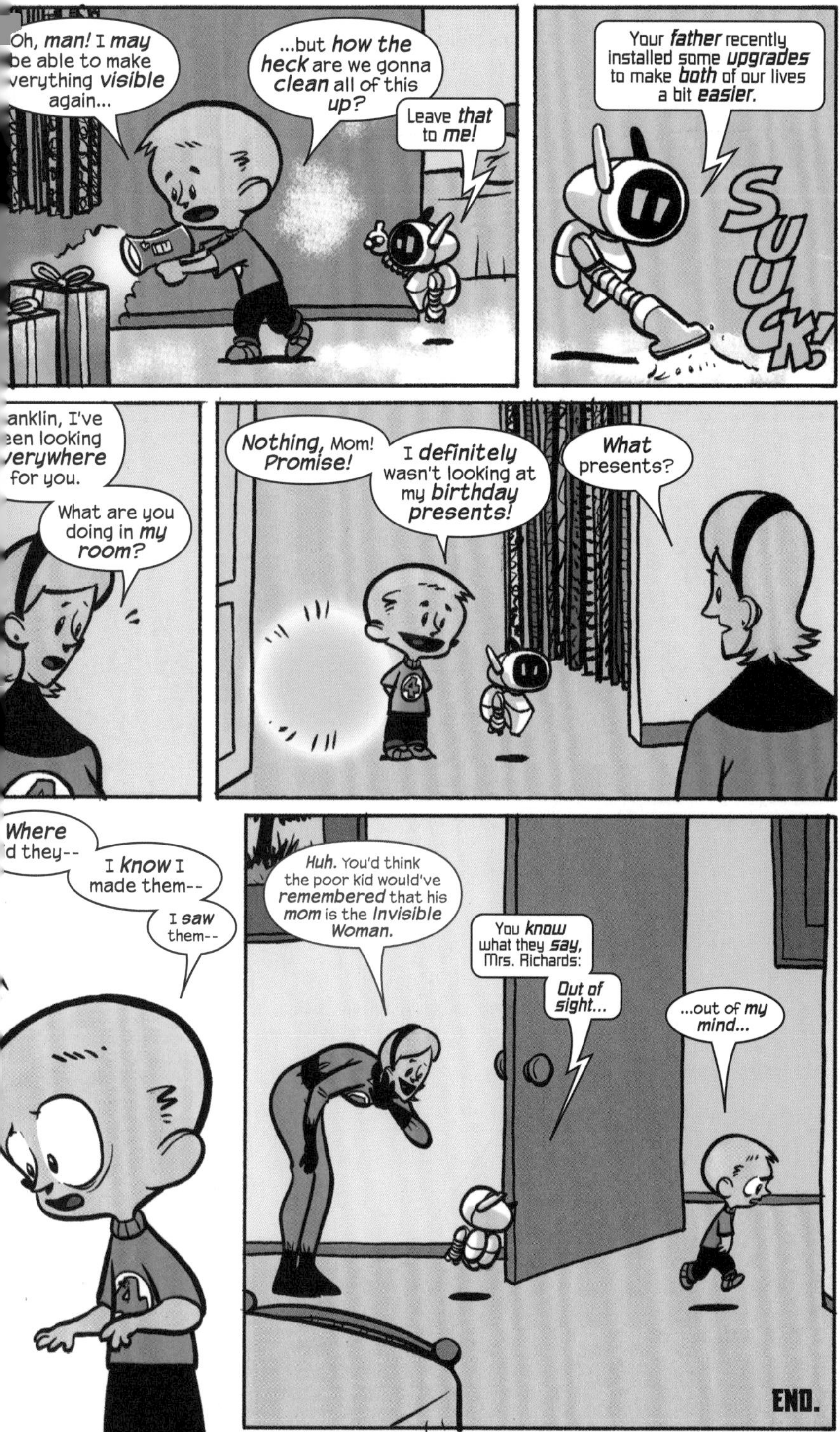

Oh, man! I may be able to make verything visible again...
...but how the heck are we gonna clean all of this up?
Leave that to me!
Your father recently installed some upgrades to make both of our lives a bit easier.
SUUCK!
anklin, I've een looking verywhere for you.
What are you doing in my room?
Nothing, Mom! Promise!
I definitely wasn't looking at my birthday presents!
What presents?
Where 'd they--
I know I made them--
I saw them--
Huh. You'd think the poor kid would've remembered that his mom is the Invisible Woman.
You know what they say, Mrs. Richards:
Out of sight...
...out of my mind...
END.

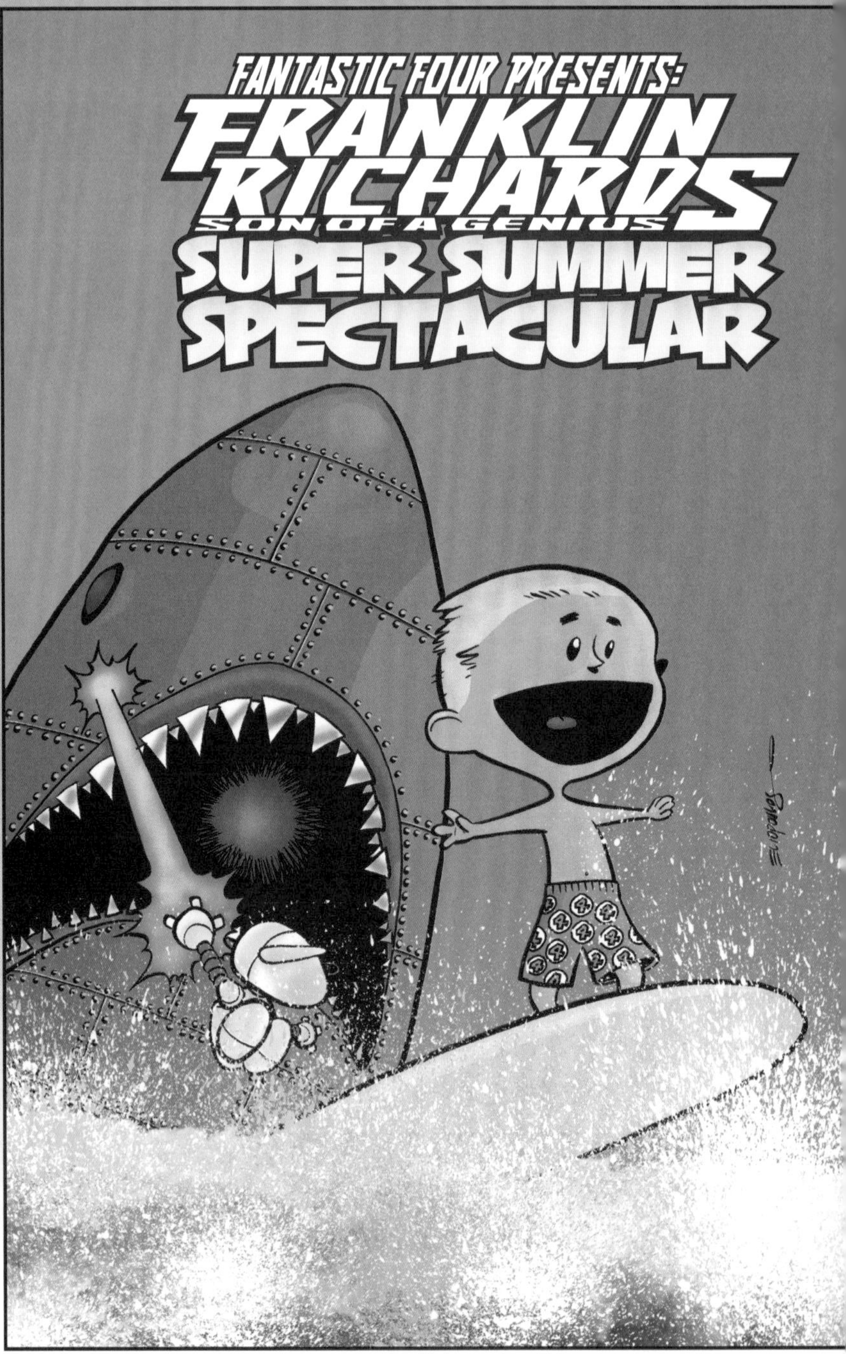
FANTASTIC FOUR PRESENTS:
FRANKLIN RICHARDS
SON OF A GENIUS
SUPER SUMMER SPECTACULAR

FRANKLIN RICHARDS SON OF A GENIUS IN: "Field of Screams"

Y CHRIS ELIOPOULOS & MARC SUMERAK

VERN KINDZIERSKI COLORS | NATHAN COSBY ASSISTANT EDITOR | MARK PANICCIA EDITOR | JOE QUESADA EDITOR IN CHIEF | DAN BUCKLEY PUBLISHER | DEDICATED TO CHARLES SCHULZ

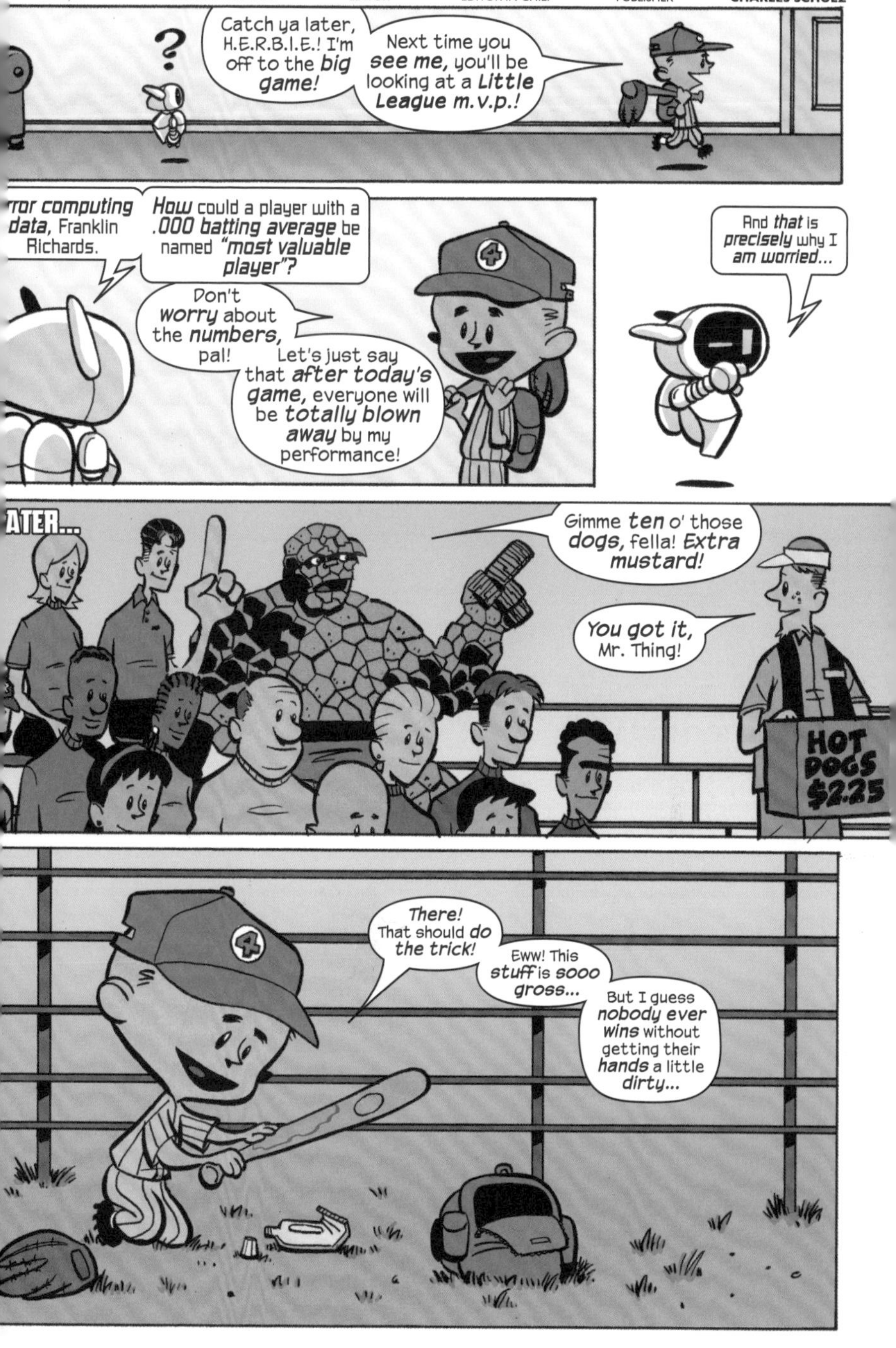

?
Catch ya later, H.E.R.B.I.E.! I'm off to the big game!
Next time you see me, you'll be looking at a Little League m.v.p.!
rror computing data, Franklin Richards.
How could a player with a .000 batting average be named "most valuable player"?
Don't worry about the numbers, pal!
Let's just say that after today's game, everyone will be totally blown away by my performance!
And that is precisely why I am worried...
ATER...
Gimme ten o' those dogs, fella! Extra mustard!
You got it, Mr. Thing!
HOT DOGS $2.25
There! That should do the trick!
Eww! This stuff is sooo gross...
But I guess nobody ever wins without getting their hands a little dirty...

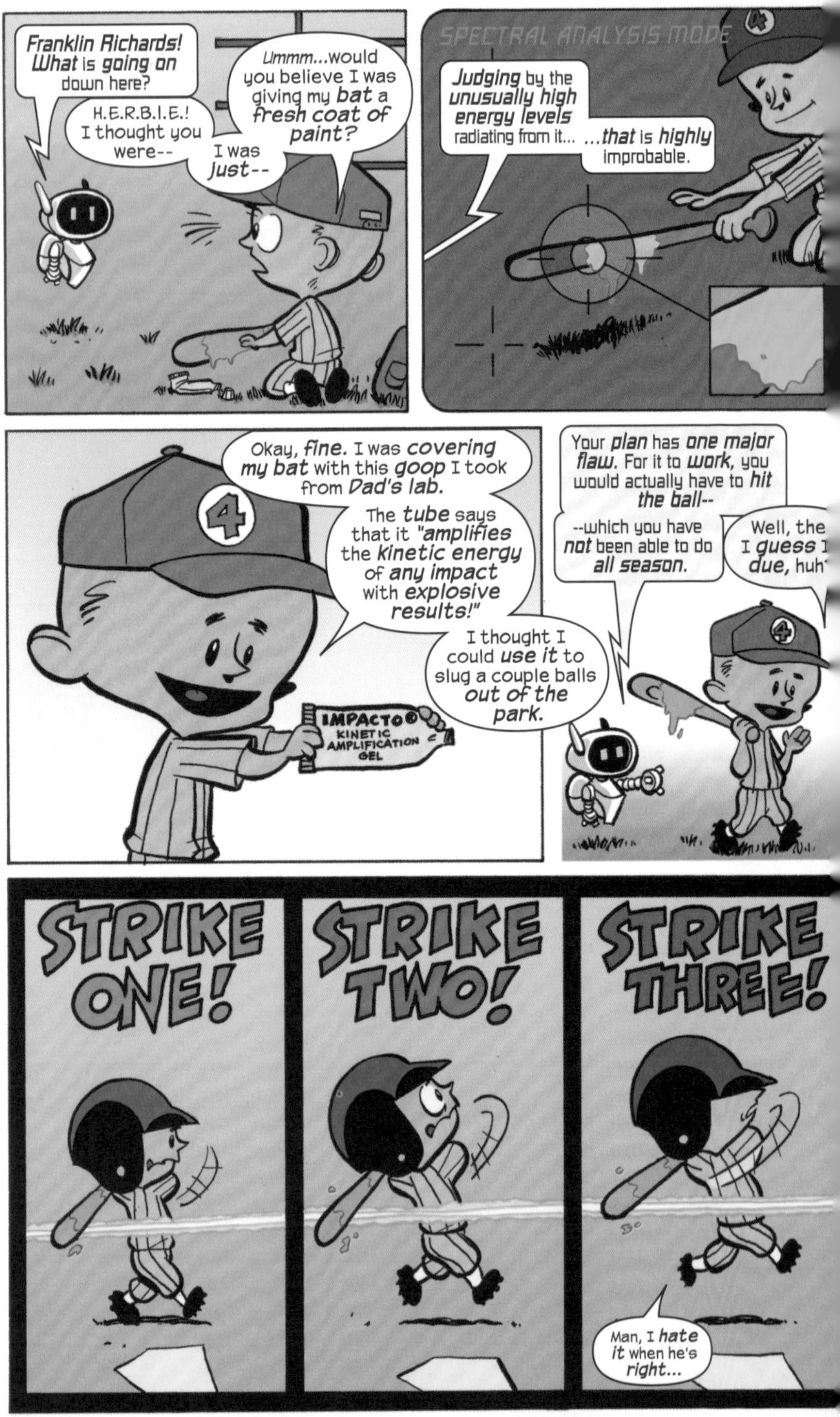
Franklin Richards! What is going on down here?
H.E.R.B.I.E.! I thought you were--
I was just--
Ummm...would you believe I was giving my bat a fresh coat of paint?
SPECTRAL ANALYSIS MODE
Judging by the unusually high energy levels radiating from it...
...that is highly improbable.
Okay, fine. I was covering my bat with this goop I took from Dad's lab.
The tube says that it "amplifies the kinetic energy of any impact with explosive results!"
I thought I could use it to slug a couple balls out of the park.
IMPACTO® KINETIC AMPLIFICATION GEL
Your plan has one major flaw. For it to work, you would actually have to hit the ball--
--which you have not been able to do all season.
Well, the
I guess
due, huh
STRIKE ONE!
STRIKE TWO!
STRIKE THREE!
Man, I hate it when he's right...

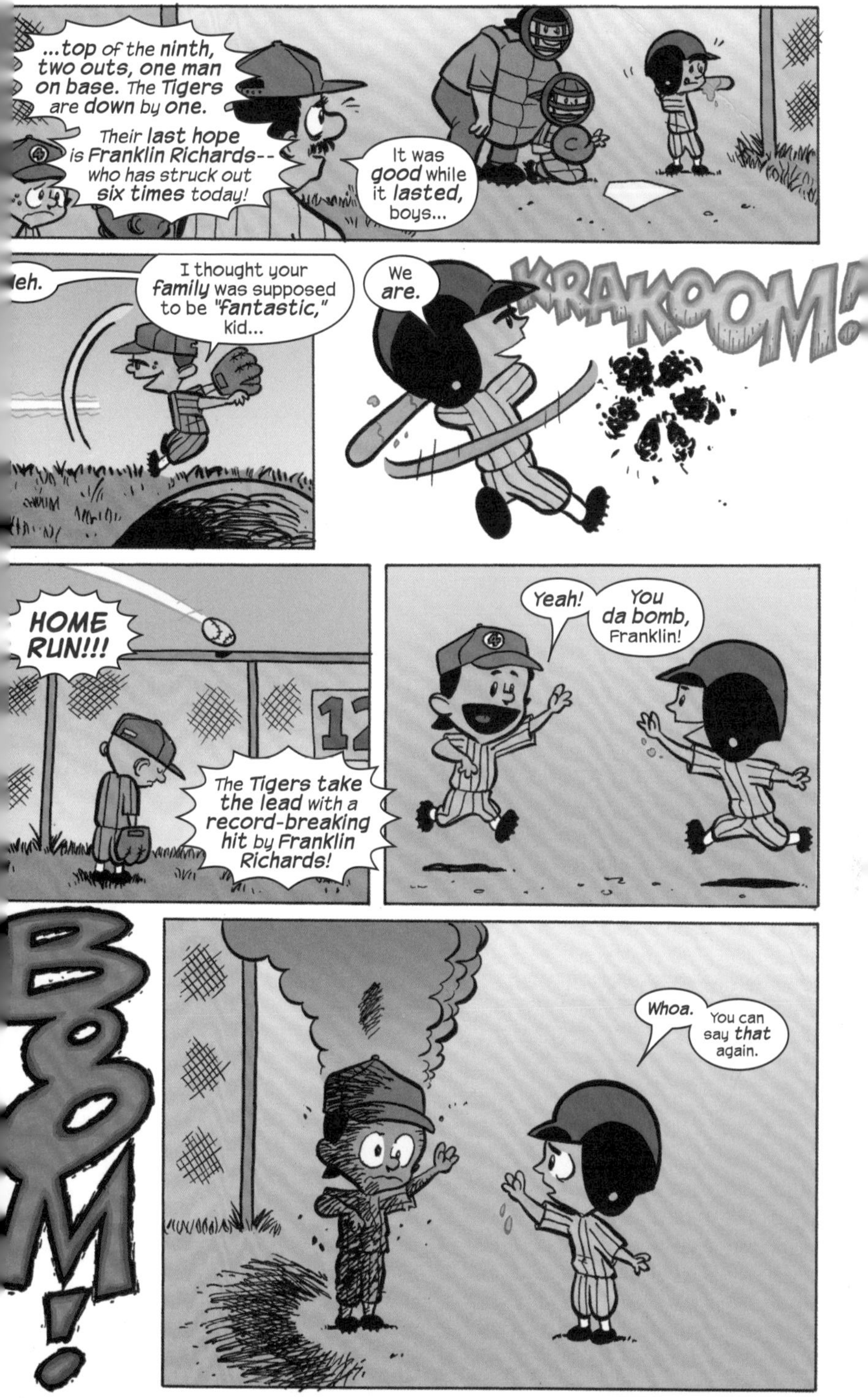
...top of the ninth, two outs, one man on base. The Tigers are down by one.
Their last hope is Franklin Richards-- who has struck out six times today!
It was good while it lasted, boys...
Heh.
I thought your family was supposed to be "fantastic," kid...
We are.
KRAKOOM!
HOME RUN!!!
The Tigers take the lead with a record-breaking hit by Franklin Richards!
12
Yeah!
You da bomb, Franklin!
BOOOM!
Whoa.
You can say that again.

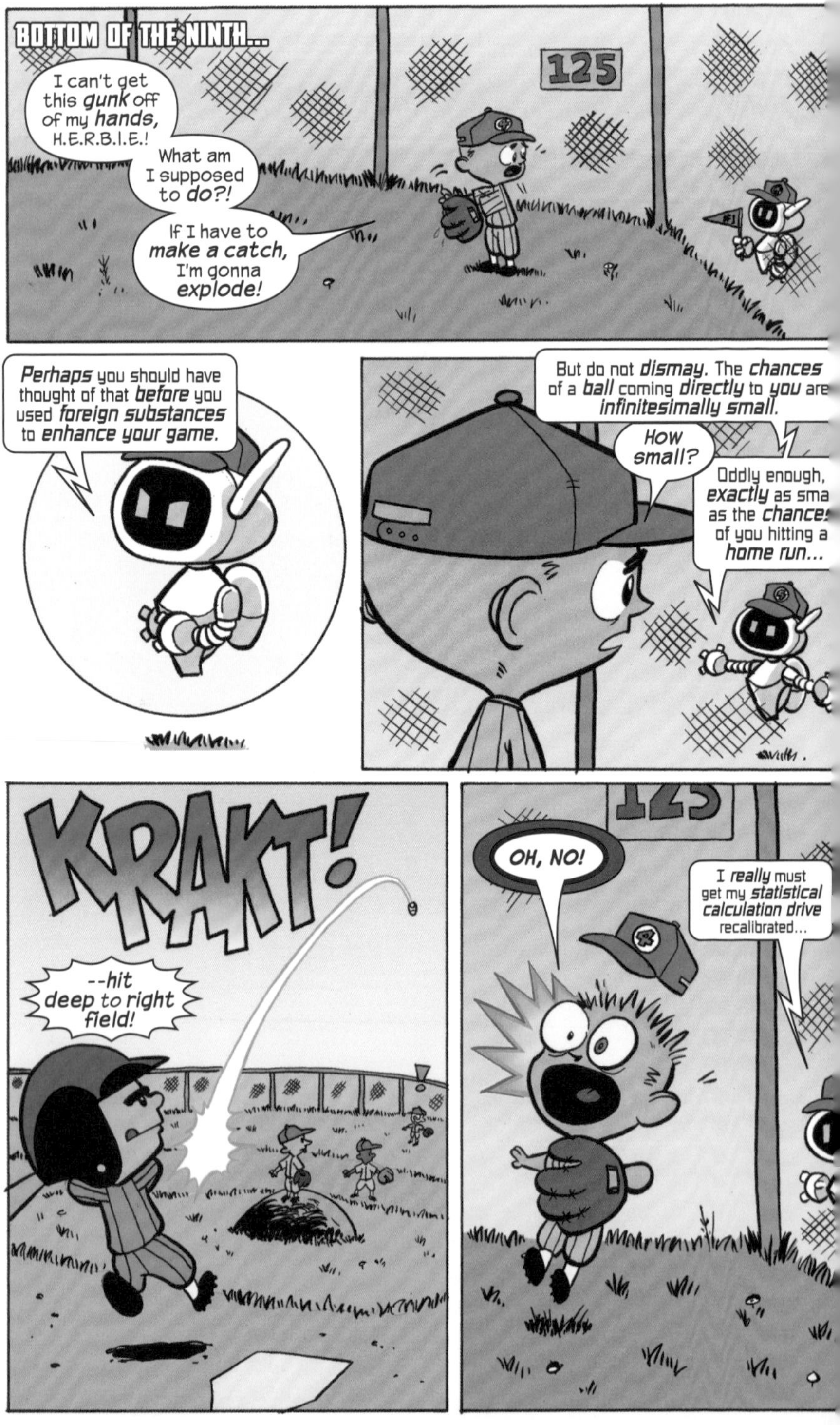

BOTTOM OF THE NINTH...
I can't get this gunk off of my hands, H.E.R.B.I.E.!
What am I supposed to do?!
If I have to make a catch, I'm gonna explode!
125
Perhaps you should have thought of that before you used foreign substances to enhance your game.
But do not dismay. The chances of a ball coming directly to you are infinitesimally small.
How small?
Oddly enough, exactly as sma as the chance of you hitting a home run...
KRAKT!
--hit deep to right field!
OH, NO!
I really must get my statistical calculation drive recalibrated...

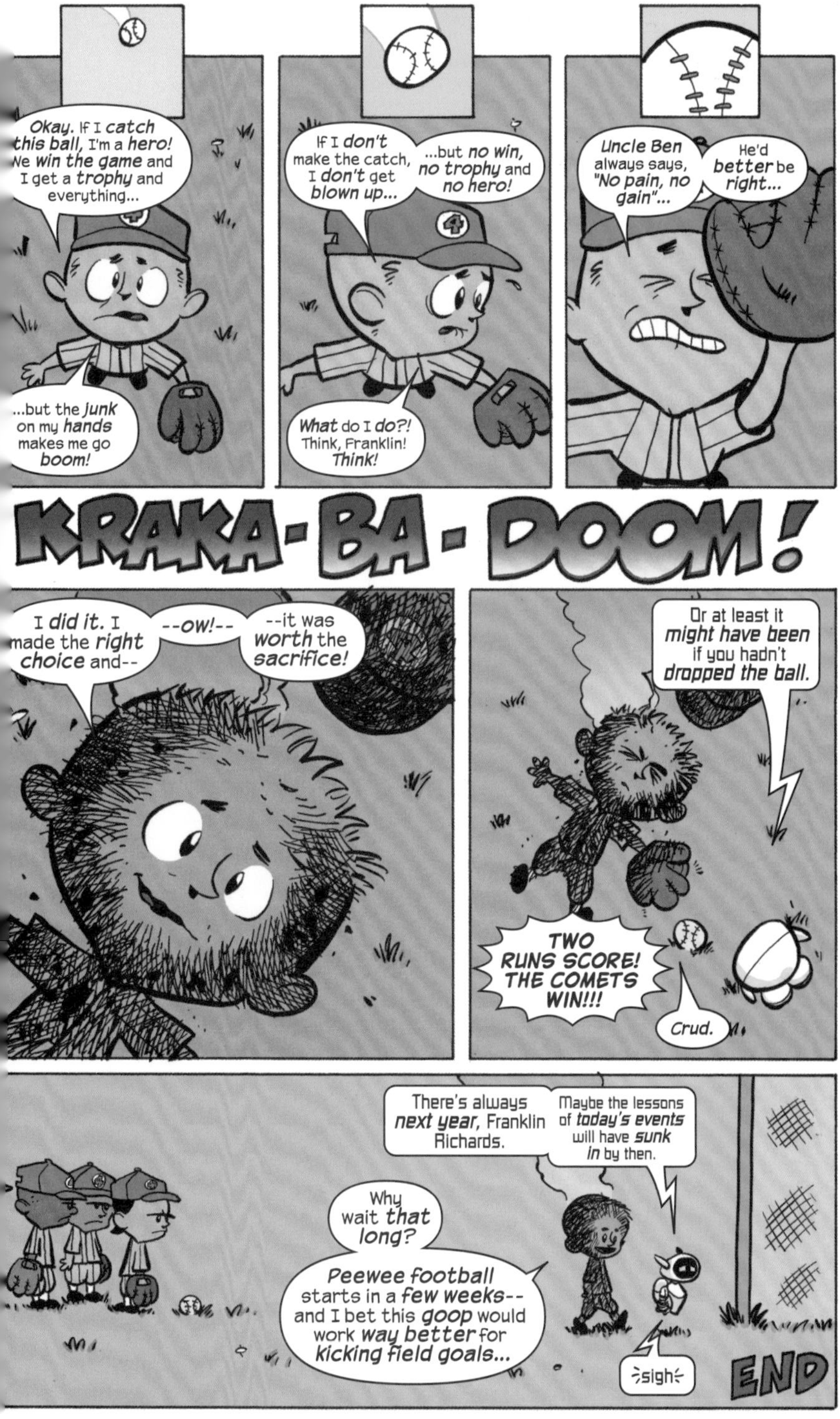
Okay. If I catch this ball, I'm a hero! We win the game and I get a trophy and everything...
...but the junk on my hands makes me go boom!
If I don't make the catch, I don't get blown up...
...but no win, no trophy and no hero!
What do I do?! Think, Franklin! Think!
Uncle Ben always says, "No pain, no gain"...
He'd better be right...
KRAKA-BA-DOOM!
I did it. I made the right choice and--
--OW!--
--it was worth the sacrifice!
Or at least it might have been if you hadn't dropped the ball.
TWO RUNS SCORE! THE COMETS WIN!!!
Crud.
There's always next year, Franklin Richards.
Maybe the lessons of today's events will have sunk in by then.
Why wait that long?
Peewee football starts in a few weeks-- and I bet this goop would work way better for kicking field goals...
sigh
END

FRANKLIN RICHARDS SON OF A GENIUS IN: "SQUID KID!"

BY CHRIS ELIOPOULOS & MARC SUMERA

LOVERN KINDZIERSKI COLORS | NATHAN COSBY ASSISTANT EDITOR | MARK PANICCIA EDITOR | JOE QUESADA EDITOR IN CHIEF | DAN BUCK PUBLISHE

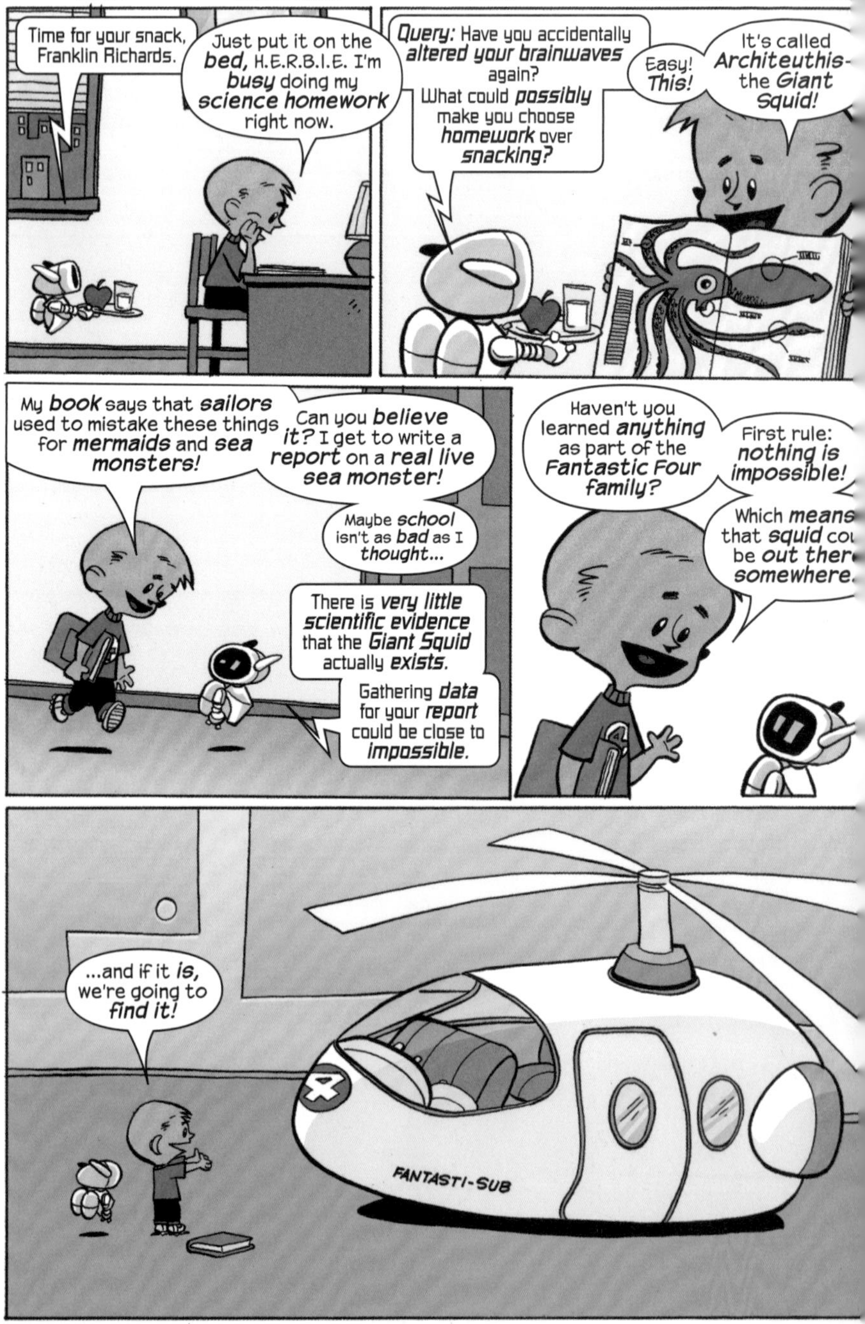

Time for your snack, Franklin Richards.
Just put it on the bed, H.E.R.B.I.E. I'm busy doing my science homework right now.
Query: Have you accidentally altered your brainwaves again? What could possibly make you choose homework over snacking?
Easy! This!
It's called Architeuthis- the Giant Squid!
My book says that sailors used to mistake these things for mermaids and sea monsters!
Can you believe it? I get to write a report on a real live sea monster!
Maybe school isn't as bad as I thought...
There is very little scientific evidence that the Giant Squid actually exists.
Gathering data for your report could be close to impossible.
Haven't you learned anything as part of the Fantastic Four family?
First rule: nothing is impossible!
Which means that squid co be out ther somewhere.
...and if it is, we're going to find it!
FANTASTI-SUB

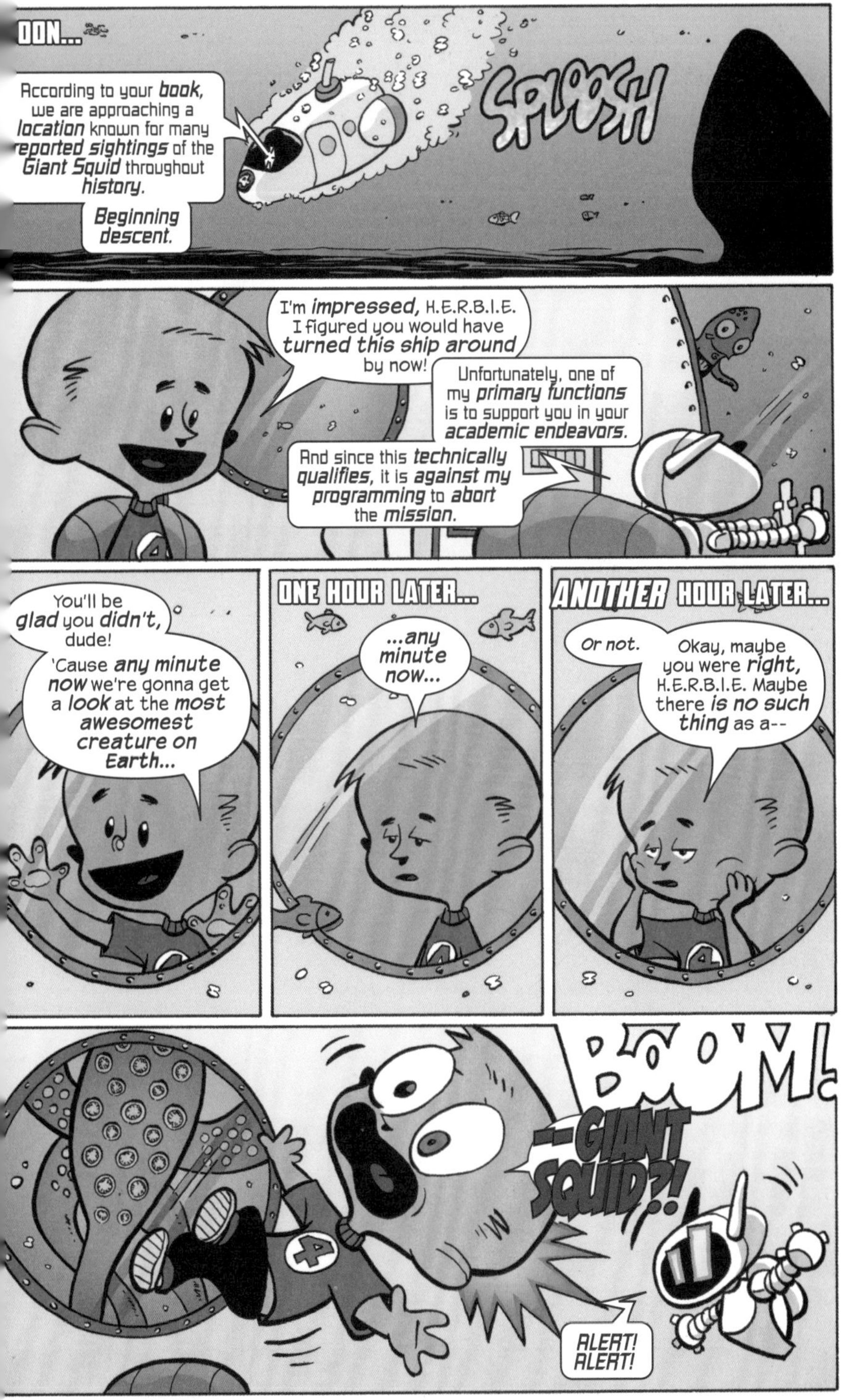

OON...
According to your book, we are approaching a location known for many reported sightings of the Giant Squid throughout history.
Beginning descent.
SPLOOSH
I'm impressed, H.E.R.B.I.E. I figured you would have turned this ship around by now!
Unfortunately, one of my primary functions is to support you in your academic endeavors.
And since this technically qualifies, it is against my programming to abort the mission.
You'll be glad you didn't, dude!
'Cause any minute now we're gonna get a look at the most awesomest creature on Earth...
ONE HOUR LATER...
...any minute now...
ANOTHER HOUR LATER...
Or not.
Okay, maybe you were right, H.E.R.B.I.E. Maybe there is no such thing as a--
BOOM!
--GIANT SQUID?!
ALERT! ALERT!

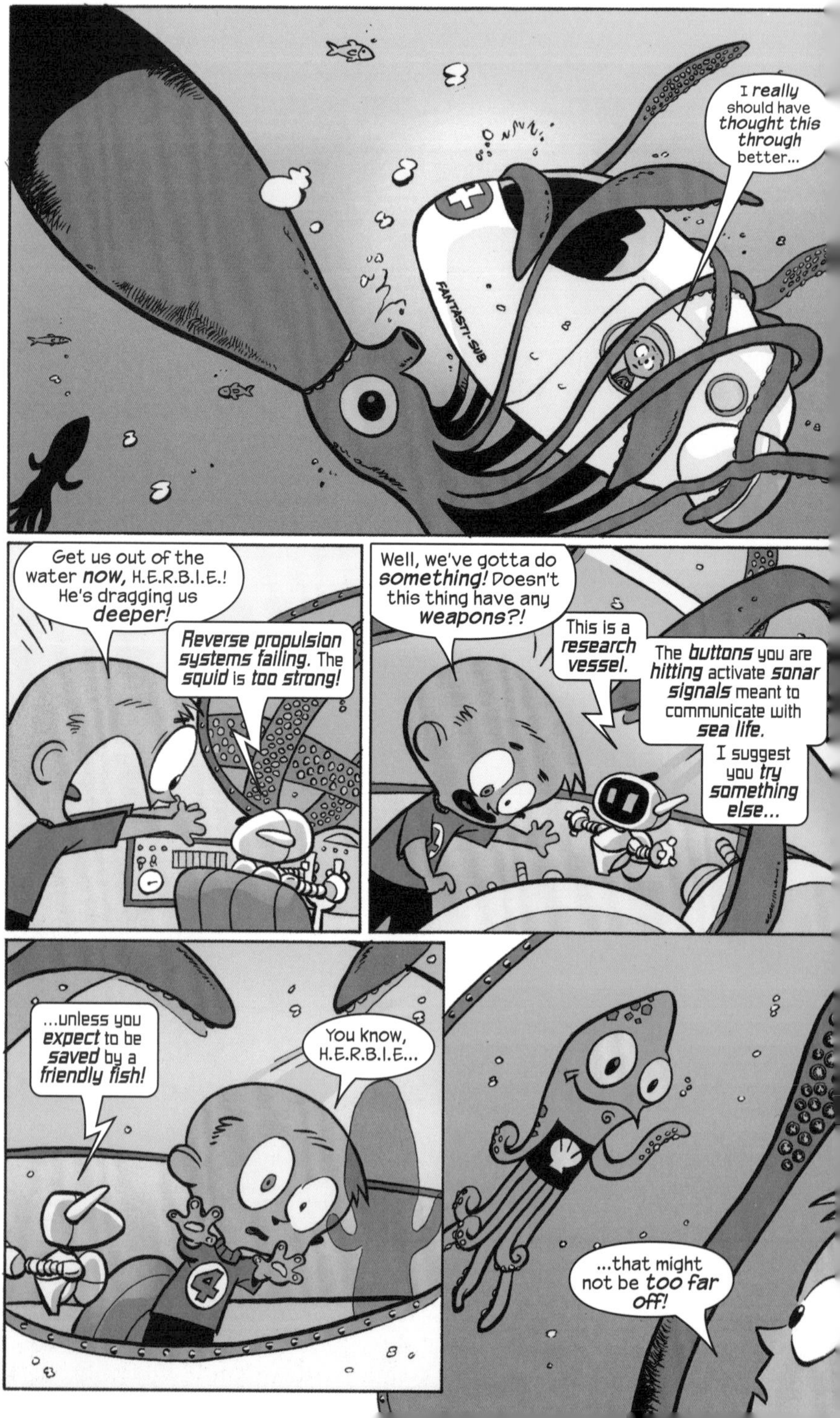
I really should have thought this through better...
FANTASTI-SUB
Get us out of the water now, H.E.R.B.I.E.! He's dragging us deeper!
Reverse propulsion systems failing. The squid is too strong!
Well, we've gotta do something! Doesn't this thing have any weapons?!
This is a research vessel.
The buttons you are hitting activate sonar signals meant to communicate with sea life.
I suggest you try something else...
...unless you expect to be saved by a friendly fish!
You know, H.E.R.B.I.E...
...that might not be too far off!

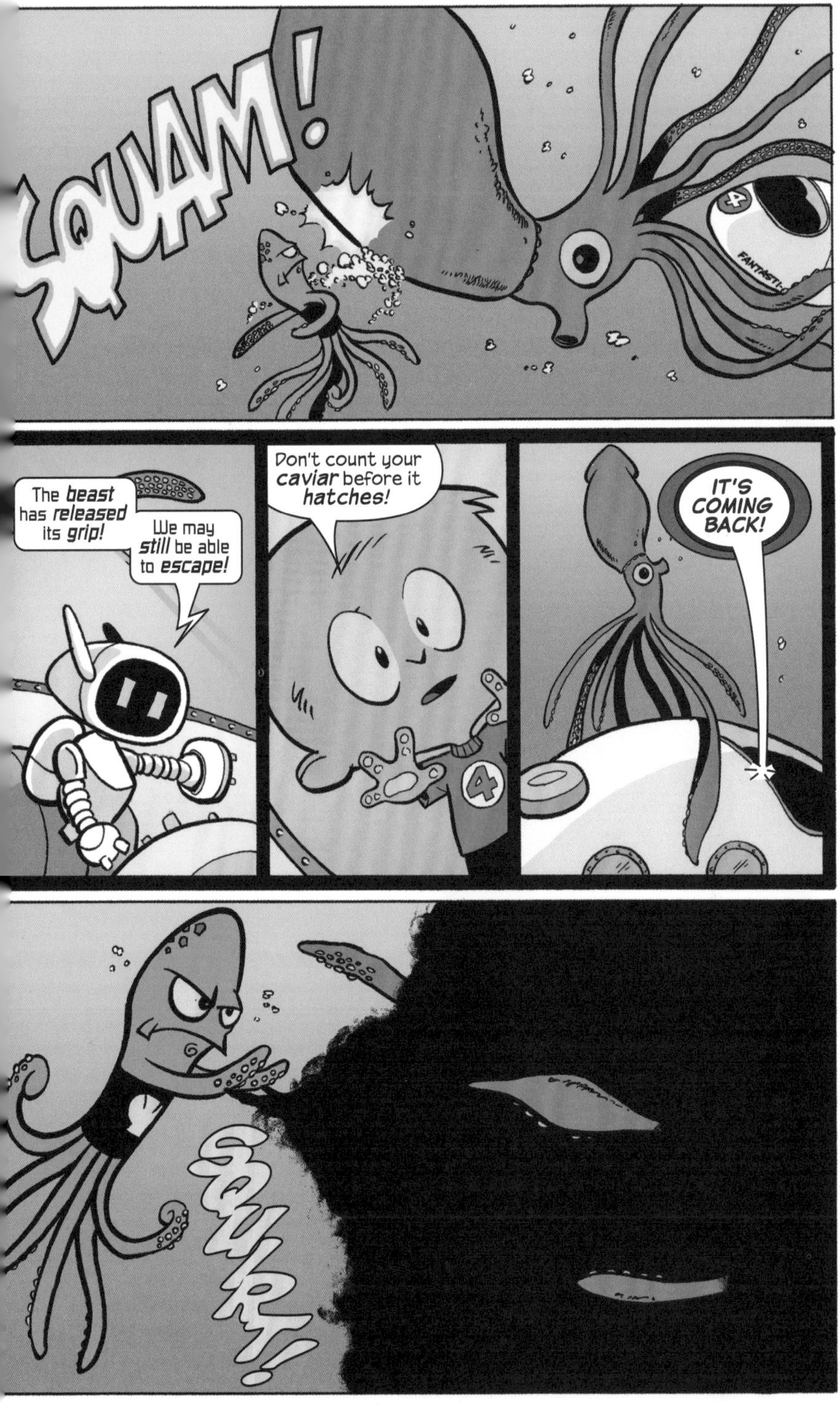
SQUAM!
FANTASTI
The beast has released its grip!
We may still be able to escape!
Don't count your caviar before it hatches!
IT'S COMING BACK!
SQUIRT!

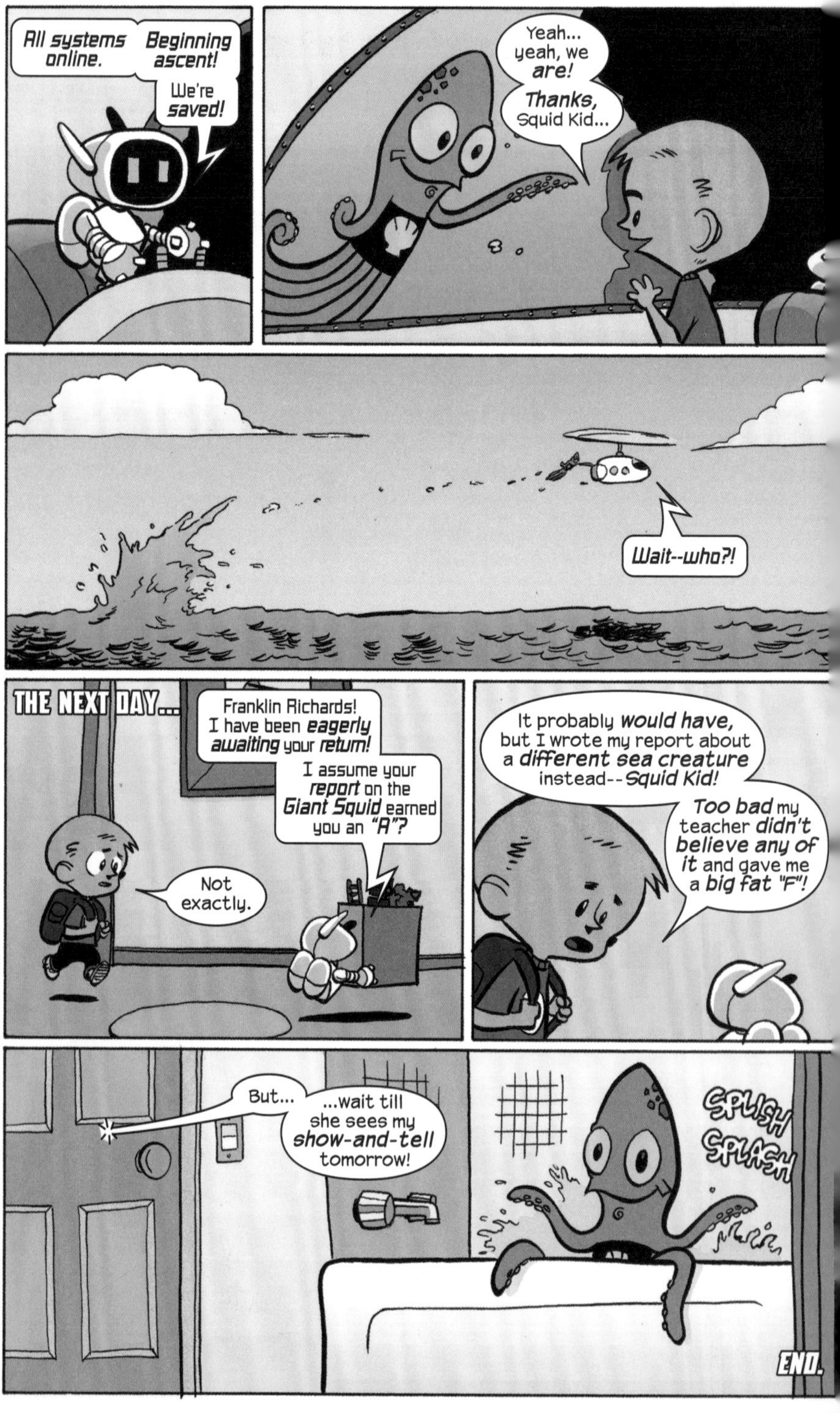
All systems online.
Beginning ascent!
We're saved!
Yeah... yeah, we are!
Thanks, Squid Kid...
Wait--who?!
THE NEXT DAY...
Franklin Richards! I have been eagerly awaiting your return!
I assume your report on the Giant Squid earned you an "A"?
Not exactly.
It probably would have, but I wrote my report about a different sea creature instead--Squid Kid!
Too bad my teacher didn't believe any of it and gave me a big fat "F"!
But...
...wait till she sees my show-and-tell tomorrow!
SPLISH
SPLASH
END.

FRANKLIN RICHARDS SON OF A GENIUS IN: **"FREAKY FRANKLIN FRIDAY!"**

Y CHRIS ELIOPOULOS & MARC SUMERAK

OVERN KINDZIERSKI COLORS | NATHAN COSBY ASSISTANT EDITOR | MARK PANICCIA EDITOR | JOE QUESADA EDITOR IN CHIEF | DAN BUCKLEY PUBLISHER

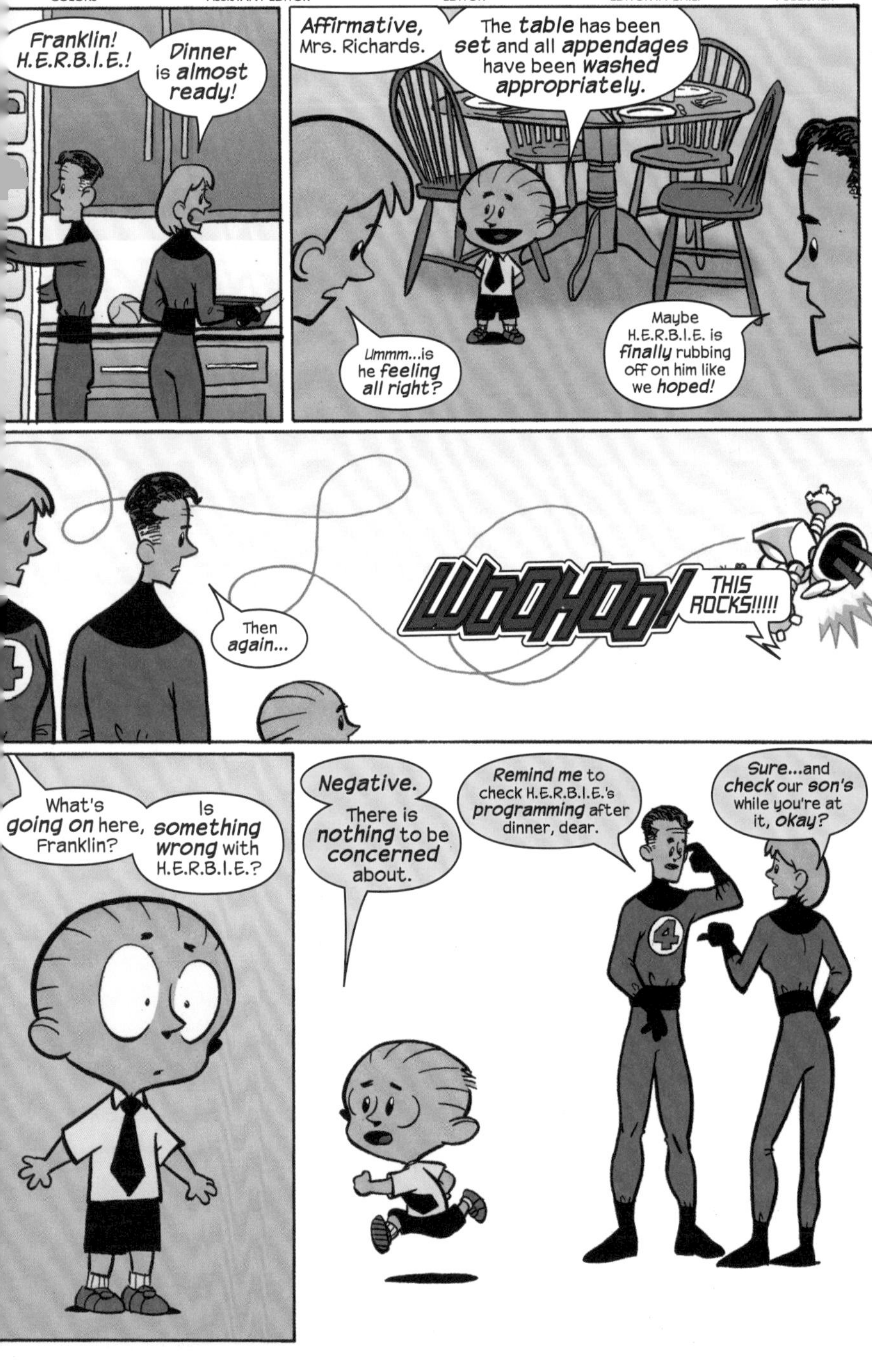

Franklin! H.E.R.B.I.E.!
Dinner is almost ready!
Affirmative, Mrs. Richards.
The table has been set and all appendages have been washed appropriately.
Ummm...is he feeling all right?
Maybe H.E.R.B.I.E. is finally rubbing off on him like we hoped!
Then again...
WOOHOO!
THIS ROCKS!!!!!
What's going on here, Franklin?
Is something wrong with H.E.R.B.I.E.?
Negative.
There is nothing to be concerned about.
Remind me to check H.E.R.B.I.E.'s programming after dinner, dear.
Sure...and check our son's while you're at it, okay?

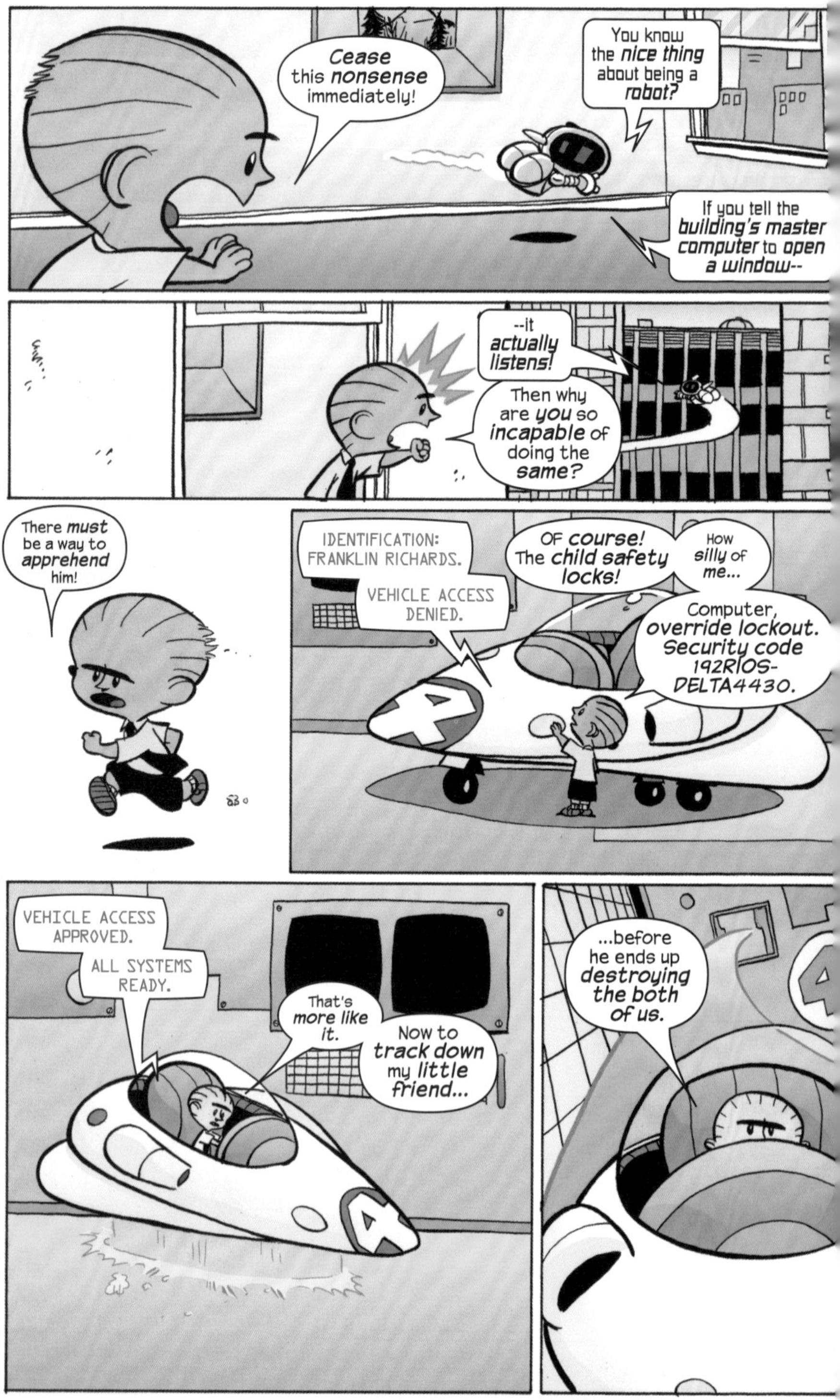
Cease this nonsense immediately!
You know the nice thing about being a robot?
If you tell the building's master computer to open a window--
--it actually listens!
Then why are you so incapable of doing the same?
There must be a way to apprehend him!
IDENTIFICATION: FRANKLIN RICHARDS.
VEHICLE ACCESS DENIED.
OF course! The child safety locks!
How silly of me...
Computer, override lockout. Security code 192RIOS-DELTA4430.
VEHICLE ACCESS APPROVED.
ALL SYSTEMS READY.
That's more like it.
Now to track down my little friend...
...before he ends up destroying the both of us.

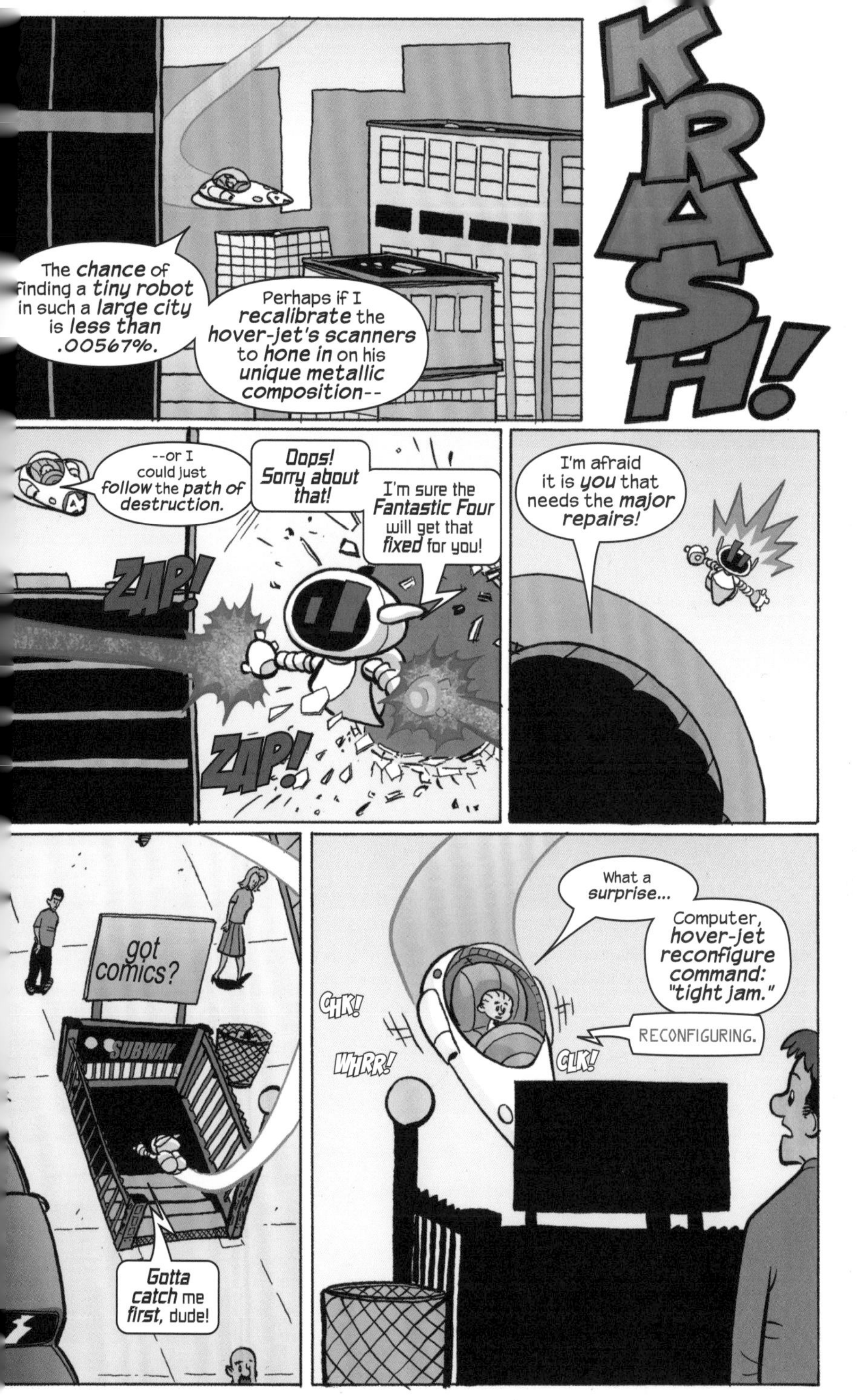
The chance of finding a tiny robot in such a large city is less than .00567%.
Perhaps if I recalibrate the hover-jet's scanners to hone in on his unique metallic composition--
KRASH!
--or I could just follow the path of destruction.
Oops! Sorry about that!
I'm sure the Fantastic Four will get that fixed for you!
ZAP!
ZAP!
I'm afraid it is you that needs the major repairs!
got comics?
SUBWAY
Gotta catch me first, dude!
What a surprise...
Computer, hover-jet reconfigure command: "tight jam."
CHK!
WHRR!
CLK!
RECONFIGURING.

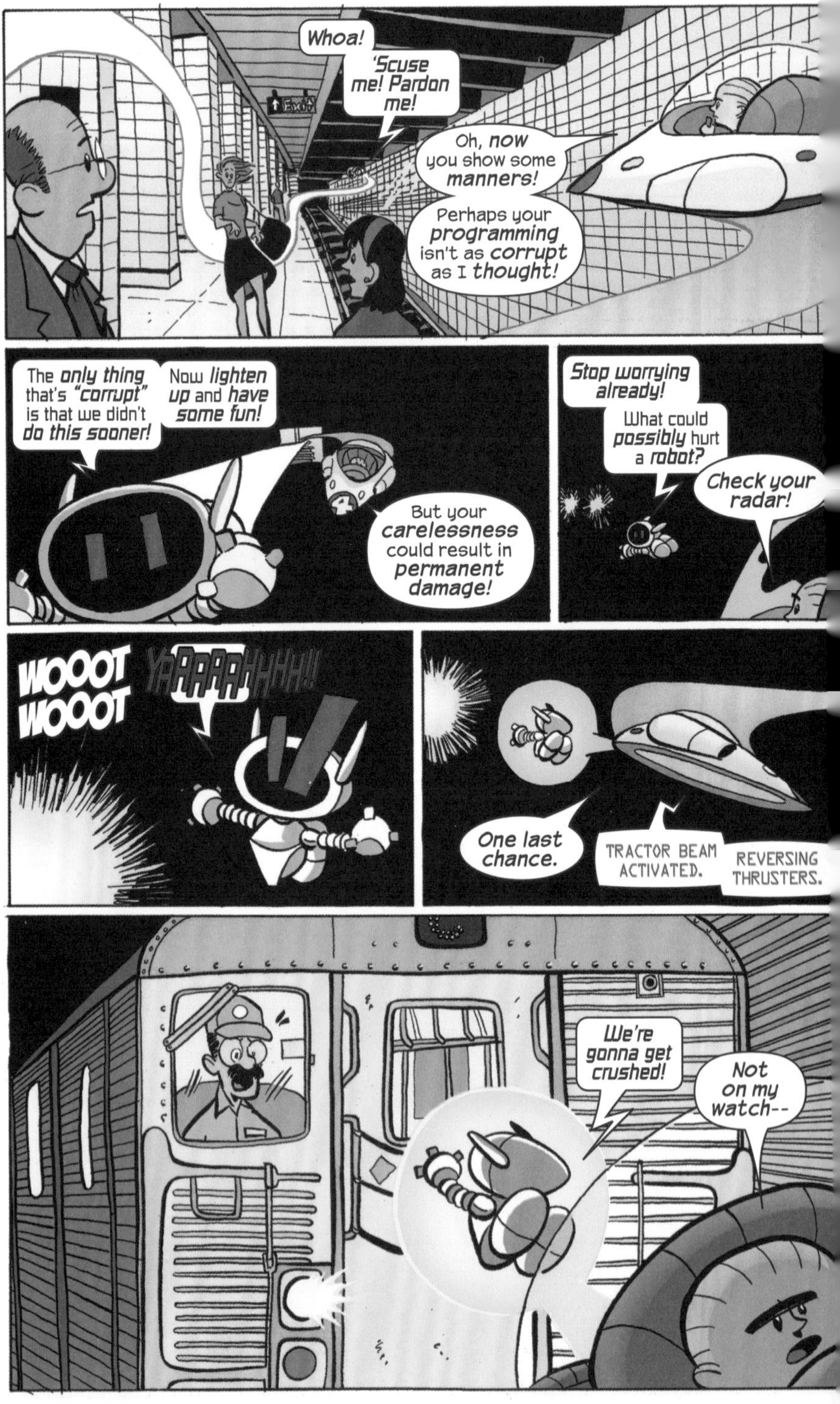

Whoa!
'Scuse me! Pardon me!
Oh, now you show some manners!
Perhaps your programming isn't as corrupt as I thought!
The only thing that's "corrupt" is that we didn't do this sooner!
Now lighten up and have some fun!
But your carelessness could result in permanent damage!
Stop worrying already!
What could possibly hurt a robot?
Check your radar!
WOOOT WOOOT
YAAAAHHHH!!
One last chance.
TRACTOR BEAM ACTIVATED.
REVERSING THRUSTERS.
We're gonna get crushed!
Not on my watch--

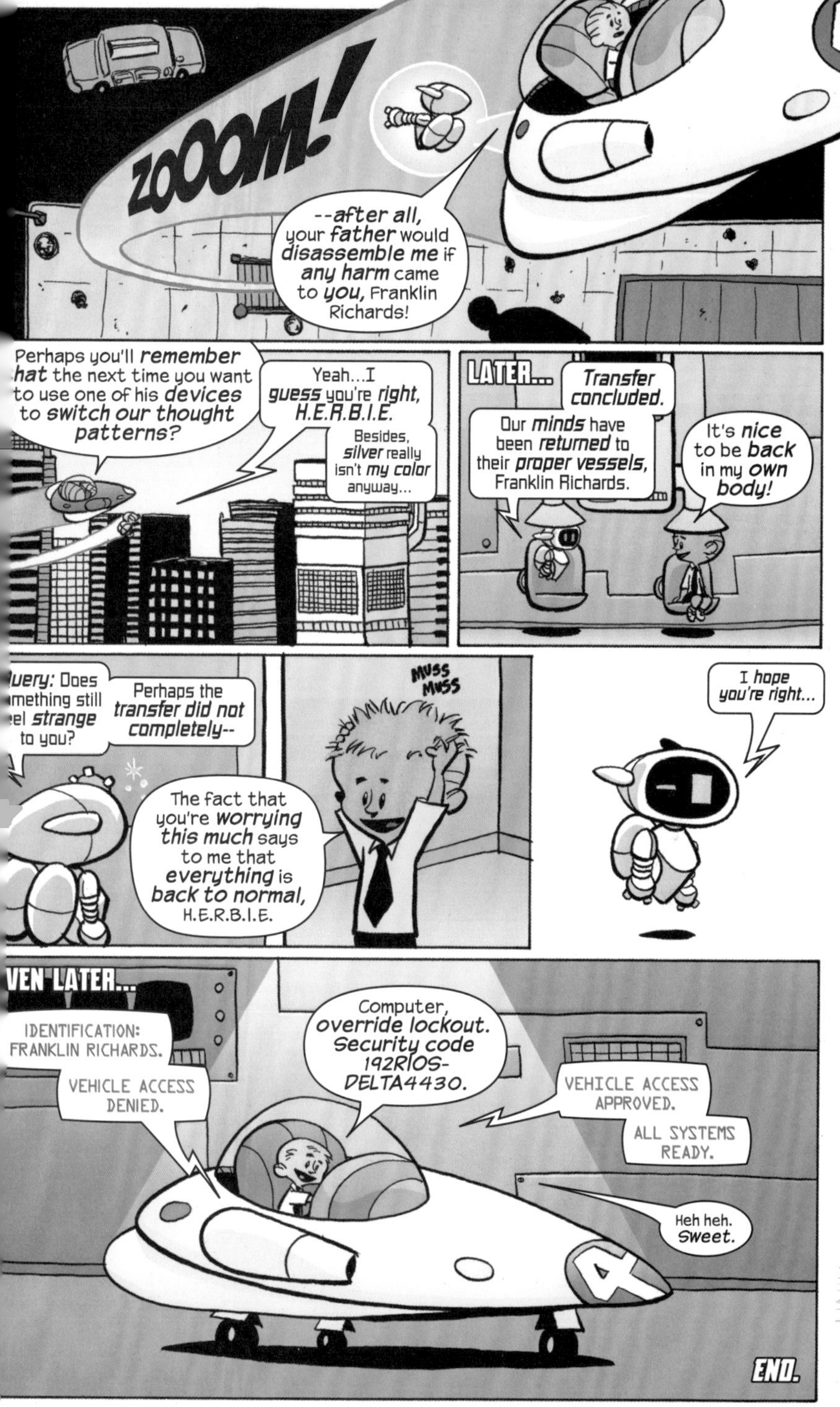
ZOOOM!
--after all, your father would disassemble me if any harm came to you, Franklin Richards!
Perhaps you'll remember hat the next time you want to use one of his devices to switch our thought patterns?
Yeah...I guess you're right, H.E.R.B.I.E.
Besides, silver really isn't my color anyway...
LATER...
Transfer concluded.
Our minds have been returned to their proper vessels, Franklin Richards.
It's nice to be back in my own body!
uery: Does mething still el strange to you?
Perhaps the transfer did not completely--
MUSS MUSS
The fact that you're worrying this much says to me that everything is back to normal, H.E.R.B.I.E.
I hope you're right...
VEN LATER...
IDENTIFICATION: FRANKLIN RICHARDS.
VEHICLE ACCESS DENIED.
Computer, override lockout. Security code 192RIOS-DELTA4430.
VEHICLE ACCESS APPROVED.
ALL SYSTEMS READY.
Heh heh. Sweet.
END.

FRANKLIN RICHARDS SON OF A GENIUS IN: # "BOUNCING BABY BOY!"

BY CHRIS ELIOPOULOS & MARC SUMERA

LOVERN KINDZIERSKI COLORS | NATHAN COSBY ASSISTANT EDITOR | MARK PANICCIA EDITOR | JOE QUESADA EDITOR IN CHIEF | DAN BUCK PUBLISHE

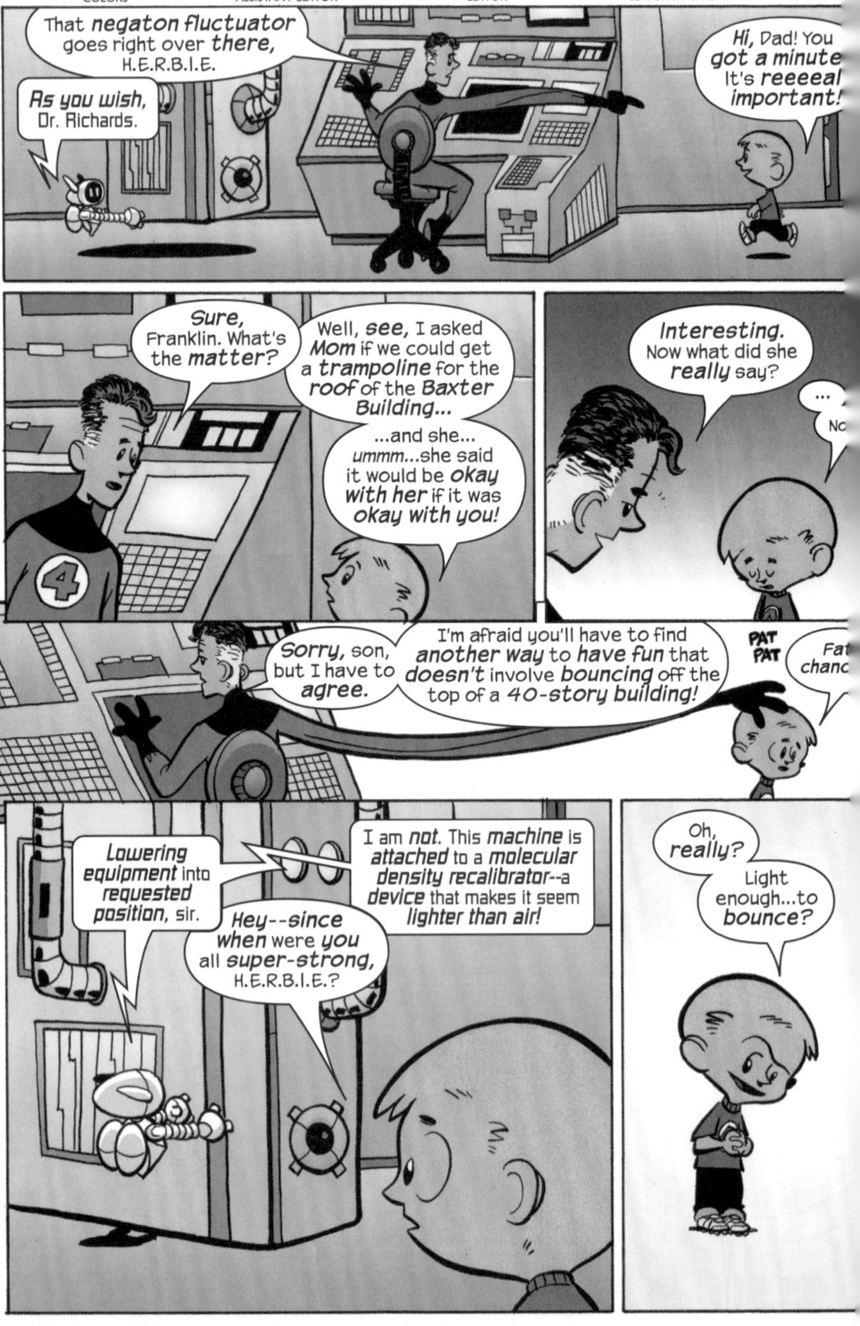
That negaton fluctuator goes right over there, H.E.R.B.I.E.
As you wish, Dr. Richards.
Hi, Dad! You got a minute It's reeeeal important!
Sure, Franklin. What's the matter?
Well, see, I asked Mom if we could get a trampoline for the roof of the Baxter Building...
...and she... ummm...she said it would be okay with her if it was okay with you!
Interesting. Now what did she really say?
...
No
Sorry, son, but I have to agree.
I'm afraid you'll have to find another way to have fun that doesn't involve bouncing off the top of a 40-story building!
PAT PAT
Fat chanc
Lowering equipment into requested position, sir.
I am not. This machine is attached to a molecular density recalibrator--a device that makes it seem lighter than air!
Hey--since when were you all super-strong, H.E.R.B.I.E.?
Oh, really?
Light enough...to bounce?

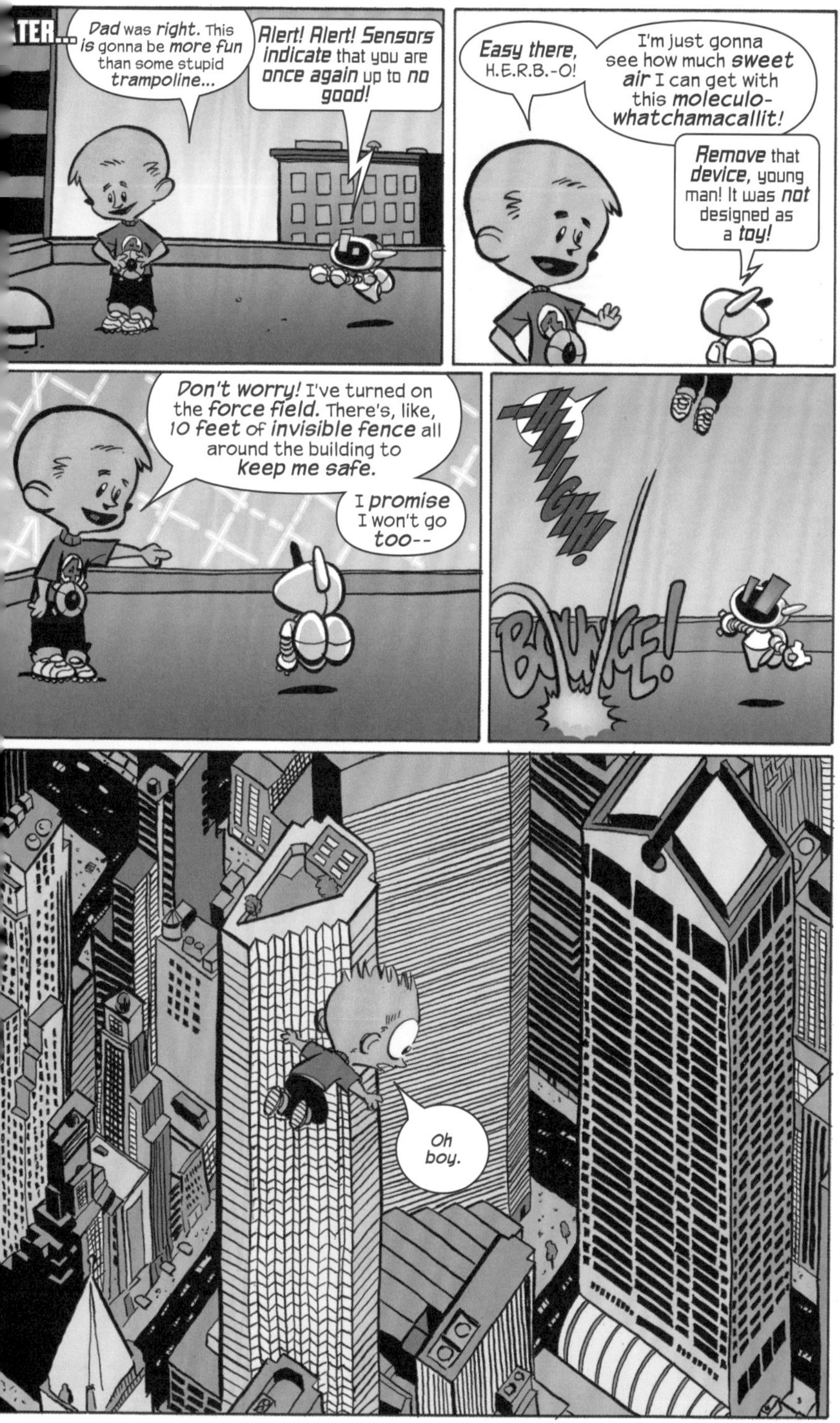
TER...
Dad was right. This is gonna be more fun than some stupid trampoline...
Alert! Alert! Sensors indicate that you are once again up to no good!
Easy there, H.E.R.B.-O!
I'm just gonna see how much sweet air I can get with this moleculo-whatchamacallit!
Remove that device, young man! It was not designed as a toy!
Don't worry! I've turned on the force field. There's, like, 10 feet of invisible fence all around the building to keep me safe.
I promise I won't go too--
Oh boy.

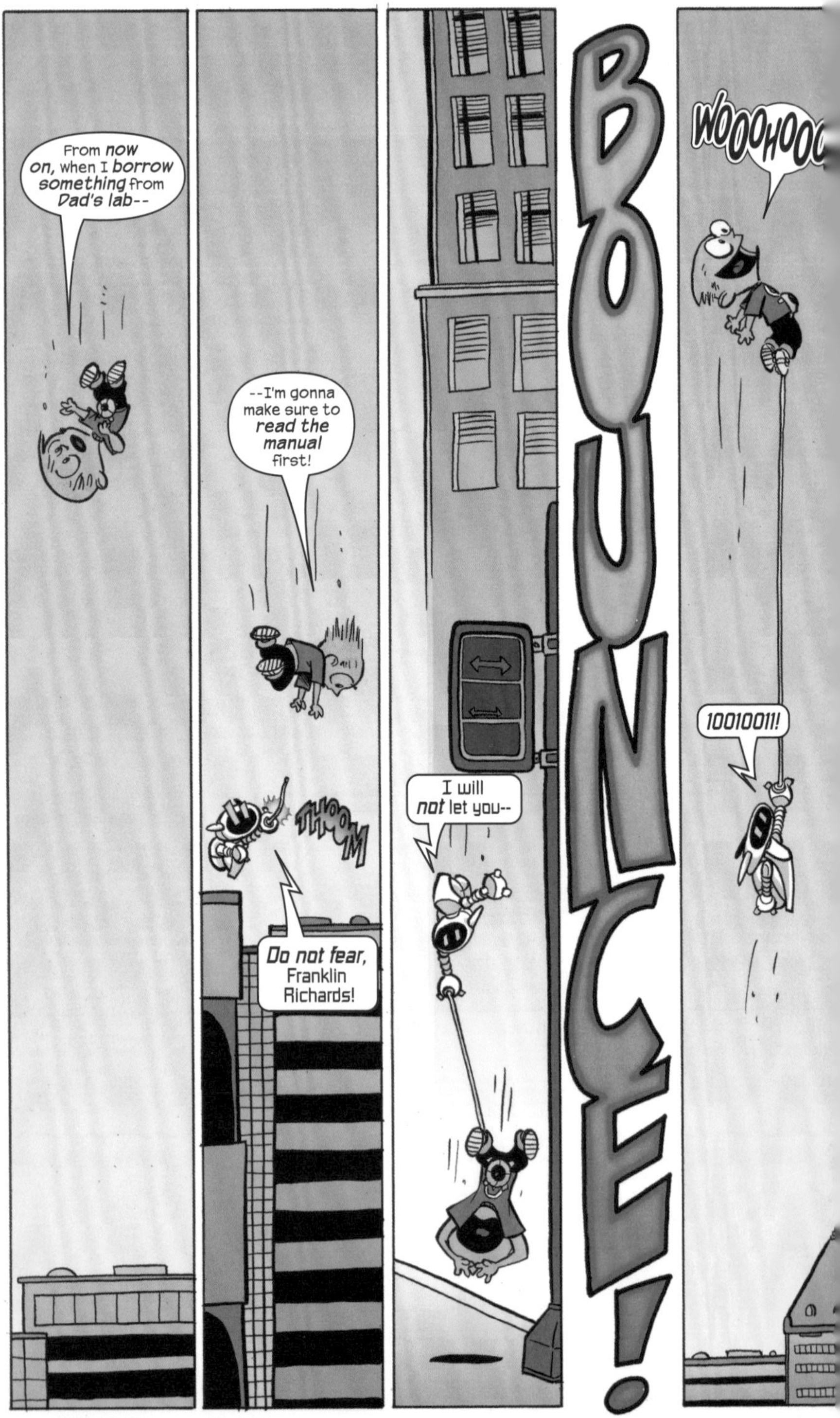

From now on, when I borrow something from Dad's lab--
--I'm gonna make sure to read the manual first!
THOOM
Do not fear, Franklin Richards!
I will not let you--
BOUNCE!
WOOOHOO
10010011!

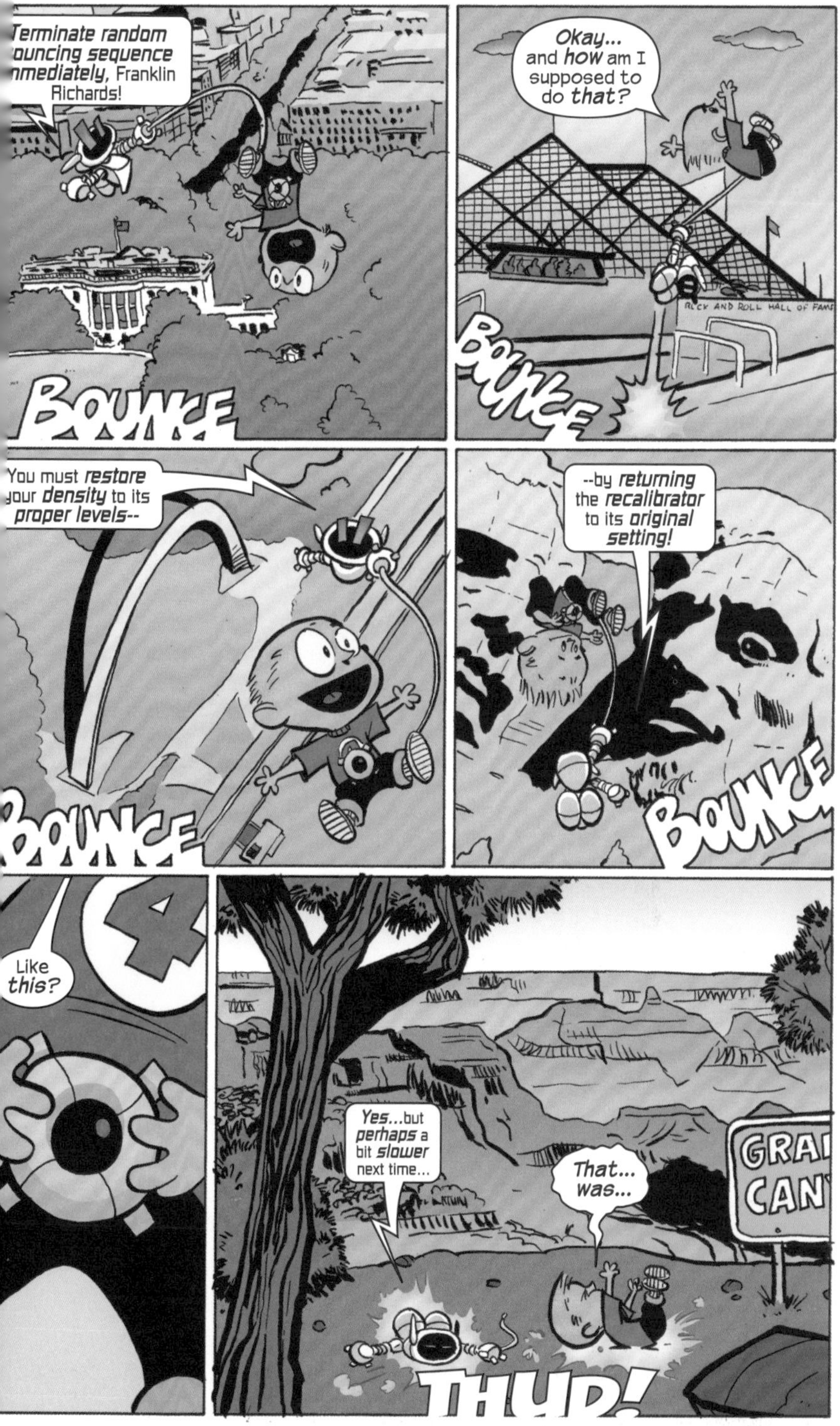

Terminate random
ouncing sequence
nmediately, Franklin
Richards!
BOUNCE
Okay...
and how am I
supposed to
do that?
RCK AND ROLL HALL OF FAME
BOUNCE
You must restore
your density to its
proper levels--
BOUNCE
--by returning
the recalibrator
to its original
setting!
BOUNCE
Like
this?
Yes...but
perhaps a
bit slower
next time...
That...
was...
THUD!

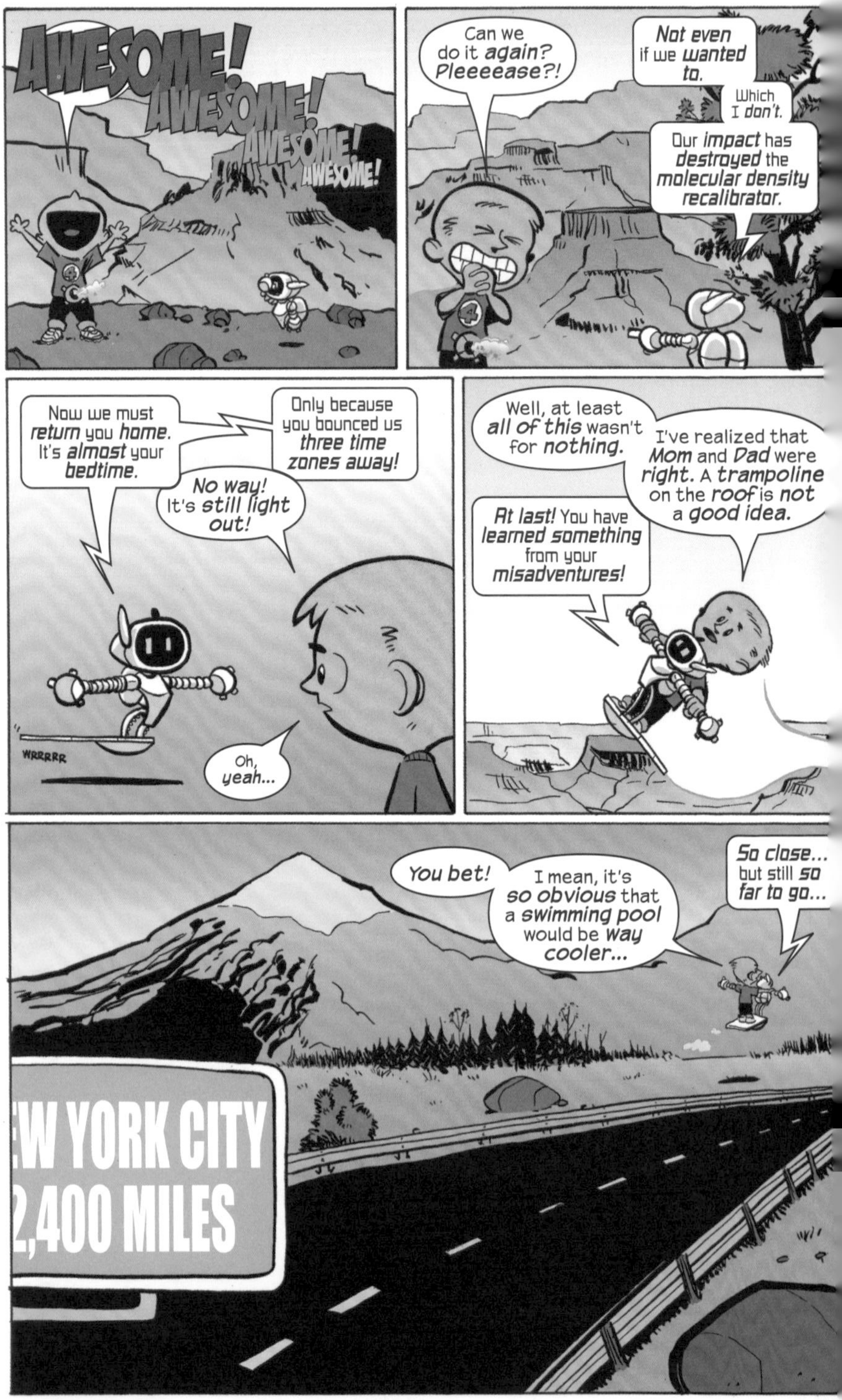
AWESOME! AWESOME! AWESOME! AWESOME!
Can we do it again? Pleeeease?!
Not even if we wanted to.
Which I don't.
Our impact has destroyed the molecular density recalibrator.
Now we must return you home. It's almost your bedtime.
Only because you bounced us three time zones away!
No way! It's still light out!
WRRRRR
Oh, yeah...
Well, at least all of this wasn't for nothing.
I've realized that Mom and Dad were right. A trampoline on the roof is not a good idea.
At last! You have learned something from your misadventures!
You bet!
I mean, it's so obvious that a swimming pool would be way cooler...
So close... but still so far to go...
EW YORK CITY
2,400 MILES

FRANKLIN RICHARDS SON OF A GENIUS IN: "COMIC BOOK FREE-FOR-ALL!"

Y CHRIS ELIOPOULOS & MARC SUMERAK

VERN KINDZIERSKI COLORS | NATHAN COSBY ASSISTANT EDITOR | MARK PANICCIA CONSULTING EDITOR | MACKENZIE CADENHEAD EDITOR

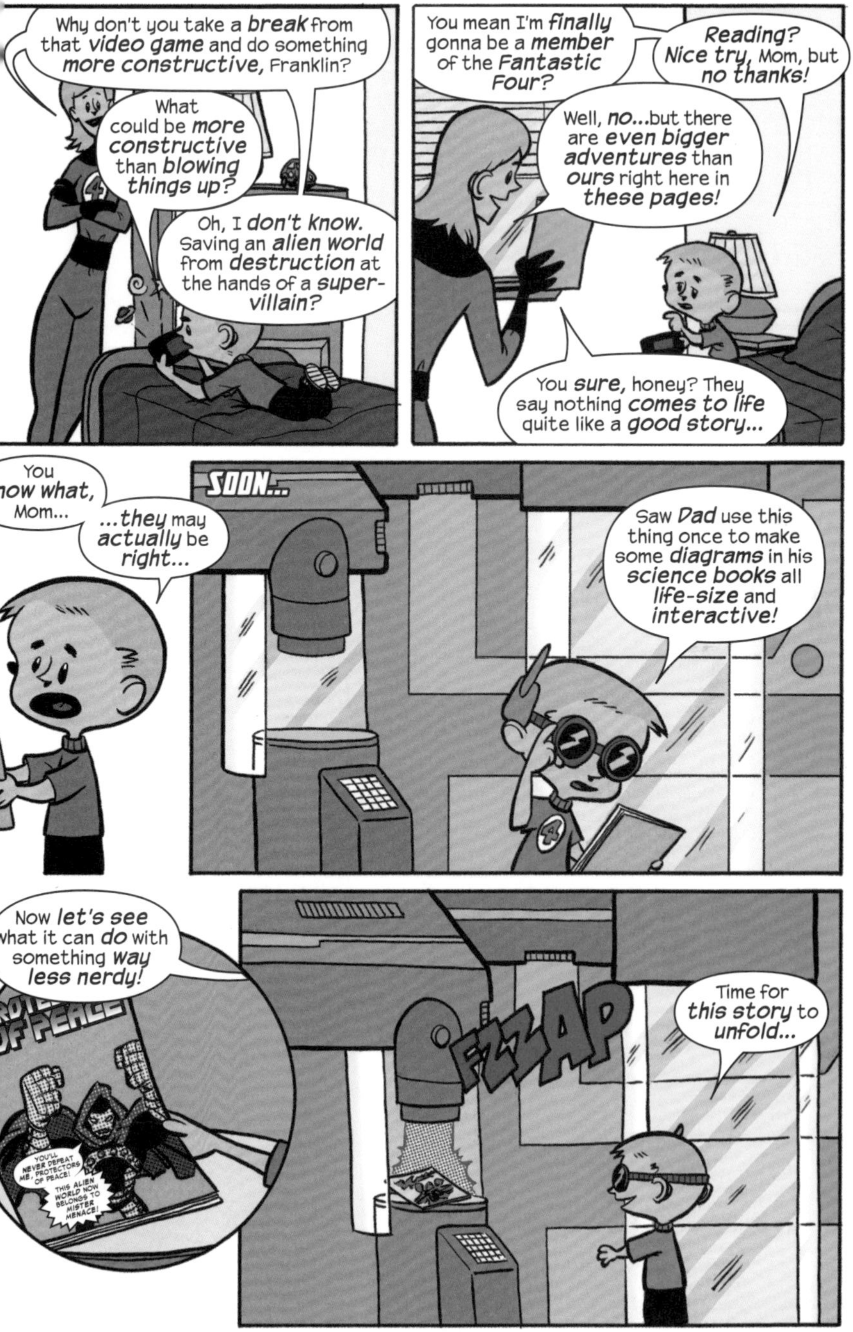

Why don't you take a break from that video game and do something more constructive, Franklin?
What could be more constructive than blowing things up?
Oh, I don't know. Saving an alien world from destruction at the hands of a super-villain?
You mean I'm finally gonna be a member of the Fantastic Four?
Well, no...but there are even bigger adventures than ours right here in these pages!
Reading? Nice try, Mom, but no thanks!
You sure, honey? They say nothing comes to life quite like a good story...
You now what, Mom...
...they may actually be right...
SOON...
Saw Dad use this thing once to make some diagrams in his science books all life-size and interactive!
Now let's see what it can do with something way less nerdy!
YOU'LL NEVER DEFEAT ME, PROTECTORS OF PEACE!
THIS ALIEN WORLD NOW BELONGS TO MISTER MENACE!
FZZAP
Time for this story to unfold...

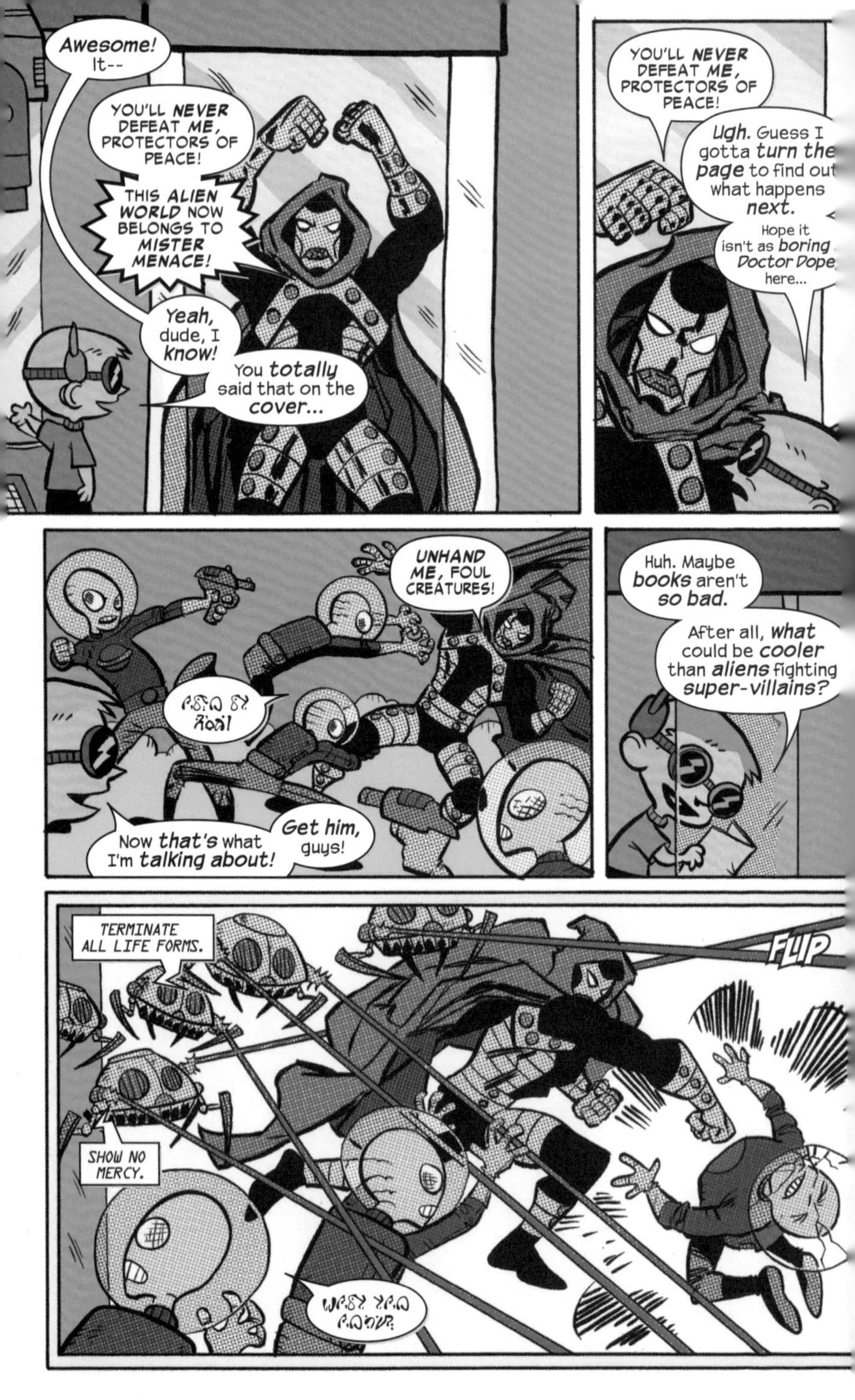
Awesome! It--
YOU'LL NEVER DEFEAT ME, PROTECTORS OF PEACE!
THIS ALIEN WORLD NOW BELONGS TO MISTER MENACE!
Yeah, dude, I know!
You totally said that on the cover...
YOU'LL NEVER DEFEAT ME, PROTECTORS OF PEACE!
Ugh. Guess I gotta turn the page to find out what happens next.
Hope it isn't as boring as Doctor Dope here...
UNHAND ME, FOUL CREATURES!
Now that's what I'm talking about!
Get him, guys!
Huh. Maybe books aren't so bad.
After all, what could be cooler than aliens fighting super-villains?
TERMINATE ALL LIFE FORMS.
FLIP
SHOW NO MERCY.

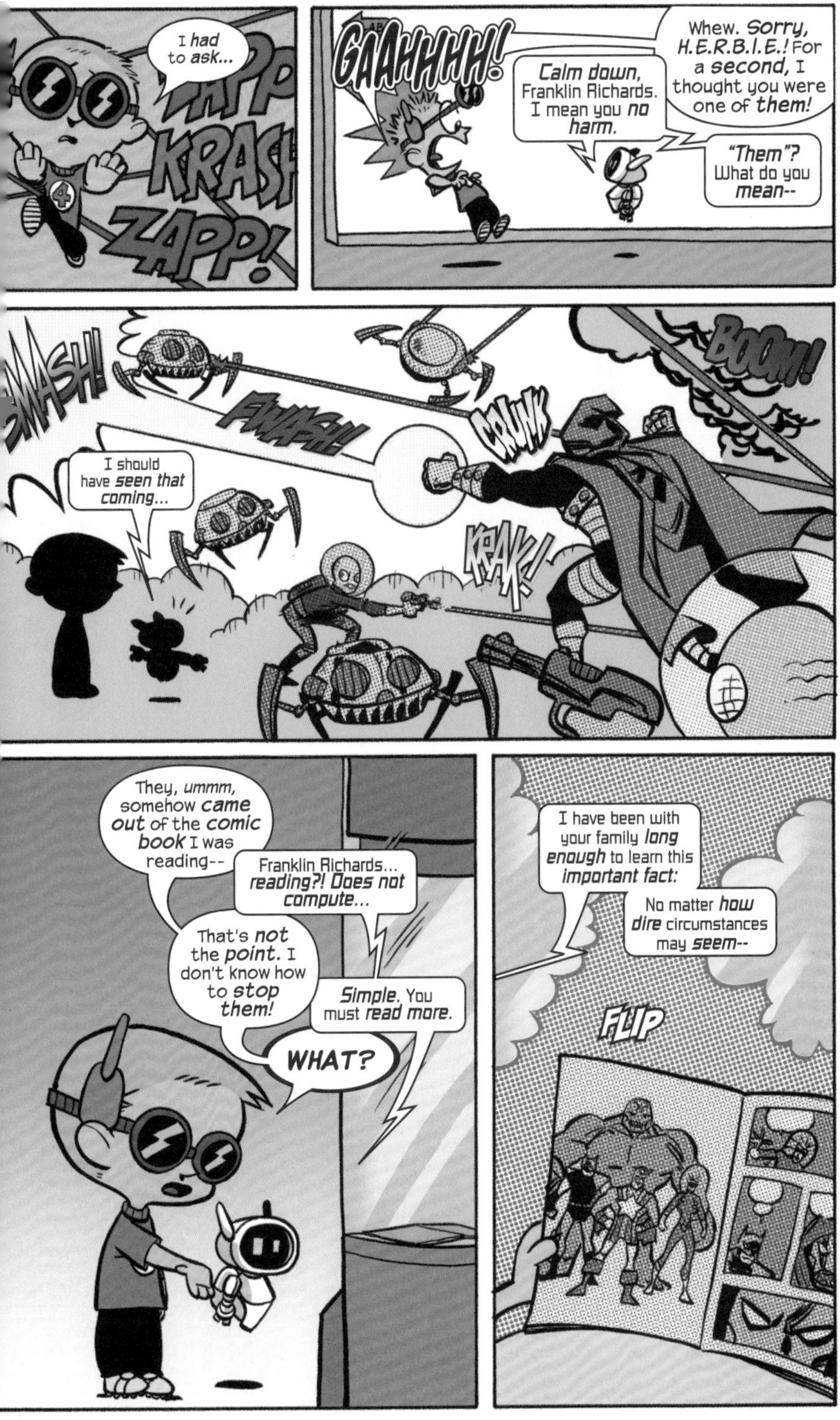

I had to ask...
ZAPP
KRASH
ZAPP!
GAAHHHH!
Whew. Sorry, H.E.R.B.I.E.! For a second, I thought you were one of them!
Calm down, Franklin Richards. I mean you no harm.
"Them"? What do you mean--
SWASH!
FWASH!
BOOM!
CRUNK
I should have seen that coming...
KRAK!
They, ummm, somehow came out of the comic book I was reading--
Franklin Richards... reading?! Does not compute...
That's not the point. I don't know how to stop them!
Simple. You must read more.
WHAT?
I have been with your family long enough to learn this important fact:
No matter how dire circumstances may seem--
FLIP

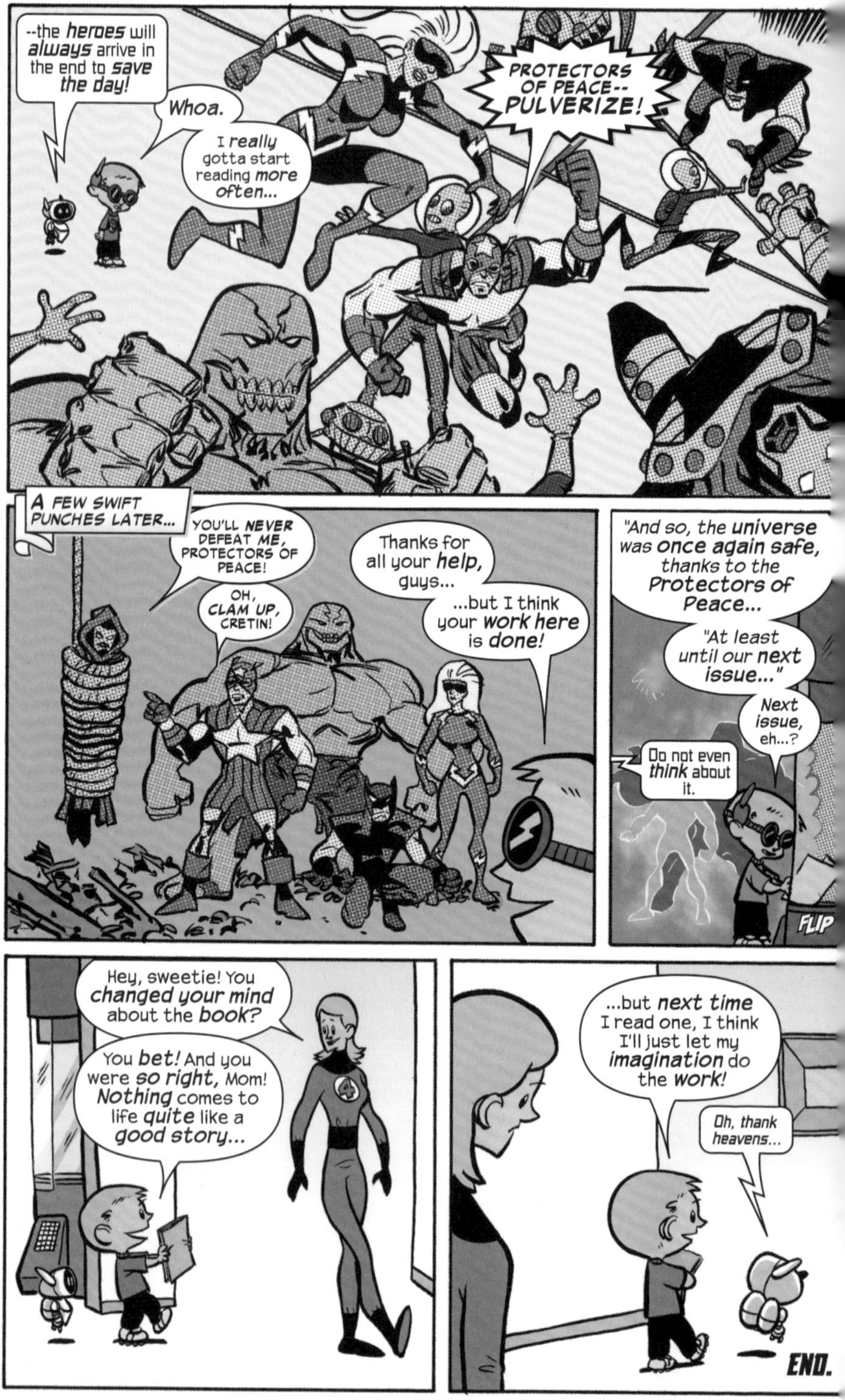
--the heroes will always arrive in the end to save the day!
Whoa.
I really gotta start reading more often...
PROTECTORS OF PEACE-- PULVERIZE!
A FEW SWIFT PUNCHES LATER...
YOU'LL NEVER DEFEAT ME, PROTECTORS OF PEACE!
OH, CLAM UP, CRETIN!
Thanks for all your help, guys...
...but I think your work here is done!
"And so, the universe was once again safe, thanks to the Protectors of Peace...
"At least until our next issue..."
Next issue, eh...?
Do not even think about it.
FLIP
Hey, sweetie! You changed your mind about the book?
You bet! And you were so right, Mom! Nothing comes to life quite like a good story...
...but next time I read one, I think I'll just let my imagination do the work!
Oh, thank heavens...
END.

RANKLIN RICHARDS' ROBOT, H.E.R.B.I.E. IN: "H.E.R.B.I.E.'S DAY OFF"

BY CHRIS ELIOPOULOS & MARC SUMERAK

GURIHIRU COLORS | **TOM VALENTE** PRODUCTION | **NATHAN COSBY** ASSISTANT EDITOR | **MARK PANICCIA** CONSULTING EDITOR | **MACKENZIE CADENHEAD** EDITOR

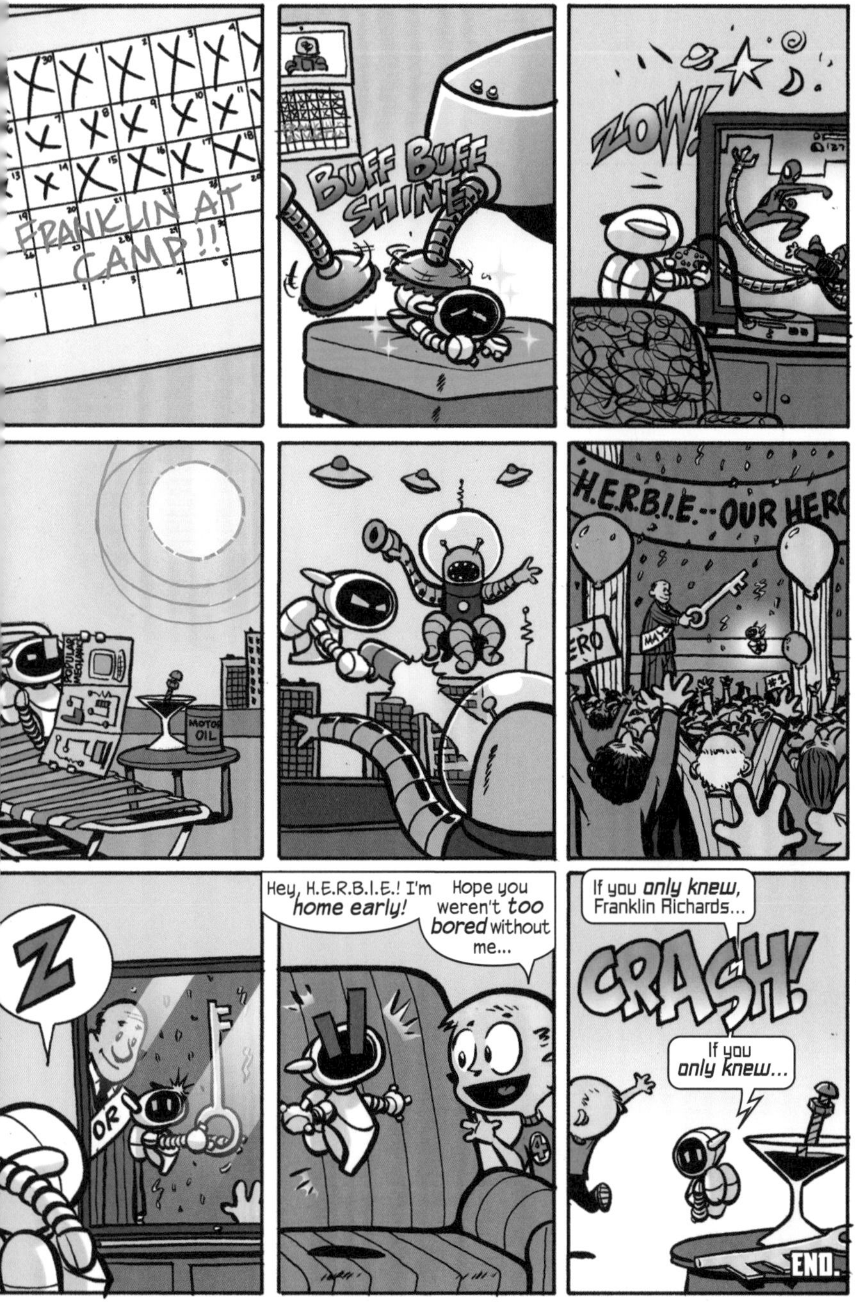

FRANKLIN AT CAMP!!
BUFF BUFF SHINE
ZOW!
POPULAR MECHANICS
MOTOR OIL
H.E.R.B.I.E.--OUR HERO
Z
Hey, H.E.R.B.I.E.! I'm home early!
Hope you weren't too bored without me...
If you only knew, Franklin Richards...
CRASH!
If you only knew...
END.

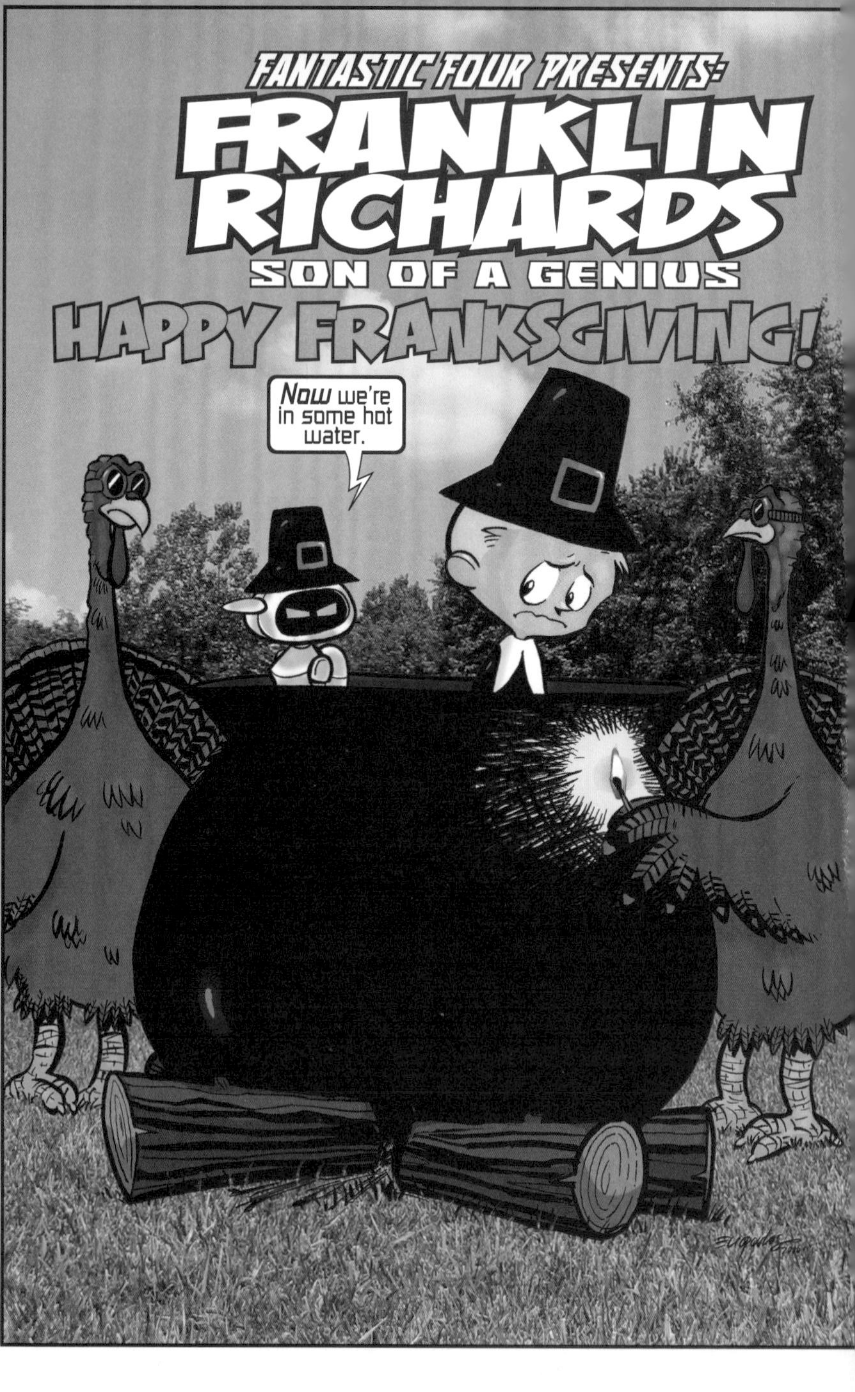
FANTASTIC FOUR PRESENTS:
FRANKLIN RICHARDS
SON OF A GENIUS
HAPPY FRANKSGIVING!
Now we're in some hot water.

FRANKLIN RICHARDS SON OF A GENIUS IN: HAMSTER HAVOC!

BY CHRIS ELIOPOULOS & MARC SUMERAK

BRAD ANDERSON COLORS · NATHAN COSBY ASSISTANT EDITOR · MARK PANICCIA EDITOR

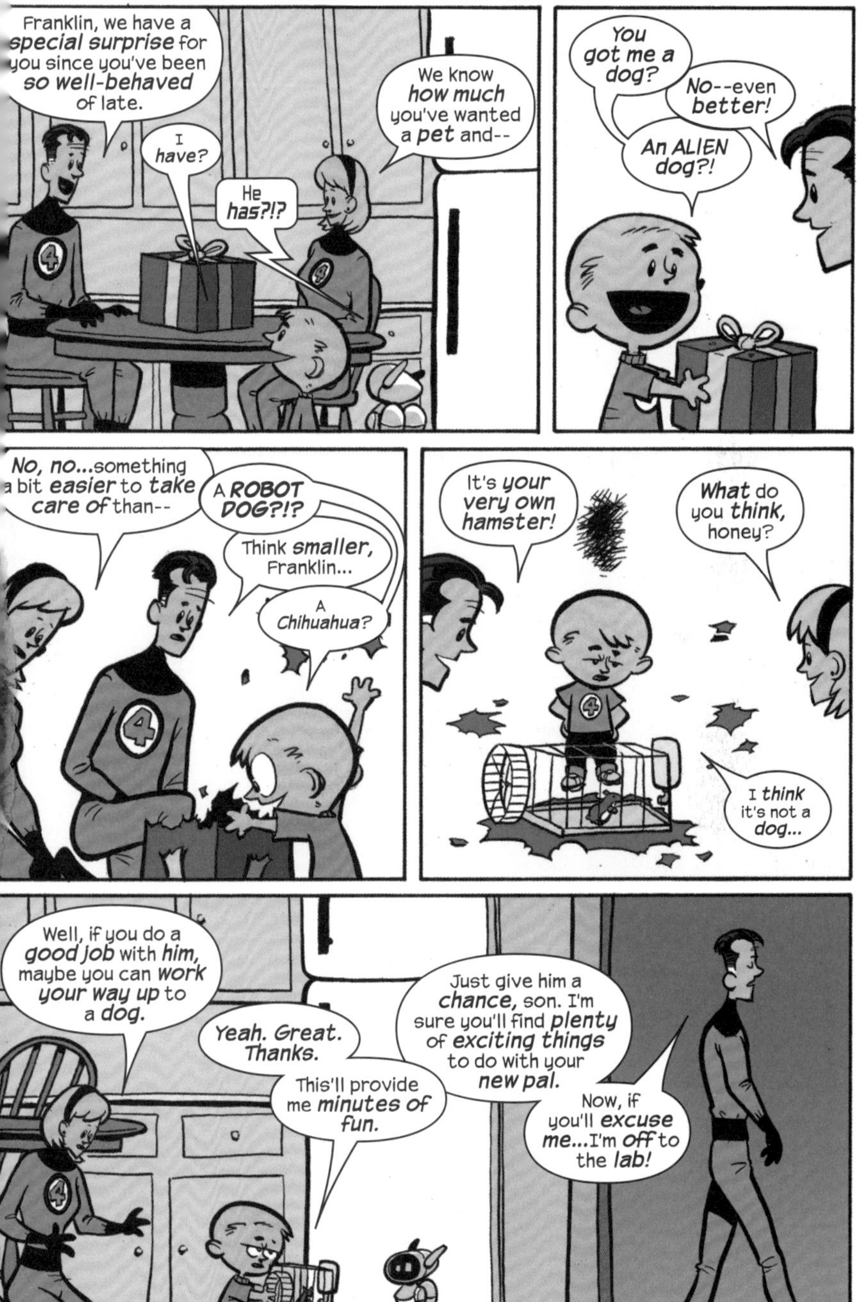
Franklin, we have a special surprise for you since you've been so well-behaved of late.
I have?
He has?!?
We know how much you've wanted a pet and--
You got me a dog?
No--even better!
An ALIEN dog?!
No, no...something a bit easier to take care of than--
A ROBOT DOG?!?
Think smaller, Franklin...
A Chihuahua?
It's your very own hamster!
What do you think, honey?
I think it's not a dog...
Well, if you do a good job with him, maybe you can work your way up to a dog.
Yeah. Great. Thanks.
This'll provide me minutes of fun.
Just give him a chance, son. I'm sure you'll find plenty of exciting things to do with your new pal.
Now, if you'll excuse me...I'm off to the lab!

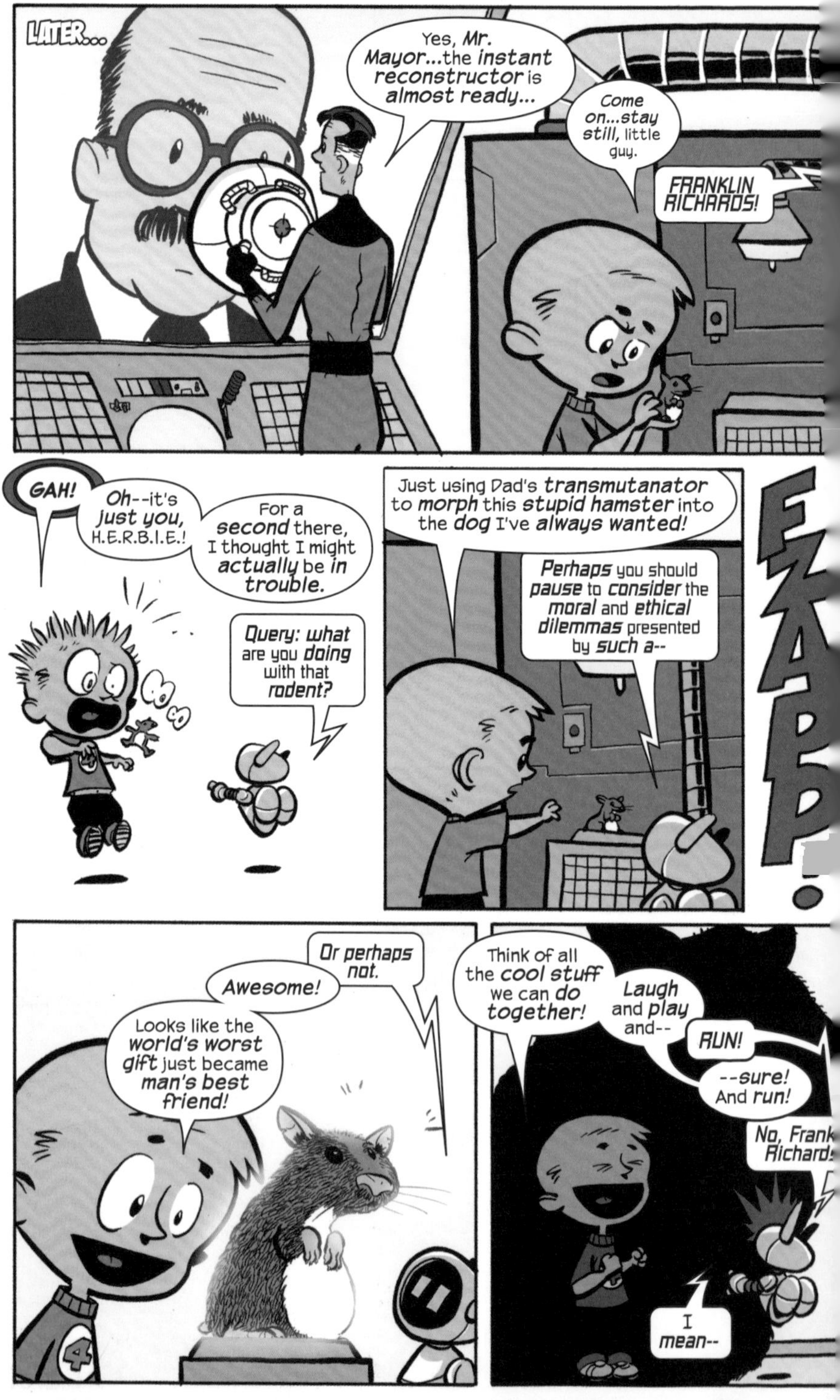
LATER...
Yes, Mr. Mayor...the instant reconstructor is almost ready...
Come on...stay still, little guy.
FRANKLIN RICHARDS!
GAH!
Oh--it's just you, H.E.R.B.I.E.!
For a second there, I thought I might actually be in trouble.
Query: what are you doing with that rodent?
Just using Dad's transmutanator to morph this stupid hamster into the dog I've always wanted!
Perhaps you should pause to consider the moral and ethical dilemmas presented by such a--
FZAPP!
Looks like the world's worst gift just became man's best friend!
Awesome!
Or perhaps not.
Think of all the cool stuff we can do together!
Laugh and play and--
RUN!
--sure! And run!
No, Frank Richard
I mean--

Maybe I should have gotten a *cat* instead...

—RUN!

Activating specimen containment protocols.

ILLEGAL MUTAGEN ISOLATED.

Good boy...easy, boy...

COMMENCING EXPULSION.

WHOOSH

SQUEE

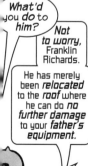

What'd you *do* to him?

Not to worry, Franklin Richards.

He has merely been *relocated* to the *roof* where he can do *no further damage* to your *father's* equipment.

But *what* if you did *damage* to him?!

My poor *dog!*

ROOF

Hamster.

Whatever!

You have *nothing* to fear.

It would take *enormous force* to *shatter* the *containment sphere*.

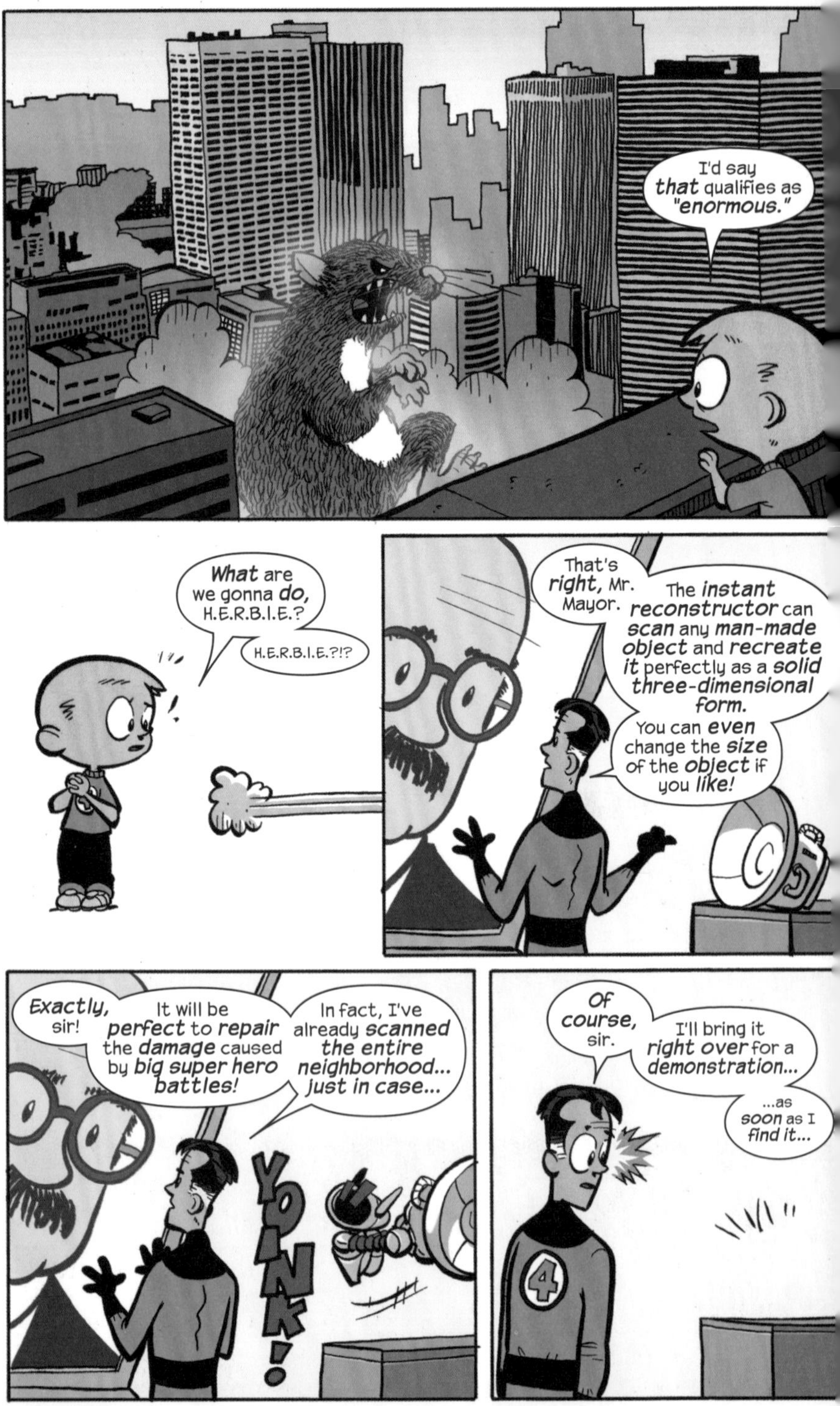

I'd say *that* qualifies as "*enormous.*"
What are we gonna *do,* H.E.R.B.I.E.?
H.E.R.B.I.E.?!?
That's *right,* Mr. Mayor.
The *instant reconstructor* can *scan* any *man-made object* and *recreate it* perfectly as a *solid three-dimensional form.*
You can *even* change the *size* of the *object* if you *like!*
Exactly, sir!
It will be *perfect* to *repair* the *damage* caused by *big super hero battles!*
In fact, I've already *scanned the entire neighborhood... just in case...*
YOINK!
Of course, sir.
I'll bring it *right over* for a *demonstration...*
...as *soon* as I *find it...*

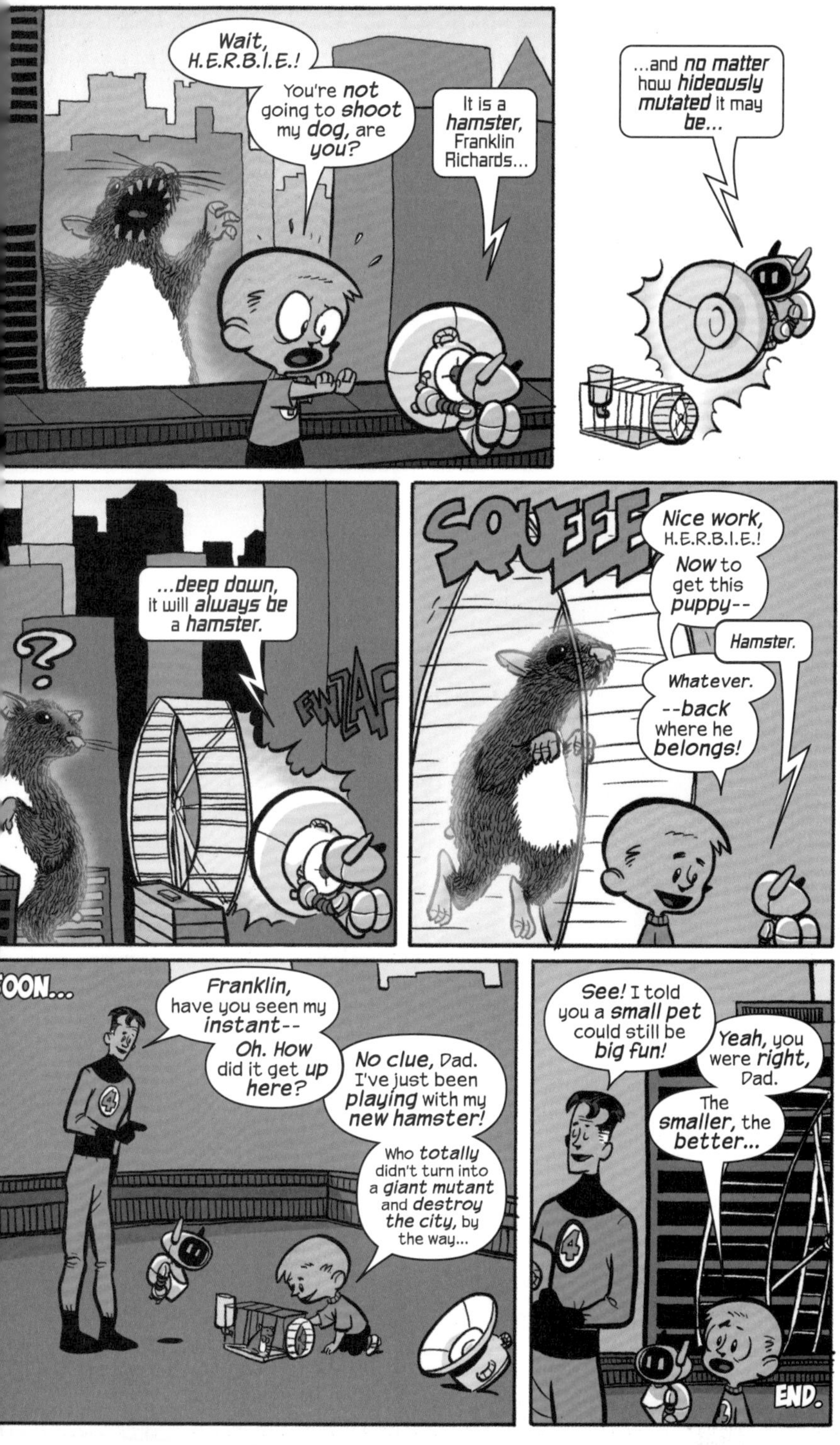

Wait, H.E.R.B.I.E.!
You're not going to shoot my dog, are you?
It is a hamster, Franklin Richards...
...and no matter how hideously mutated it may be...
...deep down, it will always be a hamster.
?
FWZAP
SQUEEE
Nice work, H.E.R.B.I.E.!
Now to get this puppy--
Hamster.
Whatever.
--back where he belongs!
SOON...
Franklin, have you seen my instant--
Oh. How did it get up here?
No clue, Dad. I've just been playing with my new hamster!
Who totally didn't turn into a giant mutant and destroy the city, by the way...
See! I told you a small pet could still be big fun!
Yeah, you were right, Dad.
The smaller, the better...
END.

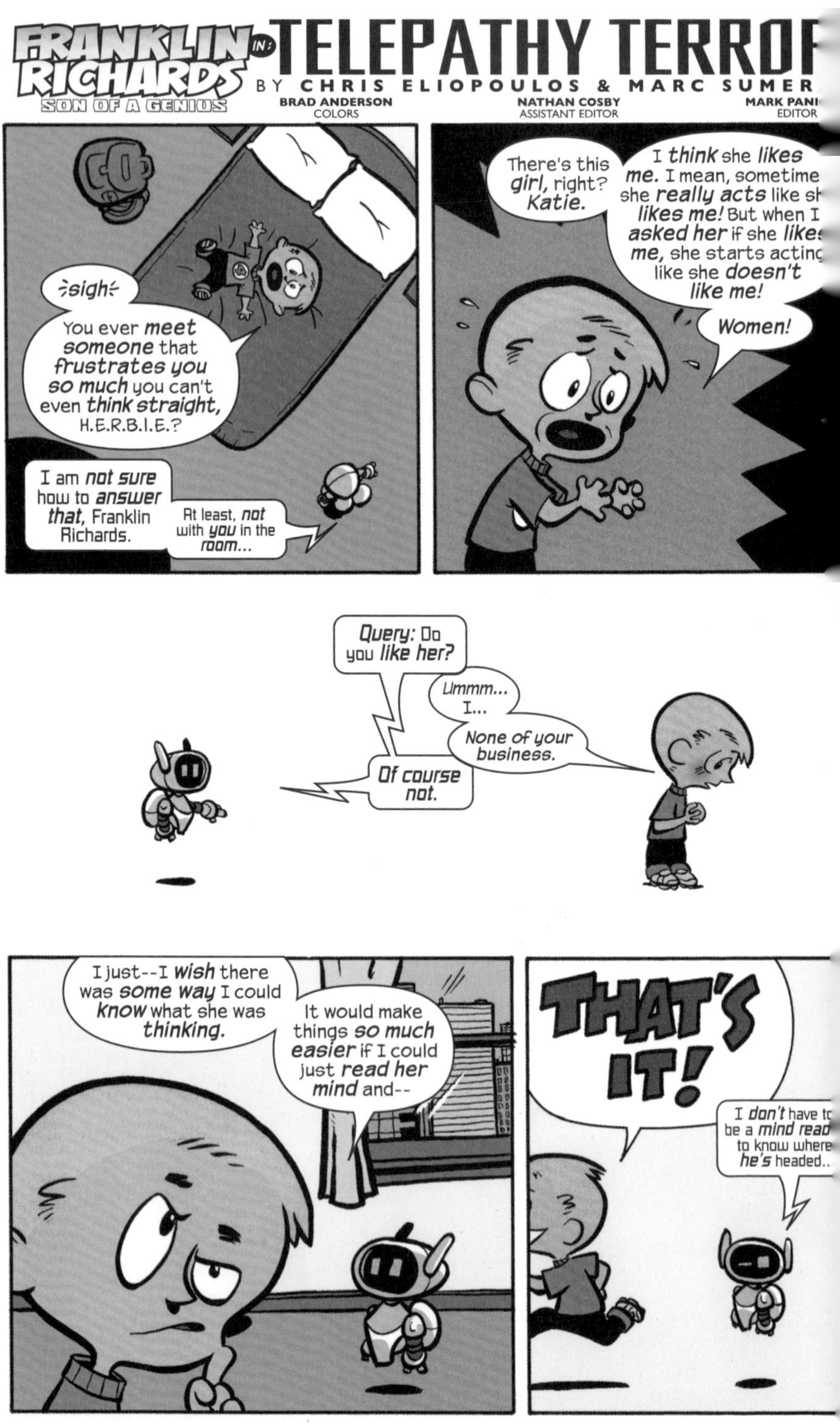

FRANKLIN RICHARDS SON OF A GENIUS IN: TELEPATHY TERROR
BY CHRIS ELIOPOULOS & MARC SUMER
BRAD ANDERSON COLORS
NATHAN COSBY ASSISTANT EDITOR
MARK PANI EDITOR
sigh
You ever meet someone that frustrates you so much you can't even think straight, H.E.R.B.I.E.?
I am not sure how to answer that, Franklin Richards.
At least, not with you in the room...
There's this girl, right? Katie.
I think she likes me. I mean, sometime she really acts like sh likes me! But when I asked her if she like me, she starts acting like she doesn't like me!
Women!
Query: Do you like her?
Ummm... I...
None of your business.
Of course not.
I just--I wish there was some way I could know what she was thinking.
It would make things so much easier if I could just read her mind and--
THAT'S IT!
I don't have to be a mind read to know where he's headed..

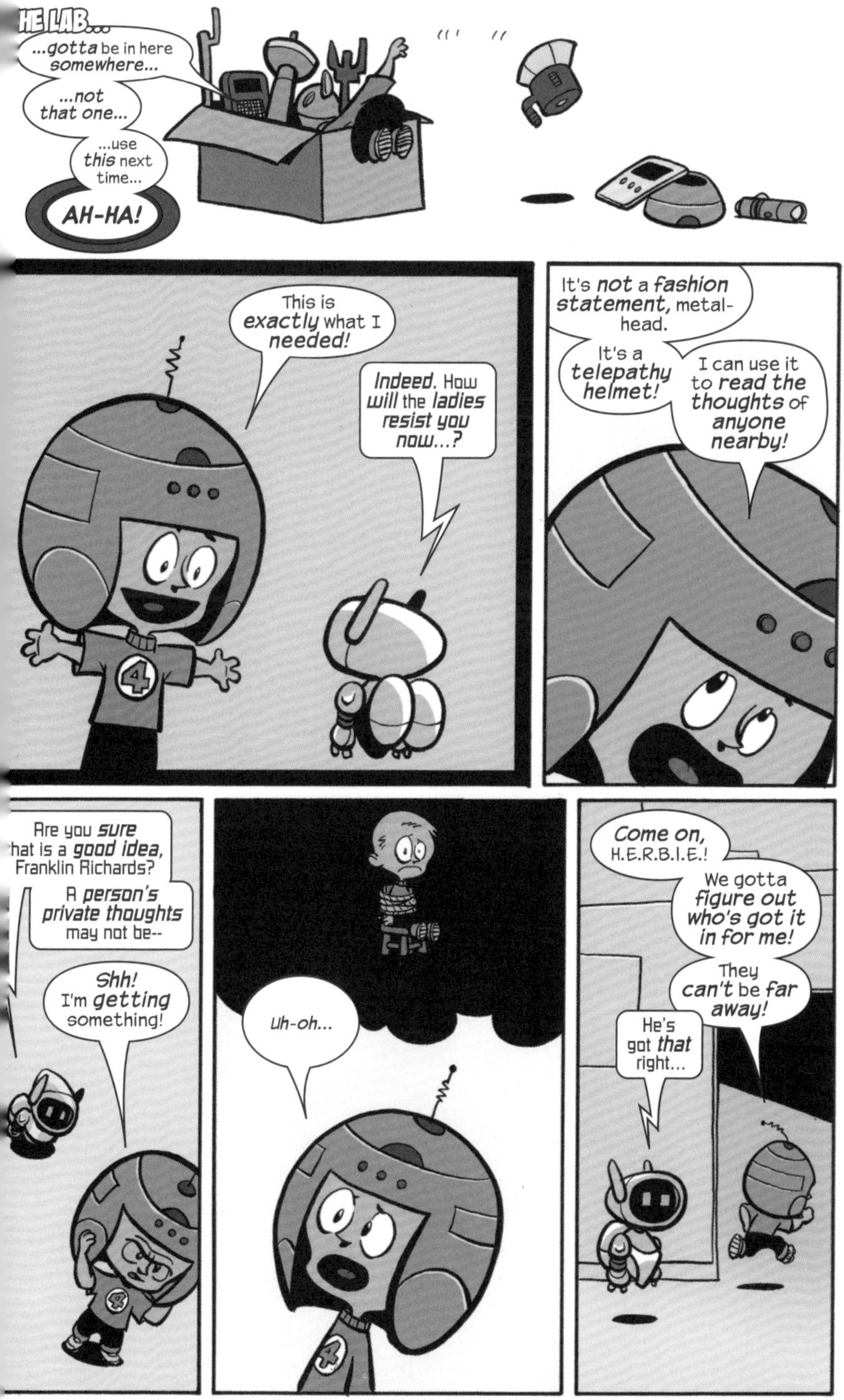
HE LAB...
...gotta be in here somewhere...
...not that one...
...use this next time...
AH-HA!
This is exactly what I needed!
Indeed. How will the ladies resist you now...?
It's not a fashion statement, metal-head.
It's a telepathy helmet!
I can use it to read the thoughts of anyone nearby!
Are you sure that is a good idea, Franklin Richards?
A person's private thoughts may not be--
Shh! I'm getting something!
Uh-oh...
Come on, H.E.R.B.I.E.!
We gotta figure out who's got it in for me!
They can't be far away!
He's got that right...

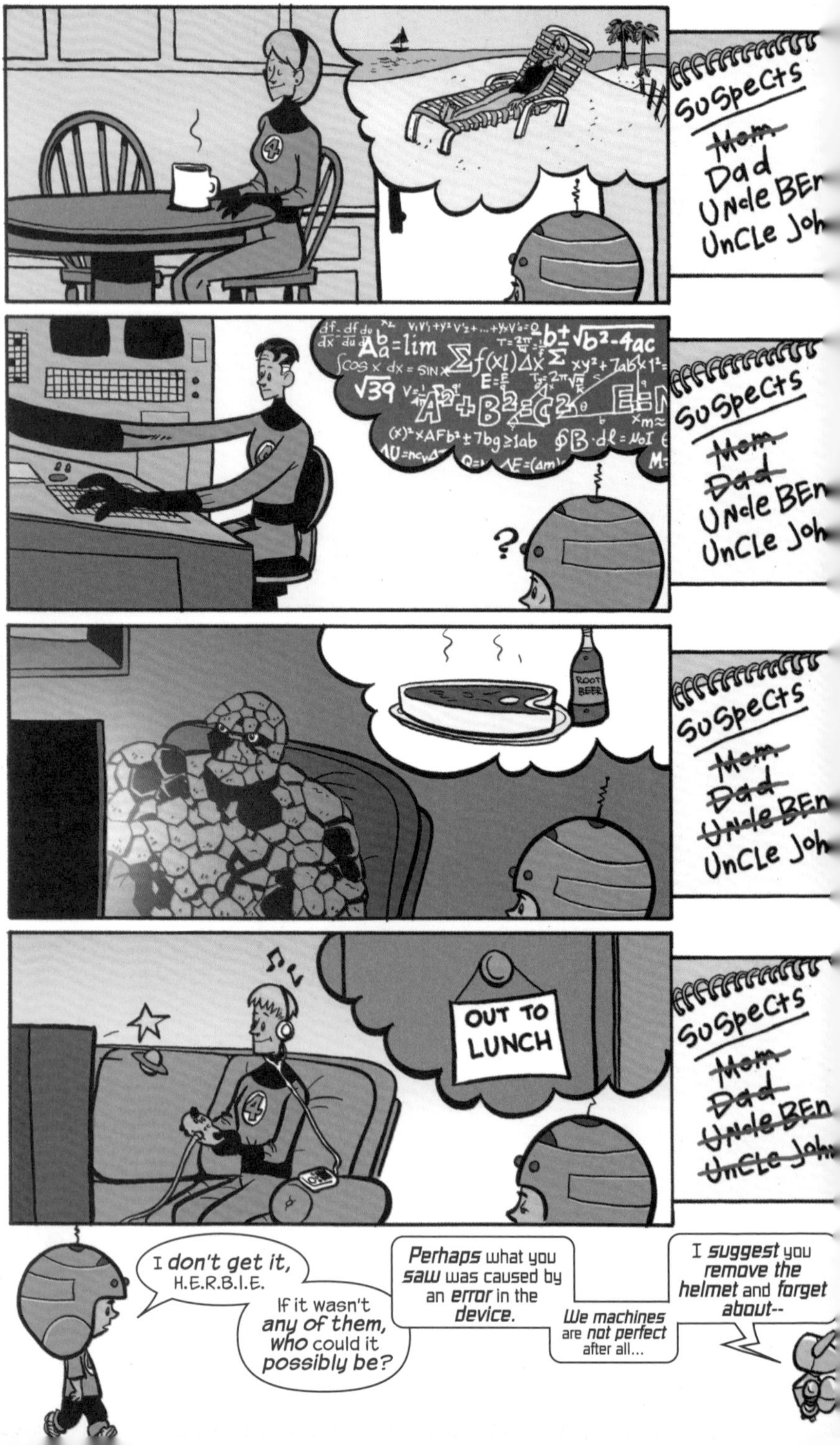

SuSpeCts
Mom
Dad
UNcle BEr
UnCLe Joh
?
SuSpeCts
Mom
Dad
UNcle BEn
UnCLe Joh
ROOT BEER
SuSpeCts
Mom
Dad
UNcle BEn
UnCLe Joh
OUT TO LUNCH
SuSpeCts
Mom
Dad
UNcle BEn
UnCLe Joh
I don't get it, H.E.R.B.I.E.
If it wasn't any of them, who could it possibly be?
Perhaps what you saw was caused by an error in the device.
We machines are not perfect after all...
I suggest you remove the helmet and forget about--

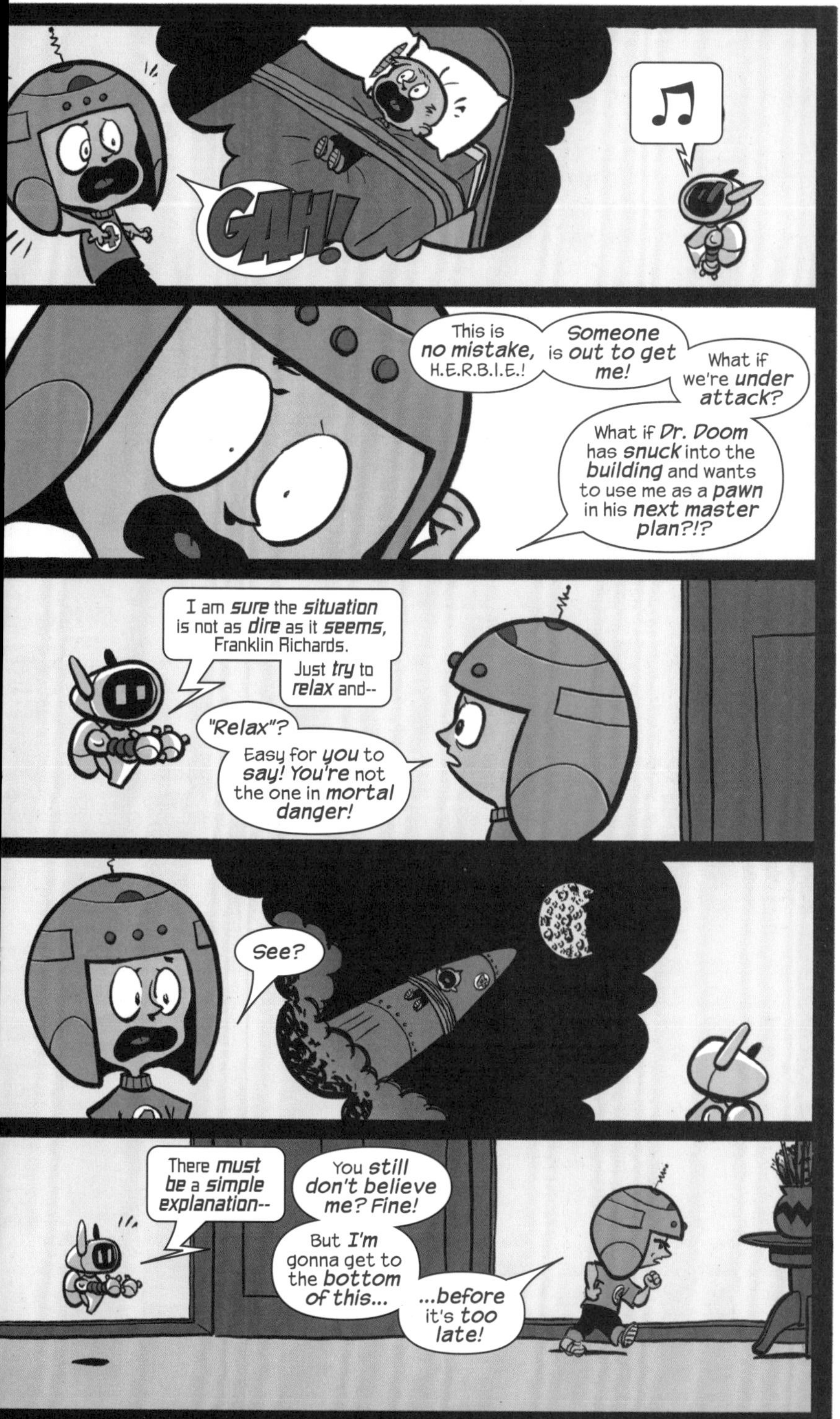
GAH!
This is no mistake, H.E.R.B.I.E.!
Someone is out to get me!
What if we're under attack?
What if Dr. Doom has snuck into the building and wants to use me as a pawn in his next master plan?!?
I am sure the situation is not as dire as it seems, Franklin Richards.
Just try to relax and--
"Relax"?
Easy for you to say! You're not the one in mortal danger!
See?
There must be a simple explanation--
You still don't believe me? Fine!
But I'm gonna get to the bottom of this...
...before it's too late!

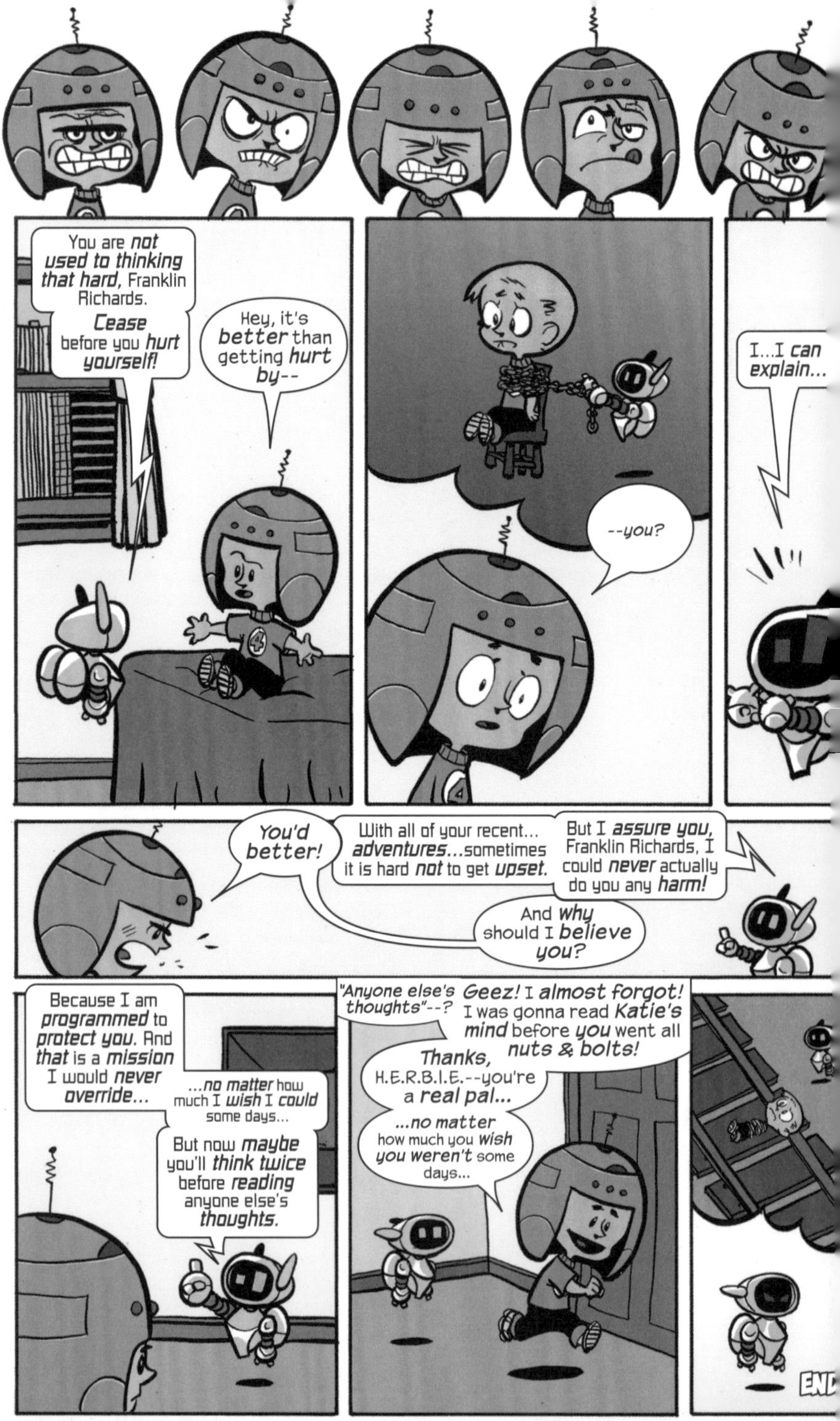

You are not used to thinking that hard, Franklin Richards.
Cease before you hurt yourself!
Hey, it's better than getting hurt by--
--you?
I...I can explain...
You'd better!
With all of your recent... adventures...sometimes it is hard not to get upset.
But I assure you, Franklin Richards, I could never actually do you any harm!
And why should I believe you?
Because I am programmed to protect you. And that is a mission I would never override...
...no matter how much I wish I could some days...
But now maybe you'll think twice before reading anyone else's thoughts.
"Anyone else's thoughts"--?
Geez! I almost forgot! I was gonna read Katie's mind before you went all nuts & bolts!
Thanks, H.E.R.B.I.E.--you're a real pal...
...no matter how much you wish you weren't some days...

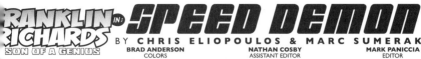

RANKLIN ICHARDS SON OF A GENIUS IN: SPEED DEMON

BY CHRIS ELIOPOULOS & MARC SUMERAK

BRAD ANDERSON COLORS · NATHAN COSBY ASSISTANT EDITOR · MARK PANICCIA EDITOR

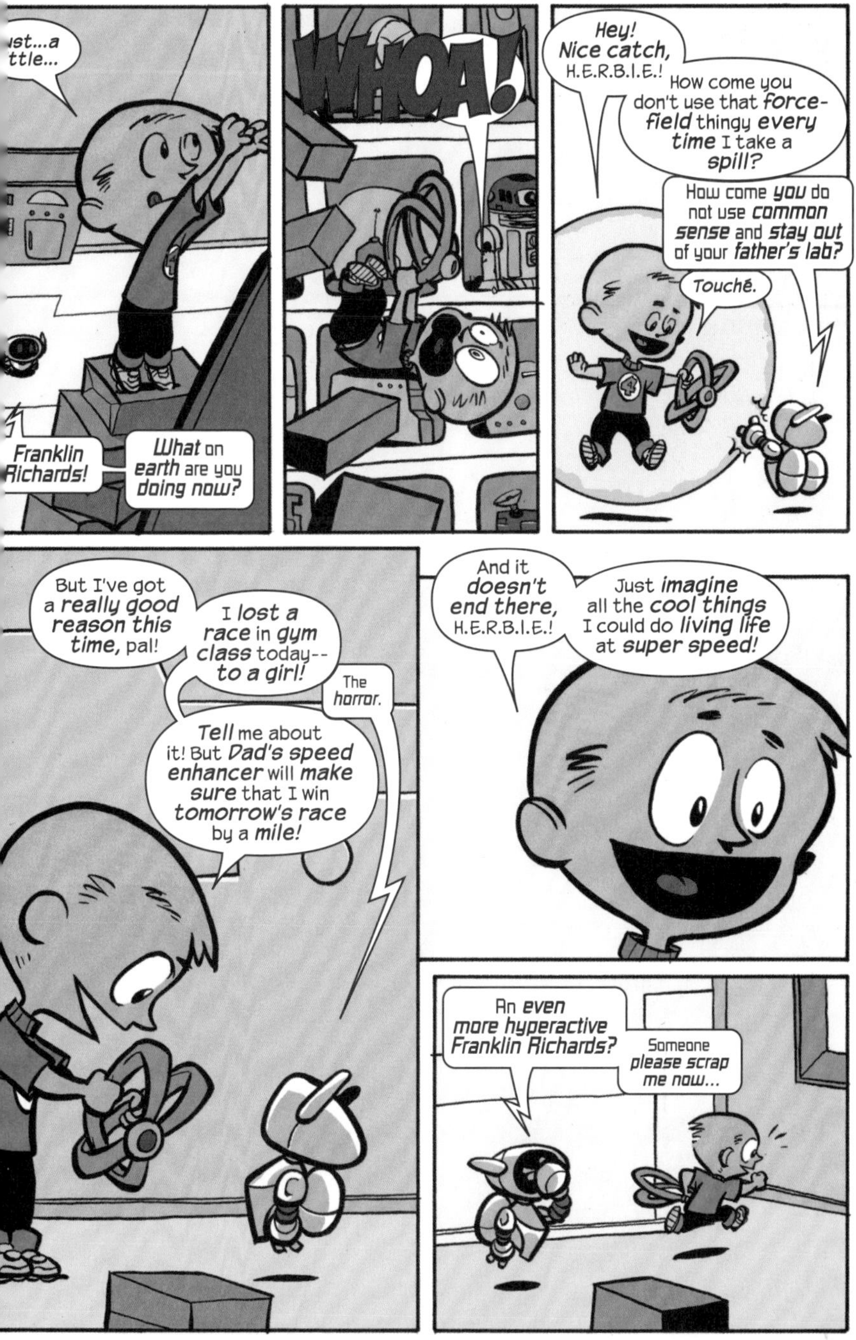
ıst...a
ttle...
Franklin
Richards!
What on
earth are you
doing now?
WHOA!
Hey!
Nice catch,
H.E.R.B.I.E.!
How come you
don't use that force-
field thingy every
time I take a
spill?
How come you do
not use common
sense and stay out
of your father's lab?
Touché.
But I've got
a really good
reason this
time, pal!
I lost a
race in gym
class today--
to a girl!
The
horror.
Tell me about
it! But Dad's speed
enhancer will make
sure that I win
tomorrow's race
by a mile!
And it
doesn't
end there,
H.E.R.B.I.E.!
Just imagine
all the cool things
I could do living life
at super speed!
An even
more hyperactive
Franklin Richards?
Someone
please scrap
me now...

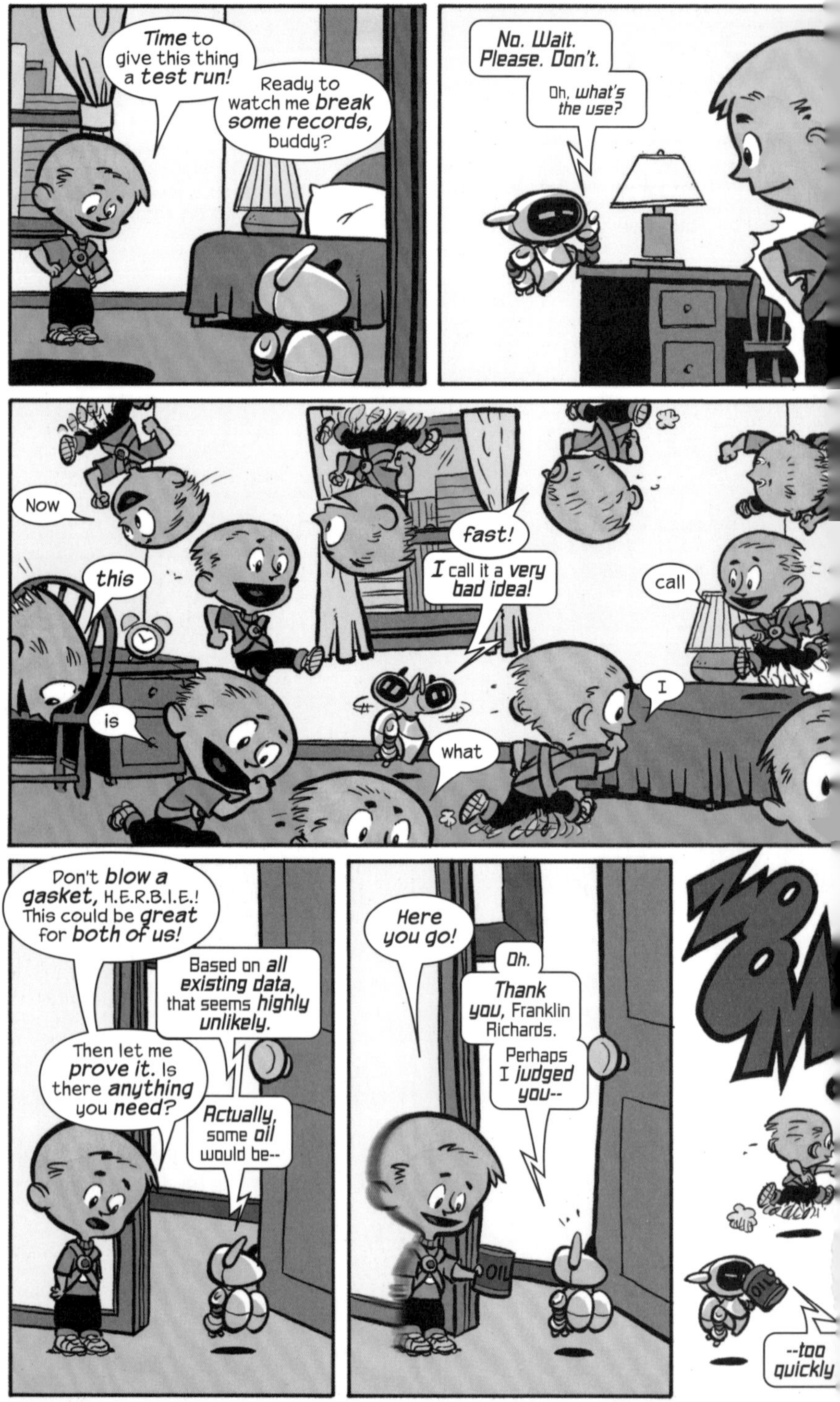
Time to give this thing a test run!
Ready to watch me break some records, buddy?
No. Wait. Please. Don't.
Oh, what's the use?
Now
this
is
what
I
call
fast!
I call it a very bad idea!
Don't blow a gasket, H.E.R.B.I.E.! This could be great for both of us!
Based on all existing data, that seems highly unlikely.
Then let me prove it. Is there anything you need?
Actually, some oil would be--
Here you go!
Oh.
Thank you, Franklin Richards.
Perhaps I judged you--
OIL
ZOOM
OIL
--too quickly

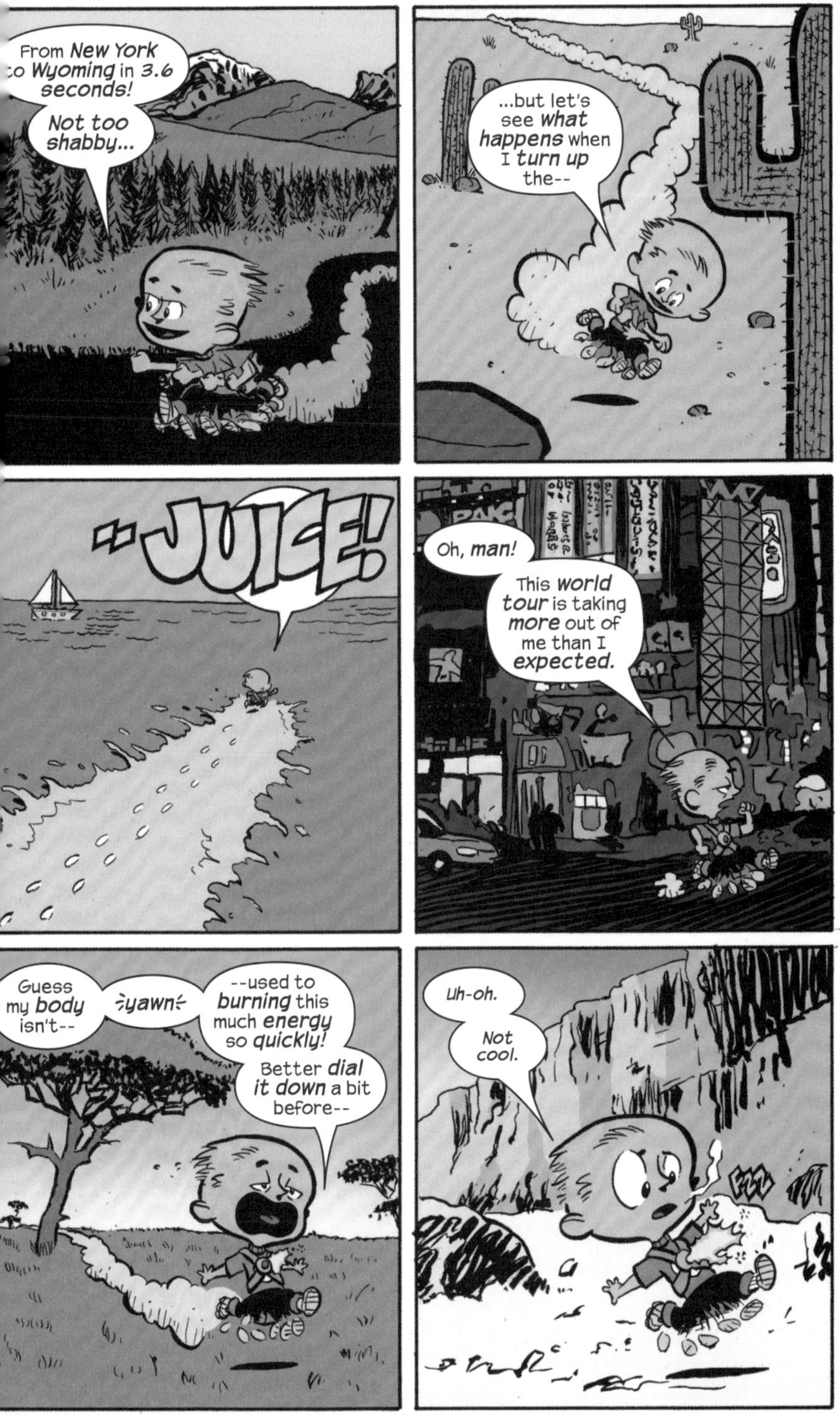

From New York to Wyoming in 3.6 seconds!
Not too shabby...
...but let's see what happens when I turn up the--
--JUICE!
Oh, man!
This world tour is taking more out of me than I expected.
Guess my body isn't--
yawn
--used to burning this much energy so quickly!
Better dial it down a bit before--
Uh-oh.
Not cool.

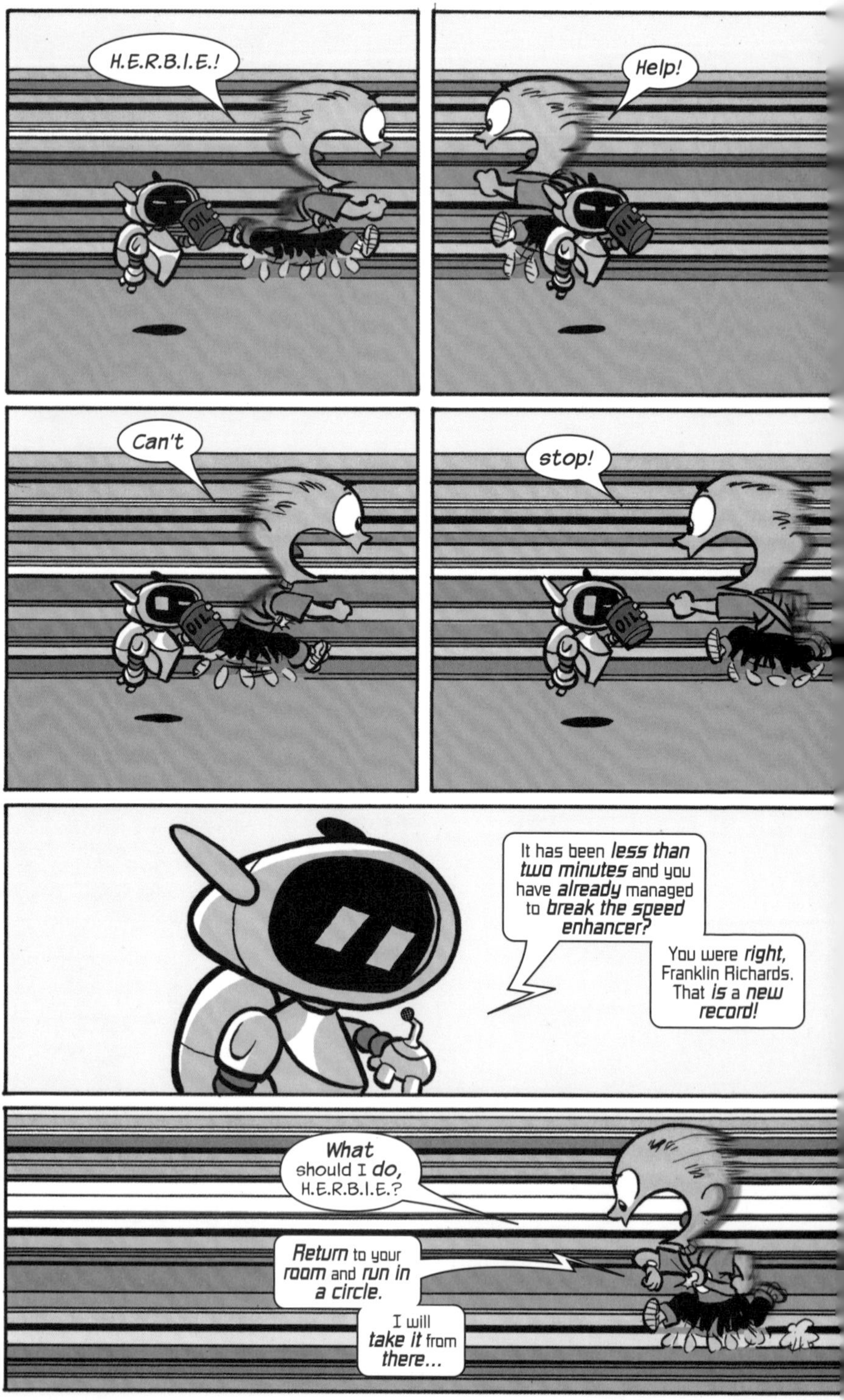
H.E.R.B.I.E.!
OIL
Help!
OIL
Can't
OIL
stop!
OIL
It has been less than two minutes and you have already managed to break the speed enhancer?
You were right, Franklin Richards. That is a new record!
What should I do, H.E.R.B.I.E.?
Return to your room and run in a circle.
I will take it from there...

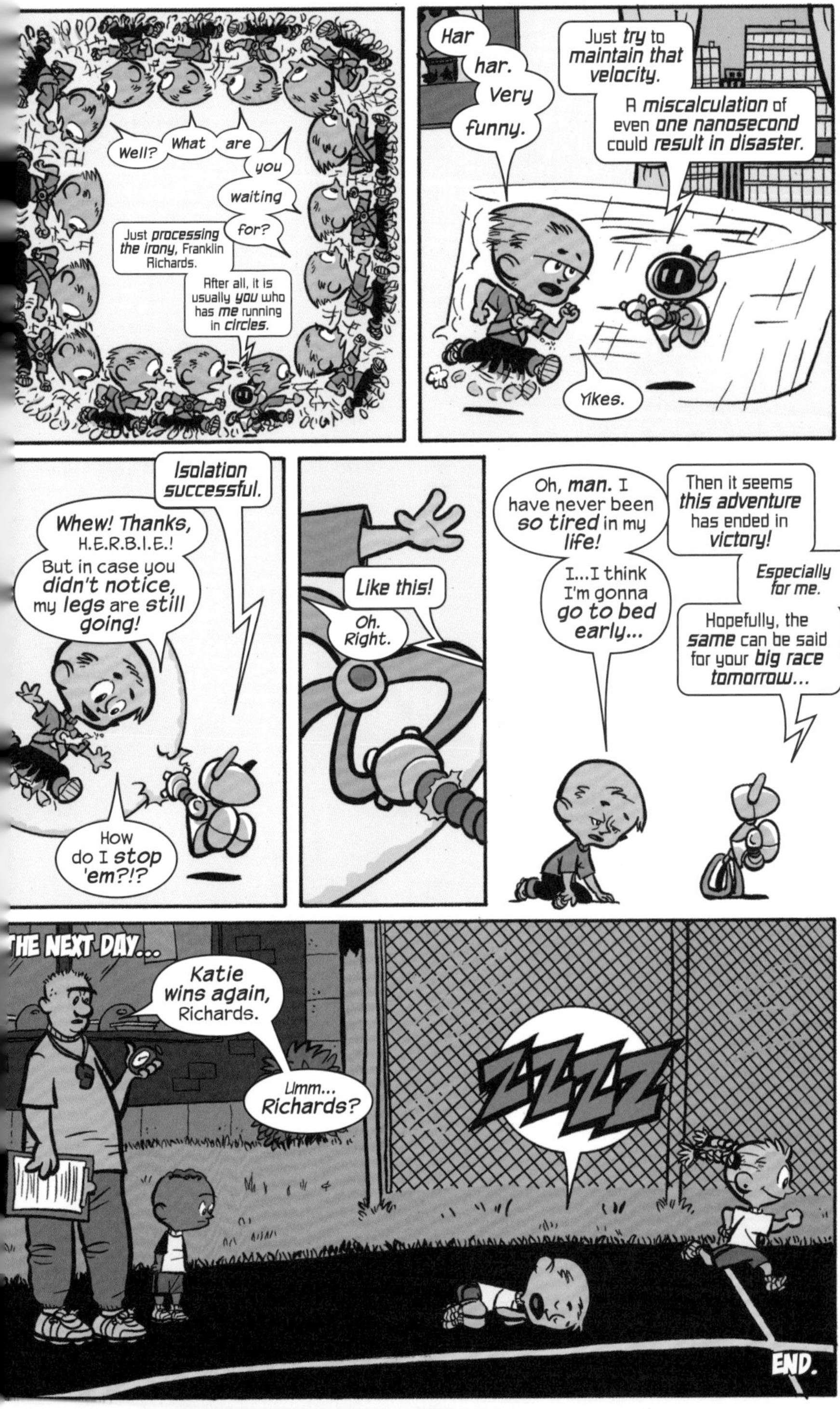

Well? What are you waiting for?
Just processing the irony, Franklin Richards.
After all, it is usually you who has me running in circles.
Har har. Very funny.
Just try to maintain that velocity.
A miscalculation of even one nanosecond could result in disaster.
Yikes.
Isolation successful.
Whew! Thanks, H.E.R.B.I.E.!
But in case you didn't notice, my legs are still going!
How do I stop 'em?!?
Like this!
Oh. Right.
Oh, man. I have never been so tired in my life!
I...I think I'm gonna go to bed early...
Then it seems this adventure has ended in victory!
Especially for me.
Hopefully, the same can be said for your big race tomorrow...
THE NEXT DAY...
Katie wins again, Richards.
Umm... Richards?
ZZZZ
END.

FRANKLIN RICHARDS SON OF A GENIUS IN: OCEAN-APE ESCAPE

BY CHRIS ELIOPOULOS & MARC SUMERA

BRAD ANDERSON COLORS
NATHAN COSBY ASSISTANT EDITOR
MARK PANICC EDITOR

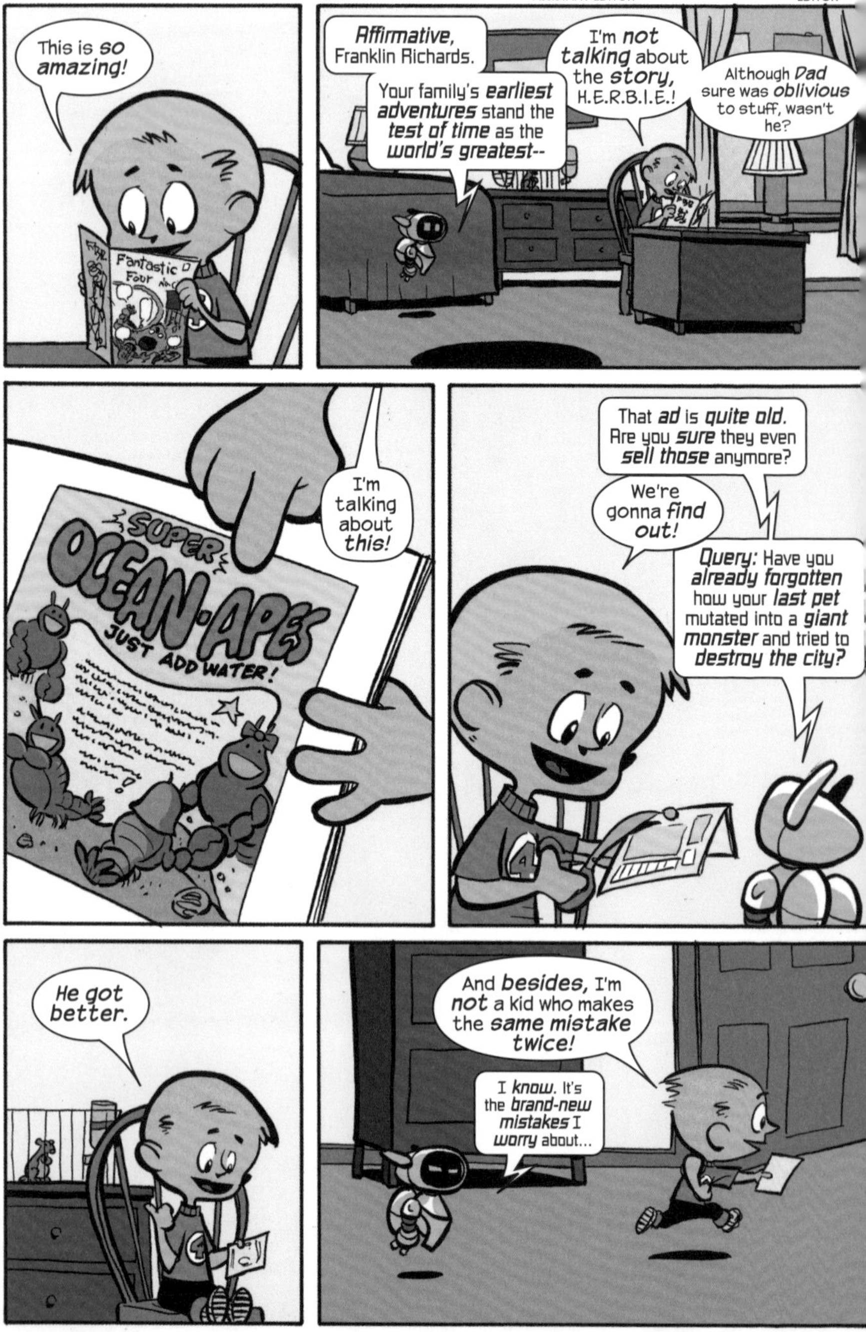

This is so amazing!
Fantastic Four
Affirmative, Franklin Richards.
Your family's earliest adventures stand the test of time as the world's greatest--
I'm not talking about the story, H.E.R.B.I.E.!
Although Dad sure was oblivious to stuff, wasn't he?
I'm talking about this!
SUPER OCEAN-APES JUST ADD WATER!
That ad is quite old. Are you sure they even sell those anymore?
We're gonna find out!
Query: Have you already forgotten how your last pet mutated into a giant monster and tried to destroy the city?
He got better.
And besides, I'm not a kid who makes the same mistake twice!
I know. It's the brand-new mistakes I worry about...

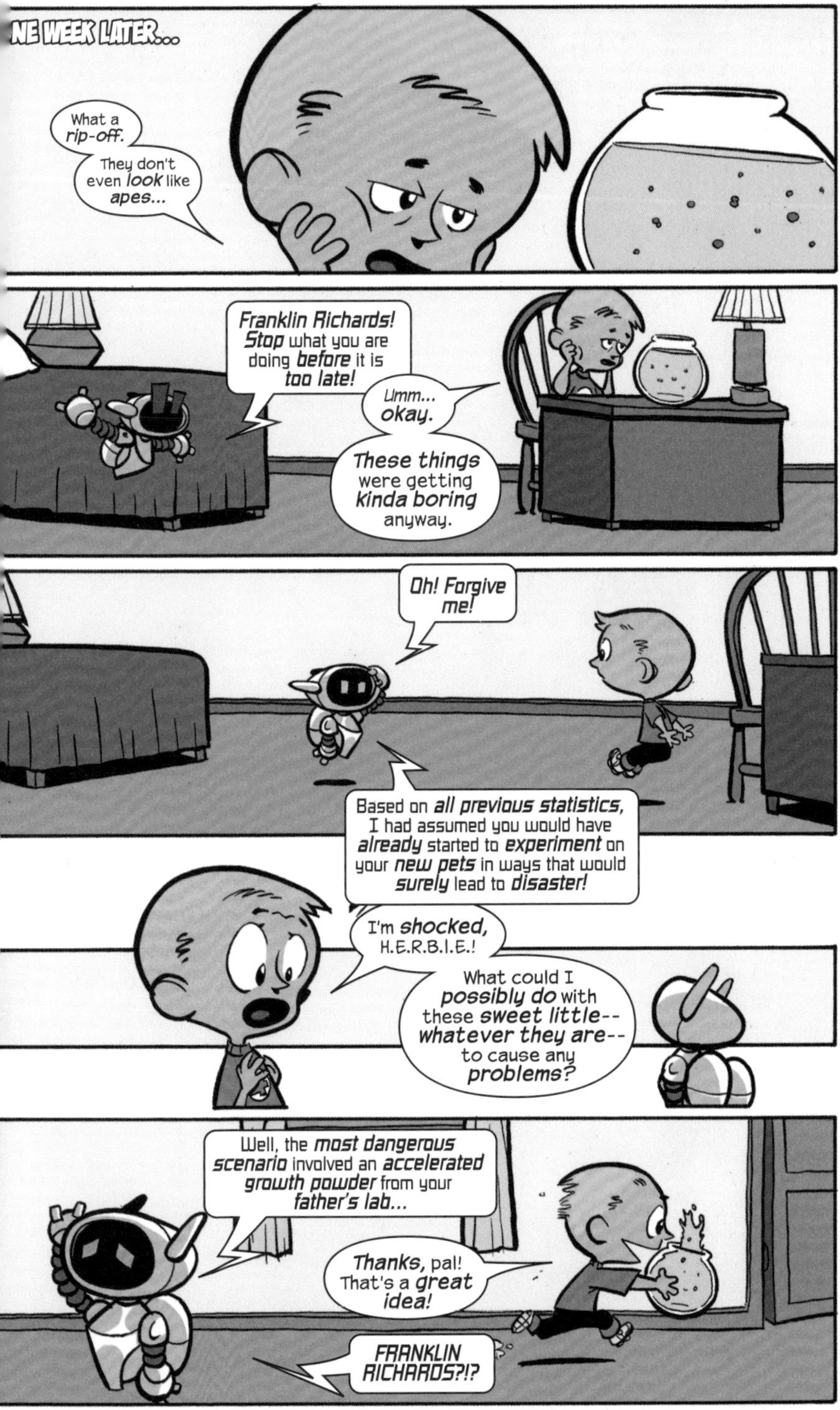
NE WEEK LATER...
What a rip-off.
They don't even look like apes...
Franklin Richards! Stop what you are doing before it is too late!
Umm... okay.
These things were getting kinda boring anyway.
Oh! Forgive me!
Based on all previous statistics, I had assumed you would have already started to experiment on your new pets in ways that would surely lead to disaster!
I'm shocked, H.E.R.B.I.E.!
What could I possibly do with these sweet little-- whatever they are-- to cause any problems?
Well, the most dangerous scenario involved an accelerated growth powder from your father's lab...
Thanks, pal! That's a great idea!
FRANKLIN RICHARDS?!?

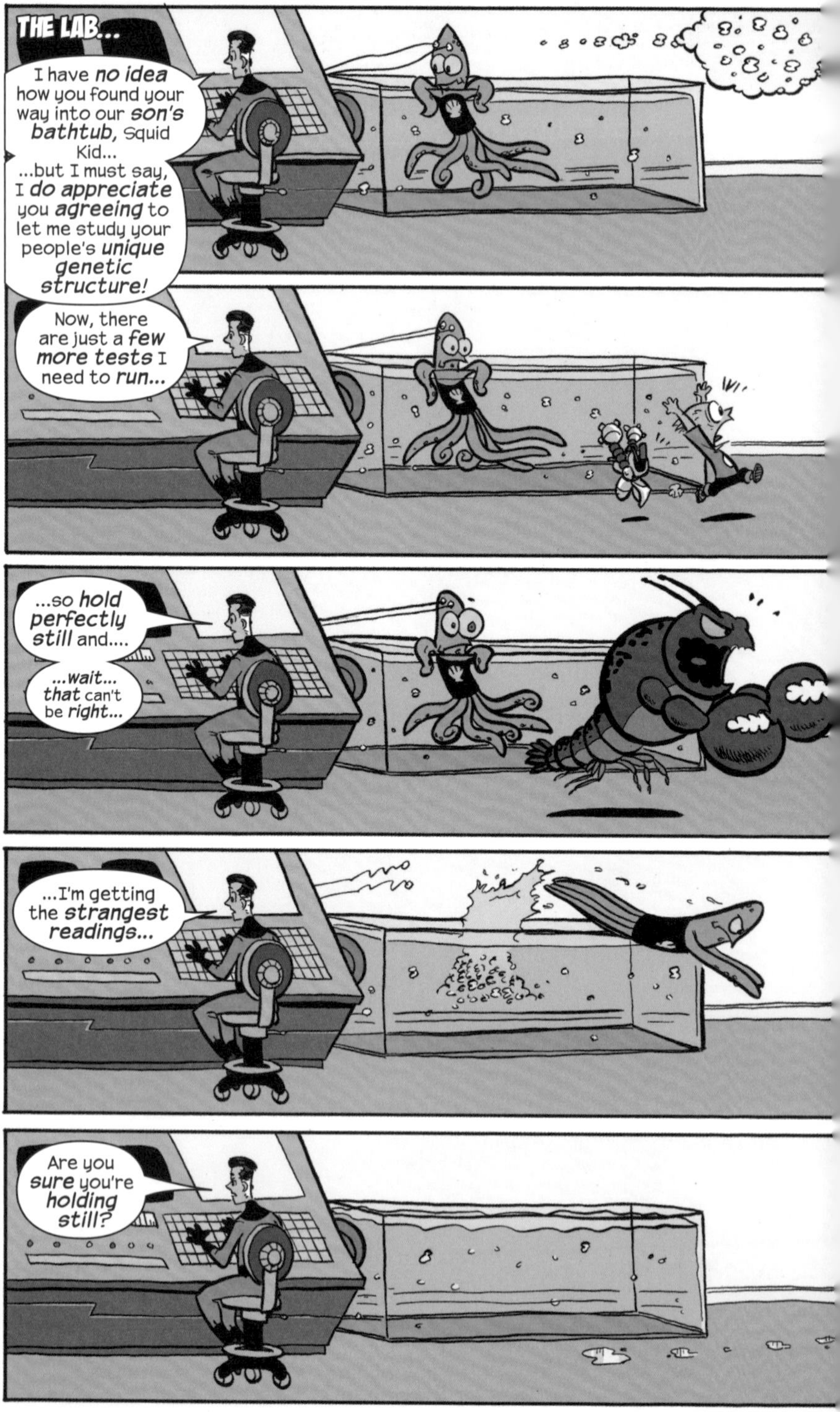
THE LAB...
I have no idea how you found your way into our son's bathtub, Squid Kid...
...but I must say, I do appreciate you agreeing to let me study your people's unique genetic structure!
Now, there are just a few more tests I need to run...
...so hold perfectly still and....
...wait... that can't be right...
...I'm getting the strangest readings...
Are you sure you're holding still?

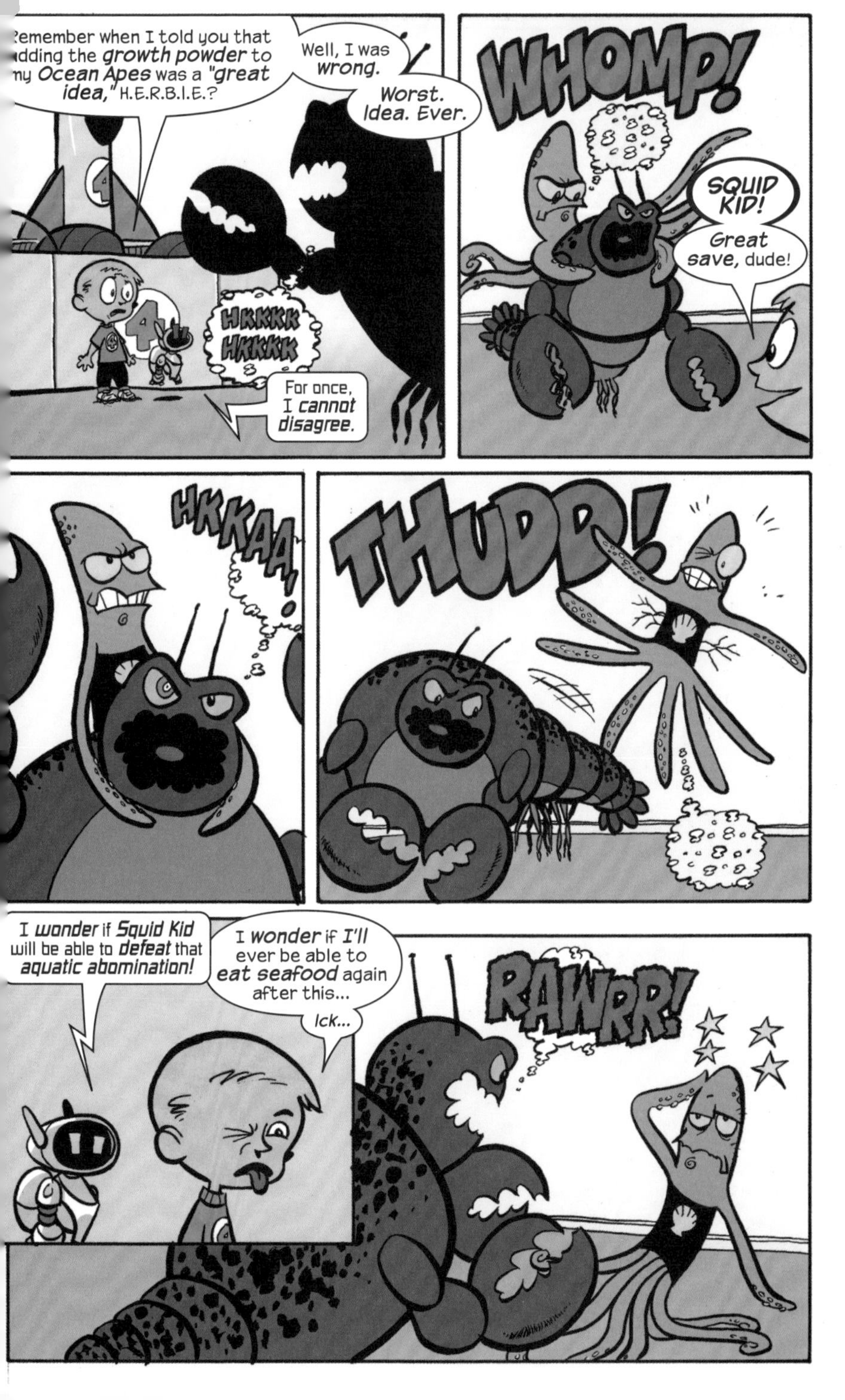

Remember when I told you that adding the growth powder to my Ocean Apes was a "great idea," H.E.R.B.I.E.?
Well, I was wrong.
Worst. Idea. Ever.
HKKKK HKKKK
For once, I cannot disagree.
WHOMP!
SQUID KID!
Great save, dude!
HKKAA!
THUDD!
I wonder if Squid Kid will be able to defeat that aquatic abomination!
I wonder if I'll ever be able to eat seafood again after this...
Ick...
RAWRR!

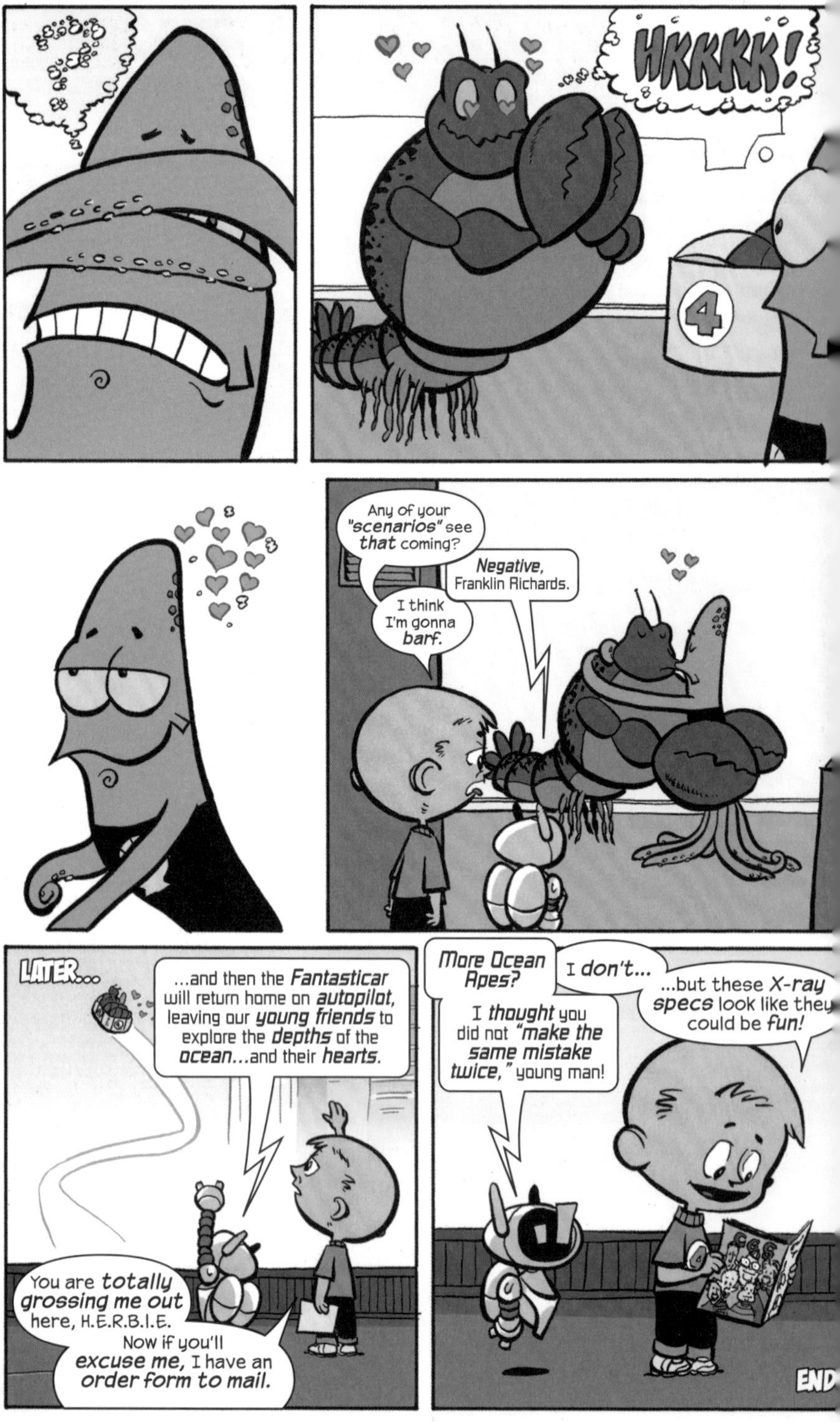
HKKKK!
Any of your "scenarios" see that coming?
I think I'm gonna barf.
Negative, Franklin Richards.
LATER...
...and then the Fantasticar will return home on autopilot, leaving our young friends to explore the depths of the ocean...and their hearts.
You are totally grossing me out here, H.E.R.B.I.E.
Now if you'll excuse me, I have an order form to mail.
More Ocean Apes?
I don't...
I thought you did not "make the same mistake twice," young man!
...but these X-ray specs look like they could be fun!
END

FRANKLIN RICHARDS SON OF A GENIUS IN: TURKEY TROUBLE!

BY CHRIS ELIOPOULOS & MARC SUMERAK
BRAD ANDERSON COLORS
NATHAN COSBY ASSISTANT EDITOR
MARK PANICCIA EDITOR

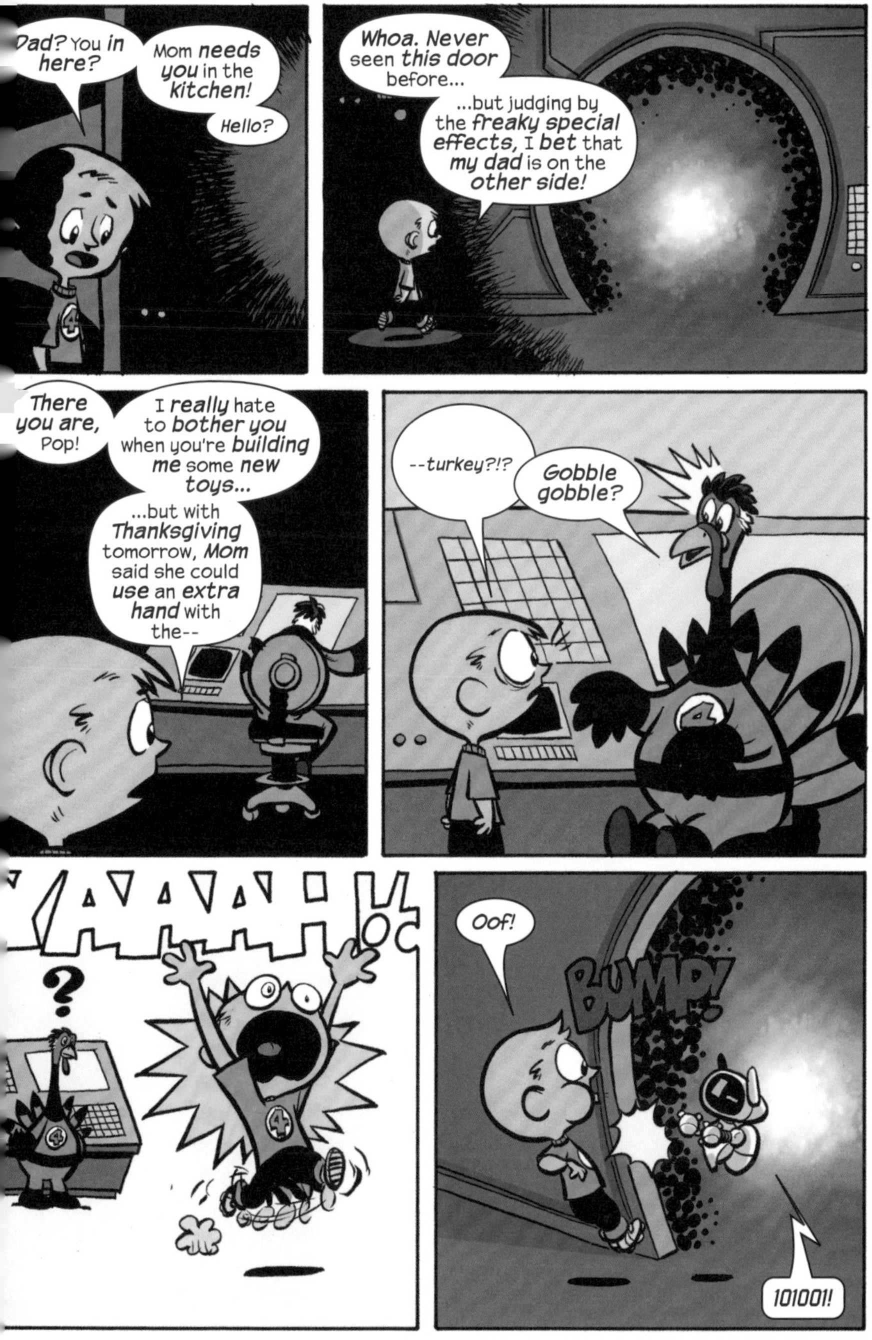

Dad? You in here?
Mom needs you in the kitchen!
Hello?
Whoa. Never seen this door before...
...but judging by the freaky special effects, I bet that my dad is on the other side!
There you are, Pop!
I really hate to bother you when you're building me some new toys...
...but with Thanksgiving tomorrow, Mom said she could use an extra hand with the--
--turkey?!?
Gobble gobble?
?
Oof!
BUMP!
101001!

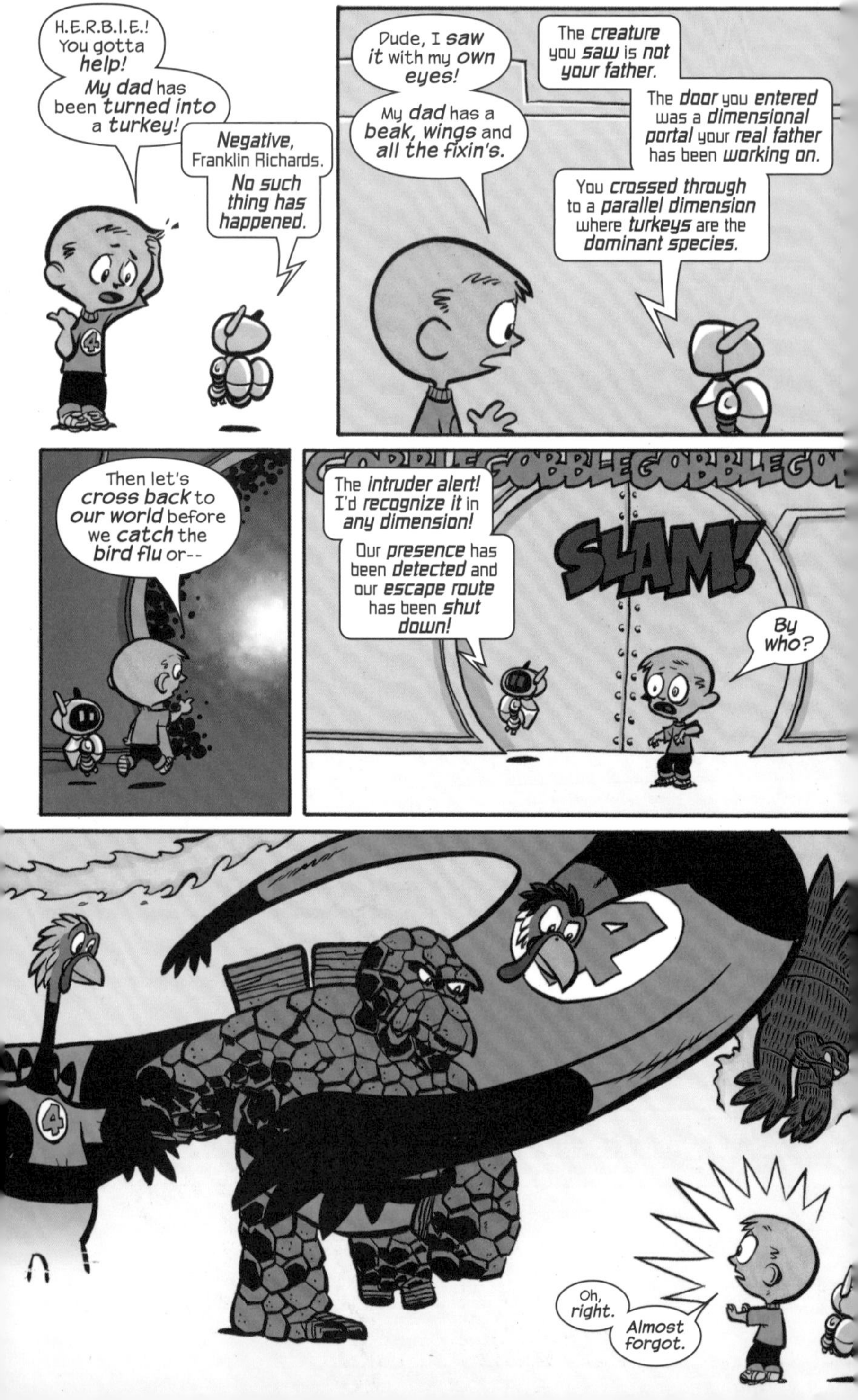
H.E.R.B.I.E.! You gotta help!
My dad has been turned into a turkey!
Negative, Franklin Richards.
No such thing has happened.
Dude, I saw it with my own eyes!
My dad has a beak, wings and all the fixin's.
The creature you saw is not your father.
The door you entered was a dimensional portal your real father has been working on.
You crossed through to a parallel dimension where turkeys are the dominant species.
Then let's cross back to our world before we catch the bird flu or--
The intruder alert! I'd recognize it in any dimension!
Our presence has been detected and our escape route has been shut down!
SLAM!
By who?
Oh, right.
Almost forgot.

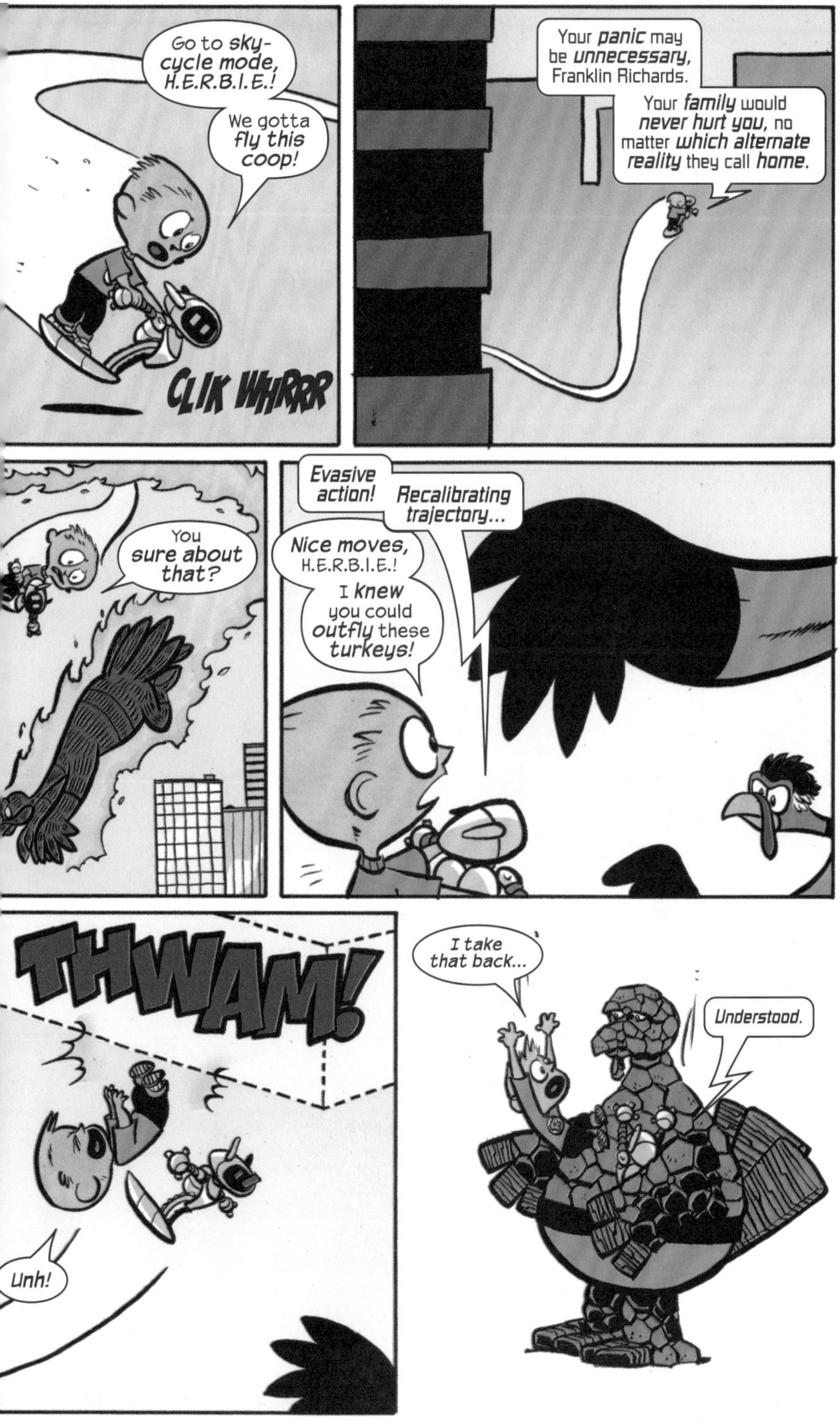
Go to sky-cycle mode, H.E.R.B.I.E.!
We gotta fly this coop!
CLIK WHRRR
Your panic may be unnecessary, Franklin Richards.
Your family would never hurt you, no matter which alternate reality they call home.
You sure about that?
Evasive action!
Recalibrating trajectory...
Nice moves, H.E.R.B.I.E.!
I knew you could outfly these turkeys!
THWAM!
Unh!
I take that back...
Understood.

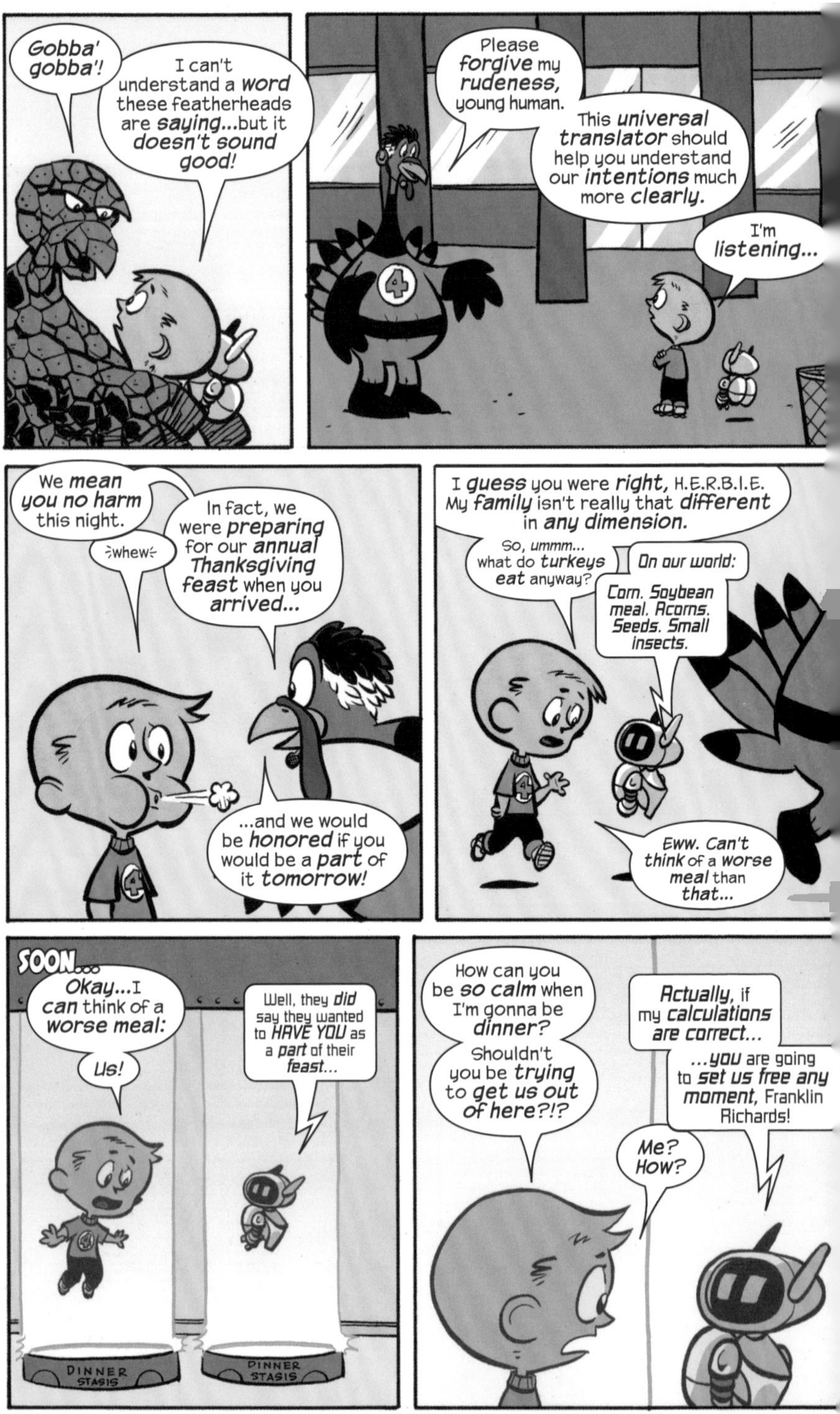
Gobba' gobba'!
I can't understand a word these featherheads are saying...but it doesn't sound good!
Please forgive my rudeness, young human.
This universal translator should help you understand our intentions much more clearly.
I'm listening...
We mean you no harm this night.
whew
In fact, we were preparing for our annual Thanksgiving feast when you arrived...
...and we would be honored if you would be a part of it tomorrow!
I guess you were right, H.E.R.B.I.E. My family isn't really that different in any dimension.
So, ummm... what do turkeys eat anyway?
On our world:
Corn. Soybean meal. Acorns. Seeds. Small insects.
Eww. Can't think of a worse meal than that...
SOON...
Okay...I can think of a worse meal:
Us!
Well, they did say they wanted to HAVE YOU as a part of their feast...
DINNER STASIS
DINNER STASIS
How can you be so calm when I'm gonna be dinner?
Shouldn't you be trying to get us out of here?!?
Actually, if my calculations are correct...
...you are going to set us free any moment, Franklin Richards!
Me? How?

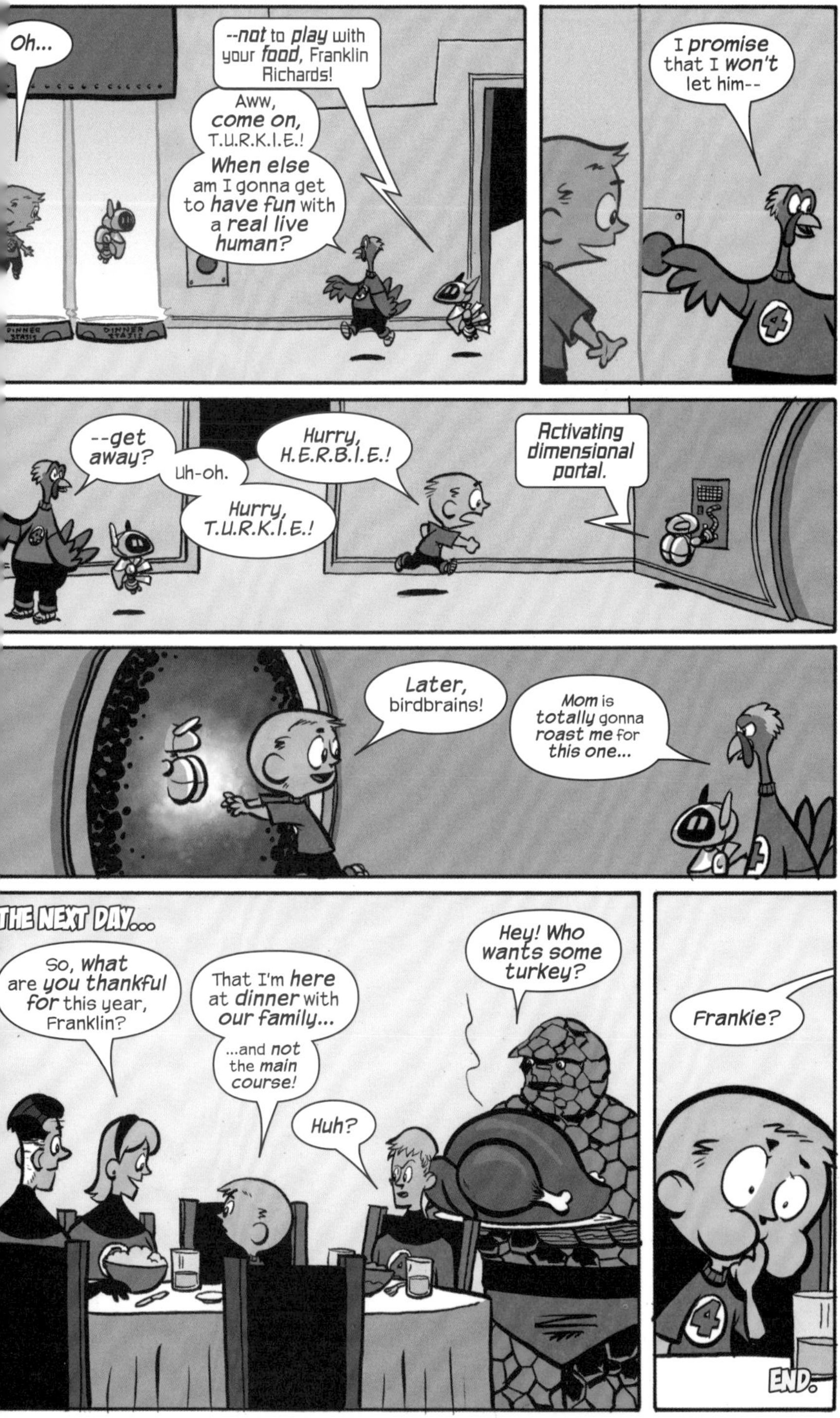
Oh...
--not to play with your food, Franklin Richards!
Aww, come on, T.U.R.K.I.E.!
When else am I gonna get to have fun with a real live human?
DINNER STASIS
DINNER STASIS
I promise that I won't let him--
--get away?
Uh-oh.
Hurry, H.E.R.B.I.E.!
Hurry, T.U.R.K.I.E.!
Activating dimensional portal.
Later, birdbrains!
Mom is totally gonna roast me for this one...
THE NEXT DAY...
So, what are you thankful for this year, Franklin?
That I'm here at dinner with our family...
...and not the main course!
Huh?
Hey! Who wants some turkey?
Frankie?
END.

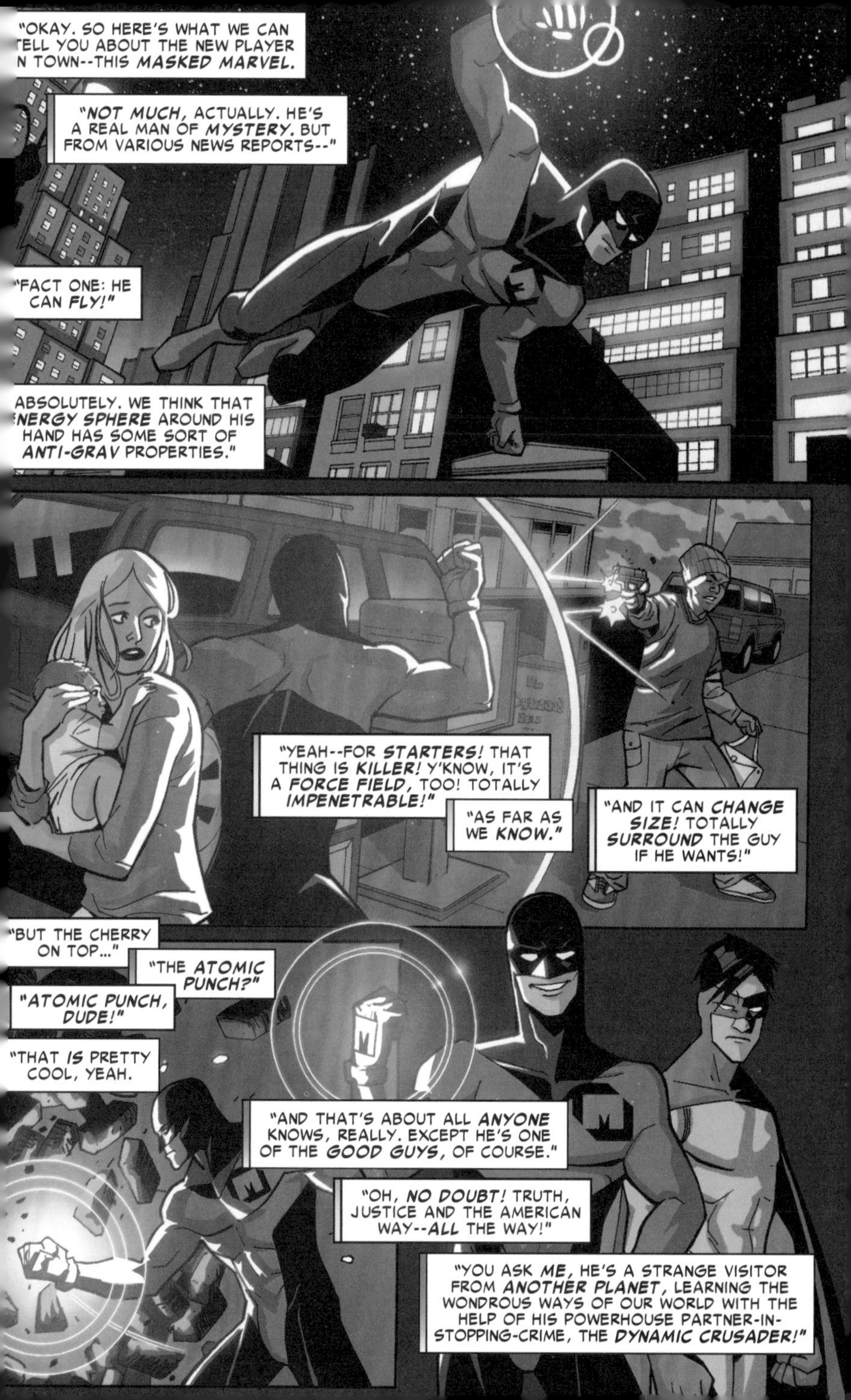
"OKAY. SO HERE'S WHAT WE CAN
TELL YOU ABOUT THE NEW PLAYER
IN TOWN--THIS MASKED MARVEL.
"NOT MUCH, ACTUALLY. HE'S A REAL MAN OF MYSTERY. BUT FROM VARIOUS NEWS REPORTS--"
"FACT ONE: HE CAN FLY!"
"ABSOLUTELY. WE THINK THAT ENERGY SPHERE AROUND HIS HAND HAS SOME SORT OF ANTI-GRAV PROPERTIES."
"YEAH--FOR STARTERS! THAT THING IS KILLER! Y'KNOW, IT'S A FORCE FIELD, TOO! TOTALLY IMPENETRABLE!"
"AS FAR AS WE KNOW."
"AND IT CAN CHANGE SIZE! TOTALLY SURROUND THE GUY IF HE WANTS!"
"BUT THE CHERRY ON TOP..."
"THE ATOMIC PUNCH?"
"ATOMIC PUNCH, DUDE!"
"THAT IS PRETTY COOL, YEAH.
"AND THAT'S ABOUT ALL ANYONE KNOWS, REALLY. EXCEPT HE'S ONE OF THE GOOD GUYS, OF COURSE."
"OH, NO DOUBT! TRUTH, JUSTICE AND THE AMERICAN WAY--ALL THE WAY!"
"YOU ASK ME, HE'S A STRANGE VISITOR FROM ANOTHER PLANET, LEARNING THE WONDROUS WAYS OF OUR WORLD WITH THE HELP OF HIS POWERHOUSE PARTNER-IN-STOPPING-CRIME, THE DYNAMIC CRUSADER!"

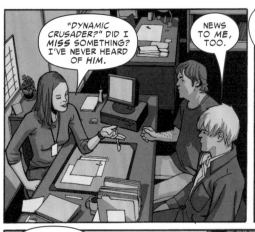

"DYNAMIC CRUSADER?" DID I *MISS* SOMETHING? I'VE NEVER HEARD OF HIM.

NEWS TO ME, TOO.

SEE, MS. BOOSE, I WAS THINKING MAYBE A *POWER MAN/IRON FIST* PARTNER-THING, Y'KNOW? ONE'S FRO *ANOTHER WORLD*, ONE'S FROM THE *STREET*...

ONE *DOESN'T* EXIST...

ADAM'S GOT A *POINT.* YOUR ENTHUSIASM'S *ADMIRABLE,* EDDIE...

...BUT HERE AT MARVEL, WE PUBLISH COMICS BASED ON *REAL* SUPER HEROES— SPIDER-MAN, FANTASTIC FOUR, X-MEN...

WE TAKE CERTAIN... *LIBERTIES* BY HIRING TALENT TO FILL IN WHAT WE *DON'T* KNOW ABOUT THEM, BUT THERE NEEDS TO BE A *VENEER* OF REALITY.

DO ANYTHING TOO *OBVIOUSLY* FALSE AND IT SHATTERS THE READER'S SUSPENSION OF *DISBELIEF.* LIKE IF, SAY, DAREDEVIL BECAME *MAYOR* OF NEW YORK CITY...

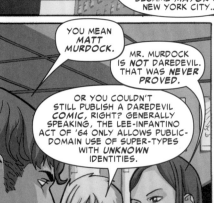

YOU MEAN *MATT MURDOCK.*

MR. MURDOCK IS *NOT* DAREDEVIL. THAT WAS *NEVER PROVED.*

OR YOU COULDN'T STILL PUBLISH A DAREDEVIL *COMIC,* RIGHT? GENERALLY SPEAKING, THE LEE-INFANTINO ACT OF '64 ONLY ALLOWS PUBLIC-DOMAIN USE OF SUPER-TYPES WITH *UNKNOWN* IDENTITIES.

LIKE THE *MASKED MARVEL,* YES. LOOK, HE'S GETTING GOOD *PRESS,* MARVEL'S INTERESTED IN DOING A BOOK, AND YOU TWO HAVE DONE *GREAT* FILL-IN WORK, SO...

NICOLE'S *RIGHT,* EDDIE. THIS IS OUR *BIG CHANCE.* WE *ASKED* HER TO LET US PITCH THIS COMIC-- LET'S NOT THROW A *CURVEBALL* LIKE SADDLING OUR HERO WITH A *SIDEKICK.*

PARTNER, NOT SIDEKICK.

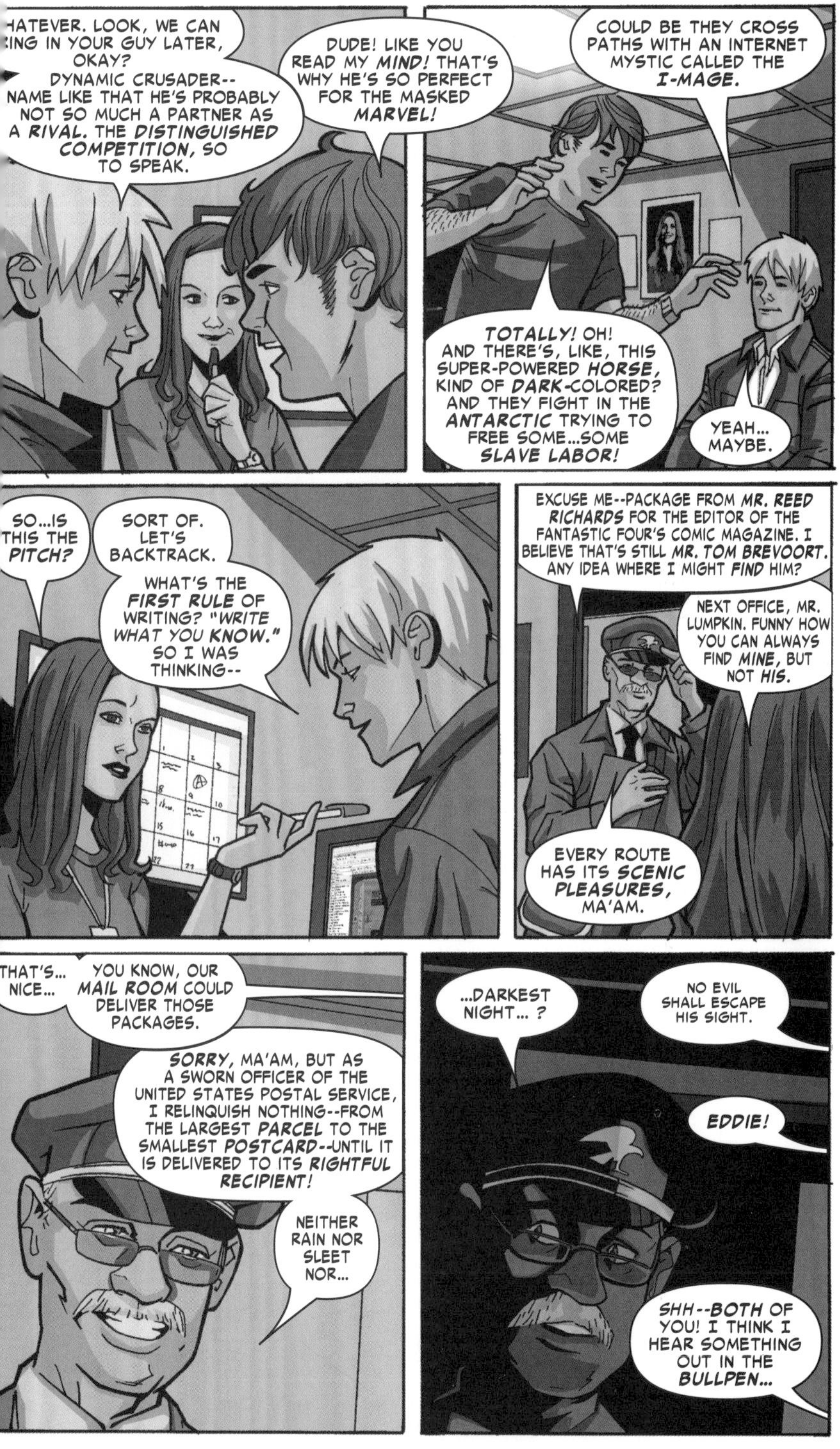
HATEVER. LOOK, WE CAN
ING IN YOUR GUY LATER, OKAY?
DYNAMIC CRUSADER-- NAME LIKE THAT HE'S PROBABLY NOT SO MUCH A PARTNER AS A RIVAL. THE DISTINGUISHED COMPETITION, SO TO SPEAK.
DUDE! LIKE YOU READ MY MIND! THAT'S WHY HE'S SO PERFECT FOR THE MASKED MARVEL!
COULD BE THEY CROSS PATHS WITH AN INTERNET MYSTIC CALLED THE I-MAGE.
TOTALLY! OH! AND THERE'S, LIKE, THIS SUPER-POWERED HORSE, KIND OF DARK-COLORED? AND THEY FIGHT IN THE ANTARCTIC TRYING TO FREE SOME...SOME SLAVE LABOR!
YEAH... MAYBE.
SO...IS THIS THE PITCH?
SORT OF. LET'S BACKTRACK.
WHAT'S THE FIRST RULE OF WRITING? "WRITE WHAT YOU KNOW." SO I WAS THINKING--
EXCUSE ME--PACKAGE FROM MR. REED RICHARDS FOR THE EDITOR OF THE FANTASTIC FOUR'S COMIC MAGAZINE. I BELIEVE THAT'S STILL MR. TOM BREVOORT. ANY IDEA WHERE I MIGHT FIND HIM?
NEXT OFFICE, MR. LUMPKIN. FUNNY HOW YOU CAN ALWAYS FIND MINE, BUT NOT HIS.
EVERY ROUTE HAS ITS SCENIC PLEASURES, MA'AM.
THAT'S... NICE...
YOU KNOW, OUR MAIL ROOM COULD DELIVER THOSE PACKAGES.
SORRY, MA'AM, BUT AS A SWORN OFFICER OF THE UNITED STATES POSTAL SERVICE, I RELINQUISH NOTHING--FROM THE LARGEST PARCEL TO THE SMALLEST POSTCARD--UNTIL IT IS DELIVERED TO ITS RIGHTFUL RECIPIENT!
NEITHER RAIN NOR SLEET NOR...
...DARKEST NIGHT... ?
NO EVIL SHALL ESCAPE HIS SIGHT.
EDDIE!
SHH--BOTH OF YOU! I THINK I HEAR SOMETHING OUT IN THE BULLPEN...

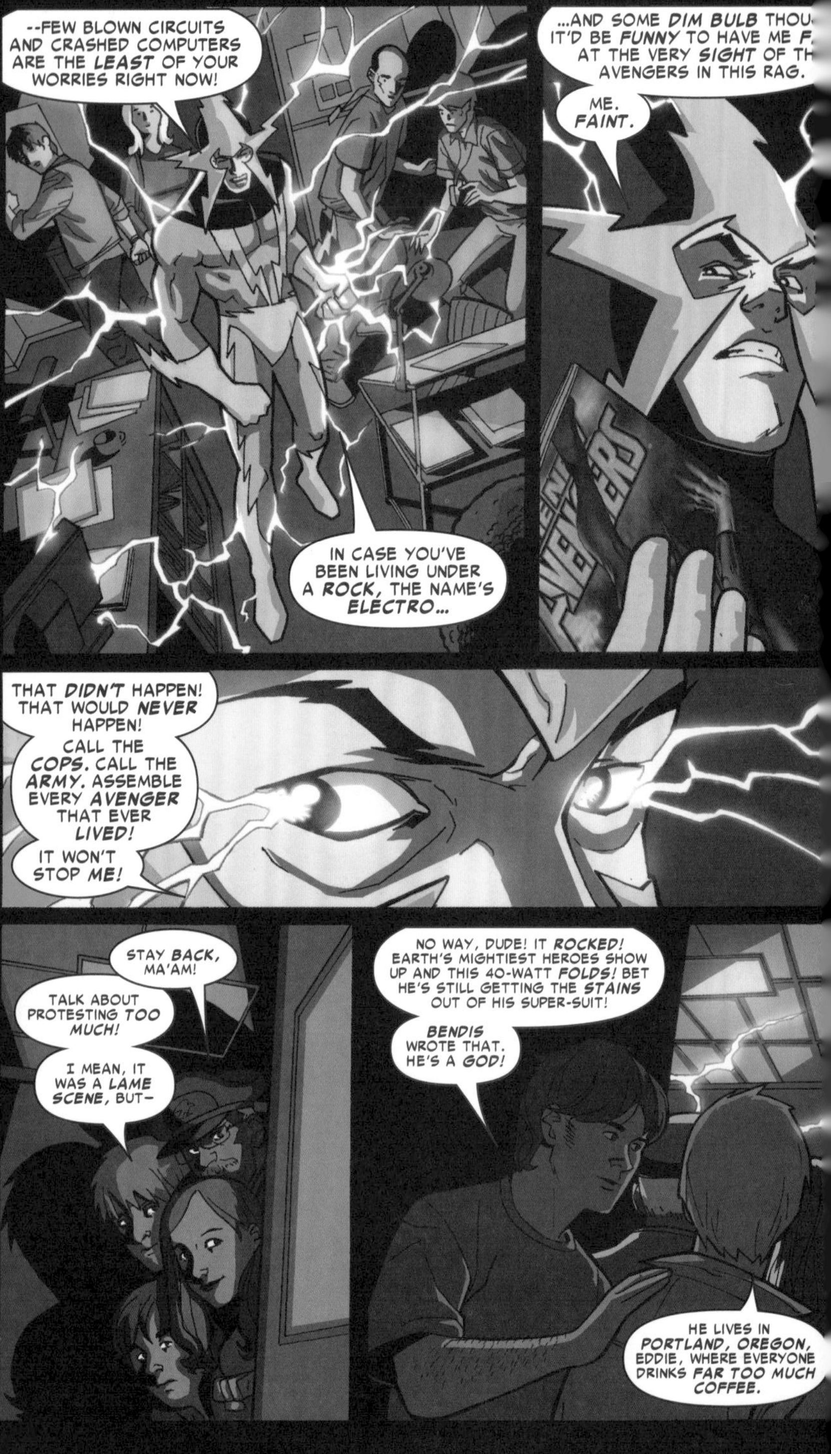
--FEW BLOWN CIRCUITS AND CRASHED COMPUTERS ARE THE *LEAST* OF YOUR WORRIES RIGHT NOW!
IN CASE YOU'VE BEEN LIVING UNDER A *ROCK*, THE NAME'S *ELECTRO*...
...AND SOME *DIM BULB* THOU IT'D BE *FUNNY* TO HAVE ME *F* AT THE VERY *SIGHT* OF TH AVENGERS IN THIS RAG.
ME. *FAINT*.
THAT *DIDN'T* HAPPEN! THAT WOULD *NEVER* HAPPEN!
CALL THE *COPS*. CALL THE *ARMY*. ASSEMBLE EVERY *AVENGER* THAT EVER *LIVED!*
IT WON'T STOP *ME!*
STAY *BACK*, MA'AM!
TALK ABOUT PROTESTING *TOO MUCH!*
I MEAN, IT WAS A *LAME SCENE*, BUT–
NO WAY, DUDE! IT *ROCKED!* EARTH'S MIGHTIEST HEROES SHOW UP AND THIS 40-WATT *FOLDS!* BET HE'S STILL GETTING THE *STAINS* OUT OF HIS SUPER-SUIT!
BENDIS WROTE THAT. HE'S A *GOD!*
HE LIVES IN *PORTLAND, OREGON*, EDDIE, WHERE EVERYONE DRINKS *FAR TOO MUCH COFFEE*.

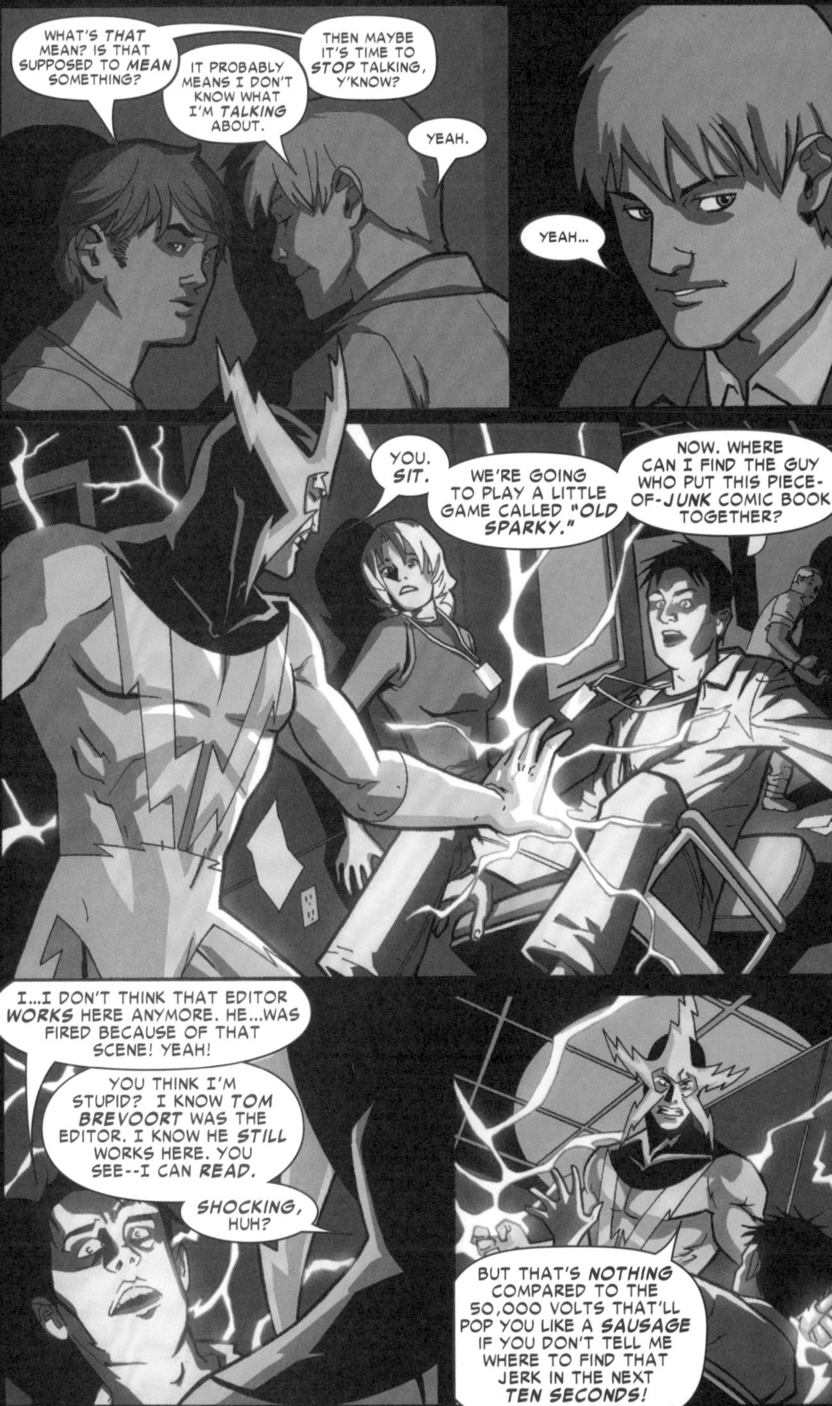
WHAT'S THAT MEAN? IS THAT SUPPOSED TO MEAN SOMETHING?
IT PROBABLY MEANS I DON'T KNOW WHAT I'M TALKING ABOUT.
THEN MAYBE IT'S TIME TO STOP TALKING, Y'KNOW?
YEAH.
YEAH...
YOU. SIT.
WE'RE GOING TO PLAY A LITTLE GAME CALLED "OLD SPARKY."
NOW. WHERE CAN I FIND THE GUY WHO PUT THIS PIECE-OF-JUNK COMIC BOOK TOGETHER?
I...I DON'T THINK THAT EDITOR WORKS HERE ANYMORE. HE...WAS FIRED BECAUSE OF THAT SCENE! YEAH!
YOU THINK I'M STUPID? I KNOW TOM BREVOORT WAS THE EDITOR. I KNOW HE STILL WORKS HERE. YOU SEE--I CAN READ.
SHOCKING, HUH?
BUT THAT'S NOTHING COMPARED TO THE 50,000 VOLTS THAT'LL POP YOU LIKE A SAUSAGE IF YOU DON'T TELL ME WHERE TO FIND THAT JERK IN THE NEXT TEN SECONDS!

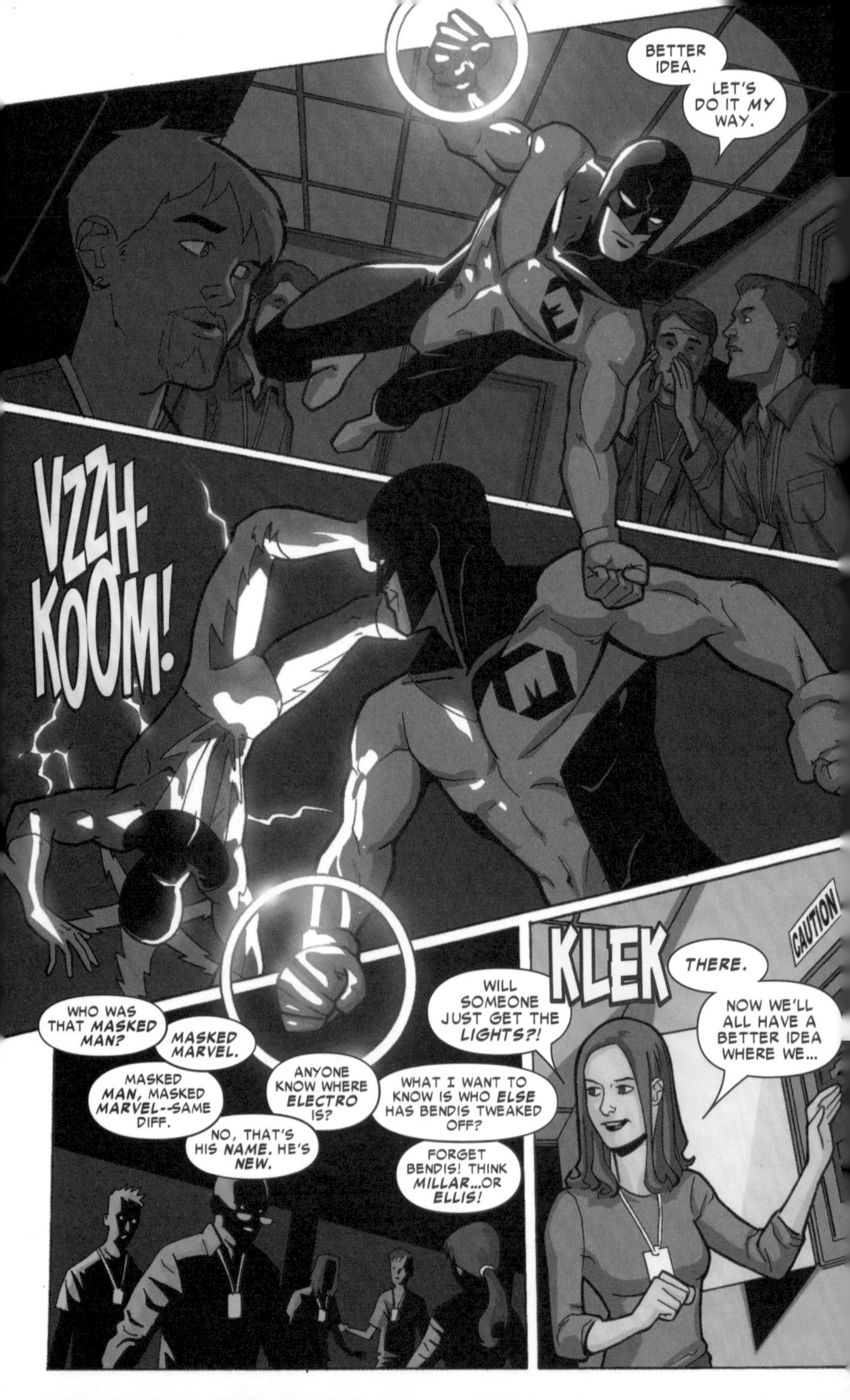
BETTER IDEA.
LET'S DO IT MY WAY.
VZZH-KOOM!
KLEK
CAUTION
WILL SOMEONE JUST GET THE LIGHTS?!
THERE.
NOW WE'LL ALL HAVE A BETTER IDEA WHERE WE...
WHO WAS THAT MASKED MAN?
MASKED MARVEL.
MASKED MAN, MASKED MARVEL--SAME DIFF.
NO, THAT'S HIS NAME. HE'S NEW.
ANYONE KNOW WHERE ELECTRO IS?
WHAT I WANT TO KNOW IS WHO ELSE HAS BENDIS TWEAKED OFF?
FORGET BENDIS! THINK MILLAR...OR ELLIS!

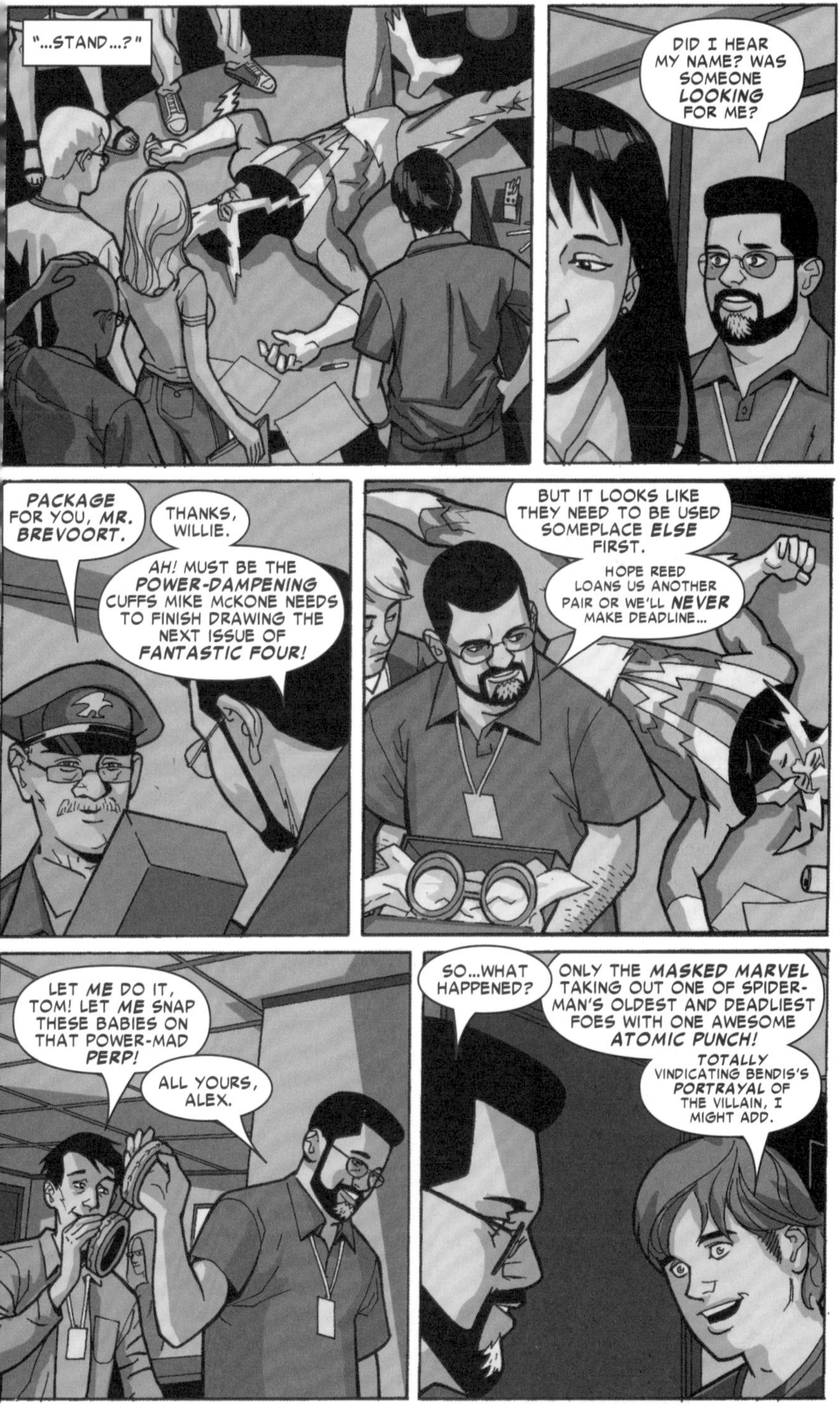
"...STAND...?"
DID I HEAR MY NAME? WAS SOMEONE LOOKING FOR ME?
PACKAGE FOR YOU, MR. BREVOORT.
THANKS, WILLIE.
AH! MUST BE THE POWER-DAMPENING CUFFS MIKE McKONE NEEDS TO FINISH DRAWING THE NEXT ISSUE OF FANTASTIC FOUR!
BUT IT LOOKS LIKE THEY NEED TO BE USED SOMEPLACE ELSE FIRST.
HOPE REED LOANS US ANOTHER PAIR OR WE'LL NEVER MAKE DEADLINE...
LET ME DO IT, TOM! LET ME SNAP THESE BABIES ON THAT POWER-MAD PERP!
ALL YOURS, ALEX.
SO...WHAT HAPPENED?
ONLY THE MASKED MARVEL TAKING OUT ONE OF SPIDER-MAN'S OLDEST AND DEADLIEST FOES WITH ONE AWESOME ATOMIC PUNCH!
TOTALLY VINDICATING BENDIS'S PORTRAYAL OF THE VILLAIN, I MIGHT ADD.

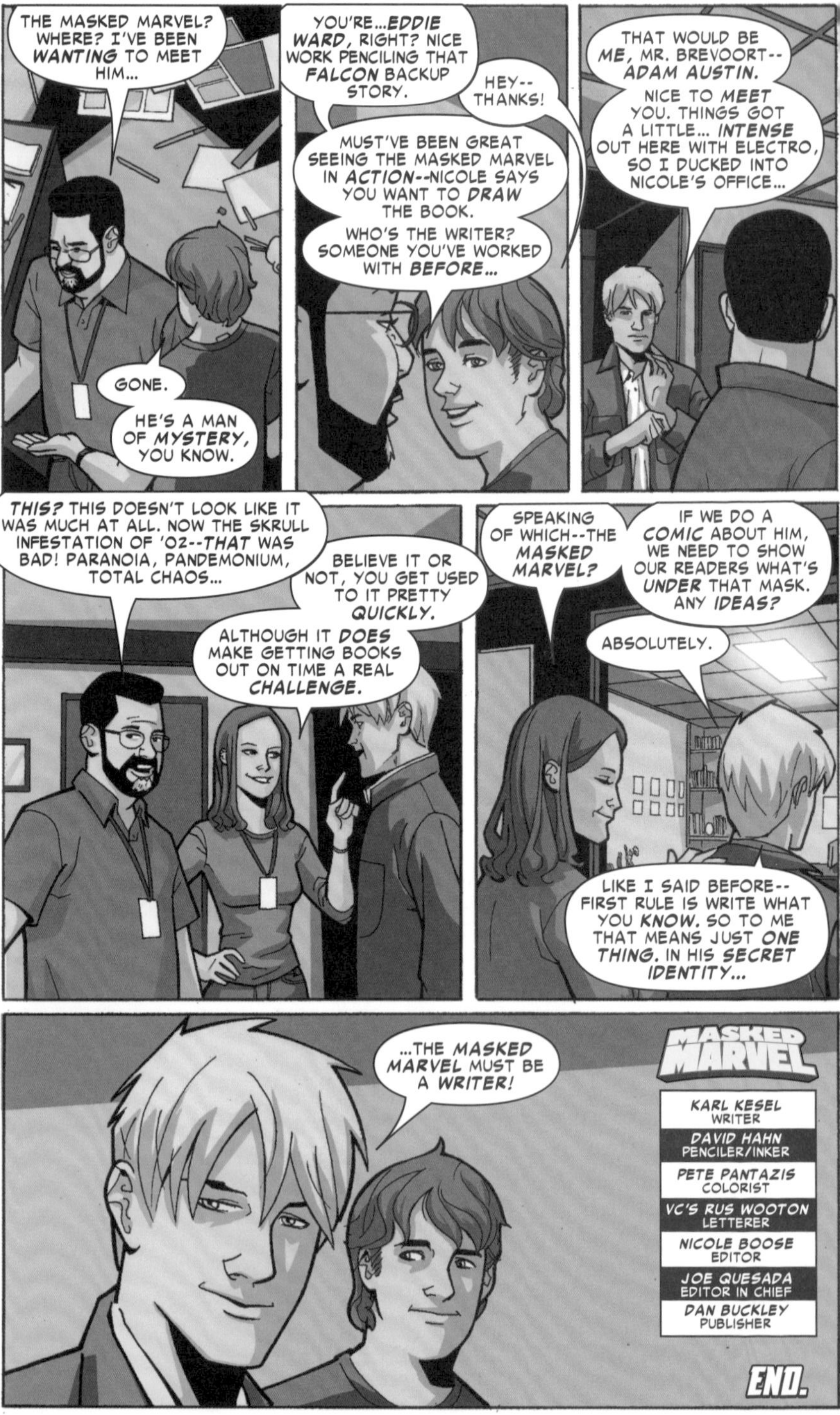
THE MASKED MARVEL? WHERE? I'VE BEEN WANTING TO MEET HIM...
GONE.
HE'S A MAN OF MYSTERY, YOU KNOW.
YOU'RE...EDDIE WARD, RIGHT? NICE WORK PENCILING THAT FALCON BACKUP STORY.
HEY-- THANKS!
MUST'VE BEEN GREAT SEEING THE MASKED MARVEL IN ACTION--NICOLE SAYS YOU WANT TO DRAW THE BOOK.
WHO'S THE WRITER? SOMEONE YOU'VE WORKED WITH BEFORE...
THAT WOULD BE ME, MR. BREVOORT-- ADAM AUSTIN.
NICE TO MEET YOU. THINGS GOT A LITTLE... INTENSE OUT HERE WITH ELECTRO, SO I DUCKED INTO NICOLE'S OFFICE...
THIS? THIS DOESN'T LOOK LIKE IT WAS MUCH AT ALL. NOW THE SKRULL INFESTATION OF '02--THAT WAS BAD! PARANOIA, PANDEMONIUM, TOTAL CHAOS...
BELIEVE IT OR NOT, YOU GET USED TO IT PRETTY QUICKLY.
ALTHOUGH IT DOES MAKE GETTING BOOKS OUT ON TIME A REAL CHALLENGE.
SPEAKING OF WHICH--THE MASKED MARVEL?
IF WE DO A COMIC ABOUT HIM, WE NEED TO SHOW OUR READERS WHAT'S UNDER THAT MASK. ANY IDEAS?
ABSOLUTELY.
LIKE I SAID BEFORE-- FIRST RULE IS WRITE WHAT YOU KNOW. SO TO ME THAT MEANS JUST ONE THING. IN HIS SECRET IDENTITY...
...THE MASKED MARVEL MUST BE A WRITER!
MASKED MARVEL
KARL KESEL WRITER
DAVID HAHN PENCILER/INKER
PETE PANTAZIS COLORIST
VC'S RUS WOOTON LETTERER
NICOLE BOOSE EDITOR
JOE QUESADA EDITOR IN CHIEF
DAN BUCKLEY PUBLISHER
END.

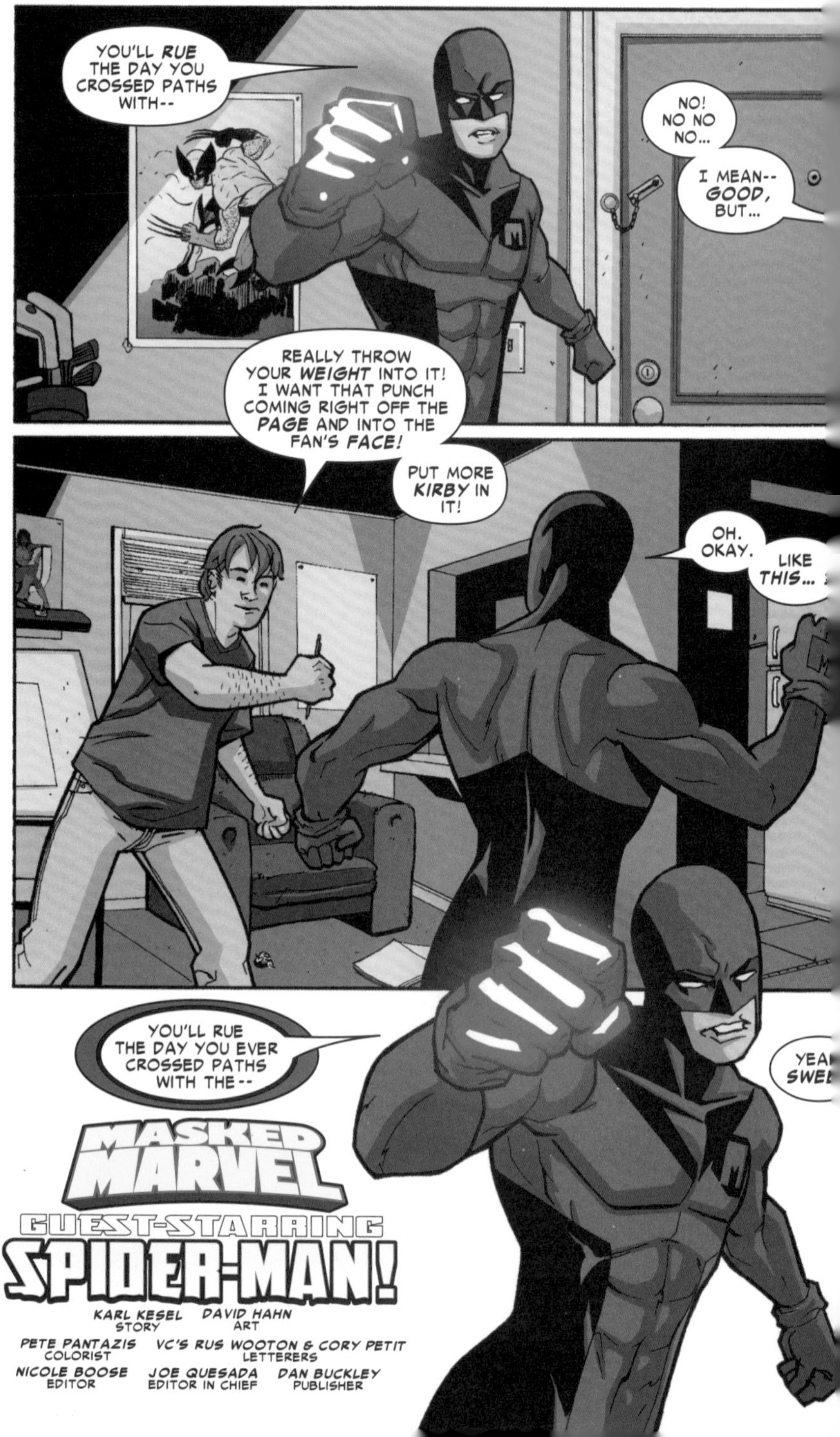
YOU'LL RUE THE DAY YOU CROSSED PATHS WITH--
NO! NO NO NO...
I MEAN-- GOOD, BUT...
REALLY THROW YOUR WEIGHT INTO IT! I WANT THAT PUNCH COMING RIGHT OFF THE PAGE AND INTO THE FAN'S FACE!
PUT MORE KIRBY IN IT!
OH. OKAY.
LIKE THIS...
YOU'LL RUE THE DAY YOU EVER CROSSED PATHS WITH THE--
MASKED MARVEL
GUEST-STARRING
SPIDER-MAN!
KARL KESEL STORY
DAVID HAHN ART
PETE PANTAZIS COLORIST
VC'S RUS WOOTON & CORY PETIT LETTERERS
NICOLE BOOSE EDITOR
JOE QUESADA EDITOR IN CHIEF
DAN BUCKLEY PUBLISHER

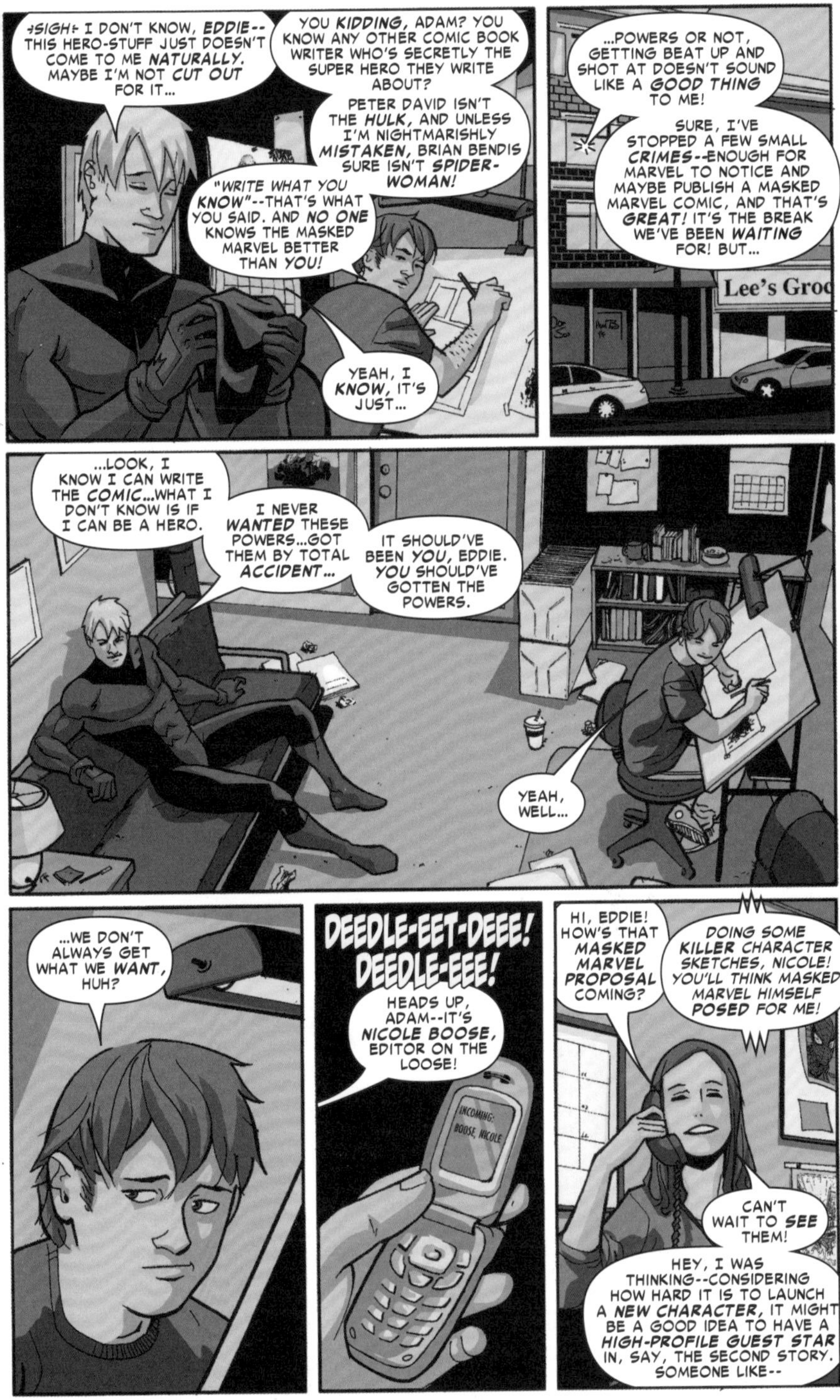
-SIGH- I DON'T KNOW, EDDIE-- THIS HERO-STUFF JUST DOESN'T COME TO ME NATURALLY. MAYBE I'M NOT CUT OUT FOR IT...
YOU KIDDING, ADAM? YOU KNOW ANY OTHER COMIC BOOK WRITER WHO'S SECRETLY THE SUPER HERO THEY WRITE ABOUT?
PETER DAVID ISN'T THE HULK, AND UNLESS I'M NIGHTMARISHLY MISTAKEN, BRIAN BENDIS SURE ISN'T SPIDER-WOMAN!
"WRITE WHAT YOU KNOW"--THAT'S WHAT YOU SAID. AND NO ONE KNOWS THE MASKED MARVEL BETTER THAN YOU!
YEAH, I KNOW, IT'S JUST...
...POWERS OR NOT, GETTING BEAT UP AND SHOT AT DOESN'T SOUND LIKE A GOOD THING TO ME!
SURE, I'VE STOPPED A FEW SMALL CRIMES--ENOUGH FOR MARVEL TO NOTICE AND MAYBE PUBLISH A MASKED MARVEL COMIC, AND THAT'S GREAT! IT'S THE BREAK WE'VE BEEN WAITING FOR! BUT...
Lee's Groc
...LOOK, I KNOW I CAN WRITE THE COMIC...WHAT I DON'T KNOW IS IF I CAN BE A HERO.
I NEVER WANTED THESE POWERS...GOT THEM BY TOTAL ACCIDENT...
IT SHOULD'VE BEEN YOU, EDDIE. YOU SHOULD'VE GOTTEN THE POWERS.
YEAH, WELL...
...WE DON'T ALWAYS GET WHAT WE WANT, HUH?
DEEDLE-EET-DEEE! DEEDLE-EEE!
HEADS UP, ADAM--IT'S NICOLE BOOSE, EDITOR ON THE LOOSE!
INCOMING: BOOSE, NICOLE
HI, EDDIE! HOW'S THAT MASKED MARVEL PROPOSAL COMING?
DOING SOME KILLER CHARACTER SKETCHES, NICOLE! YOU'LL THINK MASKED MARVEL HIMSELF POSED FOR ME!
CAN'T WAIT TO SEE THEM!
HEY, I WAS THINKING--CONSIDERING HOW HARD IT IS TO LAUNCH A NEW CHARACTER, IT MIGHT BE A GOOD IDEA TO HAVE A HIGH-PROFILE GUEST STAR IN, SAY, THE SECOND STORY. SOMEONE LIKE--

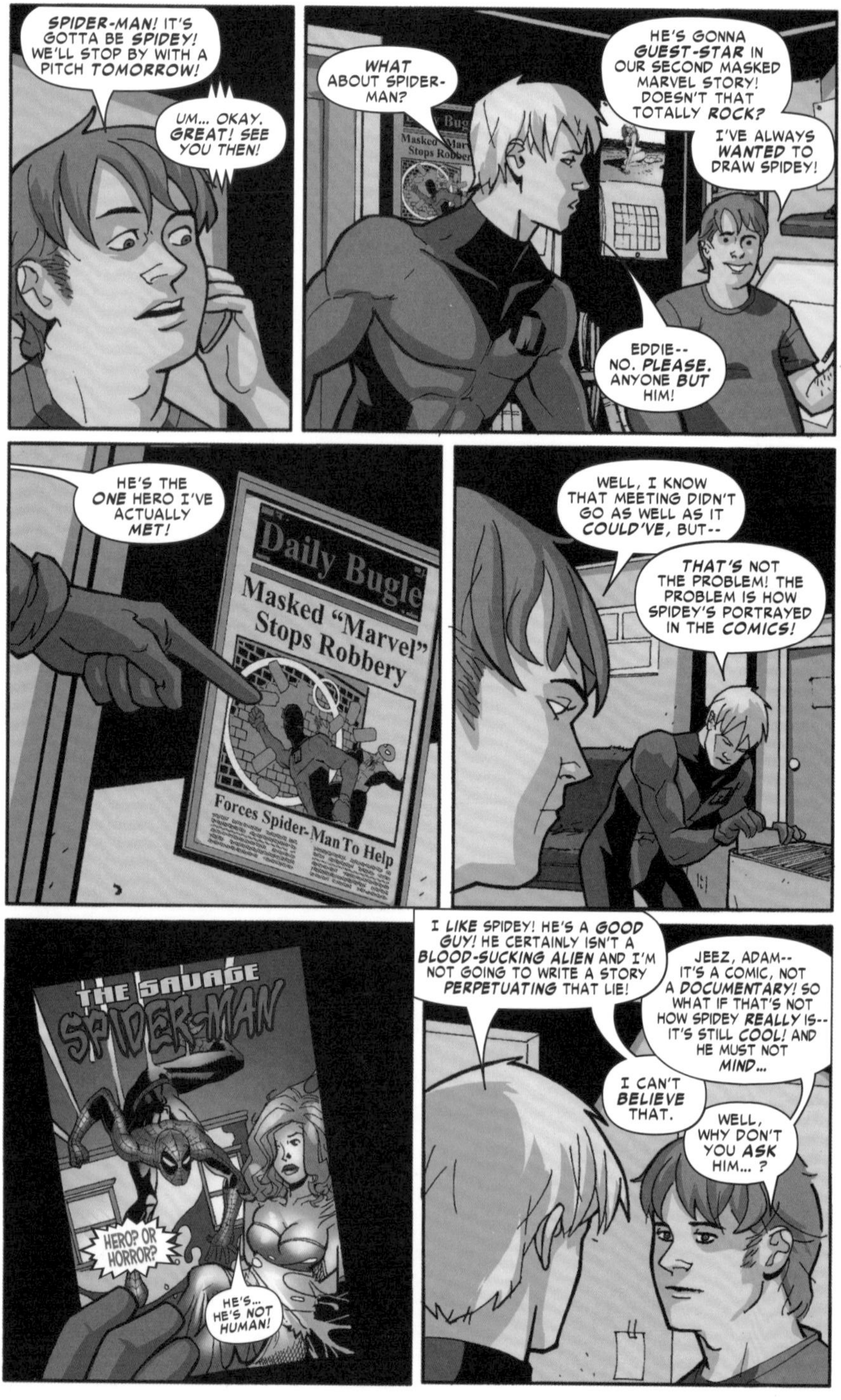
SPIDER-MAN! IT'S GOTTA BE SPIDEY! WE'LL STOP BY WITH A PITCH TOMORROW!
UM... OKAY. GREAT! SEE YOU THEN!
WHAT ABOUT SPIDER-MAN?
HE'S GONNA GUEST-STAR IN OUR SECOND MASKED MARVEL STORY! DOESN'T THAT TOTALLY ROCK?
I'VE ALWAYS WANTED TO DRAW SPIDEY!
EDDIE-- NO. PLEASE. ANYONE BUT HIM!
HE'S THE ONE HERO I'VE ACTUALLY MET!
Daily Bugle
Masked "Marvel" Stops Robbery
Forces Spider-Man To Help
WELL, I KNOW THAT MEETING DIDN'T GO AS WELL AS IT COULD'VE, BUT--
THAT'S NOT THE PROBLEM! THE PROBLEM IS HOW SPIDEY'S PORTRAYED IN THE COMICS!
THE SAVAGE SPIDER-MAN
HERO? OR HORROR?
HE'S... HE'S NOT HUMAN!
I LIKE SPIDEY! HE'S A GOOD GUY! HE CERTAINLY ISN'T A BLOOD-SUCKING ALIEN AND I'M NOT GOING TO WRITE A STORY PERPETUATING THAT LIE!
JEEZ, ADAM-- IT'S A COMIC, NOT A DOCUMENTARY! SO WHAT IF THAT'S NOT HOW SPIDEY REALLY IS-- IT'S STILL COOL! AND HE MUST NOT MIND...
I CAN'T BELIEVE THAT.
WELL, WHY DON'T YOU ASK HIM... ?

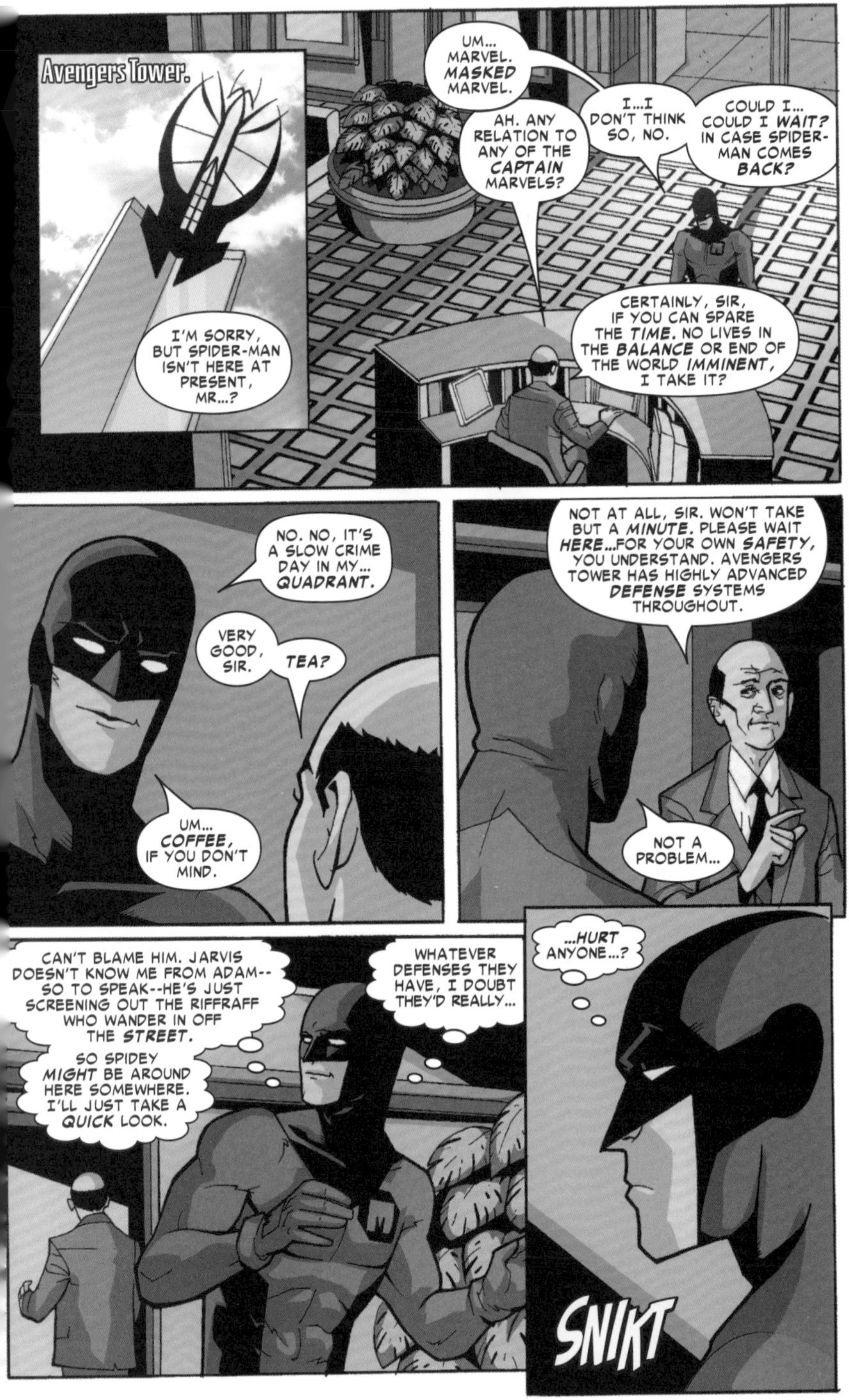
Avengers Tower.
I'M SORRY, BUT SPIDER-MAN ISN'T HERE AT PRESENT, MR...?
UM... MARVEL. MASKED MARVEL.
AH. ANY RELATION TO ANY OF THE CAPTAIN MARVELS?
I...I DON'T THINK SO, NO.
COULD I... COULD I WAIT? IN CASE SPIDER-MAN COMES BACK?
CERTAINLY, SIR, IF YOU CAN SPARE THE TIME. NO LIVES IN THE BALANCE OR END OF THE WORLD IMMINENT, I TAKE IT?
NO. NO, IT'S A SLOW CRIME DAY IN MY... QUADRANT.
VERY GOOD, SIR.
TEA?
UM... COFFEE, IF YOU DON'T MIND.
NOT AT ALL, SIR. WON'T TAKE BUT A MINUTE. PLEASE WAIT HERE...FOR YOUR OWN SAFETY, YOU UNDERSTAND. AVENGERS TOWER HAS HIGHLY ADVANCED DEFENSE SYSTEMS THROUGHOUT.
NOT A PROBLEM...
CAN'T BLAME HIM. JARVIS DOESN'T KNOW ME FROM ADAM--SO TO SPEAK--HE'S JUST SCREENING OUT THE RIFFRAFF WHO WANDER IN OFF THE STREET.
SO SPIDEY MIGHT BE AROUND HERE SOMEWHERE. I'LL JUST TAKE A QUICK LOOK.
WHATEVER DEFENSES THEY HAVE, I DOUBT THEY'D REALLY...
...HURT ANYONE...?
SNIKT

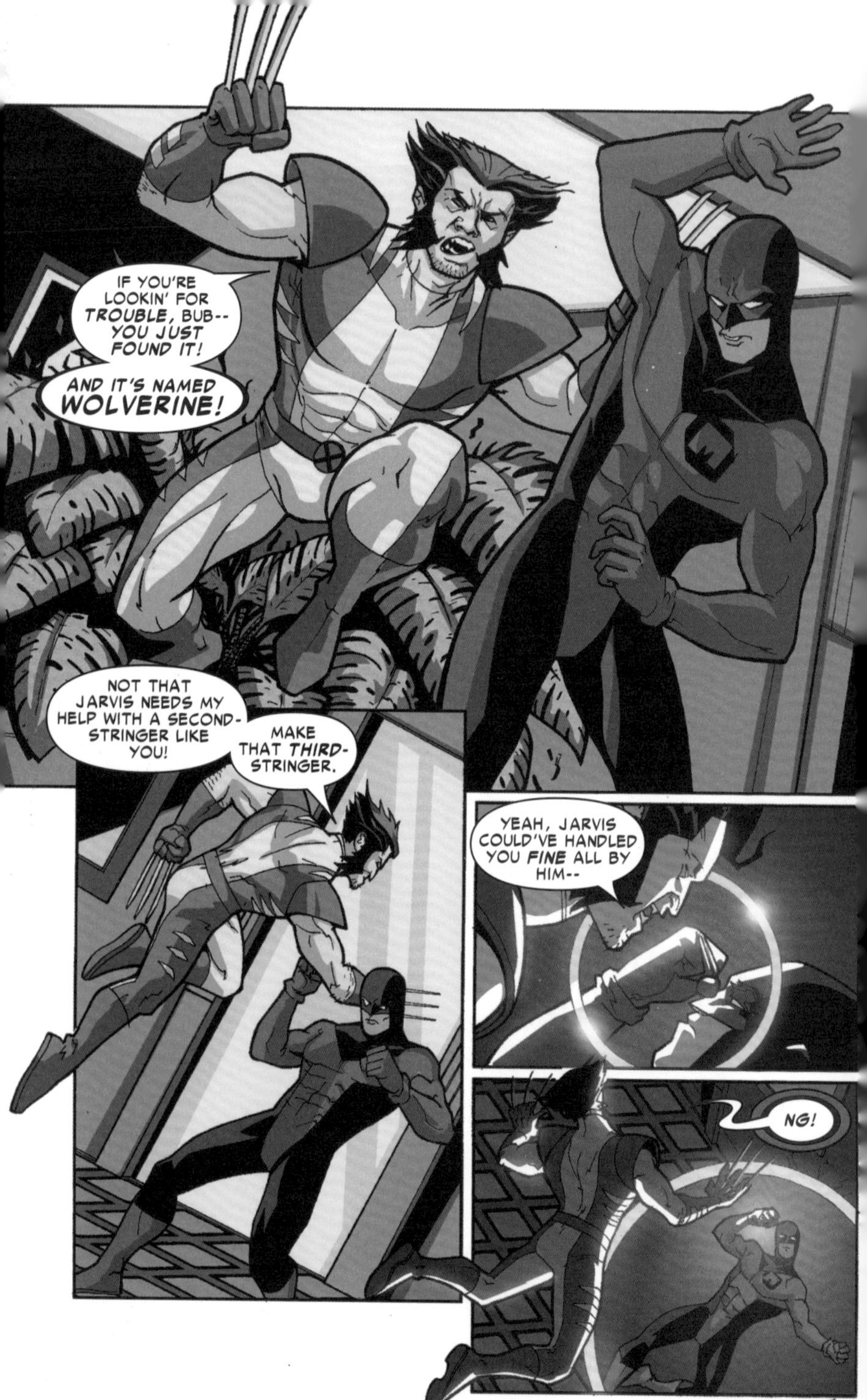

IF YOU'RE LOOKIN' FOR TROUBLE, BUB-- YOU JUST FOUND IT!
AND IT'S NAMED WOLVERINE!
NOT THAT JARVIS NEEDS MY HELP WITH A SECOND-STRINGER LIKE YOU!
MAKE THAT THIRD-STRINGER.
YEAH, JARVIS COULD'VE HANDLED YOU FINE ALL BY HIM--
NG!

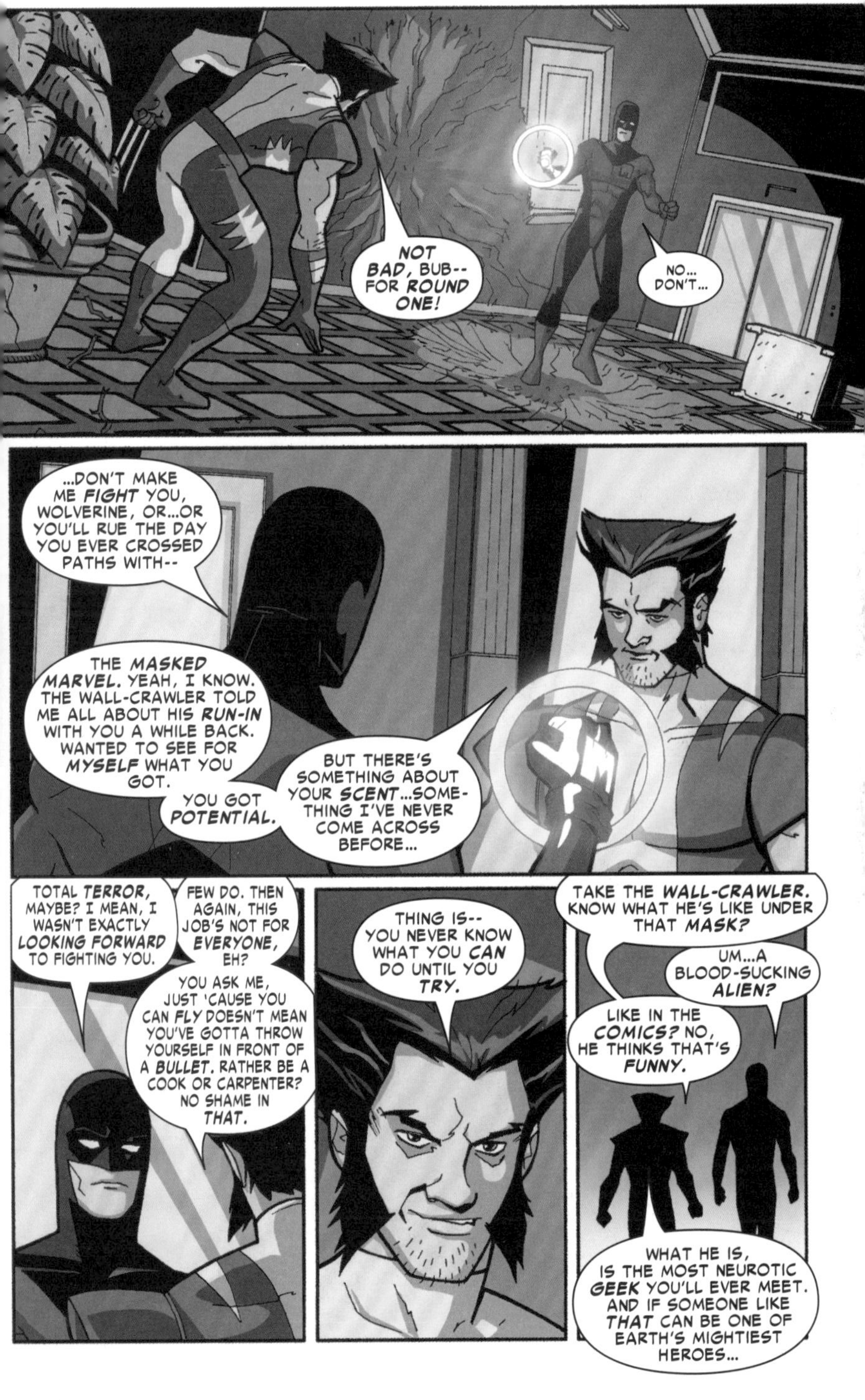
NOT BAD, BUB-- FOR ROUND ONE!
NO... DON'T...
...DON'T MAKE ME FIGHT YOU, WOLVERINE, OR...OR YOU'LL RUE THE DAY YOU EVER CROSSED PATHS WITH--
THE MASKED MARVEL. YEAH, I KNOW. THE WALL-CRAWLER TOLD ME ALL ABOUT HIS RUN-IN WITH YOU A WHILE BACK. WANTED TO SEE FOR MYSELF WHAT YOU GOT.
YOU GOT POTENTIAL.
BUT THERE'S SOMETHING ABOUT YOUR SCENT...SOMETHING I'VE NEVER COME ACROSS BEFORE...
TOTAL TERROR, MAYBE? I MEAN, I WASN'T EXACTLY LOOKING FORWARD TO FIGHTING YOU.
FEW DO. THEN AGAIN, THIS JOB'S NOT FOR EVERYONE, EH?
YOU ASK ME, JUST 'CAUSE YOU CAN FLY DOESN'T MEAN YOU'VE GOTTA THROW YOURSELF IN FRONT OF A BULLET. RATHER BE A COOK OR CARPENTER? NO SHAME IN THAT.
THING IS-- YOU NEVER KNOW WHAT YOU CAN DO UNTIL YOU TRY.
TAKE THE WALL-CRAWLER. KNOW WHAT HE'S LIKE UNDER THAT MASK?
UM...A BLOOD-SUCKING ALIEN?
LIKE IN THE COMICS? NO, HE THINKS THAT'S FUNNY.
WHAT HE IS, IS THE MOST NEUROTIC GEEK YOU'LL EVER MEET. AND IF SOMEONE LIKE THAT CAN BE ONE OF EARTH'S MIGHTIEST HEROES...

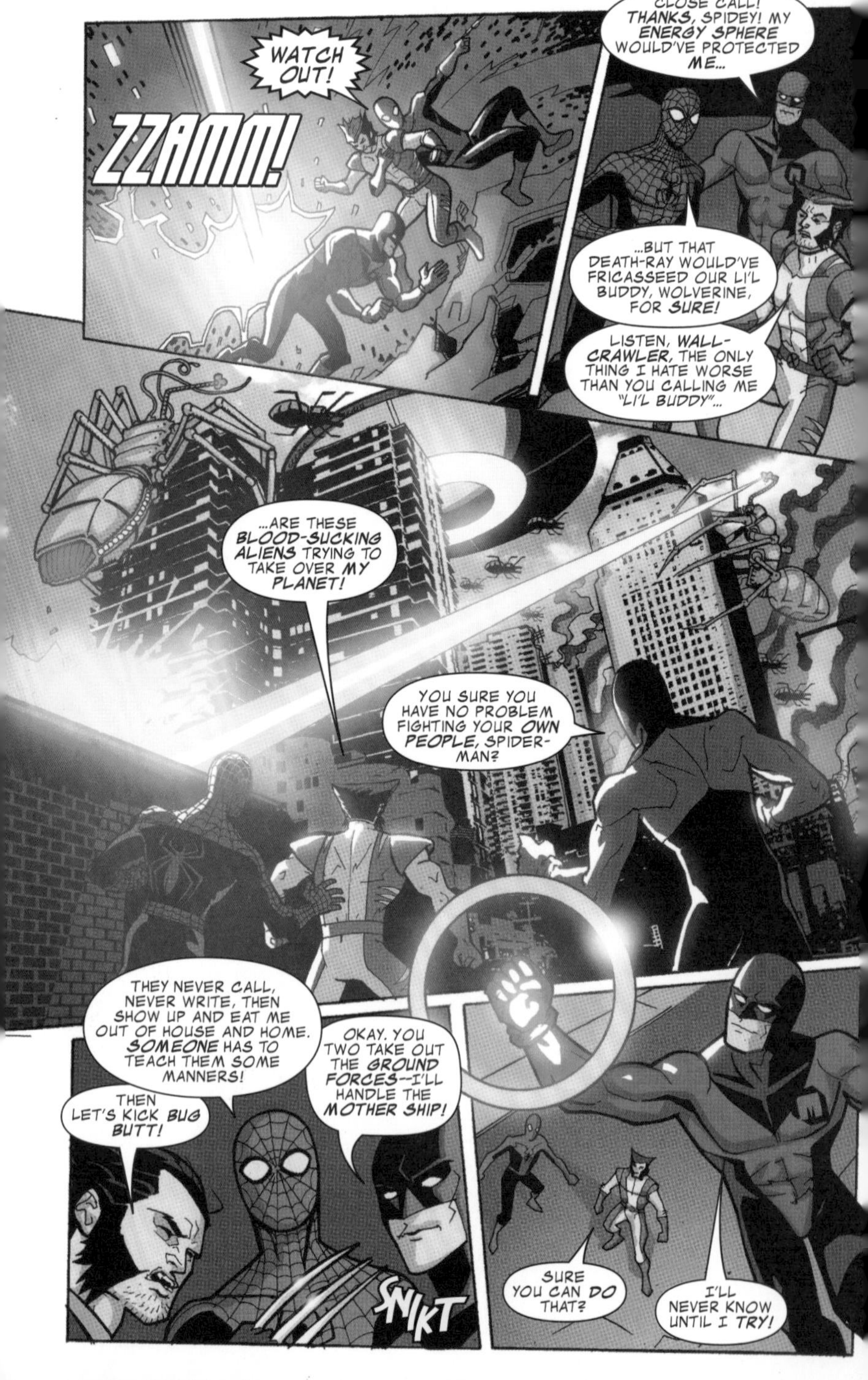
WATCH OUT!
ZZAMM!
CLOSE CALL! THANKS, SPIDEY! MY ENERGY SPHERE WOULD'VE PROTECTED ME...
...BUT THAT DEATH-RAY WOULD'VE FRICASSEED OUR LI'L BUDDY, WOLVERINE, FOR SURE!
LISTEN, WALL-CRAWLER, THE ONLY THING I HATE WORSE THAN YOU CALLING ME "LI'L BUDDY"...
...ARE THESE BLOOD-SUCKING ALIENS TRYING TO TAKE OVER MY PLANET!
YOU SURE YOU HAVE NO PROBLEM FIGHTING YOUR OWN PEOPLE, SPIDER-MAN?
THEY NEVER CALL, NEVER WRITE, THEN SHOW UP AND EAT ME OUT OF HOUSE AND HOME. SOMEONE HAS TO TEACH THEM SOME MANNERS!
THEN LET'S KICK BUG BUTT!
OKAY. YOU TWO TAKE OUT THE GROUND FORCES--I'LL HANDLE THE MOTHER SHIP!
SNIKT
SURE YOU CAN DO THAT?
I'LL NEVER KNOW UNTIL I TRY!

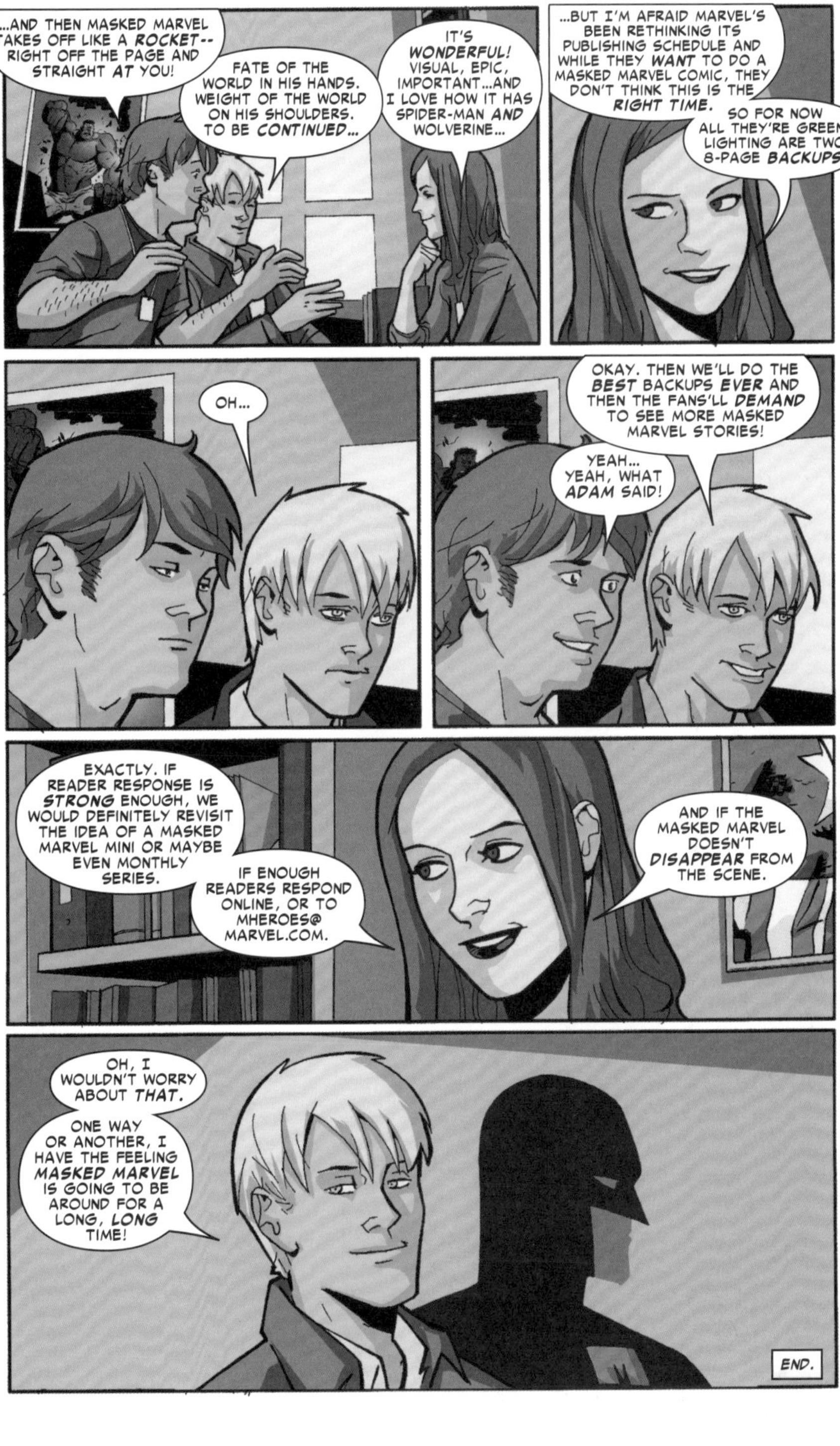
...AND THEN MASKED MARVEL TAKES OFF LIKE A ROCKET--RIGHT OFF THE PAGE AND STRAIGHT AT YOU!
FATE OF THE WORLD IN HIS HANDS. WEIGHT OF THE WORLD ON HIS SHOULDERS. TO BE CONTINUED...
IT'S WONDERFUL! VISUAL, EPIC, IMPORTANT...AND I LOVE HOW IT HAS SPIDER-MAN AND WOLVERINE...
...BUT I'M AFRAID MARVEL'S BEEN RETHINKING ITS PUBLISHING SCHEDULE AND WHILE THEY WANT TO DO A MASKED MARVEL COMIC, THEY DON'T THINK THIS IS THE RIGHT TIME.
SO FOR NOW ALL THEY'RE GREEN-LIGHTING ARE TWO 8-PAGE BACKUPS.
OH...
OKAY. THEN WE'LL DO THE BEST BACKUPS EVER AND THEN THE FANS'LL DEMAND TO SEE MORE MASKED MARVEL STORIES!
YEAH... YEAH, WHAT ADAM SAID!
EXACTLY. IF READER RESPONSE IS STRONG ENOUGH, WE WOULD DEFINITELY REVISIT THE IDEA OF A MASKED MARVEL MINI OR MAYBE EVEN MONTHLY SERIES.
IF ENOUGH READERS RESPOND ONLINE, OR TO MHEROES@MARVEL.COM.
AND IF THE MASKED MARVEL DOESN'T DISAPPEAR FROM THE SCENE.
OH, I WOULDN'T WORRY ABOUT THAT.
ONE WAY OR ANOTHER, I HAVE THE FEELING MASKED MARVEL IS GOING TO BE AROUND FOR A LONG, LONG TIME!
END.